THE *Slingerland* BOOK

by Rob Cook

SECOND EDITION

ISBN 1-888408-10-3

REBEATS

Cover concept and design by Ben Mepham @ Worm Studio 2004 bmepham@chartermi.net

Acknowledgements

The following people made this project possible, through their encouragement, advice, reminiscences, and generous sharing of drums, photos, catalogs, and other rare documents.

John Aldridge
Spencer Aloisio
David Anfuso
Gary Asher
Sam Bacco
Tanco Baart
Wayne Beavers
Donn Bennett
Dave Brown
Roy Burns
Harry Cangany
Bun E Carlos
Walter Carter
Jon Cohan
John Clark
William Connor
Mike Curotto
Rob Courtney
Barrett Deems
Norman "Scotty" Doucette
Chuck Dufkis
Ward Durrett
Chet Falzerano
Gary Forkum
Pat Foley
Sam Geati
Deborah Gillaspie
Mark Hamon
Tracey Hoeft
Dendy Jarrett
Jake Jerger
Don Knapp
Eddie Knight
Dave Kolars
Mike Lorenz
William F. Ludwig II
Rich Kalinsky
Maurie & Jan Lishon
Dave Lovvorn
Joe Luoma
Marion McLaughlin
Brian Majeski
Stephen Maxwell
Winnie Mensink
Brad Morey
Eddie Mosqueda
Nathan Moy
Liam Mulholland
Dorothy Mueller
Dan Paul
Jim Pettit
Gregg Potter
Bob Rickman
Dick Richardson
Fred Sanford
Bob Slingerland
Walter & Helen Slingerland
Brooks Tegler
Roger Turner
Ian Turnbull
Lisa (Slingerland) and Mark Wallis
Stan Werbin
Tommy Winkler
Bob Zildjian

The Author/Publisher would like to thank the Gibson Guitar Corporation for its assistance and cooperation in the production of this book. The completeness has been enhanced greatly by the their generous support. Gibson allowed access to the Slingerland Archives and purchased copies of the first edition. The contributions of Gibson's Walter Carter merit a special acknowledgement and word of thanks. Carter took photos, supplied art, and applied the editor's red pencil to early drafts. Any typos, errors, and layout inconsistencies that remain must be charged to the author. (Believe me, that list would be a lot longer if not for Walter Carter.) Other very helpful people at Gibson were Jim Landers, Wayne Beavers, Sam Bacco, Pat Foley, Josh Touchton, and, of course, Henry Juskewicz. Nearly every head of Gibson/Slingerland was accomodating: Tracey Hoeft, Dendy Jarrett, Bob Cook, J.T. Johnson, Dennis Webster, Dave Berryman, Charlie Wood, Mike Hassell, Jim Dixon, Brad Lucht, John Higgins, Walt Johnston, and Don Kremer.

PHOTO CREDITS

Sam Bacco	53,54
Donn Bennett	124
Dave Brown	122
Harry Cangany	142
John Clark	117
James Cumpsty (Rhythm)	122
Mike Curotto	16,25,34,127–131,136
Barrett Deems	42
Chuck Dufkis	51
Jake Jerger (& David Anfuso)	109–112
Marion (Slingerland) McLaughlin	7
Eddie Mosqueda	126
Stephen Maxwell	123
Nathan Moy	121,147
Dorothy (Slingerland) Mueller	47
Gregg Potter	114,141
Lowell Schiff	137
Walter R. Slingerland, Jr.	1–3,5,9,19–24,44,47
Frank Vilardi	147

All other photos were taken by Rob Cook, from Slingerland catalogs, or courtesy of Gibson.

Forward

A large part of my early recollections include Slingerland drums. My father was involved in the company all of my life until his retirement at age 65. Accompanying him to the factory and meeting the greats including Gene Krupa are times I will forever remember. Since I played drums, I had the pleasure of "sitting in" with Mr. Krupa on one occasion at the Panther Room in Chicago. I was also a member of two drum and bugle corps– Roosevelt Military Academy and Rogers Park.

We recently had the pleasure of hearing Louis Bellson in concert. He spoke of winning the Slingerland Gene Krupa contest at age 17, triumphing over 40,000 drummers. That contest was a great promotion both for the company and winners such as Bellson. There were regional contests in every state, then sectionals and the final competition in New York.

This book is a wonderful account of the business my family founded and operated for many years. Many things that I "sort of" remembered came back to me when I read them here and there are things I've learned from it that I never knew before.

Walter R. Slingerland Jr.

Dedication

The Slingerland Book is dedicated to the Slingerland family in memory of Henry Heanon Slingerland, Arthur J. Slingerland, Walter R. Slingerland, Henry Heanon Slingerland Junior, and Marion (Slingerland) McLaughlin. Slingerland family members who were interested in and helpful with this project included Walter R. Slingerland Junior and his wife Helen, Marion (Slingerland) McLaughlin, Carole McLaughlin, Dorothy (Slingerland) Mueller, Robert J. Slingerland, Mark and Lisa (Slingerland) Wallis.

The Slingerland Book is also dedicated to Spencer Aloisio. Although not a member of the Slingerland family through blood ties, I'm sure no one will object to his inclusion here. In the dozens of interviews conducted for this book, I *never* heard a critical word spoken of Spencer. Former Slingerland President Dick Richardson put it quite well: "Spencer was a really good guy and the most dedicated, hardest worker I've ever worked with in all the years I was in the music industry. There was no one like Spencer; a tremendous guy and a really good person. I don't know what it was with Slingerland– he was so loyal and I don't know why; I just have to believe he would have been loyal to whoever he was with. He went through all the transitions and whoever took over that job (head of Slingerland) he was loyal to that person and never said a word against them or the preceding person."

Rob Cook

Contents

Slingerland Endorsees

Slingerland Personnel

The Color Section

Slingerland Dating Guide

THE SLINGERLAND FAMILY

Samuel & Amalia Slingerland raised a large family on their farm in the small northern Michigan town of Manistee.

Slingerland was a conservative Lutheran with a keen business sense. In addition to farming, he supported his family with his real estate dealings.

The sons and daughters of Samuel and Amalia Slingerland

Back row l to r: Isabelle, Walter Robert, Daisy, Arthur James, Elvina (Vina), John Peter, Lillian.
Front row l to r: Lottie, Henry Heanon, Paulina Augusta.

Son Henry inherited his father's sharp sense for business. He earned spending money as a child by raising honeybees and selling the honey. His first adult business enterprise was reportedly a Great Lakes gambling boat based in Manistee. When the boat was destroyed by fire in about 1905, he moved to Chicago.

l-r Walter Robert, Henry Heanon, Arthur James II, Arthur James

The 1909 Chicago City Directory listed Heanon H. Slingerland as a music teacher, with a business address of 105 Ashland Boulevard. (A Mrs. Carrie M. Slingerland was also listed as a music teacher in the 1909 and 1910 directories at the same addresses listed as home addresses for Heanon H. Her relationship to Heanon H. is uncertain. Surviving family members are certain that he married only once, to Nona.) According to Slingerland descendants, Heanon was not a musician himself, but learned enough while working for a family-owned business to give lessons and print sheet music. (He received $4.00 per student for a month of lessons.) Apparently there came to be several divisions of this business. The operation at 105 Ashland was known as the West Side Conservatory of Music, offering vocal and instrumental instruction.

West Side Conservatory of Music
105 Ashland Boulevard
Telephone West 730
Instruction on all String and Wind Instruments, Piano, Vocal and Elocution. Private Class or Orchestra Work.
Rates very reasonable.

Heanon's brother John was listed in the 1910 directory as president of of the South Side Academy of Music at 6424 S. Halsted; presumably a similar (probably branch) operation.

The Chicago Correspondence School of Music had been established in the 1800s, and was a successful business. With the purchase of twelve correspondence ukelele lessons, the customer received a free ukulele.

After the owner died, Heanon H. Slingerland continued to work with the widow, and eventually was able to purchase the business from her. At this point (1914), he changed the name to the Slingerland Correspondence School of Music and moved to 431 S. Wabash.

STUDY MUSIC IN YOUR HOME WITH THE MASTERS. OVER 400,000 SUCCESSFUL PLAYERS OUR PUPILS OUR REFERENCE.

2249 WARD ST CHICAGO U.S.A.

Dear Friend:-

We are in receipt of your enrollment for which kindly accept our thanks.

If you will get busy and practice at least an hour a day, you will be surprised how fast you can advance. Do not attempt to play the second lesson until you have thoroughly mastered the first, and you are sure to meet with success.

You may have some friends who want to enroll. I am therefore enclosing herewith, two enrollment blanks. If you get us three pupils, we will give you a nice side-opening, keratol covered case for your instrument. When you receive your outfit, you will wonder how we can give such fine instruments and lessons, however, this advertising plan may not last long.

We have you enrolled under No. _______ therefore, in the event you send in any new enrollments, kindly make mention of this number, your name and address, and oblige.

Yours very truly,
CHICAGO CORRESPONDENCE SCHOOL OF MUSIC

S:MT

____

W.R. Slingerland

H.H. contacted his younger brother W.R. (Walter Robert) Slingerland who had taken a job with the Armour Company in Detroit after the war, and talked him into coming to Chicago to work with him.

H.H. and W.R. needed a salesman, so they called on their brother Arthur James.

Walter's son Robert also worked in sales for a brief time.

H.H. was considered the money man while W.R. was in production and day-to-day operations. A.J. worked in sales, although W.R. remembered being pressed into service on the sales front early on; at one point they found themselves with a surplus of ukes and he went door-to-door to promote their lesson plan.

A.J. Slingerland

In its early days under the ownership of the Slingerland brothers, the Chicago Correspondence School of Music imported string instruments from Germany to sell to students or give away with lesson packages. The Slingerlands were forced into manufacturing when they began to have trouble importing enough instruments to meet demand. They hired a little German guy who started making instruments in his garage. When production demands reached a point that merited in-house manufacturing, the Slingerland brothers rented a building on Diversey near California Avenue. In 1923 the first factory building was purchased by the Slingerlands, at 1815 Orchard Street. Ukuleles were manufactured first, then banjos, and, finally, guitars. Neighboring buildings were purchased as the business expanded, until the street address becamse 1815-17-19 Orchard. By the mid-1920s Slingerland boasted over 1700 dealers and laid claim to operating the worlds largest and most modern-equipped banjo factory.

By the time of Slingerland's second drum catalog (1929), Slingerland was able to boast that H.H. had been actively interested in the music field for over 29 years and through his personal efforts and supervision had instructed over a million people to play musical instruments. "So without a doubt he has taught more individuals to play than any other living man."

Marion (Slingerland) McLaughlin

The eldest of H.H. Slingerland's three children, Marion was born in 1919. (H.H. Junior was born in 1921, Dorothy in 1927.) She shared the following memories with the author in 1997.

"There are a lot of details about the family business that I cannot tell you simply because my father seldom spoke about business or financial matters at home. In those days, such affairs were private matters of the man of the house and the women and children were not involved.

My father was a gambler. I don't really know how high the stakes were. I know that when the family would go to the country club, he would retire to the lower level with the other gentlemen, and we often would not see him again until we left. Sometimes he would be very tired, and have me drive the car on the way home. In one such game he won a yacht, which was moored in Miami. My father knew that he could sell a new Ford automobile in Miami for much more than he could buy it for right here in Chicago. He bought one and loaded the whole family up for the long drive to Florida. I distinctly remember leaving the next day after classes got out for the summer at the end of my junior year of high school in 1935. The car was sold in Miami for a profit, and my father hired a captain to sail the boat, with the whole family aboard, up the East Coast, down the St. Lawrence seaway, into the Great Lakes, and right home to Chicago. The trip took six weeks.

The boat was named "Annabell" and was moored at the Chicago Yacht Club. Nearly every Sunday we would pack up a picnic and go out on Lake Michigan. Bud and I were both quite athletic, and pretty strong swimmers. I was a certified lifeguard. We would go way out on the lake, until we could no longer see land, then let the boat drift. Bud would dive off the boat; I'd climb up on the mast and dive from there. On one particular Sunday when Bud and I were swimming a good three hundred yards from the boat, a storm came up. I'd never seen a storm appear so fast. It came out of nowhere! The sky got dark, the wind blew, and the waves got so high that the boat was getting tossed about. I actually saw the propeller and rudder above the water as I swam toward the boat. I made it to the boat, and my father helped me climb aboard. I no more thatn stood up when my father told me to go get my brother. I did not question my father when he told me to do something. I immediately dove back in and went back for Bud, who was still the better part of 300 yards out. It seemed to take forever to get to him, and even longer to get back to the boat again. My father helped us into the boat, then put his hand on my shoulder. He looked at me and told me Bud would never have made it if I hadn't gone back for him.

My father put an ad in the next Sunday's paper, and sold the boat. I asked him why, and he said he wanted nothing more to do with it because he nearly lost two of his children that day.

Bud and I were very athletic; tennis and swimming were two of our passions. I didn't go out a lot, preferring to spend a lot of time on the tennis courts. I went to Oak Park High School and I'd see a lot of my classmates when I'd go along with my father to the big clubs like the Panther Room. He had a huge car, with the extra passenger seat behind the front seat, facing the rear. He often delivered drums when we went to a club– he took out that extra seat so he could fit a set of drums in the back.

I have many happy memories of my childhood growing up in the Chicago suburb of River Forest; riding bikes, playing tennis, picking grapes from Concordia's grapevines. [author note: Concordia University of River Forest is my Alma Mater.) Many of the residents of River Forest were stockbrokers, and when the crash came quite a few of them committed suicide in their garages. They'd close the garage door, open the card windows, start the car, and wait. There were a *lot* of those. We would be riding our bikes and stop to watch them carry the corpse from the garage to the ambulance. Every night my father would ask us how many we saw that day. I remember him banging his fist on the table and practically shouting "Cowards! They're all cowards! *I'll* make it!!" And he did!"

For years it was in the back of H.H. Slingerland's mind that he would return, in retirement, to farm life. An ad in the Chicago Tribune for farm land caught his attention, and in 1940 he bought the Rock River Farms (near Rockford, Illinois) from Mrs. Ruth Hanna McCormick. Mrs. McCormick was the widow of former U.S. Senator Medill McCormick. At the time (and for the preceding two decades) the farms were home to one of the nation's leading Holstein herds. The farm was just what Henry Heanon had been dreaming of. He planned to build his retirement home on one of the farm's ridges that overlooked the Rock River valley. Because of the labor shortage caused by World War II, H.H. maintained a Hereford beef herd. As soon

Slingerland Rock River Farms

as the labor pool grew again, he began a dairy herd with commercial Holstein cows. In 1944 he ventured into registered Holsteins with the purchase of a "top young sire of promise", King Bessie Supreme. Over the next two years he purchased many additional registered cows until the three milking barns were filled. Just as the herd was beginning to gain the respect of industry experts, H.H. Slingerland died, in 1946.

Gewina the super-cow

The division of assets as prescribed in H.H. Slingerland's will took the family somewhat by surprise.He left the drum business to son H.H. Junior ("Bud"), some commercial real estate to daughter Dorothy, and the farm to daughter Marion. At the time, some family members were upset, feeling that Marion had received more than her share.

According to Marion, the reason she inherited the farm was because her father did not want his dream to die with him. He knew that she was responsible enough (and animal lover enough) to continue with his vision.

Marion (Slingerland) McLaughlin (who passed away in 2002), her husband Richard (who died in 1985) and their daughter Nancy (who dies in 2003) did much more than just "keep the farm going." It became a world-class operation. They acquired herds and worked with herd and breeding consultants to develop an internationally known breeding program known as the Rock River Holsteins. The USDA in one bulletin depicted Rock River Holstein "Haven Hill Crescent Gwina Count" as the exemplary cow of the Holstein-Friesian breed. This particular cow broke numerous mile and fat production records, and is still a source of great pride for the farm. Carnation Farms, when their loss of a production record appeared imminent, insisted that the cow be monitored around the clock in order to properly document the record. The breeder's association sent a man who purchased a rocking chair and sat with the cow around the clock to document the record. Marion related another story about this cow in which an expert from the University of Illinois was sent to examine the cow when it was pregnant. He proclaimed that if she did in fact give birth that the calf would be stillborn. A healthy calf was delivered, and the cow continued to set records. The remarkable cow is buried on the farm, in a grave marked with a huge marble marker.

A disasterous fire destroyed the barn complex in 1969, after which the herd was dispersed. When they rebuilt, the McLaughlins entered the Angus business and have once again carefully bred a prize herd.

At this writing, the family farm is still going strong, and still owned by the relatives of H.H. Slingerland.

Marion (Slingerland) McLaughlin at Gewina's grave in 1997

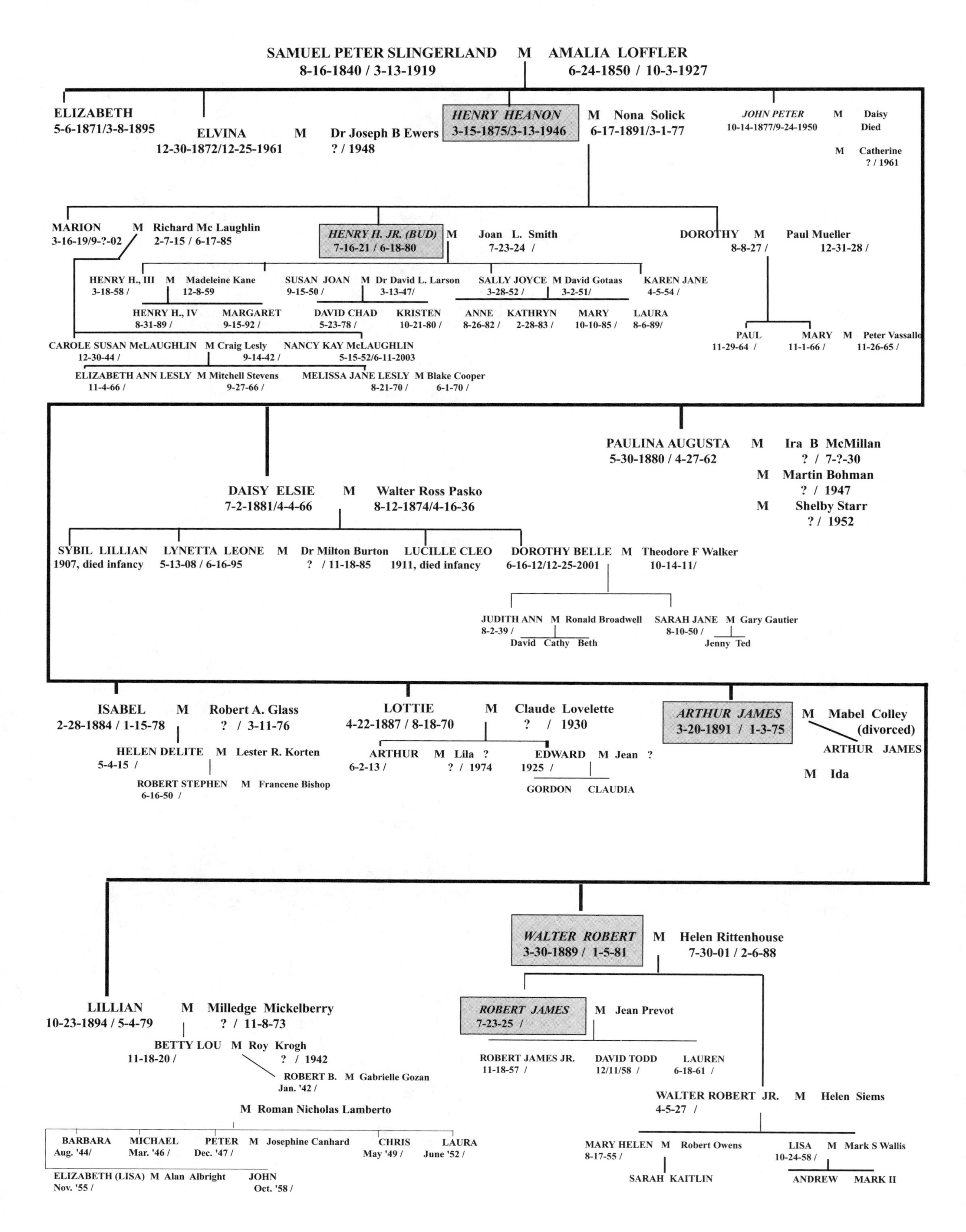
SAMUEL PETER SLINGERLAND M AMALIA LOFFLER
8-16-1840 / 3-13-1919
6-24-1850 / 10-3-1927
ELIZABETH
5-6-1871/3-8-1895
ELVINA M Dr Joseph B Ewers
12-30-1872/12-25-1961
? / 1948
HENRY HEANON
3-15-1875/3-13-1946
M Nona Solick
6-17-1891/3-1-77
JOHN PETER M Daisy
10-14-1877/9-24-1950
Died
M Catherine
? / 1961
MARION M Richard Mc Laughlin
3-16-19/9-?-02
2-7-15 / 6-17-85
HENRY H. JR. (BUD)
7-16-21 / 6-18-80
M Joan L. Smith
7-23-24 /
DOROTHY M Paul Mueller
8-8-27 /
12-31-28 /
HENRY H., III M Madeleine Kane
3-18-58 /
12-8-59
SUSAN JOAN M Dr David L. Larson
9-15-50 /
3-13-47/
SALLY JOYCE M David Gotaas
3-28-52 /
3-2-51/
KAREN JANE
4-5-54 /
HENRY H., IV
8-31-89 /
MARGARET
9-15-92 /
DAVID CHAD
5-23-78 /
KRISTEN
10-21-80 /
ANNE
8-26-82 /
KATHRYN
2-28-83 /
MARY
10-10-85 /
LAURA
8-6-89/
PAUL
11-29-64 /
MARY M Peter Vassallo
11-1-66 /
11-26-65 /
CAROLE SUSAN McLAUGHLIN M Craig Lesly
12-30-44 /
9-14-42 /
NANCY KAY McLAUGHLIN
5-15-52/6-11-2003
ELIZABETH ANN LESLY M Mitchell Stevens
11-4-66 /
9-27-66 /
MELISSA JANE LESLY M Blake Cooper
8-21-70 /
6-1-70 /
PAULINA AUGUSTA M Ira B McMillan
5-30-1880 / 4-27-62
? / 7-?-30
M Martin Bohman
? / 1947
M Shelby Starr
? / 1952
DAISY ELSIE M Walter Ross Pasko
7-2-1881/4-4-66
8-12-1874/4-16-36
SYBIL LILLIAN
1907, died infancy
LYNETTA LEONE M Dr Milton Burton
5-13-08 / 6-16-95
? / 11-18-85
LUCILLE CLEO
1911, died infancy
DOROTHY BELLE M Theodore F Walker
6-16-12/12-25-2001
10-14-11/
JUDITH ANN M Ronald Broadwell
8-2-39 /
David Cathy Beth
SARAH JANE M Gary Gautier
8-10-50 /
Jenny Ted
ISABEL M Robert A. Glass
2-28-1884 / 1-15-78
? / 3-11-76
HELEN DELITE M Lester R. Korten
5-4-15 /
ROBERT STEPHEN M Francene Bishop
6-16-50 /
LOTTIE M Claude Lovelette
4-22-1887 / 8-18-70
? / 1930
ARTHUR M Lila ?
6-2-13 /
? / 1974
EDWARD M Jean ?
1925 /
GORDON CLAUDIA
ARTHUR JAMES
3-20-1891 / 1-3-75
M Mabel Colley
(divorced)
ARTHUR JAMES
M Ida
WALTER ROBERT
3-30-1889 / 1-5-81
M Helen Rittenhouse
7-30-01 / 2-6-88
ROBERT JAMES
7-23-25 /
M Jean Prevot
ROBERT JAMES JR.
11-18-57 /
DAVID TODD
12/11/58 /
LAUREN
6-18-61 /
WALTER ROBERT JR. M Helen Siems
4-5-27 /
MARY HELEN M Robert Owens
8-17-55 /
SARAH KAITLIN
LISA M Mark S Wallis
10-24-58 /
ANDREW MARK II
LILLIAN M Milledge Mickelberry
10-23-1894 / 5-4-79
? / 11-8-73
BETTY LOU M Roy Krogh
11-18-20 /
? / 1942
ROBERT B. M Gabrielle Gozan
Jan. '42 /
M Roman Nicholas Lamberto
BARBARA
Aug. '44/
MICHAEL
Mar. '46 /
PETER M Josephine Canhard
Dec. '47 /
CHRIS
May '49 /
LAURA
June '52 /
ELIZABETH (LISA) M Alan Albright
Nov. '55 /
JOHN
Oct. '58 /

Production records did not survive, so it is not known exactly how many stringed instruments Slingerland was turning out in its heyday of the early '20s. Some insight can be gained, however, by looking at the numbers of Slingerland's competitors of the day. Martin was making only about 1,000 instruments per year. Gibson averaged around 10,000 instruments per year. The real giant of the era was Lyon and Healy, also of Chicago. Lyon and Healy's 1897 catalog claimed annual production of over 100,000 units (stringed instruments with the Washburn brand name). This number shrank as the '20s approached and sharply declined in the late '20s. It has been suggested that some of Slingerland's guitars were made (at least in part) by Regal and/or Harmony. (See the resource page, 244.)

While their instruments were not considered to be on a par with the fine instruments Martin and Gibson were producing, Slingerland was certainly one of the most prolific companies of the time. Their '20s May Bell banjo catalog claimed 1,700 dealers throughout the U.S., Mexico, South America, Canada, North and South New Zealand, and Australia. The catalog listed 10 Tenor Banjos, 5 Banjo-Mandolins, a banjo-guitar, and 7 banjo-ukes.

SLINGERLAND
MAY-BELL *VIOLIN CRAFT* GUITAR
AND TENOR GUITAR

Style 81
Price $30.00

"Slingerland Songster" No. 81

Latest creation in grand concert size, three-ply curly maple sides and back, choice spruce top, arched top and back. Finish. Chocolate brown with sunburst at bridge. Sparkling diamond inlaid headpiece, raised neck, finger guard, separate tuning pegs and adjustable bridge. Sweet, snappy, powerful tone.

Tenor Guitar No. 81T. Price....$30.00
Guitar No. 81. Price....$30.00
No. 1586—Challenge Case to fit....$ 5.40
No. 1884—Keratol, side-opening, flannel-lined case to fit....$15.00

SLINGERLAND
MAY-BELL *VIOLIN CRAFT* GUITARS

Style 82
Price $25.00

"May-Bell" No. 82

Grand concert size. Mahogany sides, back and neck. Arched spruce top, piano finish, dark brown with sunburst at bridge, finger guard rest, adjustable bridge, raised neck and rosewood fingerboard. A real sweet, snappy tone.

No. 1583—Challenge Case to fit....$4.50

SLINGERLAND
MAY-BELL *VIOLIN CRAFT* GUITARS

Style 74
Price $22.50

"May-Bell Jumbo" No. 74

Grand concert size, 2½" deeper than regular grand concert guitar. Wonderful finish in dark umber brown, sunburst at bridge, spruce top, adjustable bridge, finger guard plate and raised neck. Has very powerful snappy tone.

Jumbo Challenge Case....$8.00

SLINGERLAND
MAY-BELL *VIOLIN CRAFT* GUITARS

Style 25
Price $14.00

"May-Bell" No. 25

Grand concert size, genuine mahogany neck, back, sides and top shaded to a dark brown. Finger guard plate. Unsurpassed sweet, snappy tone.

No. 1583—Challenge Case....$4.50

SLINGERLAND MAY-BELL GUITAR

Style 11
Concert Size
Price $25.00

Sides, back and neck constructed of solid mahogany polished to a piano finish. Top is of selected and thoroughly seasoned spruce; fingerboard of solid rosewood. Top edge and soundhole bound and inlaid with vari-colored inlay woods and black ebony. The same wood inlay is brought down through middle of back and around edge. Binding of back is in black ebony. Body is concert size.

SLINGERLAND
MAY-BELL *VIOLIN CRAFT* GUITAR

Style 75
Price $15.00

This is the famous May-Bell Violin Craft constructed entirely of mahogany. It is beautifully yet conservatively finished, and has unsurpassed tonal qualities.

Features: Top, back and sides choice mahogany. Top arched, celluloid bound and guard plate, select thoroughly seasoned close grained mahogany, hand-rubbed to piano finish, neck hand-shaped mahogany, thoroughly and carefully seasoned. Large frets with pearl inlaid position dots. Finish, natural mahogany, hand polished.

No. 75—Concert size....$15.00
No. 1581—Challenge Case....$ 4.30

SLINGERLAND MAY-BELL GUITAR

Style 7
Price $16.00

A beautiful and popular model. Shaded in light and dark mahogany, perfectly blended, and has rose pearl fingerboard and guard plate. Beautiful inlay around edge and highly polished spruce top. This model has a pleasing and powerful tone. Specially constructed for Regular or Hawaiian use.

SLINGERLAND MAY-BELL GUITAR

Style 24
Price $10.00

This is the latest Slingerland May-Bell creation in a standard size guitar. Constructed entirely of select mahogany, hand-rubbed to a piano finish, and designed for the musician who concentrates upon tone and durability, yet desires conservative physical beauty, but not requiring ornate treatment. This is the usual May-Bell guitar of superior quality and workmanship.

No. 24—Standard size, supplied with white celluloid finger guard plate....$10.00
No. 1580—Challenge Case....$ 4.10

SLINGERLAND
"COLLEGE PAL" GUITARS

Style 0
Price $8.50

"College Pal"—The greatest guitar value at the smallest cost. Choice of two beautiful finishes—blended walnut or blended mahogany. Top edge bound in white ivory, fingerboard covered with white pearl; tone quality, workmanship, and materials best ever offered at this price. This guitar is a quality instrument in every detail.

No. 0—Guitar....$8.50
No. 00—Tenor Guitar....$8.50
No. 1581—Challenge Case....$4.30

SLINGERLAND
MAY-BELL TENOR GUITAR

Selected, seasoned spruce top, birch back and sides, and has top side inlaid with white celluloid.

Top edge has an additional thin black inlay, creating an attractive contrast.

Sound-hole inlaid with three rings of black celluloid.

Ebony bridge, white celluloid bridge pins, bone nut, and best patent pegs.

This instrument has full size body, is of fine construction, has great carrying power and true tone.

No. 21—Tenor Guitar....$11.00
No. 5A—Standard Guitar....$11.00
No. 1580—Challenge Case....$ 4.10

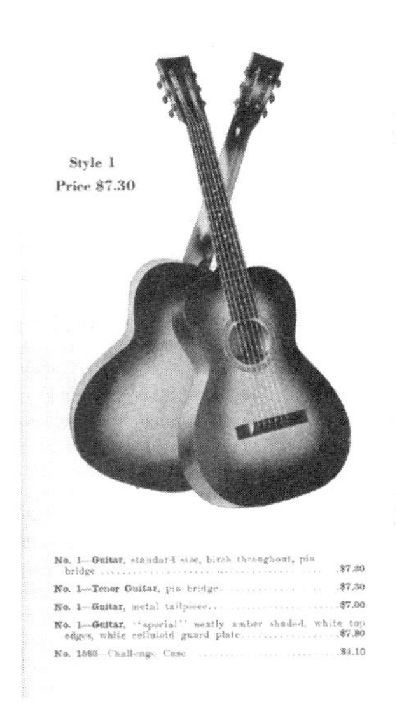

Style 1
Price $7.30

No. 1—**Guitar**, standard size, birch throughout, pin bridge $7.30
No. 1—**Tenor Guitar**, pin bridge $7.30
No. 1—**Guitar**, metal tailpiece $7.00
No. 1—**Guitar**, "special" neatly amber shaded, white top edges, white celluloid guard plate $7.80
No. 1583—Challenge Case $4.10

No. 0216
Banjo Guitar—12" Rim

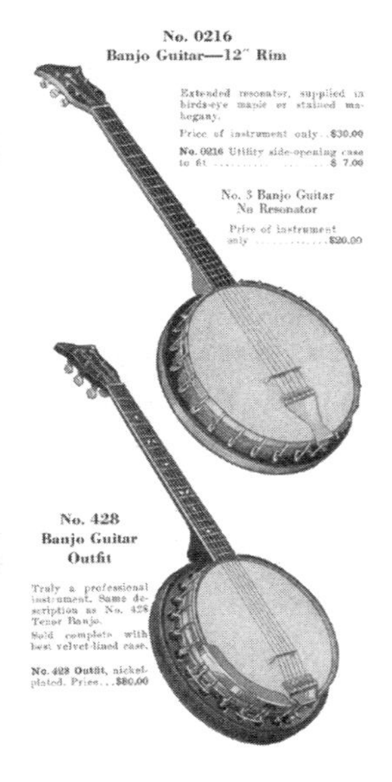

Extended resonator, supplied in birds-eye maple or stained mahogany.
Price of instrument only ..$30.00
No. 0216 Utility side-opening case to fit .... $ 7.00

No. 3 Banjo Guitar
No Resonator
Price of instrument only $20.00

No. 428
Banjo Guitar Outfit

Truly a professional instrument. Same description as No. 428 Tenor Banjo.
Sold complete with best velvet-lined case.
No. 428 Outfit, nickel-plated. Price...$80.00

No. 32 Mandolin, very popular style, stained chocolate brown, spruce top, celluloid-bound edges and guard plate. Price $7.20

No. 33 Mandolin, solid mahogany throughout, spruce top, neatly bound edges, celluloid guard plate. Price $14.00
No. 1519 Challenge Mandolin case. Price $3.30

No. 10 Banjo Mandolin. Price $13.00
With metal resonator $14.00
No. 1861 Challenge case to fit.. $ 4.20

Style 46
Price $6.90

Style 45
Price $5.90

Style 44
Price $5.00

Style 40
Price $2.70

Ukuleles No. 44, 45, 46, real professional solid mahogany. Hand polished. Real value for the money.
No. 40—Ukulele, solid birch throughout. Finished in three pleasing colors "tu-tone" finish, red, green, brown. Choice of colors.
Price each .... $ 2.70
Price per dozen $30.00
No. 41—Ukulele, "tu-tone" brown, body white celluloid bound with neat transfer .... $ 3.00

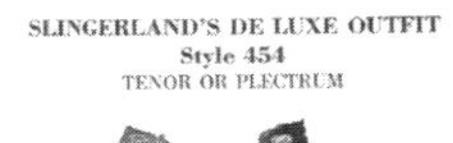

SLINGERLAND'S DE LUXE OUTFIT
Style 454
TENOR OR PLECTRUM

Price $200.00
Complete with Case

An artistic model meeting the requirements of the discriminating artist. Constructed of choice and seasoned rosewood. Resonator beautifully figured and elaborately inlaid with fancy woods. Fingerboard inlaid with fancy mother-of-pearl, hand-cut bird design.

A special feature is the new tone chamber constructed to prevent the clashing of sound waves. There are no overtones or metallic tones in the De Luxe.

Best 4-to-1 geared pegs, genuine mother-of-pearl buttons, all metal parts quadruple gold-plated and hand-engraved.

Sold complete with best grade Keratol covered, 3-ply veneered, plush-lined case.

Nickel Plate $150.00
De Luxe Outfit $200.00

SLINGERLAND
MAY-BELL "RECORDING SONGSTER" BANJO
TENOR OR PLECTRUM

Nickel Plated Complete with Case
Price $80.00

Gold Plated Complete with Case
Price $140.00

No. 432.—A beautiful solo instrument with that much desired snappy tone. Completely covered with glistening Marine Pearl. Beautifully hand-engraved. The pearl will wear a lifetime. Can be wiped with a chamois, will always hold its beautiful luster. New Patented Tone Flange. 4-to-1 geared pegs. Supplied in sea green or white pearl.

Slingerland's Professional Mute installed in any of the Professional models at an additional cost of $5.00.

SLINGERLAND'S
MAY-BELL "RECORDING NITE HAWK" BANJOS AND BANJO MANDOLIN

Nickel Plated Complete with Case
Style 428
Price $60.00

No. 428.—A beauty in appearance and a wonder for tone. A high-grade instrument at a popular price, which has made the demand for this banjo beyond expectations.

Description: Constructed of choice and seasoned American walnut. Fingerboard inlaid with beautiful diamond-shaped pearl position dots. Headpiece with mother-of-pearl ornaments hand engraved. Best 4-to-1 geared pegs.

Also supplied in Banjo Mandolin, and Four- or Five-string Plectrum Banjo, same price.

SLINGERLAND
NEW STYLE QUEEN TENOR BANJO OR BANJO MANDOLIN

Style 424
Price $30.00

An ideal Banjo with all the professional qualifications. Fingerboard and headpiece covered with Marine Pearl and hand engraved in two contrasting colors. White pearl inlay around resonator. 4-to-1 geared pegs.

No. 1734—Challenge Case to fit .... $ 4.40
No. 600—Case, three-ply veneer, keratol-covered, flannel-lined $12.80

SLINGERLAND
MAY-BELL BANJO and BANJO MANDOLIN

TENOR BANJO
Style 99-T
FOUR OR FIVE STRING PLECTRUM BANJO
Price $34.00
(Without Case)

This NEW May-Bell Banjo is professional throughout. Has large extension resonator, graceful neck, and all metal parts heavily nickel-plated. Shell, resonator, fingerboard, and head-piece covered with blue-tinted white pearl. Professional musicians consider this instrument the best banjo value on the market at this price.

No. 99—Banjo $30.00
No. 100—Banjo, same as above, only it is not covered with pearl, highly polished with edge of resonator covered with white pearl, edges bound in black. Price $20.00

Banjo Cases to fit our Resonator Banjos

No. 1734—Challenge Case, side-opening .... $ 4.40
No. 600—Three-ply veneer, keratol-covered $12.80
No. 503—Velvet-lined $15.00
No. 500—Silk plush-lined $20.00

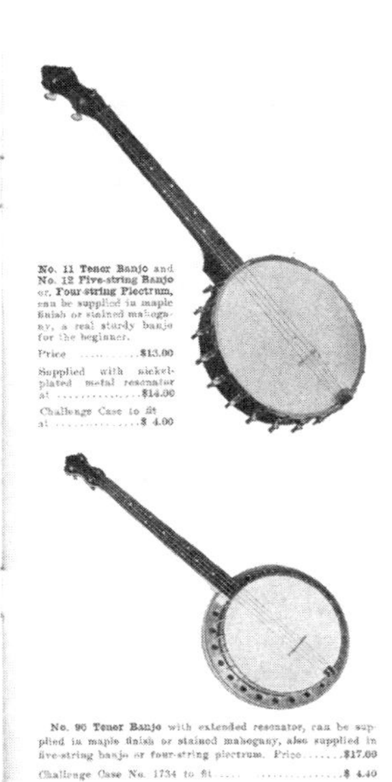

No. 11 Tenor Banjo and **No. 12 Five-string Banjo** or, **Four-string Plectrum**, can be supplied in maple finish or stained mahogany, a real sturdy banjo for the beginner.
Price $13.00
Supplied with nickel-plated metal resonator at $14.00
Challenge Case to fit at .... $ 4.00

No. 90 Tenor Banjo with extended resonator, can be supplied in maple finish or stained mahogany, also supplied in five-string banjo or four-string plectrum. Price $17.00
Challenge Case No. 1734 to fit .... $ 4.40

No. 20
May-Bell Banjo Uke

Stained walnut or birdseye maple, very sturdily built and has a very pleasing tone.
Price $7.00

No. 065
May-Bell Banjo Ukulele

Exceptionally fine Banjo, solid mahogany and walnut. Extended resonator.
Price of instrument only ..$11.00

No. 018
Banjo Ukulele

A beautiful instrument, constructed of selected and seasoned mahogany. The side of the resonator is inlaid with pearline, giving the banjo ukulele a very classy appearance. Small mother-of-pearl inlay in the headpiece. It has that banjo tone.
Price $10.00
No. 365 Canvas Case. Price $ 1.00

STANDARD OF THE WORLD

Style 024
Price $14.00

No. 024 Banjo Ukulele, genuine walnut throughout, 8-in. shell, all professional model, equipped with heavy center grooved top band, heavy cast brackets, flat head hooks, highly polished, dueo finished, natural walnut color. A very popular seller.
Price $14.00

No. 24 Banjo Ukulele, same description, but without resonator.
Price $13.00
Challenge Case to fit .... $ 3.10

Premier May-Bell Professional Banjo Ukulele
Outfit No. 30 Price $25.00

The ideal instrument for professional use, constructed of choice and seasoned American walnut, with extended resonator inlaid with beautifully colored wood inlays.
Sold complete in best Keratol 3-ply veneer, velvet-lined case.

WORLD'S FIRST PRODUCTION MODEL SOLID BODY ELECTRIC GUITAR

Slingerland continued the manufacture of string instruments at least up until the start of the second World War. Around 1939 they made a version of their electrified Hawaiian guitar with a "Spanish-style" round neck. It was the first production solidbody electric guitar that came close to post-war solid body design standards.

The Songster was a lap steel guitar with a "neck through" design. The wings were solid, making this a solid-body guitar.

Each of the pickup pole pieces were wound in opposite directions which in effect made it a humbucking pickup. The pickup appears smaller than it really is because most of the magnet and windings are concealed.

The Songster had open-back Grover tuners; very high quality for the era.

The cord was not detachable; the fabric-covered cable exited the rear of the instrument and terminated with a bakelite connector.

There were two versions of this instrument; a 24-inch scale square-neck and a 25-inch scale round neck. The round neck version had full frets and a pickguard.

THE BOSTON BACKGROUND

The traditions of Boston drummaking began with small home-based family operations in the early 1800s. The drummaking industry (and band-instrument manufacture in general) got jump-started by the Civil War. The Civil War caused a number of American firms to either begin or expand their operations not only in Boston, but in New York, Philadelphia, and Chicago.

Harry A. Bower was among the first in the long line of successful Boston drummakers who would bring Boston the reputation as the drumming capitol of the universe.

Harry Bower in his early days played tympani in the Tremont Theatre Orchestra as well as the Boston Symphony Orchestra. With his pianist wife he toured on the vaudeville stage.

In the late 1800s when Bower began his professional playing career the percussion instruments in use were not far removed from marching military instruments. Timpani were Turkish military drums originally carried on horseback, only recently placed on stands for stationary use. The snare drum was worn on a sling. When concert drummers were not wearing their snare drums, they usually placed them on chairs. Like fellow vaudevillian drummer U.G. Leedy, Harry Bower began to patent some of the gadgets he developed to make his life easier in the orchestra pit. (Leedy was beginning to take out patents at about the same time, and went on to form what would become the world's largest drum company.) In the space of just 10 years Bower took out patents for improvements in most of the basic percussion instruments of the day.

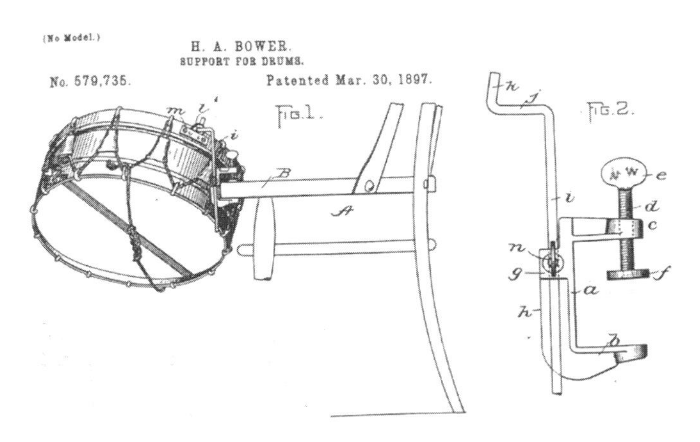

A stand for a snare drum seems like a ridiculously obvious concept in retrospect. In a time when players either wore their drums or placed them on a chair, however, this device for fastening the drum to the chair was a welcome innovation!

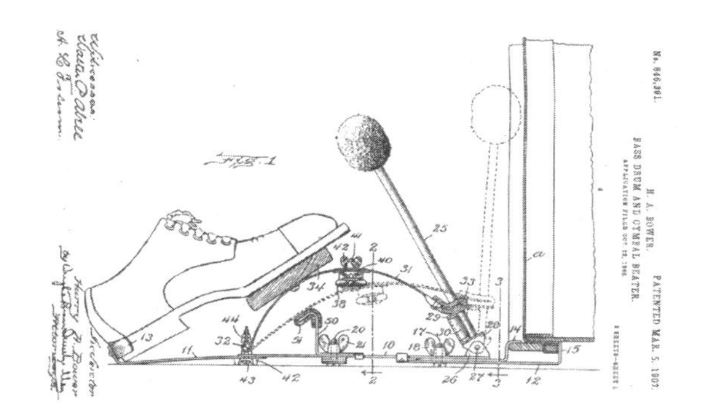

Bower (along with many of his contemporaries) was struggling to invent the drum set by developing a practical way for the drummer to play the bass drum and cymbal with his foot. This pedal was not a commercial success.

IN THE EARLY 1900'S, BOWER APPLIED HIMSELF TO DEVELOPING AN IMPROVED SNARE MECHANISM AND A TYMPANI TUNING MECHANISM

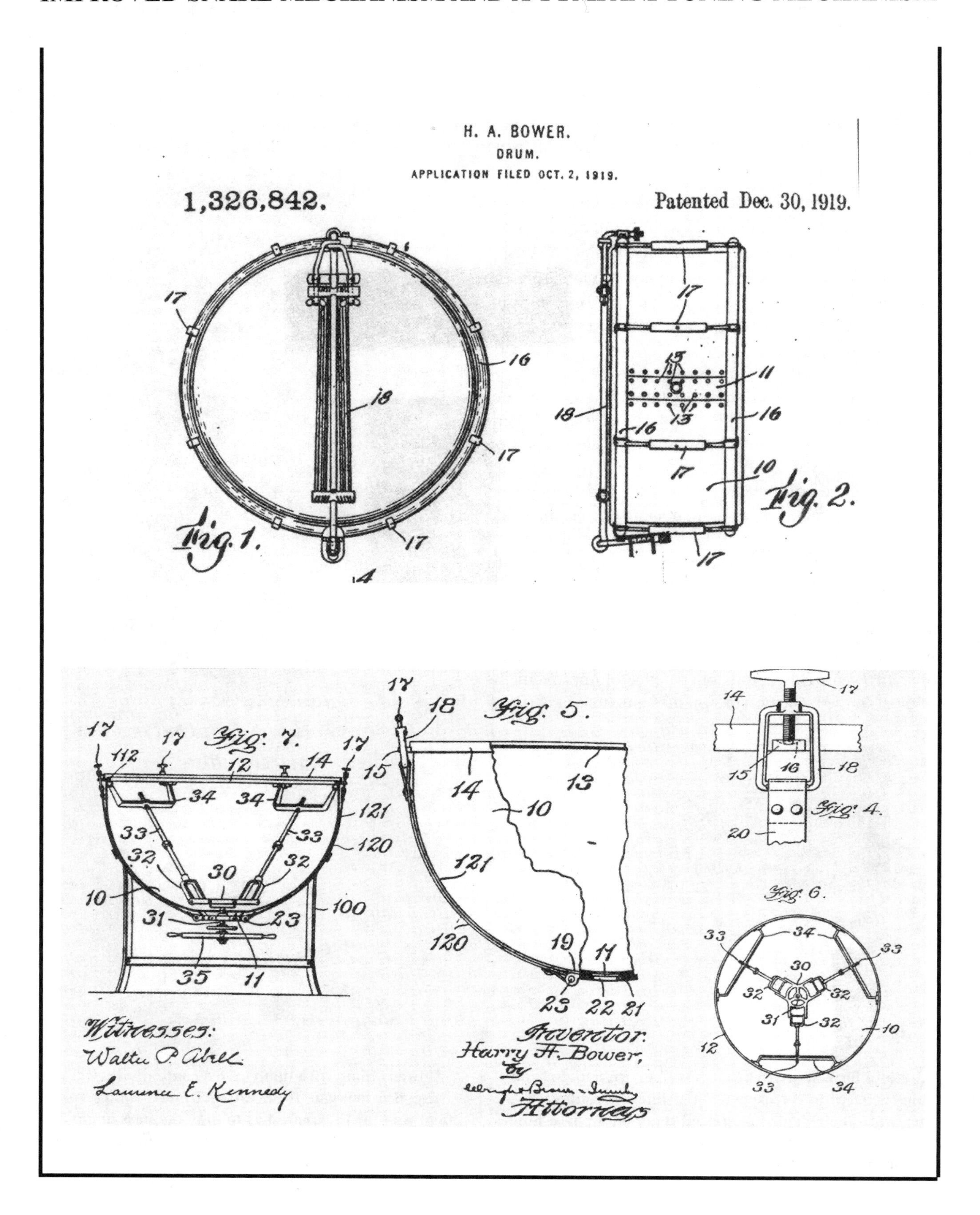

Bower sold his patents for the snare strainers, drum holders, and tympani device to fellow Boston drummaker F.E. Dodge around 1907. He continued to study snare drum technology and experiment in addition to producing what would be his most lasting contribution to American percussionists—The Bower System. The Bower System was among the very first teaching methods to treat the drums, bells, xylophone, and tympani as orchestra and band instruments rather than field instruments.

THE BOWER SYSTEM

The Bower System was endorsed by John Philip Sousa and many other leading musicians of the day. There were three volumes: Drums, Bells & Xylophone, and Tympani. The books were listed in Slingerland catalogs up until the late 1950s.

Miss Grace Tourjee, Graduate of the Bower System

Some 10 years after selling most of his patents to Dodge, Bower patented what he considered to be his crowning achievement: The Bower Drum

DODGE, NOKES & NIKOLAI

The drummaker to whom Bower sold his patents was no newcomer to Boston drummaking; Frank E. Dodge had been in business since 1868. In addition to concert and street drums, Dodge was by the early 1900s selling his own pedal, a whole line of effects, orchestra bells, xylophones, and accessories.

In 1911 the Dodge operation was sold to E.J. Nokes and E.F. Nikolai. They were able to maintain the Dodge position in the marketplace with the help of William Baker, who had been Dodge's Master Mechanic since 1898, and W.J. Blair, who was touted as one of the oldest drummakers in America. (Blair had earlier been with the well-known firm of Blair and Baldwin.)

E.J. Nokes began his playing career at the age of 10 with the Queen's Own Regiment Band in Toronto. He received the youngest honorable discharge at the age of 12 $\frac{1}{2}$ in order to take a playing job at the Grand Opera House of Toronto. Nokes was featured as a xylophone soloist with Tom Brown, Herbert Clark, and Tom Schmidt. For sixteen years Nokes played as the house drummer in Boston's Tremont Theater.

E.F. Nikolai played with one of Boston's leading dance orchestras for ten years (1902-1912) before becoming Nokes' partner.

In 1919 the firm of Nokes & Nikolai purchased the F.E. Cole banjo business.

BOWER–DODGE–NOKES & NIKOLAI–LIBERTY–**SLINGERLAND**

Around 1920, NOKES AND NIKOLAI merged with the LIBERTY RAWHIDE MFG. CO. of Chicago. Liberty originally produced only drum heads, but later began making banjos and drums. Mr. Nokes left the company a year after the merger, and went to work for C.G. Conn's retail outlet in Boston as their repair and drum corps expert. The company continued until 1928 when they sold their manufacturing equipment to the Slingerland company.

Liberty snare drum from the Mike Curotto collection

GETTING STARTED

The dominant drum companies in the early 1920s were the Leedy Company of Indianapolis and Ludwig & Ludwig of Chicago. These two firms plus a half dozen smaller ones (Duplex, Wilson, etc.) owned over ninety percent of the percussion market going into the decade. Over the next ten years the industry was buffeted by general economic chaos and changes in popular music.

By the close of the decade the banjo was out, along with the silent movie. Theater drummers no longer needed equipment. It took almost uncanny business sense for a musical instrument manufacturer to successfully adapt to these kinds of changes, and Henry Heanon Slingerland rose to the occasion.

Ulysses G. Leedy had started his company in Indianapolis around 1900 and had rapidly built it into the world's largest drum company. Leedy was the only company (and would remain so until its sale in 1929) to manufacture nearly every item in its catalog; mallet instruments, cases, heads, drums, tympani, etc.

Ludwig was started by Wm. F. Ludwig Sr. and his brother Theobold, two professional drummers who, with the help of an engineer in-law (Robert Danly), developed a popular bass drum foot pedal. The Ludwig brothers had a small shop where they sold not only their pedal, but a variety of drummers' supplies. (The Ludwigs were Leedy's exclusive sales agents in Chicago.) Wm. F. Ludwig tried on a number of occasions to convince U.G. Leedy to manufacture a metal-shell snare drum. He had played one which belonged to Sousa drummer Tom Mills and wanted one for himself in the the worst way. Leedy felt strongly at the time that the only satisfactory material for drum construction was wood, and refused to listen. The Ludwigs decided to go ahead and make their own metal snare drum. In 1912 they published their first catalog, featuring the pedal, their metal snare drum, and a line of sound-effects accessories.

Although Leedy published a much larger catalog than Ludwig and manufactured nearly everything in it, Ludwig soon caught up because of their marketing plan.Up until 1918 about 90% of the drum business was done direct with the manufacturers via mail order. After WWI, however, there was a shift of emphasis to the retail music dealers. Leedy continued its policy of exclusive distribution, selling to only one dealer per city. Ludwig sought to do business with all comers and built their volume rapidly by having several dealers in each city. Although Ludwig did not do their own plating, make their own tympani bowls, produce their own mallet instruments or trunks, etc., their marketing savvy enabled them to surpass Leedy in gross volume by 1927. In addition to establishing wider distribution, Ludwig entered the school and drum corps market about five years before Leedy.

The tremendous surge in popularity of the banjo in the '20s led both Ludwig & Ludwig and Leedy to begin the manufacture of banjos. Robert Zildjian suggests that Ludwig's banjo manufacturing was in response to a request for quotes from the military. Such military procurements were processed through a center in Philadelphia. When H.H. Slingerland learned that Ludwig had responded to a bid request for banjos he telephoned Wm. F. Ludwig and offered to refrain from bidding on drums if Ludwig would not bid on banjos. This aggravated Ludwig, who pretty much told Slingerland to mind his own business, he would make any kind of instrument he pleased. Slingerland immediately and aggressively began his drum manufacturing plans. Slingerland and Ludwig by this time owned their own tanneries and were already competing daily for the best calfskins coming out of the stockyards. While both Leedy and Ludwig already had much of what it took to get into banjo production in terms of metal and wood shops, machine shop equipment, calf head facilities, etc., it was still very expensive to actually begin banjo production. Unfortunately for both drum firms, the banjo craze was beginning to wane. Lyon and Healy, a company which in 1897 was producing 100,000 string instruments annually, in the winter of 1928 cut their instrument manufacturing to pianos and harps only!

The financial burden of gearing up for banjo production was so expensive that it crippled both Ludwig and Leedy. According to George Way (who was sales manager at Leedy through this era), Leedy's banjo losses were over $160,000 between 1925 and 1929. Gross annual sales for Leedy in these years averaged $560,000, so this was a real blow. Way felt the resultant conditions at Leedy were largely responsible for U.G. Leedy's decision to sell out to Conn in 1929, though the Leedy family cites health reasons. Wm. F. Ludwig Jr. says that losses from banjo production were definitely the cause of the financial problems which forced *his* father to sell his company to Conn— also in 1929. The same popular music trends that created tremendous problems for Leedy and Ludwig worked to the advantage of Slingerland. Their drum business grew so fast that they soon (late 1926 or 1927) had to build a larger new factory, at the corner of Belden and Wayne

As near as can be determined, this was the first type of drum sold under the Slingerland name. It was similar to the body of a banjo in its tensioning system; a banjo key was used to adjust the tension rods, which threaded into banjo clips which gripped the flanges cast in the shell. The drum was patented by Otto Geisler and appeared in the marketplace first with the Geisler badge, then the Liberty Musical Innstrument Company Badge, and finally with the Slingerland badge.

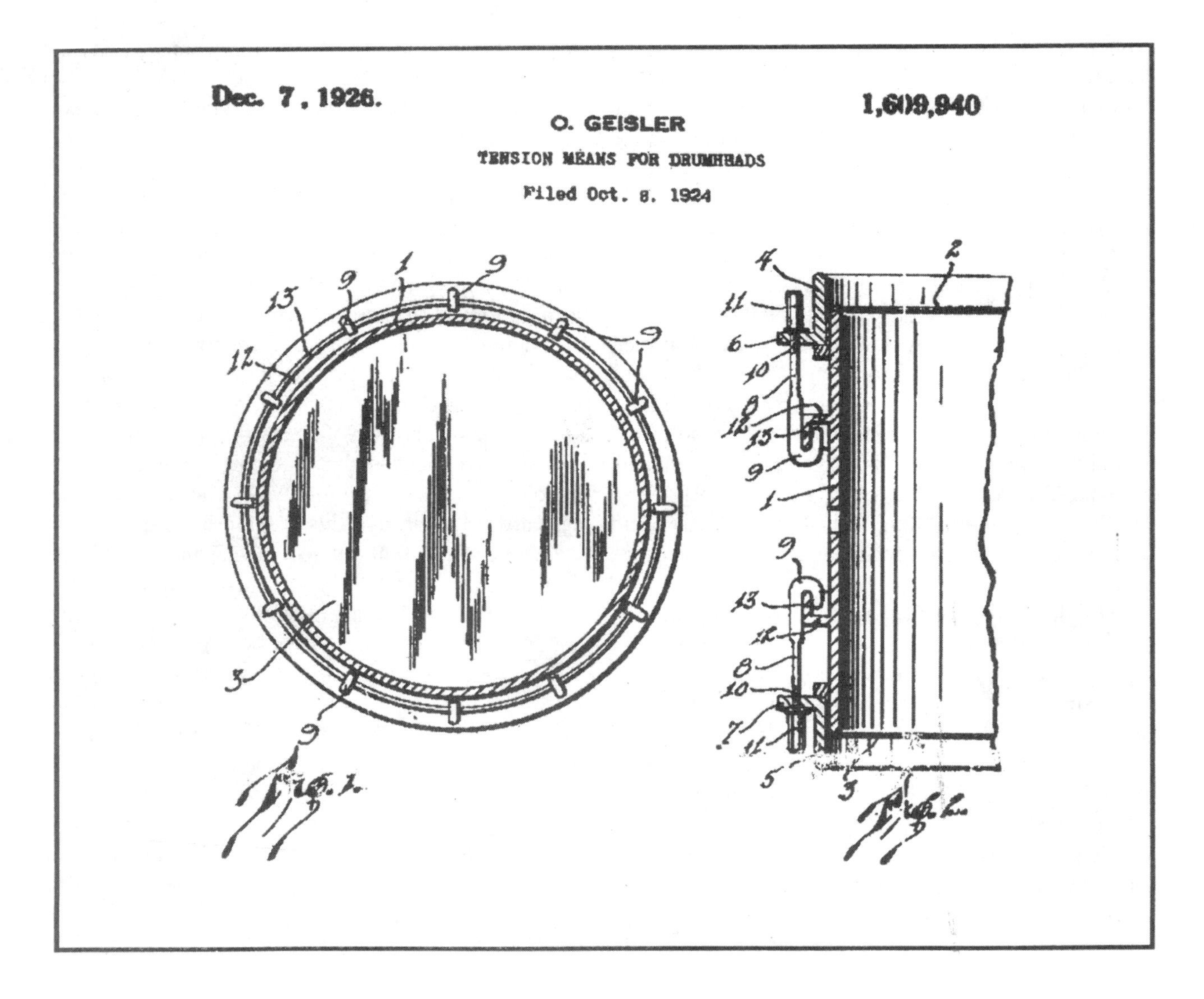

Assembly; the foreground lady is assembling brushes, the man at right is putting together stands.
Guitar assembly in the back.

Tone Flange production in the machine shop

Drumstick Turning

Metal working; plating tanks in the background

Machine Shop

Machine Shop

Cutting and planing wood for drum plies

Stacking drum plies

Clamping reinforcement hoops

Final drum assembly, head tucking

WALTER ROBERT SLINGERLAND SR.

Vice-President

The Tone Flange

Introducing the New Slingerland Patented Tone Flange

PATENTED

THRU scientific experimentation to develop the percussion instrument, which has been at a standstill for many years, the SLINGERLAND Banjo and Drum Company introduces the SLINGERLAND Patented Tone Flange Drum with its many advantageous features.

This Tone Flange eliminates the ring and overtone which drummers have worried about for years. It rejuvenates and clarifies the tone and staccato notes "pop" out like the crack of a machine gun. It also enables the drummer to make a clean "cut-off" without any overtones regardless of where his sticks may be; at the center or extreme edge of head.

One innovation that had not been done by the other firms was a "tone flange" for the snare drum. This was banjo technology applied by Slingerland to the snare drum.

photos courtesy Mike Curotto

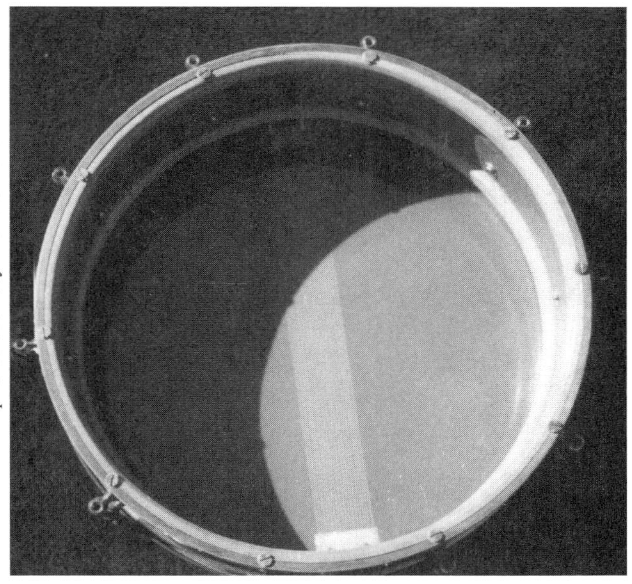

Drums equipped with the tone flange had flat wooden bearing edges into which were mounted screws aligned with each tube lug (above right.) A metal ring rested on top of the screws, the tone flange on top of the ring. Slingerland produced three styles of tone flanges. The rarest, according to collector and tone flange expert Mike Curotto, is the solid tone flange shown here. The other two, the brass with holes and aluminum with holes, are shown on page 131.

Ludwig & Ludwig and Leedy certainly suffered for their decisions to begin banjo production. Firstly, banjo sales failed to give them a return on their investment. Then, at a time when they needed extra profits from their drum devisions more than ever, they were faced with a new competitor in H.H. Slingerland. Slingerland marketed their products aggressively, giving large discounts to small dealers to build volume rapidly. Though Slingerland's drum division sales were only about $100,000.00 in 1929 (according to George Way), this came in a year when Leedy sales were down by $80,000.00, to $449,000.00. Every sale that Ludwig & Ludwig and Leedy lost to Slingerland came right off an already shaky bottom line.

Ludwig & Ludwig and Leedy might possibly have been able to weather the competitive threat Slingerland posed, and may even have been able to overcome the banjo division losses. There was, however, another death blow to the industry; the loss of the theater drummer business. The drummers who provided sound effects for silent movies comprised a significant customer base for both firms. The advent of "talkies" quickly eliminated this whole market segment; page after page of the drum catalogs became obsolete in just a couple years.

With U.G. Leedy's health failing and no qualified heir-apparent, the Leedy Company was sold to the C.G. Conn Company of Elkhart, Indiana, in 1929. Within months, the Ludwig & Ludwig company was also sold to Conn. While Conn paid the Leedy family in cash, the Ludwig family had to settle for Conn stock.

The close of the 1920's saw the Slingerland Banjo And Drum Company emerge as the largest family-owned drum manufacturing concern in existence.

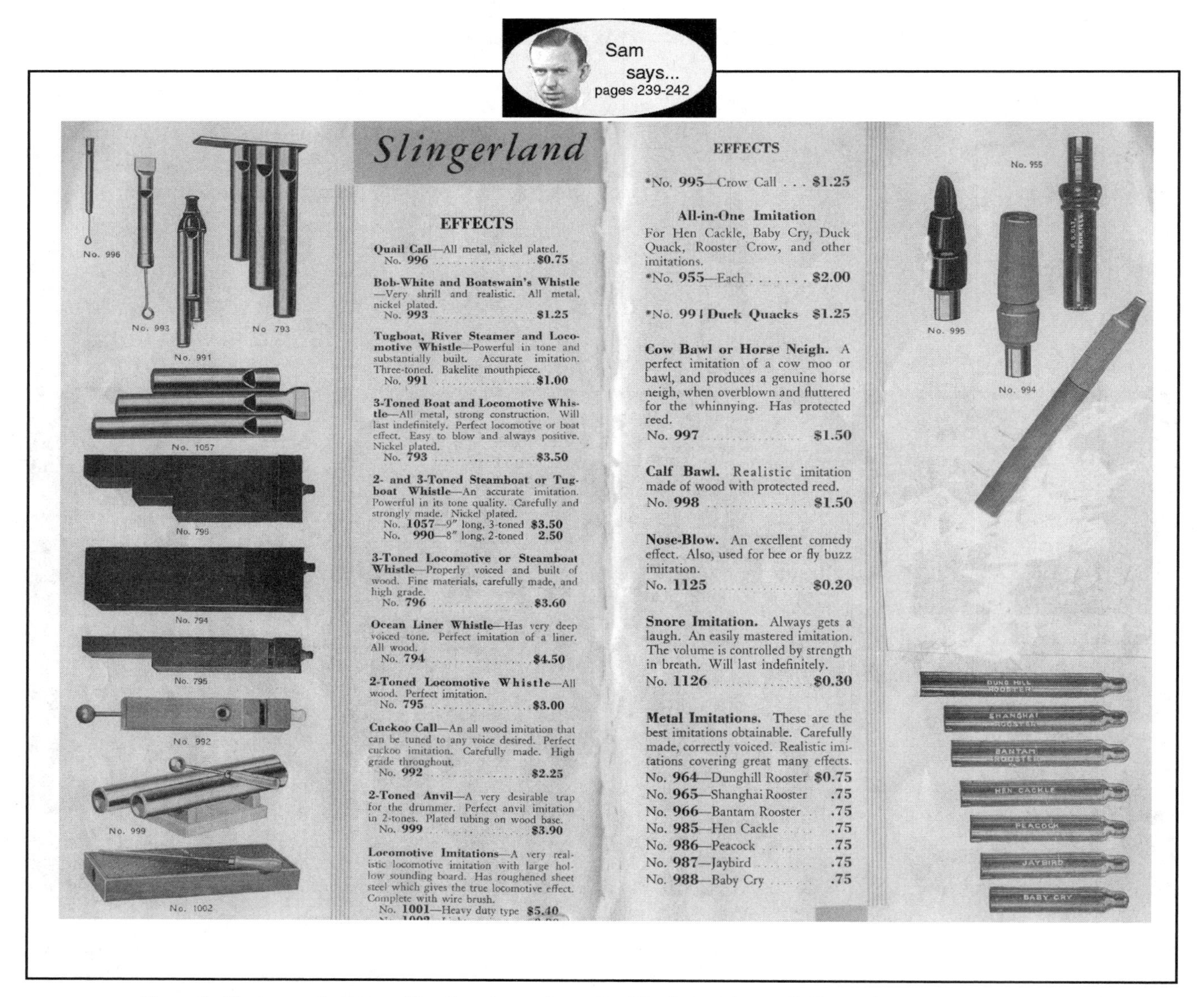

Slingerland

EFFECTS

Quail Call—All metal, nickel plated.
No. **996** **$0.75**

Bob-White and Boatswain's Whistle—Very shrill and realistic. All metal, nickel plated.
No. **993** **$1.25**

Tugboat, River Steamer and Locomotive Whistle—Powerful in tone and substantially built. Accurate imitation. Three-toned. Bakelite mouthpiece.
No. **991** **$1.00**

3-Toned Boat and Locomotive Whistle—All metal, strong construction. Will last indefinitely. Perfect locomotive or boat effect. Easy to blow and always positive. Nickel plated.
No. **793** **$3.50**

2- and 3-Toned Steamboat or Tugboat Whistle—An accurate imitation. Powerful in its tone quality. Carefully and strongly made. Nickel plated.
No. **1057**—9" long, 3-toned **$3.50**
No. **990**—8" long, 2-toned **2.50**

3-Toned Locomotive or Steamboat Whistle—Properly voiced and built of wood. Fine materials, carefully made, and high grade.
No. **796** **$3.60**

Ocean Liner Whistle—Has very deep voiced tone. Perfect imitation of a liner. All wood.
No. **794** **$4.50**

2-Toned Locomotive Whistle—All wood. Perfect imitation.
No. **795** **$3.00**

Cuckoo Call—An all wood imitation that can be tuned to any voice desired. Perfect cuckoo imitation. Carefully made. High grade throughout.
No. **992** **$2.25**

2-Toned Anvil—A very desirable trap for the drummer. Perfect anvil imitation in 2-tones. Plated tubing on wood base.
No. **999** **$3.90**

Locomotive Imitations—A very realistic locomotive imitation with large hollow sounding board. Has roughened sheet steel which gives the true locomotive effect. Complete with wire brush.
No. **1001**—Heavy duty type **$5.40**

EFFECTS

*No. **995**—Crow Call ... **$1.25**

All-in-One Imitation
For Hen Cackle, Baby Cry, Duck Quack, Rooster Crow, and other imitations.
*No. **955**—Each **$2.00**

*No. **991 Duck Quacks** **$1.25**

Cow Bawl or Horse Neigh. A perfect imitation of a cow moo or bawl, and produces a genuine horse neigh, when overblown and fluttered for the whinnying. Has protected reed.
No. **997** **$1.50**

Calf Bawl. Realistic imitation made of wood with protected reed.
No. **998** **$1.50**

Nose-Blow. An excellent comedy effect. Also, used for bee or fly buzz imitation.
No. **1125** **$0.20**

Snore Imitation. Always gets a laugh. An easily mastered imitation. The volume is controlled by strength in breath. Will last indefinitely.
No. **1126** **$0.30**

Metal Imitations. These are the best imitations obtainable. Carefully made, correctly voiced. Realistic imitations covering great many effects.
No. **964**—Dunghill Rooster **$0.75**
No. **965**—Shanghai Rooster .75
No. **966**—Bantam Rooster .75
No. **985**—Hen Cackle .75
No. **986**—Peacock .75
No. **987**—Jaybird .75
No. **988**—Baby Cry .75

Sound-effects products used by theater and vaudeville drummers: all discontinued by 1941

SLINGERLAND IN THE 1930S

As can be seen in the graph below, Slingerland's growth in the drum marketplace was spectacular for a firm that had been in this business for only a couple years. They were already gaining rapidly on the two giants of the industry, Leedy and Ludwig & Ludwig.

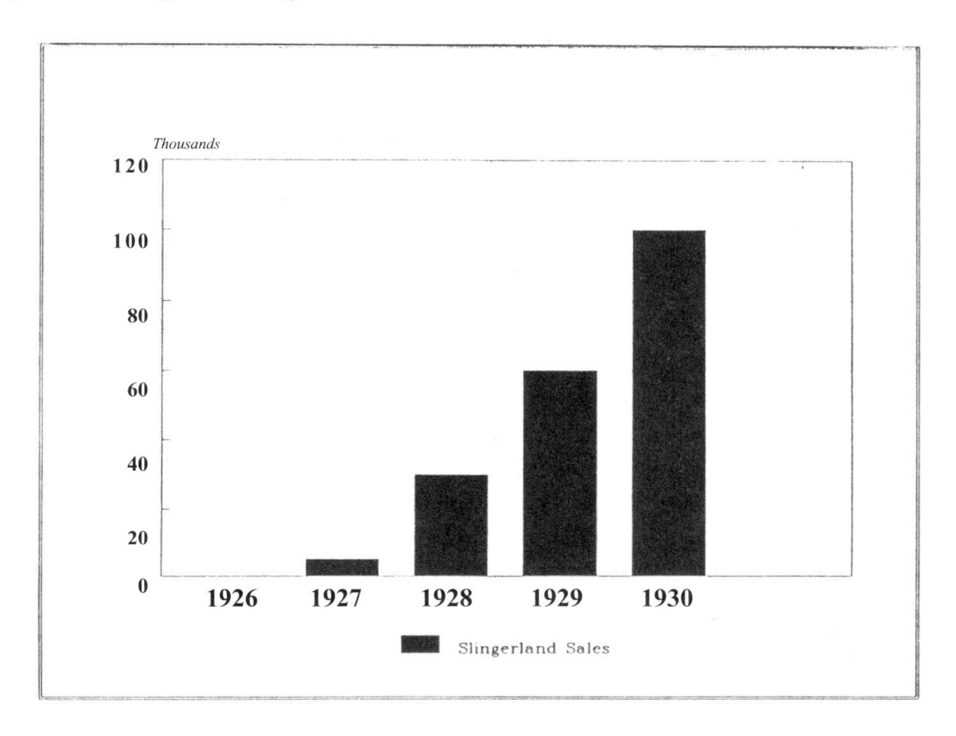

The three keys to Slingerland's continued growth and success were:

Shrewd business sense

H.H. Slingerland had built his business on very sound financial footings. His company was in good enough shape to weather the loss of the theater drummer business, the decline in the popularity of the banjo, and even the stock market crash.

Sam Rowland

George Way once wrote that Slingerland was about to give up on the drum business, but the hiring of Way's former assistant Sam Rowland changed their fortunes.

Gene Krupa

Krupa almost single-handedly popularized the drum set as a solo instrument, and in the process brought recognition (and sales) to Slingerland.

It would seem that combining Leedy and Ludwig & Ludwig under one parent corporation (Conn— which also owned numerous band instrument companies and other music-related firms) would have resulted in a near monopoly and a death knell for competitors. This was, however, not to be the case. Conn's first big mistake (in the opinion of Leedy sales manager George Way) was to move Leedy out of Indianapolis to Elkhart. Shortly after that move, Way tried to interest investors in backing a new drum company to be started up back in Indianapolis. Why? To quote Way's proposal: "Leedy and Ludwig drums are now being made in Elkhart. The metal parts are being made in the Conn plant and assembly is being done in the Buescher plant. The Ludwig sales office is in Chicago and the Leedy sales office is in Elkhart. The craze on the part of the officials of the Conn Company for standardization, along with the fact that much of the quality and service have been seriously impaired, has created a very unpleasant atmosphere in the field. It is interesting to note that no manufacturer of a general line of musical instruments has ever been successful in making drums. There are many reasons for this, the principal one being that drums are very much of a specialty. During the last twenty years the Conn Company has attempted four different times to make their own drums, but were never successful. And the new regime is likely to fail in the fifth attempt— even though they have acquired the Leedy and Ludwig companies— for many reasons. This is especially so if the few [employees] who understand the drum business should pull away or if a new company should be inaugurated. Since the Leedy company moved to Elkhart there have been hundreds of complaints received because of poor quality and service. At Indianapolis the administrative, sales, and factory officials were closely interwoven, whereas here [Conn, Elkhart] there is a decided wall between each group. The writer and our traveling representative have been told by our various dealer friends, to say nothing of dozens and dozens of professional friends throughout the country, during the last year, that they would heartily support a new organization that presented the right models made in the right way."

These words would certainly be prophetic. Conn would indeed eventually fail at the drum business and get out of it altogether, in 1955. The market would indeed support new companies, although rather than the company George wanted to start the new major players would be WFL and Slingerland. At the time that Way first prepared his proposal (1932), he did not consider Slingerland to be a serious long-term competitor in the drum business. By 1936 when he updated his proposal, his opinion had changed. Slingerland was making big-time progress, and their window of opportunity had never been wider.

Here is how George Way sized up the companies in the marketplace in his 1932 proposal seeking backing for a new drum company (quoted verbatim).

Manufacturers In The Field

THE LEEDY MANUFACTURING COMPANY was established by a single man (Mr. U.G. Leedy) at Indianapolis in 1895. The first accessories were made in the basement of the theater in which he was employed. Shortly after, he took a room in an office building, taking in a partner, and from then on the business became the largest exclusive drum factory in the world in terms of buildings, floor space, and investment. The Leedy Manufacturing Company is the only firm that ever reached the goal of making the entire line of drummer's instruments and accessories, and, while they did not do the greatest volume of business, they always enjoyed the prestige of being the house of superior workmanship.

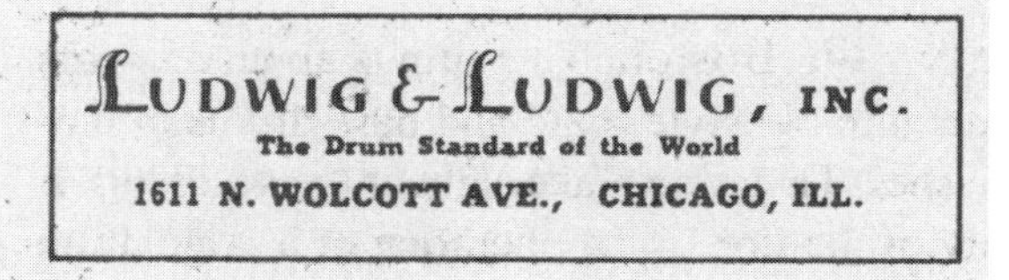

LUDWIG & LUDWIG, former professional drummers of Chicago, and at one time selling agents for the Leedy Company, started to manufacture about 1909. They never reached the stage of manufacturing the complete line, but owing to the fact that they catered to the jobber and sold on the open market to all comers, having several dealers in each city, their volume in 1927 surpassed that of the Leedy Company, reaching approximately $800,000.00 for that year. Another

THE NOVAK DRUM COMPANY, of Chicago. A former drummer with very limited ideas and a very small shop, employing only four or five people. Makes a business of supplying extremely cheap merchandise to such houses as Montgomery-Ward and Sears-Roebuck. This firm is not recognized by either the professional or the amateur drummer. Their total business cannot possibly reach more than $50,000.00 a year, if that much. They also manufacture a cheap line of ukuleles and guitars.

THE WILSON DRUM COMPANY of Chicago went out of business in 1928. Mr. Wilson was formerly a workman for the old Lyon and Healy drum department, which he bought out about 1915. Lack of original ideas and business ability was the cause of final failure. However, in 1926 his business undoubtedly totaled $50,000.00 or $60,000.00.

J. C. DEAGAN
DEAGAN BUILDING
BERTEAU AVE. & E. RAVENSWOOD PK.
CHICAGO, ILL.

J.C. Deagan, Inc. Chicago. This firm is about 30 years old. They make the mallet-played instruments only and had practically no competitors until Leedy finally produced a superior line of these instruments in 1922. Deagan has hardly changed a model for 20 years. However, as they were so long the leaders in this field, they still have a very good name and their business undoubtedly runs $300,000.00 a year.

Kohler & Liebech, Chicago. This firm has been established about twelve years. Both men were formerly workmen at Deagans. They make mallet-played instruments only, have no catalog and do not solicit professional or amateur sales. They do a very small amount of business with the music stores, confining most of their activities to supplying mallet-played instrument parts to organ factories for theatre organs. Have a very small shop and their business can not possibly exceed $50,000.00 a year.

GEORGE B. STONE & SON, INC.
Professional Drum Makers Since 1890
61 HANOVER STREET
BOSTON, MASS.

Geo. B. Stone & Son, Boston This firm is about 35 years old. They manufacture old style snare and bass drums in limited sizes and finishes. They also make eight or ten accessories. The main activity of the firm is the operation of a large drum school. It is doubtful if their manufacturing activities exceed $25,000.00 a year.

WALBERG & AUGE
86 Mechanic Street - - Worcester, Massachusetts

Walberg & Auge, Worchester, MA. This firm discontinued the making of snare and bass drums five or six years ago. They are admittedly not wood workers, but have confined their efforts to metal parts such as trap holders, music stands, etc. They do a fair business among jobbers and some direct business with the dealers. Almost every drum catalog carries two or three of their special holders, which are very good. Their total business in drum accessories probably reaches $60,000.00/year. This firm is about 28 years old. They also manufacture several other articles.

DUPLEX MANUFACTURING COMPANY, Inc.
SAINT LOUIS, MISSOURI
2815-2817 Henrietta Street
Service and Dependability

Duplex Mfg, Inc. This is the oldest drum shop now in existence, being about 45 years old. It is very small, employing only five people. They only make metal snare drums, pedals, and a few holders. Their wood drums, both snare and bass, are assembled products. However, they have three or four outstanding articles that keep them going. The biggest year they ever had was around $20,000.00.

ODD SHOPS There are four or five drummers operating retail drum shops in various cities and who manufacture one or two specialty accessories such as pedals, practice pads, sticks, etc. and who sell them locally. They are not known outside of their own vicinity. However, the total business of these firms no doubt reaches about $20,000.00 a year. Most of the articles they make are hand made and could not be considered serious competition to legitimate manufacturers. They sell mostly to pupils and local professionals.

Fred Gretsch Manufacturing Company, Brooklyn, N.Y. This is a large general musical instrument jobbing house, also importers. However, they do some manufacturing and probably sell about $12,000.00 of very cheap snare and bass drums per year. They do not manufacture anything else in the drum line.

Wells Manufacturing Company, Brooklyn A very small shop employing three or four men who do not make an assembled product, but supply wood shells to other drum factories such as Duplex, Stone, and a few jobbers who make up cheap models. Their business could not exceed $15,000.00 per year.

Established 1865

ALBERT HOUDLETT

The Houdlett Company, Brooklyn Another firm that operates very similar to Wells as mentioned above. However, they make other musical instrument accessories

THE SLINGERLAND TEXT FROM WAY'S ORIGINAL PROPOSAL, 1932:

The Slingerland Drum And Banjo Company of Chicago have been in business for 20 years or more. Their main line consists of all grades of banjos, guitars, ukuleles, etc. and they only added drums within the last two years. This action was taken due to a hard feeling over the fact that the Ludwig Company introduced a line of banjos in competition. Their drum business at this time probably does not exceed $100,000.00 per year. Most of their drum merchandise is decidedly inferior and they have nothing of an original nature to create a high standing in the field. Most of their business is being gotten by granting exhorbitant discounts to the small dealer. Unless they change their tactics in the near future and find means of introducing some high grade and original models, they will not get any farther.

THE REVISED SLINGERLAND TEXT FROM WAY'S 1936 PROPOSAL:

The Slingerland Drum and Banjo Company of Chicago have been in business for 20 years or more. Their main line consists of all grades of banjos, guitars, ukuleles, etc. They added drums in 1927. This action was taken because of hard feelings over the fact that the Ludwig Company introduced a line of banjos in competition. Their drum business did not exceed $60,000.00 in 1929. Most of their merchandise is very similar to Ludwig's. They were about to give up the manufacture of drums in 1930, when Sam Rowland (a former Leedy executive) joined them and the company has become the third largest in the drum field, due to his efficient management.

As George Way pointed out in his 1932 proposal, Slingerland was selling enough drum merchandise to sting their competitors, it was a marginally profitable division of their operation and, according to Way, they were about to give up the manufacture of drums in 1930 when Sam Rowland joined them. Rowland had been an important part of the Leedy team in Indianapolis but did not remain with Leedy when Conn moved Leedy operations to Elkhart.

SAM C. ROWLAND

Sam Rowland, originally from Crawfordsville, Indiana, started his career as a professional drummer. He spent twelve years in the top vaudeville pits, two years with circus bandmaster Fred Jewell and with the Indiana University Concert Band and Orchestra. He settled in California where he headed the drum department at the Los Angeles Wurlitzer music store while moonlighting with Dick Stokes' Californians, a popular West Coast orchestra.

In February 1927 he moved to Indianapolis to join Leedy as Assistant Advertising Manager (George Way was advertising manager).

Rowland chose not to move to Elkhart with Leedy as a division of Conn, electing instead to move to Chicago and work for Slingerland.

Rowland left Slingerland in early 1937 to join the Ludwig family, who were starting a new drum company. The new company was at first called The William F. Ludwig Drum Company. Conn still operated *their* Ludwig drum division, and their lawyers saw to it that the name of their new competitor was changed. The Ludwig family shortened the name to WFL. According to Wm. F. Ludwig II, one of the reasons Rowland left Slingerland was a telephone conversation he overheard. He heard H.H. Slingerland (in the office next to his) telling someone about the new Ludwig operation. Slingerland reportedly was derisive in in comments, saying, "There's no fool like an old fool!" and predicting that the new Ludwig company would not be in operation for a full year. When Rowland brought that story to Ludwig as an employee, he inspired a rallying cry of "A year and a day!" at Ludwig. Rowland took to Ludwig a complete Slingerland product line review in the form of handwritten notes in a 1936 catalog. Many of his notes are quoted in this book. (See index.)

Rowland later worked for yet another of the major players in the drum business as sales director for the Gretsch company in New York.

Sam Rowland's 1936 Slingerland Catalog Notes

When Sam Rowland left Slingerland to join the Ludwig family, one of the first things he did was to sit down with the most current Slingerland catalog (1936) and jot notes next to many of the products. These notes will undoubtedly be useful to collectors and historians, as in many cases they indicate why a particular item was discontinued, where the idea came from, and even how many were sold. The notes are transcribed in their entirety on pages 239–242. Many of the products he commented on are illustrated throughout this book; most are identified with this "Sam Says" graphic:

Sam
says...
pages 239-242

Rowland had a tremendous amount of influence in the drum corps world. His American Legion Corps won several State Championships and one National Championship. At the Illinois American Legion convention of 1933, Corps under his instruction won the first four places. Rowland spearheaded Slingerland's progress in the marching marketplace, editing the marching publications shown on this page.

On Parade (1931) A 16-page manual for instructors of newly organized Corps. Promoted as a manual capable of enabling an instructor to develop a playing and marching Drum and Bugle Corps within two weeks.

The Drum Corps Handbook (1931) A 75-page manual meant to provide new ideas to existing corps. Inluded sections on baton twirling and drum and bugle music for "G", "D-Crook" and "Baritone" bugles prepared by nationally recognized authorities. Also included Drum Major signals, Flash Stick twirling, Tenor and Scotch drum beat combinations, etc.

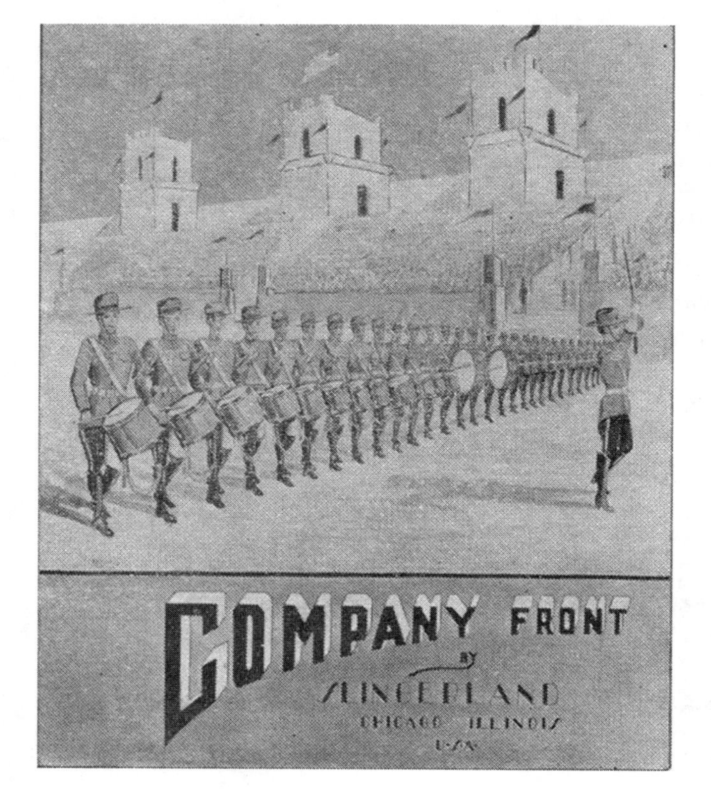

Company Front (1931) This booklet included organizational information such as instrumentation notes and marching formations, but the main focus was on equipment; new bugle models, accessories, and "every other known new item".

PATENT BATTLES

Relations between Ludwig and Slingerland had never been cordial, and seemed to worsen as the years passed. By the late twenties they were bitter competitors in several arenas.

As George Way mentioned in his proposal, the competition became more intense and tinged with animosity as soon as Ludwig began banjo production.For the next forty years there would be threats of legal action from both corners, a number of which actually developed into litigation. Lawyers for both sides were frustrated by the fact that it was more important to win the lawsuits than to reach amicable compromises. At one point (much later, in 1947) even Wm. F. Ludwig Sr. grew weary of the bickering; a letter to H.H. Slingerland explained that the lawyers were being bypassed in this correspondence because it was just too hot to expend the extra effort. “Couldn't,” he asked, “we just talk about this situation and work it out ourselves?”

Slingerland was never known as an innovative company. Many of its products were patterned after other items already in the marketplace. An early example is the Shur-Grip holder. Slingerland developed a whole line of hardware (cowbell holder, tambourine holder, trap-holder, etc.) around this unit. Shortly after its introduction in the early 1930’s (when Ludwig was a division of Conn), Conn’s patent attorney advised Slingerland that the Shur-Grip trap holder was in violation of a patent they held in the name of L.B. Greenleaf. H.H. asked his patent attorney for a history of the Greenleaf patent. The response informed him that six of the eight original Greenleaf claims in his patent application had been denied because of similarities to previously issued patents such as the toilet mirror and lamp holder. The patent Greenleaf finally was granted was based on only two of his original claims. (Slingerland’s attorney took the position that there was no infringement on the Greenleaf patent because the Shur-Grip holder featured no tilter.)

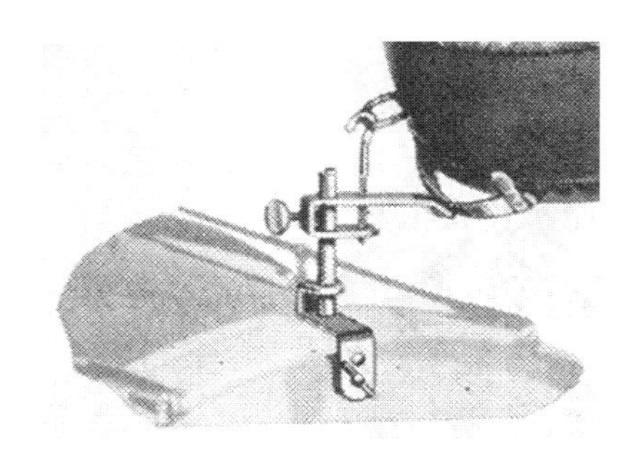

Slingerland Shur-Grip Holder

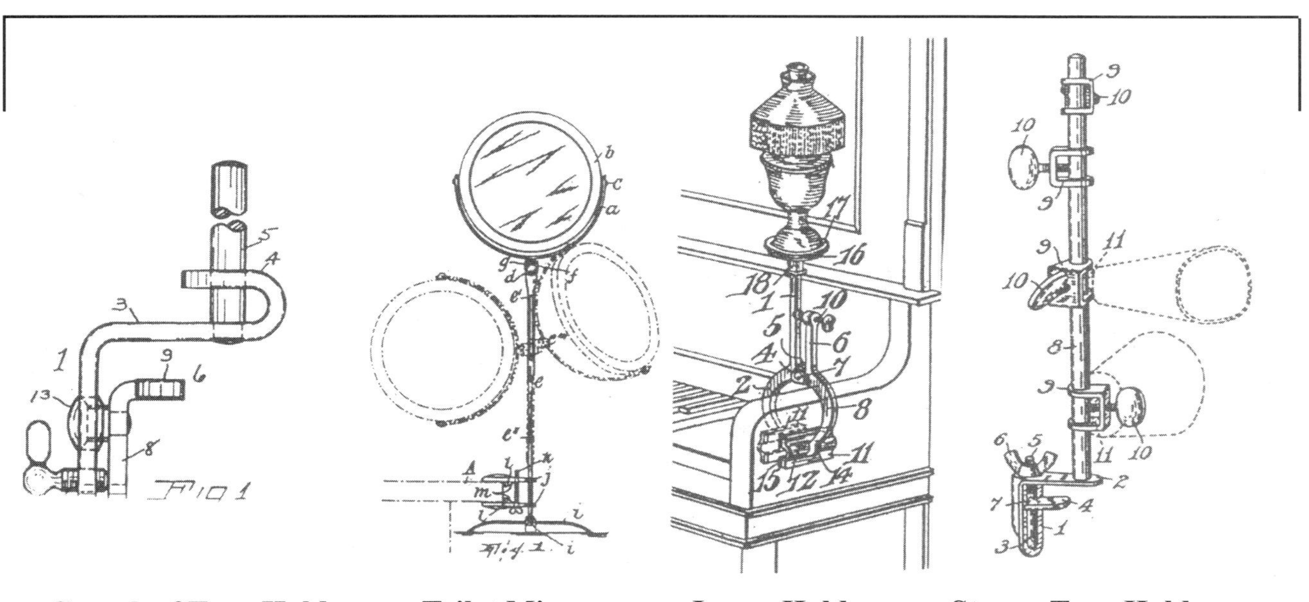

Greenleaf Trap Holder **Toilet Mirror** **Lamp Holder** **Strupe Trap Holder**

Slingerland ended up paying Conn $100.00 for the right to produce the Shur-Grip clamp, though the final license was actually granted not on the Greenleaf clamp but on a patent in Cecil Strupe’s name.

Conn's patent attorney also had a problem with Slingerland's Duall snare drum.Walter Soderburg of Duluth, Minnesota, had filed the patent for this drum in 1932. In 1933 Slingerland purchased the patent assignment from Soderburg and made it the crown jewel of the Slingerland snare drum line. In June of 1934 Conn's lawyers notified Slingerland (in the same letter which notified them of patent infringement by the Shur-Grip holder) that the drum constituted patent infringement of the Danly snare drum. They ordered Slingerland to not only cease and desist from manufacturing the items, but also to account to Conn for the sales of both articles.

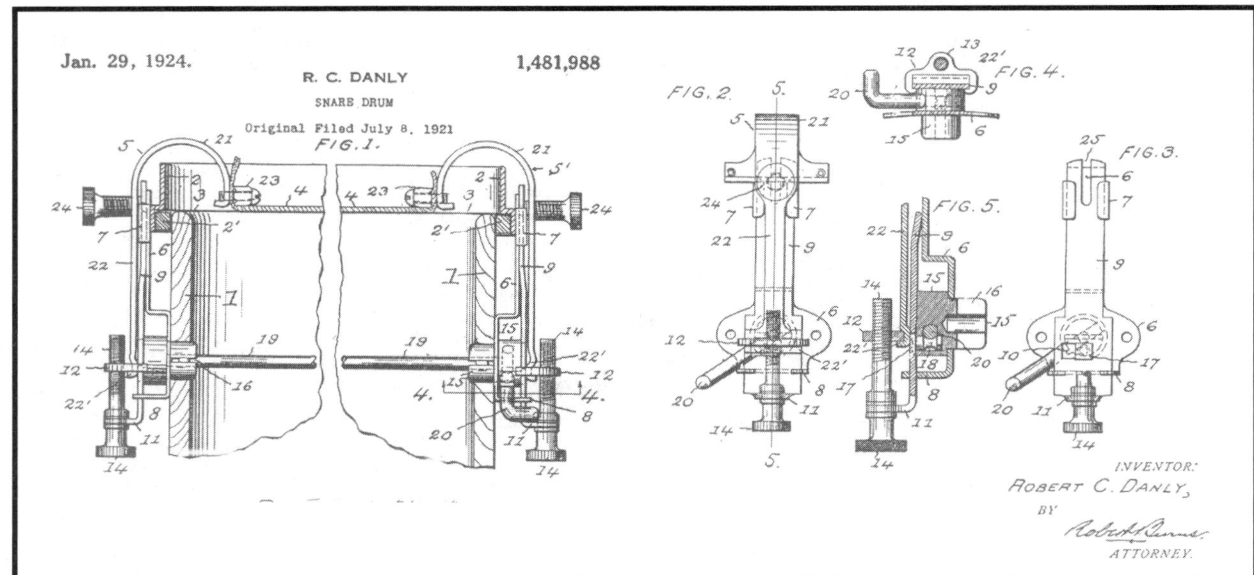

Drawings from the patent papers on the R.C. Danly snare drum. Robert Danly was Wm. F. Ludwig Sr.'s brother-in-law, and the man who designed the bass drum pedal that got the Ludwig brothers started in manufacturing. The feature claimed as unique and patentable was the internal shaft (#19 in the drawing) which connected to the snare mechanism, facilitating simultaneous release of both ends of the snares.

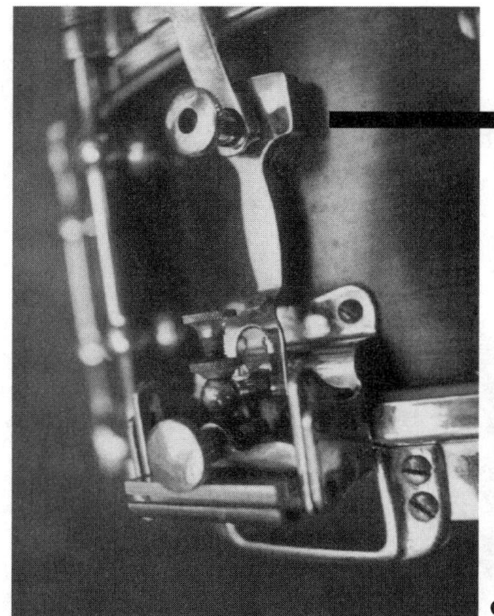

rod through drum,

parallel to snares

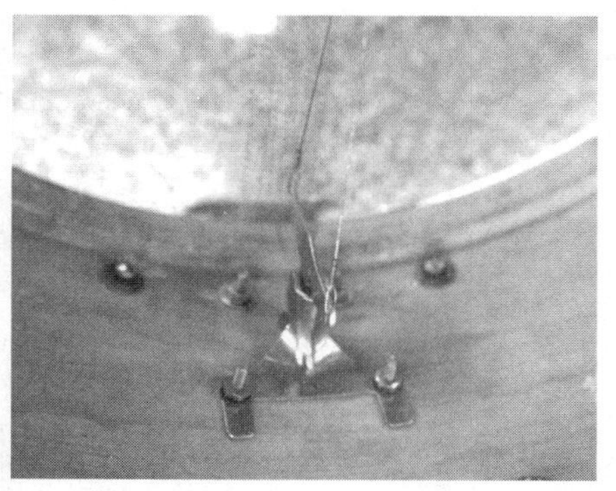

One Duall surfaced which instead of a rod has a cable system connecting the two sides. This drum is in the Mike Curotto collection.

There were fairly major design differences between the Slingerland (Soderburg) and Ludwig (Danly) snare drums, but key to each was the internal "parallel" mechanism. Conn counsel claimed that the only differences resulted from Slingerland's overcomplicated efforts to disguise the Danly mechanism. H.H. Slingerland resented this suggestion and invited Conn counsel to visit his office for a firsthand demonstration of the superior working snare mechanism.

GENE KRUPA

The next important factor in the growth and development of the Slingerland company after Sam Rowland's contributions of the early thirties was the affiliation with Gene Krupa.

It would be hard to overstate Krupa's importance not only to Slingerland, but to the development of Swing music, the drummer as a solo instrumentalist, and even the development of the drum set as we know it today.

At the age of about 9, Krupa worked running errands in a neighborhood music store near his home on the south side of Chicago. He wanted to take up a musical instrument, and since the drums were the cheapest instruments in the wholesale catalog that came to the shop, he set his sights on drums. At the age of 16 he entered St. Joseph's College, a preparatory seminary for the study of the priesthood.

Krupa was still 16 when a friend told Gene about theater drummer/teacher Roy Knapp, and Gene sought Knapp out. According to Knapp's memoirs, Knapp was downstairs in the musician's room of the Capitol Theater at 79th and Halsted when the doorman called down to him, "Hey! There's a maniac up here who wants to see you!" Knapp went upstairs to kind Krupa and his sister. Krupa had a pair of timpani sticks and was beating on the walls, the chairs, his belly... everything. From that day on, Krupa studied with Knapp. He took lessons in Knapp's theater pit, on the stage, and in the musician's dressing rooms. According to Knapp, Krupa already, at age 16, considered himself a helluva drummer and he wanted to study timpani under Knapp. Knapp talked him into sudying primarily drums. "He was a beautiful student," said Knapp, "the greatest talent I ever had to work with. He'd get what I was giving him almost while he was sitting there taking his lesson. He had a great sense of rhythm, of course, and it was easy for him to get the time-counting system I gave him." (Knapp later taught at the Dixie Music House until it burned in 1937. He then started his own drum school and was known for decades as the Dean of Chicago percussion.)

Krupa left the seminary after one year to play the drums. He played with three or four local orchestras over the next 8 years, including "The Austin High School Gang" which included Benny Goodman.

Krupa had before 1935 already made somewhat of a name for himself among the "hot jazz musicians", but he found himself stalled in a frustrating Chicago gig with Buddy Rogers. Rogers was a versatile and competent musician, but wasn't playing the jazz that Gene was really aching to play. Krupa tried to make the best of his situation, offering to give Rogers some pointers on how to play a drum solo. (As part of his act, Rogers took solos on nearly every instrument.) Rogers rebuffed Krupa, adding to his frustration.

John Hammond (Benny Goodman's manager) came to Chicago on behalf of Goodman, to recruit Krupa for the jazz band that Goodman was putting together. The opportunity to play the kind of music he really like was irresistable to Krupa, so he joined Goodman in New York although it meant a cut in pay. The gig Goodman was assembling his band for was the radio broadcast *Let's Dance* sponsored by Nabisco. The show ran from December 1934 until May 1935, airing late at night in New York, which put it in prime time on the West Coast. Unbeknownst to everyone including the bandleader, a tremendous following was building in California. Following the Nabisco broadcasts, the Goodman band tried "stepping up" to a fancy hotel gig at the Roosevelt Hotel. This was a very bad move, as the Roosevelt clientele (and management) was expecting more of the music they'd enjoyed from the previous band— Guy Lombardo and his Royal Canadians. Goodman's swinging jazz was as far removed from that as any music of the day.

Goodman then took the band on a cross-country tour which was filled with more of the same disappointments for band and audiences alike: empty dance floors, customers demanding refunds, angry ballroom owners. By the time the band made it to California, Goodman was ready to quit.

Things went much better in Oakland, where the band realized for the first time that the *Let's Dance* broadcasts had made them some fans. (Air time by a local DJ had also helped.) This time people were standing in line waiting to get into the dance.

Next on the schedule was a month-long engagement at the Palomar Ballroom in Los Angeles. The owner had heard about disasters at the last few venues, and was trying to cancel the band. Knowing this, the band opened with some of their "sweeter" numbers, which met with polite applause. Benny, figuring he had nothing left to lose, called for Fletcher Henderson's arrangement of "King Porter Stomp" which featured a hot Bunny Berrigan solo. This was exactly what the fans had been waiting for, and the roof came off. From that moment on the band's success was phenomenal. Instead of cutting the band's month-long engagement short, the management insisted on extending it. By the time the band left California on the cross-country tour home, the word had gone out and the popularity of their new music had spread like wildfire. Every date was another conquest, culminating in spectacular engagements at the Congress Hotel in Chicago (six months, with radio broadcasts heard by millions) and the Paramount Theater in Times Square.

Krupa was the ideal drummer for Benny Goodman's band as it introduced the new sound of the '30s; he was a flamboyant and flashy showman. Goodman himself by contrast was rather staid on the bandstand— sometimes even characterized as dour. As the leader of the band "making all the noise", however, Goodman also became a major celebrity. Almost overnight Goodman and Krupa became two of the first jazz musicians to enjoy the same fame and adulation as the movie stars and major sports figures of the day.

According to Wm. F. Ludwig II, Krupa's affiliation with Slingerland began right after his triumph at the Congress Hotel in Chicago.

Krupa had bought his first drum from Frank Gault at Frank's Drum Shop of Chicago. During his Austin High School days, Gene had played Ludwig drums that his father bought at Chicago's major music retailer Lyon and Healy. Krupa's father wanted him to have a new drum set after the Congress Hotel gig, and called the Ludwig & Ludwig sales office to see if he could get a special deal in light of his son's burgeoning fame. Sales manager Fred Miller explained that he did not have the authority to make that kind of decision; they would have to discuss it with higher-ups in Elkhart. Mr. Krupa instead went to the yellow pages where he found a listing for the Slingerland Banjo and Drum Company. (Krupa later told Ludwig that he hadn't wanted to go to a banjo company, but his father talked him into giving it a try.) Mr. Krupa got H.H. Slingerland on the phone and told him about Gene's success. Slingerland agreed to give them a set of white pearl drums wholesale. Slingerland ads of the 1940s bragged that Krupa had been playing Slingerland Radio Kings exclusively since 1929. There were no Radio King models that early, though it is possible Krupa played Slingerland drums earlier than the 1935 incident related by Mr. Ludwig.

Krupa photo personalized for Frank Gault: "To Frank Gault, the man who sold me my first drum– a sincere thank you for that– also in sincere appreciation of your friendship. Gene Krupa 1939"

With his movie-star good looks and his dynamic yet musical approach to the drum set, Krupa brought the drummer to center stage. Krupa explained to Slingerland's Sam Rowland that what he really needed to help him make the drum set into a solo instrument were tunable tom-toms. (Up to this point tom-toms had tacked heads and were considered more of a special-effects drum or novelty.)

Krupa with one of his earliest Slingerland kits, late 1920s.

Slingerland's Sam Rowland had some snare drum tube lugs installed on tom-toms for Krupa, and Slingerland showed the set with the world's hottest endorsee on the cover of the next (1936) catalog. This feature was an immediate hit with drummers everywhere and Slingerland was recognized as *THE* progressive drum company.

When Sam Rowland left Slingerland to join the Ludwig family in starting their new drum company in 1937, he went through the latest Slingerland catalog (1936) and made notes on nearly every page. These insights helped Ludwig learn from Slingerland's mistakes and profit from their successes.Rowland's notes on this page: "I designed for Krupa, modernized them for catalog, and they should be adopted immediately. Orders are coming in fast. Could be revised by applying one lug in center so as to match construction of snare drums and bass drums."

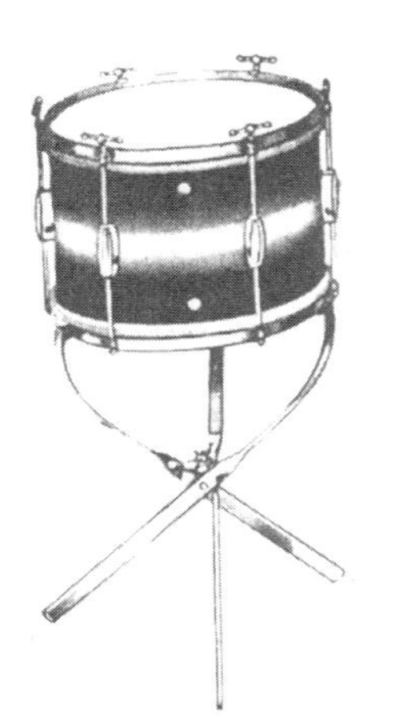

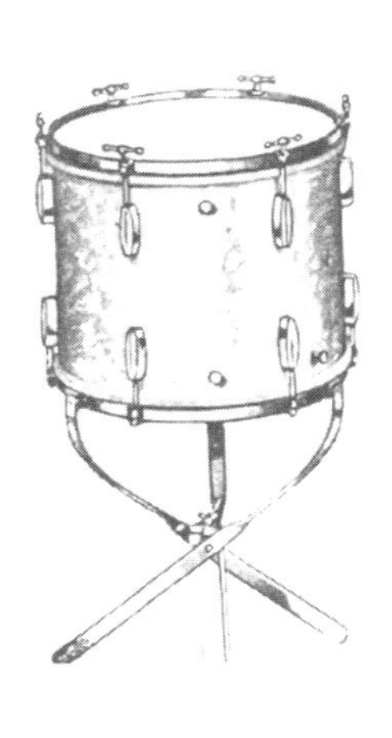

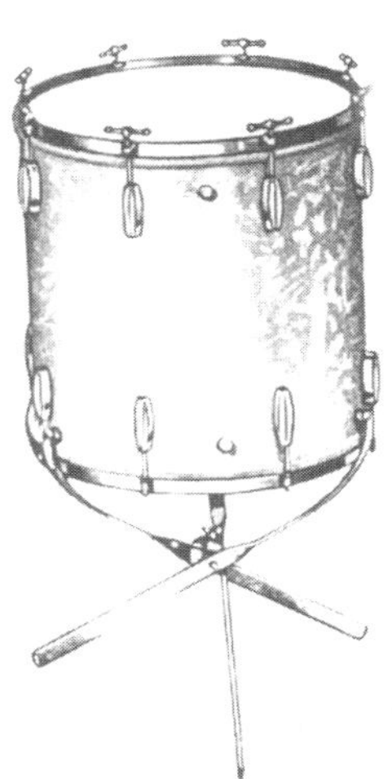

First catalogued separate tension tunable tom-toms

Krupa getting some help with timpani from Saul Goodman. Krupa continued to study throughout his career. In addition to Goodman, he took lessons from Lawrence Stone in Boston, James Moore in New Haven, Connecticut, and Hymie Gurlooker in Pittsburgh. "Wherever there was a teacher," he said, "I wanted to study." He continued to take lessons from Roy Knapp throughout his career as their relationship evolved from teacher-student to that of percussion

Krupa giving a clinic at Franks Drum Shop in Chicago. Roy Knapp set up his teaching studio in Franks after his drum school closed. Although Krupa gave many clinics throughout his career, he did not really consider himself much of a teacher. He founded a drum school in New York with Cozy Cole in 1953 which employed twelve teachers by 1959. Krupa did not feel comfortable in the role of teacher, and eventually left the school.

(top) November, 1957, with the University of Michigan Marching Band, a halftime show honoring Irving Berlin (above) January, 1967, in clinic at Franks Drum Shop (right) July, 1973, Accepting the first *Gene Krupa Award* from New York's Professional Percussion Center

As Slingerland's top endorsee, Krupa appeared on the cover of every catalog from 1936 to 1967.

1936

1937–1939

1940–1941

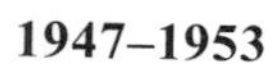

1947–1953

1955–1957

1959–1961

1962–1963

1964–1965

1967

The affiliation with Gene Krupa had a direct influence on the sales of Slingerland drums (and, no doubt, even the sales of Slingerland's competitors, as the popularity of the drummer as a solo artist grew). Prior to this phenomenon, endorsees were glad to sign just for the exposure they received through publicity photos and catalog mentions. Slingerland recognized that Krupa deserved more than just publicity and equipment discounts, and began providing him with free equipment. It was soon obvious to all that he deserved much more. William F. Ludwig II repeatedly tried to lure Krupa into a WFL endorsement deal. In the late 1930s he managed to arrange a meeting with Krupa's manager to discuss it. Ludwig was told that it would cost $35,000.00 in cash to have Krupa. Ludwig phoned his father and begged him to take the deal, but was refused. Finally, in 1947, Krupa signed an endorsement agreement which paid him a share of the profit from every drum that the Slingerland company sold. Krupa had the option of taking his payment in cash at the end of each year (it was a 10 year agreement) or developing a partnership position with Slingerland. He chose the cash.

From this time on, manufacturers were faced with the difficult problem of placing a dollar value on endorsements. This is not to say that this situation would not have developed without Gene Krupa, but he certainly accelerated its growth.

Luckily for Slingerland, Krupa was loyal, a gentleman, and not greedy. According to former Slingerland sales manager Brad Morey, President Bud Slingerland once asked Krupa to come to Chicago to make a personal appearance at the annual NAMM music convention. Krupa signed autographs for hours, until his hand practically bled. After the convention Bud sent Gene a check for $2,000.00. Gene returned the check with a note explaining that he didn't really do anything to *EARN* the payment.

MAIN OFFICE AND FACTORY
1325 BELDEN AVENUE
CORNER WAYNE AVENUE

PHONE LINCOLN 4240-4241

CABLE AND TELEGRAPH ADDRESS
BANJODRUM—CHICAGO

WORLD'S LARGEST

CHICAGO, ILLINOIS

October 1, 1946

The undersigned, Mr. Gene Krupa, and H. H. Slingerland, Jr. hereby enter into the following contract.

H. H. Slingerland, Jr., doing business jointly as co-partner with Mrs. H. H. Slingerland, Sr. in the Slingerland Drum Company, does hereby agree to transfer to the Krupa Reserve Account of Mr. Gene Krupa three quarters of one per cent (3/4 of 1%) of gross annual sales of drums each year for a period of ten (10) years effective this date. Mr. Krupa reserving the right to either draw this amount out or to apply this amount toward an interest in Slingerland Drum Co. The value of the business to be determined by the average book value plus eight (8) times the average net profits for the years 1945, 1946 and 1947.

Mr. Gene Krupa hereby agrees to use, play and endorse Slingerland Drums only and to promote good will.

This contract to continue for ten (10) years at which time the contract can be renewed by the parties.

Krupa suffered a heart attack in 1960, which forced him to cut down on his playing. He cut down to playing six months of the year, half of which was at New York's Metropole club. He announced his retirement in 1967 but after three years was back out making appearances with the original Benny Goodman quartet. His last public appearance was with the quartet at Saratoga Springs, New York. By the time of that performance, it was clear that the Leukemia he had been diagnosed with was severely weakening him.

Knowing that the end was near, some of Krupa's best friends in the drum world put together a testamonial dinner for him in New York. The primary organizers were Louis Bellson and Buddy Rich. (Rich cancelled two important dates for the event.) Held on Wednesday, August 15, 1973, the dinner turned out to be less than two months from Gene's passing on October 16th.

Barrett Deems, Gene Krupa, and Buddy Rich. The three were close friends. Deems was a pallbearer at Krupa's funeral. The day before the funeral, he phoned Bud Slingerland to see if Bud wanted to ride to the funeral together. Bud told Barrett that he would arrange for a car for him, but that he was not going to be able to attend. Stunned, Barrett asked why. Bud explained that he was taking his son to the Notre Dame football game that day; tickets were very hard to come by. Deems never forgave him.

Buddy and Gene at the testamonial dinner in New York City less than two months before Krupa's passing.

Krupa's final resting place, Holy Cross Cemetary, Calumet City, Illinois. **(For directions, see page 243.)**

SLINGERLAND IN THE 1940S

General economic conditions as the U.S. inched closer and closer to all-out involvement in the war had people tightening their belts. Raw materials (particularly brass) got harder and harder to get, even before the U.S. actually joined the war. The U.S. government, through the War Production Board, put restrictions on the use of all metal used by the drum companies; only 10% of a drum's weight could be metal. Most of the drum companies still managed to produce a few drums with wooden lugs and counterhoops, wooden stands, etc. Both of Conn's drum divisions made drums with wooden lugs and hoops. WFL developed a drum which was lugless; tensioning was accomplished by means of an internal ring (and bearing edge) which pressed harder on the head as the side-mounted tension rods were tightened. By the end of this era, WFL was selling drums which very closely resembled Slingerland's.

Slingerland's line of wooden wartime drums were the Rolling Bombers. Henry Adler (owner in the '40s of a popular New York City drum shop) recalls that since there were no restrictions on drum *parts* Slingerland was able to skirt the War Production Board's restrictions by shipping him drums in kit form. Henry would order drums the same way he normally would, but when his shipment arrived it would consist of shells, bags of hardware, etc. Slingerland fared a little better than its competitors through the 1940s, a decade best remembered as an era that virtually shut down all industry unrelated to the war effort. Slingerland was on very sound financial footing, well able to weather a few lean years. H.H. decided to sell the tannery just after the war, though it's not known whether this was belt-tightening due to slim sales the last few years or simply a move to streamline his operations. At the time the tannery was sold, Slingerland was the last drum company to own its own hide-processing facilities. United Rawhide (founded in 1950) eventually became the main supplier of calf heads to all the major drum companies. Although plastic drum heads would not become commercially viable for a few years, they really got started during the war. According to Wm. F. Ludwig II, the reconaissance planes flying over German-occupied sections of Europe were using cellulose photographic film, which frequently broke. The War Department put a very high priority on the development of a more suitable material for this film. An English company, Imperial Chemical Industries, invented the polyester film that almost literally saved the day. In addition to working quite nicely for photographic film, the polyester film had most of the qualities required to make a synthetic drum head. This development certainly did not escape the attention of the Slingerland family; Remo Belli first learned about Mylar during a visit with Bud Slingerland. It is virtually impossible to say who "invented" the plastic (Mylar) drum head— it's more a question of who perfected it. And that is a very big question indeed, resulting in a number of lawsuits. The major players, however, unquestionably included Ludwig, Remo, Evans, Rochon (Camco), and Slingerland.

The manufacture of Leedy and Ludwig & Ludwig drums in Elkhart (both were divisions of Conn through this era) came to a virtual halt as Conn converted its manufacturing capabilities to the production of altimeters, ammunition boxes, and other military supplies. The government was empowered to evaluate the capabilities of manufacturing facilities and determine what products they could make and how much they could charge.

What about the other big drum companies? There really weren't any. Gretsch and Rogers would not become major players until after the war. The very young WFL produced a few drums for the military but was still struggling to become a market presence. It had just opened its doors in 1937, and the first year was literally hand-to-mouth. They were picking up steam but were still a very young company.

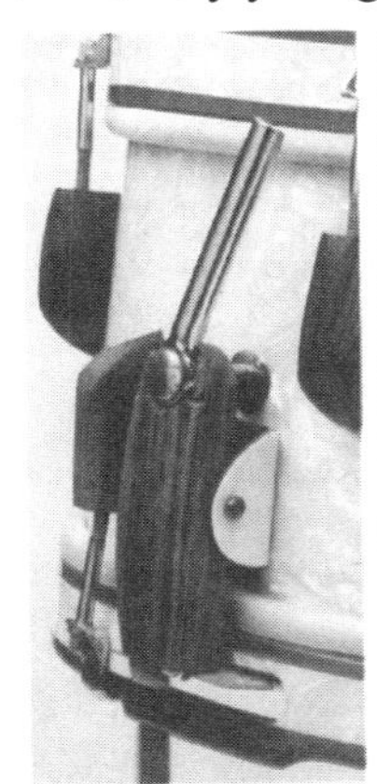

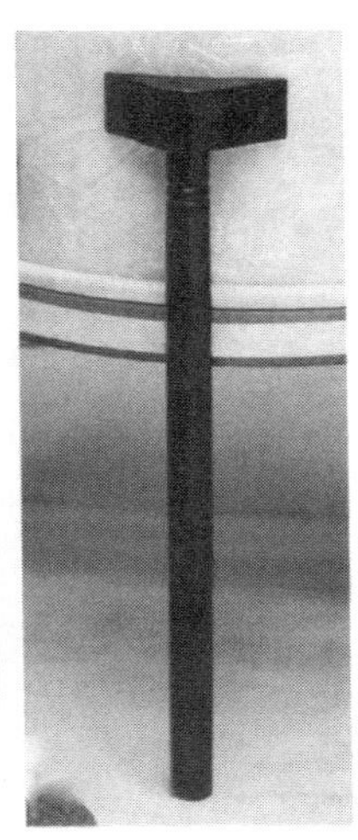

photos by Marty Berglin, courtesy of Joe Luoma

Strainer, butt assembly, floor tom legs– all were made from wood to meet the War Production Board's requirement that no more that 10% of the outfit (by weight) could be made of metal.

Slingerland family and personnel during the 1940s

Almost more important to the Slingerland story during the '40s than the war itself are the family personnel changes in the company. Entering the decade, the top echelon of the firm consisted of H.H. Slingerland, Sr. along with his two younger brothers Arthur James and Walter Robert. After a family disagreement, Arthur left the company in 1943. He remained in Chicago and started a company which distributed all kinds of musical accessories. H.H. Jr. (Bud) served a stint in the service during the war, but got out before the war was over and went to work for his dad. When H.H. Slingerland, Sr., died on March 13, 1946, his brother Walter became President. Walter's son Robert J. Slingerland worked at the plant for a brief time in sales as soon as he got out of college in 1949. (Walter Robert Junior also spent some time working at the factory.) When Walter Robert retired in 1954, Bud became President.

	1940	1941	1942	1943	1944	1945	1946	1947	1948	1949	1950	'52
H.H. Slingerland Sr.	(Pres.) ———						dies					
H.H. Slingerland Jr.				joins company ———								becomes Pres.
Arthur James	———		leaves									
Walter Robert	———					becomes president ———						retires '54
Robert J.									joins company - - -			leaves '51

SLINGERLAND FAMILY PERSONNEL TIMELINE, 1940S

(L-R) Walter Slingerland Sr., Walter Slingerland Jr., Robert Slingerland (Walter Jr. was enrolled at the Roosevelt Military Academy in Aledo, Illinois.)

Upon his retirement from the drum company Walter Robert remained active. He purchased land outside Chicago which was farmed. To control growth and development the rural area was incorporated. He was one of the founding fathers of Schaumburg, Illinois, serving as original trustee for thirteen years and building inspector for eight. The village has become a major Chicago suburb. A street and park in Schaumburg bear the name of this widely respected citizen, who died at the age of 91 of Chronic Obstructive Pulmonary Disease.

George Way and Slingerland

Walter Robert Slingerland **George Way**

George Way started his career as a vaudeville and circus drummer around 1910. After several years of extensive touring with minstrel shows and other acts, Way settled in Edmonton, Alberta, where he started the Advance Drum Company. In 1921 Way accepted an offer from the Leedy Drum Company of Indianapolis to become their sales manager. For over 20 years Way directed not only the sales and promotional efforts at Leedy, but also designed a number of products. Unlike Slingerland, Leedy virtually shut down during WWII. Way started a wholesale drummers' supply house specialing in calfskin heads. (Dozens of dealers and prominent percussionists had come to rely on his expertise to select their calfskin heads.) Though he was selling nearly as many drum heads single-handed as Leedy had been selling before the war, Way's business was not very profitable and he took a job with American Rawhide in Chicago. Though he was with Amrawco only about a year, Way had time to continue his design work, laying out a new type of drying rack for the skins being processed. For a few months in 1946, George Way was sales manager at Slingerland. By this point in his career, Way was 55 years old, and looked upon by many as a little old-fashioned and stodgy. Way did not feel that Slingerland was 'market driven' enough and complained to a friend that that the company was more interested in making money than in really trying to help the working drummer.

It could be argued that Slingerland missed a golden opportunity by not giving George a freer rein; he may have given Slingerland the kind of boost Sam Rowland had 16 years earlier. On the other hand, Way was no longer one of the "young turks" and his business acumen certainly did not match that of the Slingerland family. Way left Slingerland to head west where he started a drum shop in Hollywood. He sold his interest in the shop a year later and returned to work for Conn in Elkhart.

George Way designed the H.H. Ball Bearing pedal during his short term at Slingerland. This pedal was one of the first to feature enclosed spring mechanisms. The two enclosed springs were individually adjustable. The text and photo are from the 1949 catalog when the pedal made its debut. The pedal was discontinued by catalog #54 (1953).

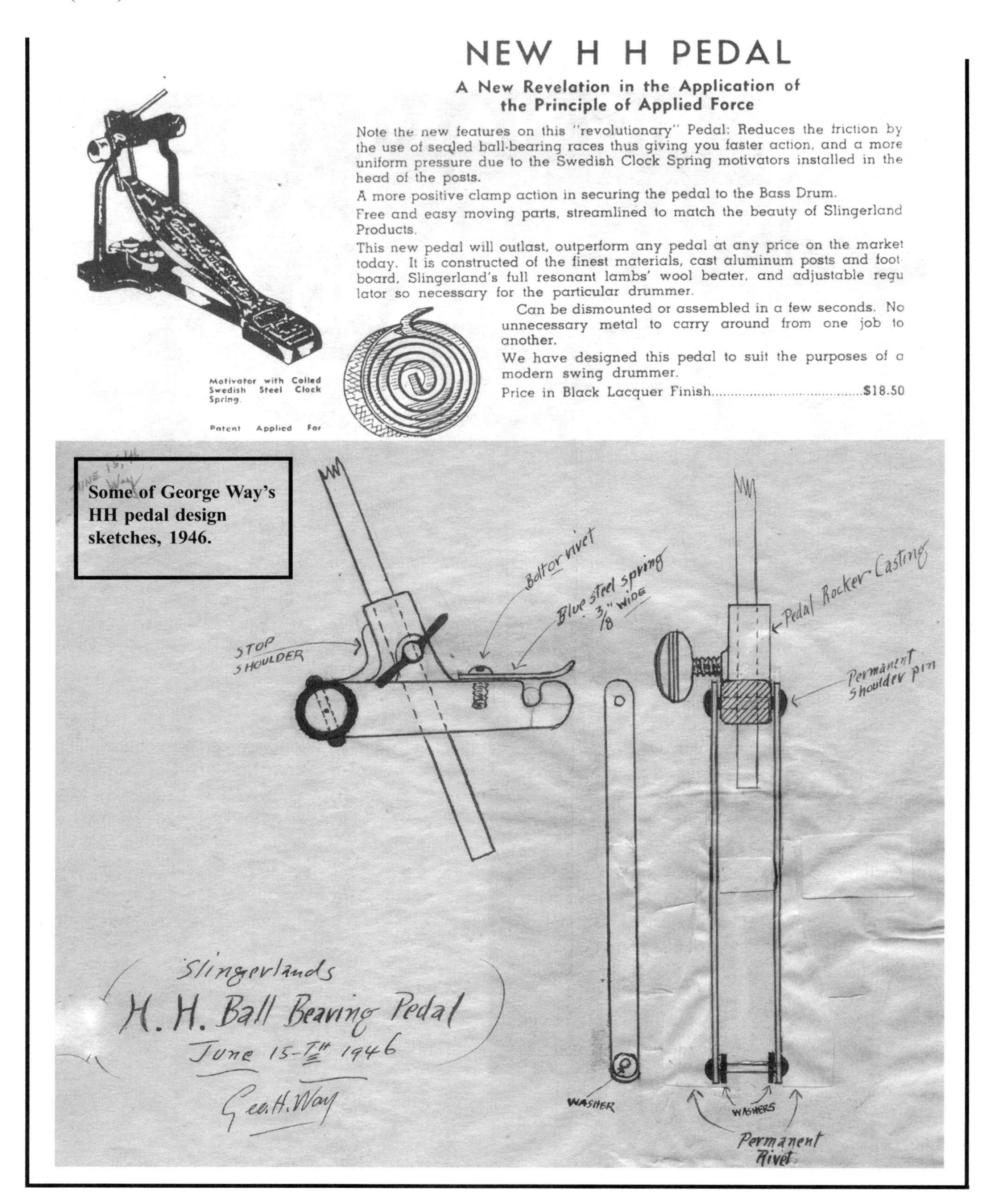

NEW H H PEDAL

A New Revelation in the Application of the Principle of Applied Force

Note the new features on this "revolutionary" Pedal: Reduces the friction by the use of sealed ball-bearing races thus giving you faster action, and a more uniform pressure due to the Swedish Clock Spring motivators installed in the head of the posts.

A more positive clamp action in securing the pedal to the Bass Drum.

Free and easy moving parts, streamlined to match the beauty of Slingerland Products.

This new pedal will outlast, outperform any pedal at any price on the market today. It is constructed of the finest materials, cast aluminum posts and foot board, Slingerland's full resonant lambs' wool beater, and adjustable regulator so necessary for the particular drummer.

Can be dismounted or assembled in a few seconds. No unnecessary metal to carry around from one job to another.

We have designed this pedal to suit the purposes of a modern swing drummer.

Price in Black Lacquer Finish..$18.50

Motivator with Coiled Swedish Steel Clock Spring.

Patent Applied For

Some of George Way's HH pedal design sketches, 1946.

SLINGERLAND IN THE 1950s

The drum companies that survived the hardships of wartime did very well in the postwar days, at least in terms of sales. According to Leedy & Ludwig's plant supervisor Leonard Pickel, the customer demand had most of the major companies scrambling to get raw materials and parts anywhere they could— even from competitors.

Big bands were no longer the rage; the trend in the '50s was to be-bop and Latin. The catalogs of all the major drum companies reflected these changes with smaller bass drums and expanded Latin offerings. Slingerland's lugs and hoops got a facelift in the '50s (see the dating guide section), and by the end of the decade all plating was chrome, no nickel.

Slingerland did not merely survive the wartime era— it emerged from the war poised to dominate the market. While Conn's combined (Leedy & Ludwig) drum divisions were grossing in the neighborhood of $800,000.00 in the years from 1949 through 1953, Slingerland's gross sales were growing from slightly under $3 million in 1949 to over $4 million in the mid '50s. Sales started a slight downward trend toward the end of the '50s, as the postwar boom slowed down and the competition became stiffer. The Ludwig family business, operating as WFL until 1955 when rights to their family name were reacquired, was growing rapidly while both Gretsch and Rogers were becoming major players.

BUD SLINGERLAND became President in 1950 and remained the guy in charge for the next 20 years.

H.H. (Bud) Slingerland Jr. was born on July 16, 1921. It wasn't long after the death of his father (March 13, 1946) before Bud was in charge of Slingerland— he became president in 1950. Bud was a quiet, strong-willed man. While not entirely humorless, he certainly was serious most of the time.

A careful money manager, Bud was perfectly willing to pitch in and work to save some wages. Spencer Aloisio was taken aback when he started working at Slingerland as a high-school student to see Bud, the president of the company, out in front of the plant mowing the lawn.

While not a drummer, Bud Slingerland appreciated the value of employing drummers to work in a drum factory. Factory workers, sales reps, office staff— most were drummers.

Maurie Lishon (Franks Drum Shop, Chicago) discovered an interesting aspect of Bud Slingerland when he returned a carful of mismatched blue sparkle drums. Bud could see no problem, but instructed a worker to take care of Maurie. The worker later explained to the perplexed Lishon that Bud was color blind.

Bud Slingerland was a cautious traveler. William Connor, former President of Slingerland's Solar Musical Instrument Company, recalls that he almost always traveled by train when he visited Solar in Shelbyville, Tennessee. Occasionally in the winter he would fly down, but he didn't like it. When he was riding in Connor's car with him, Bud would constantly quiz him about the speed he was maintaining, the tire pressure and when it was last checked, and other safety concerns. It took a great deal of resolve for Bud to get up the nerve to board the plane for Switzerland when he visited there in the mid '60s. He studied the different airlines and the different types of planes before finally deciding to fly on Swissair figuring that the Swiss were such discriminating craftsmen when it came to all things mechanical that they were bound to have the safest planes in the air. Once in the air over the Atlantic, Bud got up out of his seat to stretch his legs. He wandered up to the cockpit, this being in the days when the cockpit was not sealed off from the passenger compartment. He noticed that the pilot and co-pilot were both busy. He asked why the autopilot was not flying the plane and was told that it was broken! Bud returned to his seat visibly shaken.

Above all else, Bud Slingerland was a canny businessman. His investments, his capital expenditures at the factory, the way he monitored the activities of his sales force; all demonstrated a sharp business acumen. In the 1960s when he decided to do some manufacturing in Tennessee, he set up the facility there as a new corporation. The stockholders were his children, and the corporation's only customer was Slingerland. The President of the corporation (William Connor) was really the man responsible for operating the plant, designing the machinery, etc., and his commissions were based on profitability.

SLINGERLAND ACQUIRES LEEDY

The Conn company had purchased both the Leedy and Ludwig drum companies in 1929. (Such actions would probably not have been permitted in later decades by federal antitrust laws, as Conn, Slingerland, and Ludwig dominated the market.) The Leedy family quit drummaking altogether at that point, as company founder U.G. Leedy was ill and his sons were not old enough to take over the business. Wm. F. Ludwig Sr. worked for Conn (first in Elkhart, then based in Chicago) in the early '30s, but finally quit and decided to go back into the drum business for himself. He started the William F. Ludwig Drum Company in 1937. Conn's lawyers made it clear to Ludwig that they owned the Ludwig name and he would have to change the name of his new company. Mr. Ludwig decided that if he couldn't use his name he could at least use the initials and changed the name to the WFL Drum Company.

Conn never was able to operate its drum divisions in the black. They tried combining the two divisions in 1950, establishing the Leedy & Ludwig line. Still unable to operate the drum division profitably, Conn finally decided to get out of the drum business altogether. They put the word out that the whole division was for sale, and Wm. F. Ludwig Jr. jumped at the opportunity to get the family name back. Ludwig called Bud Slingerland and proposed that they cooperate and buy Leedy for Slingerland, Ludwig for WFL. Bud agreed, and in May of 1955 they signed a deal they worked out with Leland Greenleaf at Conn. Much of the existing inventory was sold to a large East Coast dealer, and the mallet-instrument department went to Jenkins, a manufacturer in Decatur, Indiana.

For four months, Bud Slingerland and Bill Ludwig Jr. spent three days a week in Elkhart trying to sort out who'd get what. This was not a pleasant experience for the two men. There had been no love lost before this transaction, and this certainly did not bring them any closer. Every single piece of machinery turned into a major dispute. When it was all over Bill Ludwig Jr. finally asked Bud the question that had been on his mind throughout the negotiating.... what did Slingerland want with the Leedy name? Bud's somewhat arrogant reply stunned Ludwig; he said that up until now the number one drum dealer in every town was a Slingerland dealer, and the number two dealer was a Ludwig (WFL or Leedy & Ludwig) dealer. From now on the number two dealer would be a Leedy account, and Ludwig would have to market his products through the "third string".

By 1956 Slingerland had a Leedy catalog out, though it was basically the same as the last Leedy & Ludwig catalog (#53A). The cover used the same endorsee photos and most pages were identical. The endorsee situation would change markedly in the next few years, with none of the Conn-Leedy endorsees still appearing in the last Slingerland-Leedy catalog 10 years later. There were new endorsees added, though the roster definitely dwindled. The best known Leedy endorsee at the end was Shelly Manne.

DON OSBORNE

Don Osborne was born in 1928. While still a teenager, Osborne became not only one of the Chicago areas better drummers, but also took many of the better tenor sax gigs.

At the age of 21, Osborne won Slingerland's second Gene Krupa drum contest. (The winner of the first contest had been Louis Bellson.)

While for the most part there was a drastic change around 1949 from big bands to smaller combos, quite a few of the Chicago area bands managed to hang on by working college dates, hotels, etc. Don Osborne played for one of the finest, the Bill Russo Experiment In Jazz. (Russo later joined the Stan Kenton Orchestra as arranger and composer.) From Russo's band, Osborne went on to work with Ralph Marterie, the Tex Beneke Orchestra, and scattered dates with Serge Chaloff, Chubby Jackson, Anita O'Day, Buddy Greco, and others.

Osborne was asked to join Stan Kenton as well as Woody Herman, but did not want to live on the road. He took a day job in the office at a Chicago pickle factory, and was working there when Bud Slingerland recruited him. He started with Slingerland in 1954 in the advertising and sales department, and continued to freelance with such names as Cy Touff, Sandy Mosse, Ira Sullivan, and Audrey Morris in the London House in Chicago. He later was named Vice President under Bud and was the first President of Slingerland after the family sold the firm.

DON OSBORNE, JR.

At the age of 15 (a sophmore at Chicago's Taft High School) prodigy Donny Osborne Junior was not only performing at the Slingerland trade show exhibits but doing clinics at the legendary Franks Drum Shop of Chicago and even sitting in with the Buddy Rich Big Band whenever they were in town.

The main Slingerland factory from 1928 through 1959. It is identified as #3 because of the first building at 1815 Orchard and the drum head facility near the stockyards.

As the '50s drew to a close, Slingerland production facilities were vastly overcrowded. Although Slingerland was laying claim to being the world's largest drum company, they were still in the rather ramshackle building theyd been in for 30 years. The plating was all being farmed out; there was no in-house plating. There was no room for storing surplus inventory or materials. Raw materials were ordered in quantities that were so close to actual production numbers that any transportation disruptions had immediate effects on production.

Bud's search for someone to make him a machine that could gold-foil hot-stamp his drum sticks led him to central Tennessee, the pencil-making capital of the world.

He had been using a hand-operated machine and wanted an automatic machine that would be adjustable to all the different diameters. He found just who he was looking for in Shelbyville, Tennessee: William Connor. Connor designed a machine to do the job Bud described around 1957 or 1958, and Slingerland used the machine for many years. Bud had Connor build several other machines over the next couple of years and finally tried to talk Connor into moving from Tennessee to Chicago to help lay out and supervise a new drum factory. Connor, however, had seen enough northern winter weather as a boy in Flint, Michigan.

The first time that William Connor came to Chicago to deliver equipment to Slingerland, they were still in the the factory at Beldon and Wayne (above). "I went up there to deliver the rotating table drill for drilling holes for lugs," he remembers. "It was an overnight trip, and it got down to seventeen degrees below that night. My car started up okay because it had been in the hotel garage. When I got out to the plant, it turned out the night watchman had fallen asleep and the plant had frozen completely up. It was sometime the middle of the next afternoon before it even started to get a little bit warm in the plant. Machines of that type won't even run unless everything is warmed up to at least room temperature, so I had to stay an extra day that trip."

The same building as it appears today. Although no longer related to either drum production or the Slingerland family, it is known as The Slingerland Condominium Association.

SLINGERLAND IN THE 1960S

Slingerland's manufacturing facilities were desperately overcrowded by the end of the 1950s. A little of the pressure was taken off by the Shelbyville, Tennessee, operation but Bud Slingerland still needed to move forward with his plan to expand and modernize the Chicago operations.

Bud once (in the early '50s) took Robert Zildjian aside and told him about a hot stock tip that he'd gotten from a friend at the country club. He made it clear that he expected reciprocity: "You should be getting tips like this, too," he told Zildjian. "keep your ears open, and let me know!" In about 1959, Bud again took Zildjian aside. "You remember that stock I told you about?" Zildjian did remember, but had not taken advantage of the tip. Bud told him that he'd just cashed in on the investment he'd made back when he first told Zildjian about the stock and had cleared well in excess of a million dollar profit. "You see?" asked Bud, "I'm going to use the profit from that stock tip to build a brand new factory!" And he did.

photo by Tom Kinahan

The Chuck Davis Quartet, entertaining the firefighters

The Niles Bugle, July 30, 1959

Jazzmen played while the former Kolb residence burned at 6630 Milwaukee last Saturday afternoon. Slingerland Drum Company, new owners of the property, held a picnic for employees on the grounds where a new building will soon be erected. In celebration of the new intended residence of the famous company the musicians played "There'll be a hot time..." while Niles Firemen burned down the old frame buildings on the property. The Kolb family first owned this property in 1867 and lived here until 1955 when the property was sold. Louis Kolb continued his florist shop here until two weeks ago. Kolb's sister related that grandchildren of the present family felt so bad about the end of the Kolb era at the address that they stayed away from the fire.

> *"I was told that when they moved, Bud had everyone who worked with electrical devices (drilling, soldering, etc.) bring extension cords from home to work with them so they could keep working while the electrical system was being finished up."*
> ***William Connor***

The 45,000 square-foot Slingerland factory at 6633 N. Milwaukee Avenue in Niles, built in 1960. A 19,800 square-foot addition was constructed in 1973.

6633 N. Milwaukee, 1970

Reception room **Section of wood shop** **Final assembly of drums**

Assembly of tympani & accessories **The plating room** **Shipping & final inspection**

SLINGERLAND'S SHELBYVILLE, TENNESSEE, MANUFACTURING FACILITY

When Bud Slingerland established his manufacturing facility in Shelbyville, Tennessee, he did not set it up as a conventional branch or division of his Chicago manufacturing operation. He formed a whole different company, the Solar Musical Instrument Company. Solar Musical Instrument Company had only one customer: the Slingerland Drum Company. The directors of the Solar Corporation were Bud, his mother, and his sister. The stockholders were Bud's four children. The President was William Connor, former owner of the machine shop that Bud bought out to start Solar.

CONNOR'S SHELBYVILLE SHOP, 1964

"It all started as a result of an inquiry from Slingerland to me," Connor recalled. "I was building all sorts of production machinery for the pencil industry, printing pencils and pens, that sort of thing. Bud Slingerland wanted an automatic machine that would be adjustable to all the different diameters and so forth. I designed him one, and it worked fine. He ran that machine for many years.

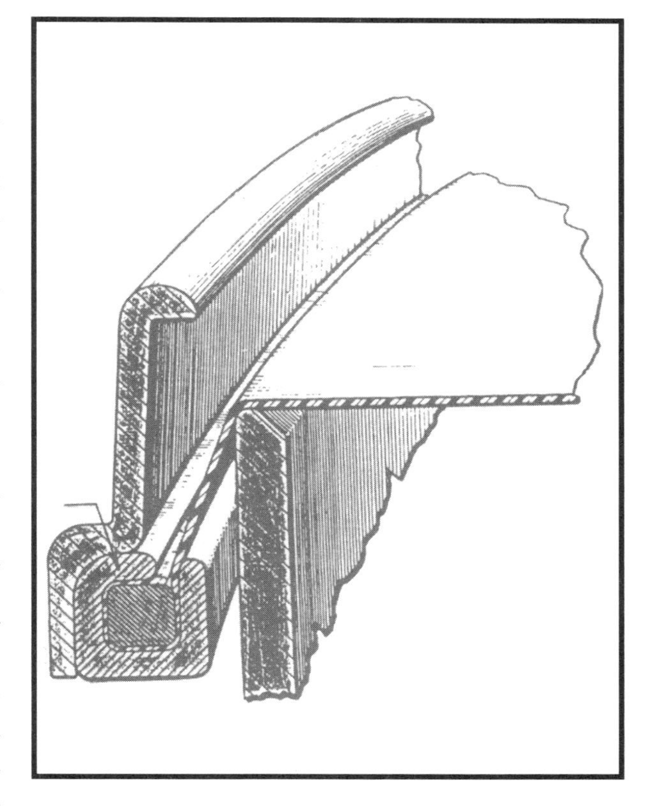

"They were still using calfskin heads at the time. Bud was going to the stockyards or slaughterhouses and buying leather, the calfskin. That material, while it worked, was never really satisfactory because it wouldn't stay tuned. With changes in humidity the calfskin heads had to constantly be adjusted— even while playing. Ludwig, I understand, came up with a way to mold a Mylar drum head, mounting it in an aluminum hoop-frame and crimping it in. Slingerland wanted to do the same thing, and presented me with the problem. He had tried to have people in his plant, then other people in Chicago do this for him, but hadn't been successful. So I did a small (probably 14") head. Bud sent me samples of the materials he thought we could use, and I built a machine to mold a channel with the open edge on top. The Mylar was molded to give it a collar, and inserted in the channel. Then an insert was put in and the channel was crimped over the insert to secure the Mylar."

Assembling the parts

The spinning operation, trimming excess mylar

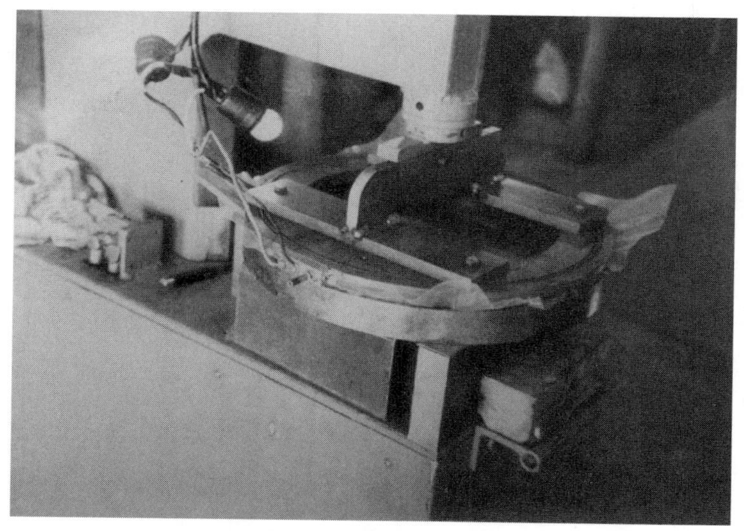

Pressing a 14" head

"It was more of an art than a science. There were a lot of little tricks to doing it. We had to have little rollers that would go down inside because the channel is UP, and if you try to go around the other way, it's going to collapse. There were five or six sets of rollers involved; bending, rolling, keeping the twist out of it. All power driven. It took a while to find every one of the problems one at a time. A few months. Bud paid for all the development."

"It was a nice operation. Pretty soon I had three or four guys working for me, making drum heads. We were knocking out about a thousand a day. Whatever size Bud wanted. He'd give me a list of what he wanted for the week, I'd order the materials, and get 'em all in. By that time I'd made molds for all the sizes."

"As soon as I showed him that we COULD do it, he bought my machine shop. I'd wanted to sell the shop; at this time we were in a mild recession as far as machinery was concerned and I was looking for something else. I was quite willing to sell him my machine shop and go to work for him. The organization was completed in October of 1962, about three years after I first set up the machine shop to work on Bud's projects. We sold the drum heads to Slingerland. This was done at a price that he set, which I'm sure gave him room to make a profit at the Slingerland end, but also allowed for a nice profit for us at Solar. Obviously what he was doing, and there's certainly nothing wrong with it, was transferring some money from his company to their (his kids') company. The prices were fair. The prices that he paid us were considerably under market price for the things, so there was a normal profit for us and a normal profit for him. The drum heads were a very profitable thing- I imagine it'd be a good business to be in today!"

- WILLIAM CONNOR, President, Solar Musical Instruments

Discussing the Shelbyville operation with William Connor.....

RC: Did you ever reach a point with the drum heads where you thought it just wouldn't work?

WC: Oh, no. I knew it would work. I'm an optimist and this is what I do. I'm an inventor and I saw no reason why it couldn't be made to work; it was just a matter of working out the details and making it work in a production situation. I knew it'd be successful before it was over with, and it was. Once we got it going, we had three of four who worked as a team. They'd know what they were going to do first thing in the morning. Say they were going to make a thousand 14" heads. They'd start out by making all the parts; one guy would be over here molding, somebody'd be rolling hoops, and they'd get together as a team and assemble them, crimp them. A lot of times they'd get the order for the day all done a couple hours ahead of time; maybe six hours of work would do it. Then they'd start on the next days, 'cause I'd worked out a system where I paid them on a piece-work basis. They were making considerably more than minimum wage. Bud didn't like that. He kept wanting me to put them back on minimum wage. I told him "Bud, it'll end up costing us MORE to put them just on the wage! We won't get nearly the satisfaction out because this way they can put in a couple hours work ahead of time and they end up with time to clean the place up, they're willing to do the repair work, and we're farther ahead no matter how you look at it!" We ended up making a good bit of money for him!

RC: What was the next project after drum heads?

WC: I think drums came next because he couldn't keep up with the orders at the Niles plant. So we tooled up and made a complete assortment of shell sizes.

RC: The same way he was making them in Niles?

WC: The only variation was that he was using maple for the reinforcement hoops, and we were using oak. We found that we could easily get the oak locally and it was very workable. You could roll it, heat it, and make a beautiful hoop. I had to go all over the country to find poplar for the core material. The inner and outer plies were mahogany. I found a place in Louisville where I could get the mahogany veneer for the facings. The grain ran parallel to the axis of the drum on the core material. It was all put in a form that was heated. The form was in two halves so it would open up for shell removal. We'd clamp it together, put the mahogany in, put the core material in, the other layer of mahogany, a hoop at the bottom and a hoop at the top. (Glue was brushed on the wood just before the wood was put in the mold.) Then came the tube apparatus. The tube would be put inside and blown up and we'd heat the mold so it'd dry fairly quickly. As it turned out, we used an assortment of inner tubes; automobile, aircraft landing wheel, just about anything that was the right size.

RC: Were the drums completely assembled in Shelbyville?

WC: Oh, yes. I made machines to do the drilling. Bud shipped die-cast lugs down here for a while and I'd have them polished and plated. Later we had a local die-caster make lugs for us. We made the pedals, the pedal assemblies. I believe he shipped the castings down here becasue he had a good source for the castings. We did all the machining on the castings; drilling, putting the pins through them, assembly— all that stuff. We assembled a lot of hardware.

RC: At the peak of your production, how many drums would you say you were making in Shelbyville?

WC: I'd say that over the two or three years we were making drums we probably put out a grand total of around 5000 shells.

RC: Any idea how that compared with Niles?

WC: I'm sure their capability was a great deal more than that. He had more equipment and more people in Niles.

Pretty soon we started making drumsticks, using machinery that was brought down here from Chicago. He didn't have a real good source for hickory up there. There's a lot of hickory grown around here and I was able to find enough hickory to do it. We never did make any money on drumsticks. We lathed them, dipped them, lacquered them, painted and shipped them. I never really did like the drumstick business too much although I had asked for it. I thought we would make a better operation out of it than we did.

After drumsticks, then we got started on guitars. That was really a nightmare. You see, with all of these projects, I was told to go figure out a way of doing it. I was getting paid a percentage of the profits, and the startup costs on these extra projects came out of those profits. With something like guitars, the startup costs were extensive, as this was a whole new business. I had no idea how guitars were made. I went to Chicago and talked myself into a tour of the Harmony factory, and went up to Kalamazoo to visit Gibson. I'd met a cabinetmaker through a sports car club who I hired to make the guitars, a J.W. Gallagher. His son is still making guitars. I told him what I needed to do, and he didn't have much cabinet business at the time so he agreed to come and try the guitar project. We started just in a little corner, to get a feel for it. Bud helped us by buying several guitars for us to look over; Gibson and two or three other brands. We sawed them up— just put them right through the band saw! That was awful hard to do, destroying those guitars just to see what was inside them. It worked, though. Gallagher started making handmade guitars to get the feel of it. In the meantime I was trying to find wood. I went to several places for mahogany; Louisville, Knoxville, and other places. I finally found a company that imported mahogany in big slabs for the furniture industry. I was able to buy planks and we got that shipped down here. That was primarily for the necks. I finally found rosewood and mahogany veneer for the shells and for the fretboard. We needed spruce for the tops, and that was the hardest. I had lived in Portland, Oregon for a while and I knew that spruce was available out there so I started calling dealers out there until I finally found a guy who could ship me a carload. We were also able to buy a few tops, but they were scarce because guitars were selling like crazy at the time. We made little machines to accurately space the frets on the fretboards, and we sawed all the fret slots in one whack.

Our major problem was that we decided these was no way we could compete with the cheaper guitars on the market, the imported ones, with the type of equipment and setup that we had available to us and the amount of money we had to invest. If we could have invested a lot more time and bought some new equipment, we probably could have made a cheap guitar in mass production. But that would have taken a much larger operation than we had to work with. Gallagher and I figured that we could make a higher-priced guitar with some hand labor in it, a really nice one. And we did. We made a few really nice guitars. Instead of selling ones for $125.00 we could have produced fewer units and sold them for $400.00 to $500.00 and we would have ended up making some money. Bud didn't see it that way, though. He wanted to go for the mass-produced guitar and get the price down. There was no way we could do it, and I couldn't argue with him. When he made his mind up about something, *that was it*! I tried never to argue with him; I just accepted what he said, and if that was the way he wanted it, that's the way it was. He was a very good businessman, and he and I got along quite well.

RC: Your association ended before the end of the decade though?

WC: Yes. I finally realized that he was never really going to let me make anything out of the deal. I didn't feel that I was really benefiting financially from all the work I was doing. The bonuses I received were what we had agreed on, but the money was being pulled out of profits to go into the new products he wanted us to develop here. As a result we never really showed the profit we should have. I wasn't really out searching for another job, but one came along, with an apparel company developing automatic sewing equipment. I gave Bud 60 days' notice and he decided to shut the place down. He didn't want to send someone else down here to run it.

The whole experience of working with the musical instruments was very interesting. I think most of the frustrations I had were because he was so tight. I wasn't able to try a lot of the things that I'm sure would have worked very well. I found out, though, that Bud was not what I would call a leader in the industry, he was a follower. If somebody came up with something new, he'd develop his version of it.

The end of the line for Leedy— Leedy had clearly been a second line for Slingerland since they purchased the division in 1955. Very few innovations were made in the line, and gradually the line became basically Slingerland drums with the Leedy nameplate attached. Rights to the Leedy trademark were included with each sale of Slingerland up until the Gibson purchase of Slingerland in 1994, at which time Leedy remained the property of Gretsch.

THE BIG SLINGERLAND-LUDWIG DRUM HEAD LAWSUIT

As mentioned in earlier chapters, little love was lost between the Ludwig and Slingerland families. They were bitter competitors from the days Wm. F. Ludwig Sr. and H.H. Slingerland Sr. battled for choice skins at the Chicago stockyards: Ludwig for drums and Slingerland for banjos.

There was never any doubt that when Slingerland began making plastic drum heads, they copied the way Ludwig was making heads. Bud had been trying unsuccessfully in Chicago to copy the Ludwig drum head. (The problem was in finding a way to mold a collar into the mylar.) He finally took a Ludwig head to William Connor and showed him what he wanted to do.

Connor had not been manufacturing the heads for long before he had a personal visit from Wm. F. Ludwig Sr. "It was during the winter of 1962," says Connor, "In January or February as I recall. The shop door opened and in walked Mr. Ludwig. It was a very cordial conversation, but he basically wanted to know what we were doing. I knew what he was there for; I'd been half expecting him. I explained what we were doing. He told me we were not supposed to be doing that, because he had a patent on the process. I explained that I understood he had a patent but that I also understood that there were some problems with the patent, and that I thought we were probably in the clear. He didn't like that, but he didn't seem mad or upset when he left. A month or so later (by the time we'd moved into a new building that was under construction so we could do some other things we had planned) I got served with papers to appear in Federal Court."

The case dragged on for over two-and-a-half years, with a judgment finally handed down in September 1965.

As far as Ludwig was concerned, they were battling Slingerland. Technically, the lawsuit was between Ludwig and the Solar Musical Instrument Company. Bud Slingerland claimed in depositions that Solar was an independant company his family happened to own stock in. The president of Solar (Connor) was not a Slingerland employee, and Slingerland was just another Solar customer. Solar, he testified, fully intended to sell their products to many different customers. This simply was not true. Slingerland had always been a family-owned business, and Solar was owned and controlled by the Slingerland family. Solar had only one customer for its products: Slingerland. Slingerland claimed to have no control over Solar's pricing, profitability, or procedures. This also was simply not true.

Connor is of the opinion that the whole lawsuit could have been avoided if the two sides had gotten together and agreed to share the technology. It probably could have been settled in a manner that let Ludwig's patent stand, with a licensing arrangement for Slingerland that would have kept anyone else from using it. Slingerland, however, was determined to destroy the patent he was being sued over. Emotions ran hot on both sides. Connor recalls that one day (well into the trial) Wm. F. Ludwig Jr. came to Bud Slingerland's hotel room with several associates. They were supposed to be trying to find a way to come to an agreement, but they were both hard-headed and would not settle. They argued back and forth more and more vehemently until they almost came to blows. It was very close to a fist fight, with the pair challenging each other to go to the gym and put on gloves.

Key to the Slingerland contention that the Ludwig patent was invalid because of prior art was a rumor that Bud had heard about Ludwig having seen this type of drum head in Switzerland long before he filed his patent. He was eventually able to convince the judge of this, though both he and Ludwig found it neccessary to travel to Switzerland personally as they prepared for the trial. (Both visited the Swiss shop of one Oscar Bauer on the same day, attempting to determine what had been seen and discussed back in 1958.) Additionally, statements were entered which had to be taken through the American Consulate in Zurich. These statements complicated matters, as the lawyers argued about difficulties of translating words such as "Trommelfellbefestigung-konstruktionen". (Ludwig Sr. spoke German, but neither Slingerland nor his lawyers did.)

After months of high-powered legal maneuvering, the time came for the Nashville judge to make a decision. With everyone in the courtroom waiting in anticipation, the judge shook his head and announced that he'd have to think about this one. He promised to let everyone know his decision as soon as possible.

When the decision came, it supported Slingerland's claims that the patent should not have been issued because of prior art.

SLINGERLAND IN THE 1970S

When Ludwig's sales were jump-started by Ringo Starr of the Beatles in the '60s, Rogers and Slingerland also benefited. These three firms went into the '70s as the major drum companies. (Gretsch certainly had a presence but other than Charlie Watts of the Rolling Stones maintained a lower, jazz-oriented, profile.) Slingerland entered the '70s poised to fight for a larger market share; they had Buddy Rich back (he'd been an endorsee in the'30s, see the endorsee section), they were signing more hot rock drummers, and were determined to make inroads in the marching market. In spite of the many executive changes, Slingerland's direction in the '70s was consistent: The endorsee roster was updated, new outfit finishes and configurations were shown off in striking new catalogs, the mallet instrument business was re-entered in a big way with Deagan, and major inroads were made in the marching percussion field. Where sales had been hovering right around the $4 million mark since the late '40s, they nearly doubled by the end of the '70s.

SLINGERLAND TIMELINE–1970S

1970 1971 1972 1973 1974 1975 1976 1977 1978 1979

Owner:

(Bud Slingerland to 1970)

Crowell, Collier, MacMillan--

(Sold to Mardan Corp 1980)

President:

(Bud Slingerland to 1970)

Don Osborne ---Larry Linkin-------------------------------

(Bill Young 1980)

Sales Manager:

(Don Osborne to 1970)

Gary Beckner ------------------------------------Spencer Aloisio --------------------------------------- (to 1986)

Sales (in millions):

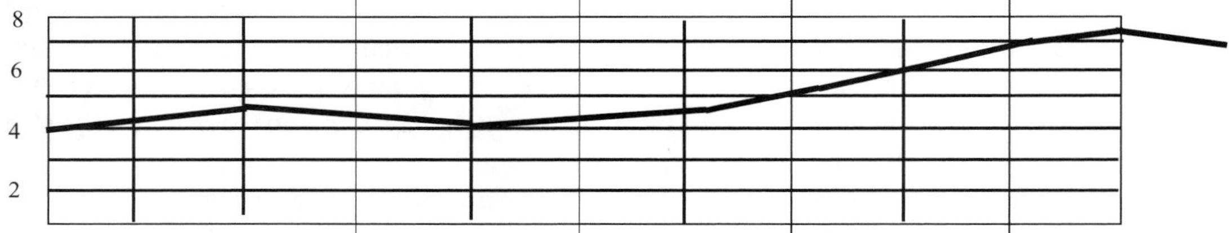

8
6
4
2

Gene Krupa Dies

Buddy Rich Fired

Louis Bellson Signed

Copper, Denim, custom coverings

Blakrome

New Lacquers, Chrome

Headmaking discontinued, Remo deal struck

Silver & Black Niles Oval badge used throughout the 70's ---

Dual Super Strainer Discontinued

First reissue Radio King

Brass hoops replaced by steel

TDR Strainer Introduced

lots of new outfit configurations

Deagan Distribution Begun

Deagan Acquired

Jenco Distribution Ceased

Cut-a-way marching percussion, Marching market penetration

Fred Sanford begins consulting

Fred Sanford becomes contracted consultant

From the Slingerland family to corporate ownership

Bud Slingerland's decision to retire in 1970 at age 48 was prompted, he told friends, by the news that he had cancer. He lived another ten years– long enough to undoubtedly recognize that he would have faced major hurdles had he decided to continue the family business. He could see that the marketplace was feeling more competitive pressure from the Japanese firms, and that his equipment was for the most part old and worn. To continue making premium quality equipment was going to require heavy investment in new equipment which would price him right out of the ballgame. Fortunately for him, this was an era of corporate acquisitions. Norlin bought the Gibson Guitar Company, CBS bought Rogers, Fender, and Rhodes, and the publishing conglomerate Crowell, Collier & MacMillan (CCM) was interested in joining the party. The purchase agreement was negotiated, and 1970 marked the end of the Slingerland family's 42 year association with drum manufacturing.

Crowell, Collier, and MacMillan had all been publishing firms, which merged to form a New York-based corporation. In the sixties CCM deepened their penetration of the educational market. Then, beginning in 1967, the firm began acquiring school-music related companies. Between 1967 and 1970 they bought the U.S. School of Music (a small retailer of musical instruments), the C.E. Ward Company (manufacturer of band uniforms and choral robes), G. Schirmer Inc. (music publisher), Slingerland, C. G. Conn Ltd., and Uniforms by Ostwald. The Conn and Ostwald acquisitions finally attracted the attention of the U.S. Justice Department. The government filed an antitrust suit in February, 1970, claiming (in a bit of a reach) that since CCM owned a drum company, a musical instrument retailer, a music publisher, and a uniform firm, they therefore had the resources and interest to also enter the business of manufacturing band instruments. In purchasing Conn, the suit claimed, CCM eliminated a potential competitor and was therefore guilty of monopolistic practices. The suit was not successful in forcing CCM to divest itself of some of the new companies. Within hours of the Justice Department's announcement of the suit, CCM announced that it would vigorously fight the charges.

Although Conn was the second largest independent U.S. manufacturer of band instruments at the time with net sales of $28.9 million in the fiscal year ending April 30, 1968, the company's bottom line was miserable. The net profit for the same period was under $43,000.00, or only 0.15%. CCM undoubtedly saw this slim profit margin as an opportunity and a challenge; it would be up to their corporate minds to trim the fat andgenerate some dividends. Slingerland's bottom line in the years prior to the CCM buyout is not a matter of public record, for until the 1970 sale of the company Slingerland was wholly family-owned. It is clear, however, from the way Bud Slingerland manipulated profits during the Shelbyville years that he had the business acumen to present the Slingerland Drum Company the way CCM would find it attractive— either as a cash cow or as a marginally profitable firm which could, with a little big-city management, turn *into* a cash cow.

As far as the dealers and endorsees were concerned, the Slingerland future never looked brighter than it did in the '70s: completely reworked catalogs full of new outfit configurations in new colors with hot endorsees, a marching percussion line that quickly grabbed a huge market share, the Deagan acquisition. Certainly little changed out in the plant; again, most of the production personnel remained unchanged. What *did* unfortunately change was a rather critical factor. For the first time since the firm's inception, it was no longer controlled by an individual who understood not only all of the company's people and processes, but (perhaps even more importantly) the marketplace as well. Up until this point, whenever a major decision such as tool replacement or plant expansion came up, the able patriarch was there to make the call. And once the call was made, action was immediately taken. Now any major decisions would have to be directed "upstairs" and plant personnel would become increasingly frustrated at the lack of response from up there.

When the changeover was made and Bud left, the presidency was given to sales manager Don Osborne and Gary Beckner was named sales manager. Beckner, like most of the Slingerland staff, was a drummer, and an ambitious one. He was responsible for the TDR strainer as well as other Slingerland innovations of the early '70s such as the copper finish. In spite of his accomplishments, there was friction not only between Beckner and Osborne, but also between Beckner and some of the field salesmen who took their complaints to Osborne, deepening the rift between he and Beckner. (One source suggested that Osborne was beginning to feel that Beckner was after his job.) It finally came to a head in about 1974. Osborne summoned Beckner to his office. Knowing that there was about to be a showdown, Beckner asked Spencer Aloisio and Charles Engdahl to accompany him. They did, but were put in a rather awkward position. To jump to Beckner's defense would have jeopardized their own positions, so they had to stand by while Osborne fired Beckner. Aloisio was then given Beckner's job of sales manager.

SPENCER ALOISIO

Spencer Aloisio was born May 15, 1948. His first formal music training came in the form of a few piano lessons from the nuns at the Catholic grammar school he attended in Norridge (a Chicago suburb). His dad was a big band follower who loved music and had kind of a natural talent to play along with the records on the drum set he kept set up in the house. (Mr. Aloisio never studied or performed in public even as an amateur, playing at home for his own enjoyment.) Spencer got the bug from that, and fell into the after-school routine of playing along to Count Basie records or anything else handy.

When his dad finally asked him if he wanted to take up an instrument in the school band, Spencer chose the saxophone. He took lessons for a couple of years and spent a year in the high school band, but didn't really enjoy the sax. In the meantime he'd continued his record accompaniment on the drums, and finally decided drums were really his instrument. He took drum lessons for about a year at a local music store to get started before his dad suggested a more advanced instructor. Mr. Aloisio had a friend who was a trumpet player gigging with a talented drummer, so he offered to see if the drummer did any teaching. The drummer turned out to be Don Osborne Sr., who certainly was teaching. He had more prospective students than he could teach, so he auditioned them. It was through his weekly lessons with Osborne that Spencer not only refined and developed his natural abilities as a drummer, but also developed an association with Slingerland. Osborne was sales manager at the time and arranged a summer job for Spencer over the summer of 1966. While it was great to be packing up brand new drums which he knew were being shipped out to be played by guys who had the same professional ambitions as he, Spencer says that after a while it got a little overwhelming. "I used to think "there's got to be an end to this", but the drums just kept rolling down the line.... We just kept packing them up and shipping them out. I guessed *everybody* was trying to trying to do the same thing I was!"

When Spencer enrolled at Chicago's DePaul University, he was able to maintain his part-time job at Slingerland with a three day class schedule that left him two full days to work at the drum factory. That schedule continued through 1967 and 1968 until his

school schedule no longer left full days open and he was starting to play in bands so he finally had to quit Slingerland.

Spencer left town for military service early in 1971 and returned after his six-months active in August looking for something to do. He called Osborne who immediately offered him a job at Slingerland. This time instead of factory work like packing up drums Spencer was groomed for office work.

As soon as he'd been shown the ropes he was given a position in the sales department. He eventually would become sales manager, then vice president. Though he was stuck with many difficult situations through some of Slingerland's most turbulent years, Spencer remained loyal and dedicated. Dealers, endorsees, competitors and supervisors all have the highest praise for the job Spencer Aloisio did for Slingerland.

Spencer stayed with Slingerland until their last year in Chicago, leaving in 1986 just before the move from Niles to Algonquin. He was contacted by Fred Gretsch about coming to work for the Gretsch-owned Slingerland, but declined. At this writing, Spencer Aloisio works at the Chicago Musician's Union.

Spencer Aloisio, 1994

Osborne replaced by Linkin

Don Osborne Sr.'s frustrations with the corporate mindset, combined with personal problems, had made it increasingly difficult for him to do his job effectively. An outspoken and strong-willed man (like his dear friend Buddy Rich), he often found it neccessary to blow off a little steam. Late one Friday night in 1977 he made the mistake of phoning New York to give Jim McIlhenny a piece of his mind about the way they were handling things at Slingerland. By the end of the conversation he got carried away and told them what they could do with the job. When longtime friend Maurie Lishon (proprietor of Franks Drum Shop of Chicago) found out what had happened, he tried to start a campaign to get Don his job back. He called several other prominent industry leaders and urged them to write letters on Don's behalf. Maurie contacted McIlhenny directly on Osborne's behalf. The response from CCM's Jim McIlhenny was sympathetic but unyielding. It was his policy, he explained, to consider rehiring anyone whom he had found it neccessary to fire. If, on the other hand, they had quit, the policy was not to take them back.

At the time of Osborne's departure from Slingerland, Larry (Link) Linkin had been running trade shows for the National Association of Music Merchants (NAMM). Although he was a clarinet player rather than a drummer, Link accepted the job offer from Jim McIlhenny because he knew "Mac" and looked forward to the opportunity to work under him, feeling there was a great deal he'd be able to learn. Unfortunately for both men, there was a corporate shakeup only about 30 days after Link started at Slingerland, and McIlhenny was suddenly out of the picture.

Linkin's management style was ideally suited to the Slingerland situation. He was able to delegate responsibility and hold people accountable without riding herd on them. According to everyone interviewed, it was a very relaxed yet productive atmosphere in the Slingerland offices.

Sales increased dramatically, mallet instrument manufacturer Deagan was acquired, a large marching percussion market share was grabbed, and it would have seemed on the surface that everything was coming up roses for Slingerland. Link, however, knew better and was faced with the same frustrations as his predecessor. Seeing that the company was "going to hell in a handbasket," Link did not hesitate when he was offered the position of retiring NAMM president Bill Gard in 1980.

MARCHING PERCUSSION

In much the same way that Sam Rowland breathed new life into Slingerland in the early '30s by developing the drum corps business (see chapter four), Fred Sanford had a tremendous impact on the company's fortunes in the 1970s.

FRED SANFORD

June 22, 1947–January 23, 2000

The interview here was conducted in about 1994. Sanford has since passed away; he lost his battle with cancer on January 23, 2000. He was surrounded by family members who reported that Freddy died as he lived– with courage and good humor, and the "Freddy smile" to the end.

Fred Sanford grew up in Casper, Wyoming, where his first serious involvement with percussion started in the seventh grade when he became a member of the Casper Troopers Drum Corps. He spent a total of nine years with the Corps.

After High School, Fred moved to Southern California to attend college. To earn spending money he worked with a High School corps, the Anaheim Kingsmen. Through the next couple of years they became the state champions of California.

The Grad Assistant to the University's marching band was working with a new corps up in Northern California, the Vanguard, and contacted Fred about coming up to San Jose. With Fred's help and guidance, the Santa Clara Vanguard became an award-winning corps.

An interview with Fred Sanford:

RC: You started working with the Santa Clara Vanguard in about 1968?

FS: Yes. I graduated in 1970 and taught High School in Bergenfield, New Jersey. I kept working with them and writing programs, coming back from New Jersey to California.

RC: What kind of equipment were most of the corps using when you started working with the drum corps?

FS: Ludwig was by far the strongest. Slingerland was second, and trying hard. Rogers was on the scne in those days also, but most of the groups that I'd been working with were playing Ludwig. The instrumentation was pretty simple– we're talking about 12"x15" snare drums, single tenors the same size, and this was before tuned bass drums so we were using maybe a couple of 28" bass drums and a couple pair of cymbals. The Vanguard had some Ludwigs, then we got a set of Rogers in 1971 which was when we won our first national title.

RC: When was your first contact with Slingerland?

FS: In 1972, when I got a phone call from Larry McCormick who informed me that Slingerland was in the process of designing a new drum, the TDR. He was calling to ask if it would be possible for the Santa Clara Vanguard to work with Slingerland on the development of this drum.

RC: What was Larry McCormick's position? Was he employed by Slingerland?

FS: No. He had his own company, McCormick Enterprises. He'd started a little garage operation with sticks and mallets and stuff like that. His business was growing and he was becoming a dealer for various things so he had some kind of vested tie-in to this as well. I agreed to at least look at the drum, and that was the first time I met Gary Beckner, I guess his position was ales manager at the time. He had come up with a brand new finish that was new and unique; a copper finish. By this time timp-tom trios, as they were known, were legalized in drum corps.

RC: Did you start working for Slingerland when you first met Gary Beckner and saw the new drums and finishes?

FS: No, I didn't really work for them– I was more of a consultant and clinician. I really didn't have that much direct contact with the factory. But we continued to play Slingerland drums and established a good rapport with the company– especially Gary Beckner and Spencer Aloisio. The first time I was contractually linked to Slingerland was not until Larry Linkin first became President. Once again I got a call from Larry McCormick. Larry Linkin had called Larry McCormick and asked for help: he was a clarinet player and needed some help figuring out who was who in the marching band scene. I became an in-house consultant. I didn't move to Chicago, but I traveled back there several times a year and worked on R&D projects and educational projects. I received a monthly retainer and we were essentially using the Santa Clara Vanguard as a field-fs;testing ground for all the things we were working on.

By this time the instrumentation we were working with in drup corps had expanded itself– you know, with multiple tenors, marching tenors, marching typmani, and at that time you were permitted a marching bell and xylophone. This was about the time that Slingerland bought Deagan, so I got involved with Deagan as far as the development of the marching bell and xylophone set. Further on the rules were expanded to allow the marimba as well.

RC: It sounds like you were pretty well removed from the politics of executive heirarchy?

FS: I do remember that there were numerous company heads that Larry Linkin had to report to at different times and that he was going through quite a bit of frustration becausenothing ever seemed to be stabilized.

RC: From an equipment standpoint, what do your think your biggest contribution was?

FS: I worked with Bill Hollerich on the slapshot strainer, but much more significant was the cutaway tom-tom, which has pretty much become the standard of design for any of those types of instruments.

RC: Was there talk of patenting that?

FS: A little bit, but no one pursued it. You know, I wish I had a quarter for every one of that style of drum that got sold! I'm not even sure it *could* have been patented, though it certainly was a unique design. The design, like most things of that nature, developed out of a need. Traditional tom-toms were very stuffy sounding outdoor and we wanted to open them up a little more. When I first discovered this, I was doing some work with Remo. They had just introduced the roto-toms and they were fiddling around with some shell materials.

We were down in North Hollywood at the plant and we were fooling around on the back lot with some mylar cylinders. I noticed that even just half of a shell, or half of a mylar reflector; gave the same resonance as a full shell. Physically I didn't know why– I just knew that it worked. Ludwig at that time was working on the scoop idea, putting a lot of bucks into developing that, but the cutaway eventually became the standard. I think it was 1977 when we first used it. Slingerland was not geared up to make shells deep enough, so we had to use Jasper shells.

RC: It wasn't long after that before Link couldn't get the money to tool up for any kind of new project. Did

Slingerland's first cutaway shells, by Fred Sanford

you run into that?
FS: Yes, there were a couple of things– one was the fiberglass shells. We did produce a nice fiberglass conga, and had Alex Acuna and Don Alias endorsing it.
RC: Your association with Slingerland lasted until about 1980?
FS: Yes. In 1980 I got a call from Ludwig's Frank Baxpehler. Slingerland had been making major inroads in the marching business and Ludwig was feeling the pinch. Ludwig was peaking out at the time, and Frank asked if I'd move to Chicago and work for Ludwig full time. That was my twelth year with Santa Clara and I felt it was time to take my career to the next step. So I resigned from Santa Clara and moved to Chicago.

The person charged with filling Fred Sanford's shoes at Slingerland was Ward Durrett. Here are his comments:
WD: I first became noticed by Slingerland when I was with McCormick Enterprises. Over the course of a couple of years as Fred Sanford phased himself out and had gone to Ludwig they needed a marching percussion guy.
RC: You got there just before the change of ownership, when Dan Henkin bought the company?
WD: Yes.
RC: Did the change in ownership change your life at Slingerland any?
WD: Not really, because I came just about at the same time the change was made. Actually I was hired by Tom Burzicki who was the transition guy for Danny Henkin. (He also was the president of Selmer when I was at Ludwig.) So the entire thrust of what I did was under the Henkin banner. Burzicki was an accountant and was an interim guy between Link and Bill Young. He's the guy who developed the Spirit series– that was his idea. The Pearl export has just been introduced and was driving everybody crazy. Tama's Swingstar was in the low-end too. Tom redesigned the manufacturing process around the Spirit series. The Bill came in. Bill was very much of an entrepreneur and knew what he wanted to do, so he ended up just going on to something else.
RC: What was the status of the mallet and marching stuff at the time you came to Slingerland?
WD: The TDR had been out for five or six years and the slapshot strainer had just come out. Actually I took over the last stages on that– it was about three-quarters of the way done. The cutaways were still strong. All the stuff that Fred and Link had developed was still pushing real well, and from the marching perspective it kept Slingerland real visable. The numbers were nowhere near what, say, Ludwig was doing, but the visibility was real good. At the 1980 Winter Olympics one of the corps at the opening ceremonies used Slingerland, stuff like that.

When Slingerland wanted to lure the Bridgeman away from Ludwig, one of the things that Dennis Delucia wanted to do was different powder coatings and different plating. I went out to Dennis and took him a number of different shells with different colors, and different colored hardware. (This was in 1981.) He went for the black drums with the brass hardware. That's where the "Black Gold" thing started. Slingerland carried that for about three or four years until it kind of folded. That whole process got transferred over to the outfits but that's where it all began. It was pretty effective on the drum set line.
RC: Was Slingerland feeling any competitive pressure on marching gear from the imports at the end of the Mardan (Dan Henkin) regime?
WD: No, not yet. They had just gotten into the outfit stuff. Yamaha was talking about bringing in some stuff, and Pearl had just started to bring in a few pieces.
RC: So probably of the three divisions (marching mallets and outfits) the marching line was the strongest?
WD: Yes, and it was pretty much carrying things. That era was really the height for that division.

> **"It was a good sales staff; Phil Hulsey, John Clark– a lot was happening from 1977 to 1979. Sam Geati was a big part of that, as well as Brad Morey."**
> **Fred Sanford**

Excerpt from 1980 Slingerland ad

1980–1986
SLINGERLAND AT THE EDGE

After such a strong showing in the 1970s in spite of the detachment on the part of the corporate owners, Slingerland was poised to enter the '80s as one of the serious contenders in the percussion industry. Significant penetration of the marching percussion market had been accomplished, and a new line of inexpensive outfits was being imported to compete with Pearl and Tama. Deagan's sales in 1980 peaked out at just over $1.2 million, up over twofold from the sales in 1977 when Slingerland acquired Deagan. Having laid claim to the title of "world's largest drum company" in two different eras, it appeared Slingerland was coming back again. Instead, the eighties turned out to be the decade that nearly saw the Slingerland name disappear for good.

The folks at McMillan came to the realization by the end of the '70s that what they did best was publish, and they were ready to get out of the music business. They came up with a buyer who wanted Conn, but was not particularly interested in Slingerland. It was a package deal, though, so Slingerland was sold to Elkhart's Dan Henkin along with Conn. Henkin's first fiscal year began on January 31, 1980.

Henkin's name was a familiar one to industry veterans. He'd made his money on ventures such as the Gemeinhardt flute company, and was now bent on rebuilding the Conn dynasty. He even bought the Elkhart mansion that Colonel Conn had built, and lived in it. (Still does, at this writing!) Henkin's Mardan Corporation did business as the C.G. Conn Co. Ltd., with music divisions that included Deagan mallet percussion, Conn brass and saxophones, Scherl & Roth string instruments, Artley flutes, picclolos, etc.

The "Henkin Regime" was kicked off with a lavish party in Elkhart. A big tent was set up on the grounds of Henkin's estate, and guests from across the country were invited for the weekend. Doc Severinsen, who was a good friend of Henkin's and a vice president of development in Henkin's Conn division, played for the guests, along with Louis Bellson.

Henkin visited the Niles plant long enough to introduce himself around and say hello but didn't spend any time there. Over the next four years (the term of his ownership) Henkin rarely visited the Slingerland plant. "I don't think Dan had any great love for the drum business from the beginning," remembers Aloisio. "He worked his deal with McMillan to get Conn, and Slingerland was just part of that package."

Slingerland's plant executives would have to travel to Elkhart for meetings, from which they generally returned feeling angry and frustrated. Bill Young, who had succeeded Larry Linkin as President, finally decided that he was better off resigning. He had a vision for Slingerland, but was unable to steer toward it because he was not able to muster support from Elkhart. Even worse, he could not even continue to operate at the same level the company had built up to without some badly needed tooling— one of Larry Linkin's main complaints.

Succeeding Bill Young's fairly short tenure as president was Dick Richardson. Richardson was president of Musser when he got the offer from Henkin and made a bit of a splurge for the first year or so. At the end of that first year (May 2, 1983) Richardson composed a letter to his dealers. The letter encouraged dealers to make time at the upcoming NAMM music convention to visit the Slingerland booth to check out the progress they were making. The "New Slingerland", according to the letter, had embarked on a program of product updating, improvement, and innovation. Getting more specific, Richardson called attention to the development and production of the Magnum series of hardware, the slapshot strainer as standard on all TDR snare drums, and Slingerland's position as the exclusive original equipment manufacturer for May EA drum miking systems. The letter went on to point out that Slingerland was now distributing Sabian cymbals. The Spirit set was becoming well established as the most outstanding value in the medium price range. The Deagan mallet instrument manufacturing operation, reported the letter, had been moved into the Slingerland plant, and they'd updated the manufacturing process and revamped the Deagan product line.

Behind the scenes, however, Richardson was having the same problems that had faced Linkin and Young. Ward Durret recalls that Richardson returned from meetings in Elkhart "simply *livid*! And he was a very laid-back guy. It drove him out of the industry!" reports Durret. "Nobody in the industry has seen him since!

It was my understanding that he was hired with an agreement that would provide him an opportunity to purchase the Slingerland division eventually."

Durret was becoming equally frustrated. Typical of the situations that made him feel the Slingerland operation was of little interest to the owner (and a turning point in Durret's feelings toward the company) was the lost opportunity for exposure at the Los Angeles Olympics. Durrett had been approached by the Olympic Organizing Committee about Slingerland's possible involvement as a sponsor. Official sponsorships started at a minimum price of $250,000.00. Sponsors could either pay in cash, or, if they had a product the committee needed, could provide "payment in kind". For the manufacturers of durable goods, the actual goods remained the property of the manufacturer and they were free to sell the the merchandise after the Olympics. The committee was proposing to Durrett that Slingerland provide drums for the opening ceremonies. They also needed other band instruments, so Durrett worked up a proposal which called for Mardan divisions to provide not only the Slingerland drums, but also sousaphones from the Conn division and trumpets from King. The proposal included a plan for selling all the instruments after the Olympics were over, so there was, in Durrett's view, very little risk and a great deal to gain— the exposure afforded by the sponsorship would far exceed anything Slingerland would be able to afford otherwise. The total value of the instruments came up to about $280,000.00, and the Olympic committee was willing to split the sponsorship between the three divisions since all were part of one corporation. The proposal was submitted to Henkin in Elkhart, who turned it down. Henkin *did*, however, work a deal with the Olympic Committee to provide the tubas and trumpets. When he saw that, Durrett concluded that Henkin had no intention of sinking a dime into Slingerland, and he left. He'd been doing some teaching and decided to go back to teaching full time. "The tooling was just plain worn down," he recalls, "from thousands and thousands of stampings. The stuff was still good, but it was only the design concept that was still good; we were not able to actually make good equipment. But it would have cost thousands and thousands of dollars to retool all that stuff. It was an interesting environment to work in, and it was full of idea people, people who really worked their brains out trying to make it work. But these people could only take it so far before the circumstances of ownership came into play. It was my understanding that when Dick Richardson took the presidency of Slingerland he was eventually going to get ownership of the company. By the time that opportunity had finally arisen, there was nothing left to buy!"

The Slingerland that Richardson described to dealers in his 1983 pre-NAMM letter was the Slingerland he wanted to buy: a marching division that was setting standards and deepening market penetration, an outfit division that was going head to head with the imports, and a newly revitalized and streamlined "in-house" Deagan division. Over the next couple of years, however, all three areas would go flat. Deagan, although it had been completely moved by May 1983, never did resume production under the Henkin regime. (Deagan did not resume production until June 1, 1985.) Fred Sanford was busy at Ludwig taking back the marching business that Slingerland had been building at the expense of Ludwig and Rogers in the late 1970s. Ward Durrett left Slingerland and was not replaced with a marching percussion expert. By this time Pearl and Yamaha were beginning to have an impact on the marching scene also. The remaining area, outfits, was hit by a triple whammy: inability to produce high-quality merchandise, increasing competition from the imports, and a general downturn in the economy which had a tremendous effect on Americans' discretionary spending. The 1983 oil crisis caused skyrocketing prices of all petroleum-related products such as drum covering material and drum heads.

Slingerland's Cancer

One industry insider (a publisher privy to industry statistics and gossip) points out that during the CCM era, Slingerland's fixed assets were not properly depreciated. This means that the company's fixed assets (buildings, inventory, machinery) were not actually worth as much money as its balance sheet indicated. For a family-owned business with no need for outside financial help, that is not a problem except for tax considerations. For a corporate division expected to yield a return for its stockholders, that's a major problem. The health of a company is gauged by the profit and size of dividends, measured as percentages of company worth. An overvalued company is simply unable to produce acceptable profits and dividends.

When someone sells an overvalued company and the purchaser must borrow to buy the company, the purchaser soon finds that the profits are not sufficient to make the payments on the financed amount.

Henkin finally became determined to sell the Slingerland division. He came to Spencer Aloisio with a proposal that included a financing plan, but Aloisio politely declined. Henkin cast about for other potential buyers, even considering approaching prominent Slingerland endorsees. He finally came up with a buyer from within the ranks: Slingerland accountant Larry Rasp and his wife Sandra. The Rasps set up a corporation, the Sanlar Corporation. In order to put the financing package together, the Niles building was not included with the business; Rasp would lease the building to do business in. Henkin arranged a short term $685,000.00 note for Rasp and the deal was closed on November 8, 1984. In spite of the help that Henkin provided in making the deal float, Rasp's venture was doomed from the start. In a letter written just two days before the closing, Rasp's lawyer pointed out to him that although he had some good ideas and plans, there was a serious problem of undercapitalization. The lawyer felt it was critical to the firm's success to attract some non-music industry investment capital, and he strongly urged Rasp to get someone started writing up a complete analysis of the company: its history, market position within the industry, the marketing strategy, etc. He offered to review the project to help polish it and develop a business plan. The load was lightened a little when the Deagan division was sold to Yamaha.

The agreement between Henkin and Rasp included a number of clauses which almost immediately led to disputes. The biggest problem, from which no doubt all others were in one way or another related, was related to cash flow. Slingerland suppliers were not being paid by Rasp for goods and services which Henkin had received. The purchase agreement had spelled out a payment plan timetable for these payables, which was not being met. Some of the suppliers were turning to Mardan (Henkins corporation) for payment. Other disputes involved the dollar value Mardan had placed on the inventory, existing leases of Slingerland equipment to parties unknown to the new owner, routing of payments received on Old Receivables, access to Sanlar financial records by Mardan personnel, and lost or lapsed trademarks, patents, and copyrights.

It's a wonder that Rasp had any time at all to run Slingerland; he was very busy dealing with not only the disputes between him and Henkin, but had plenty of fires to put out with his vendors— lawsuits were everywhere. Cash flow forced Slingerland from the building on Milwaukee Avenue that had been home since it was built in 1960. The move was to Algonquin, another Chicago suburb. Slingerland did manage to publish a catalog in 1985, but it reflected the squeeze the company was feeling. The catalog was only 20 pages, and the only outfits in it besides the Spirit series were four Magnum outfits. The tympani and marching equipment were gone, Deagan was of course gone, and all that remained of the Latin line was two congas and a couple Timbale sets. There were no endorsees listed. It was a strain to even produce the few products that remained in the catalog. Slingerland had gone from a company that was trying valiantly to build acceptable products on worn and outdated tooling to a company that was trying desperately to keep its head above water. Spencer Aloisio finally bowed out, in January 1986. Less than two months later (on March 15th, 1986) Slingerland entered Chapter 11 bankruptcy, citing $3.3 in liabilities. Rasp indicated that he saw the Chapter 11 protection from creditors as an opportunity to restructure the company.

Before the end of 1986, Rasp struck a deal with Fred Gretsch Enterprises. Gretsch got the Slingerland name and assets, which were moved to the Gretsch warehouse in South Carolina. Gretsch stuck their own stickers over the Algonquin address on the last Rasp Slingerland catalog. Virtually nothing in the catalog was still being produced, but there were plans to keep the Spirit series drums, so the catalog was still considered a useful sales tool.

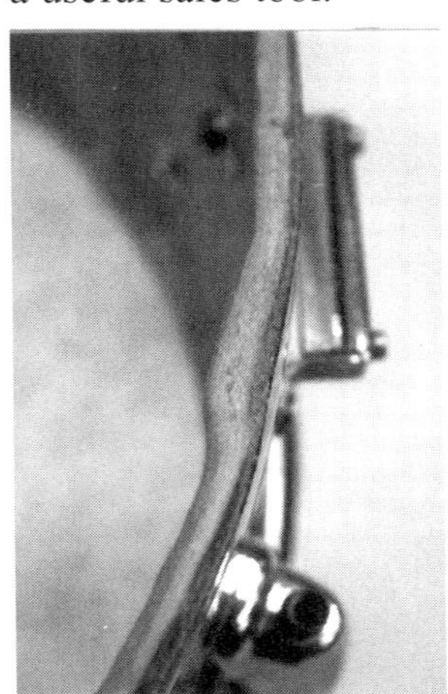

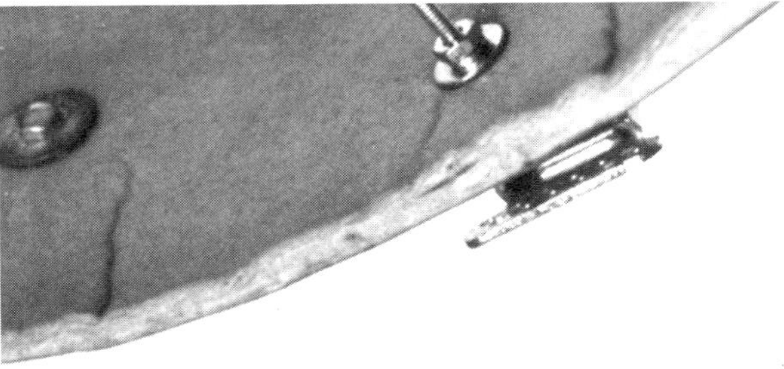

One of the last product developments of the Rasp era was a shell made of *cardboard*. As could be expected, the acoustic properties and durability of the bearing edges on these drums were dreadful.

THE GRETSCH/HSS ERA
(1986–1995)

The Slingerland story from the time of Slingerland's sale to Fred Gretsch Enterprises up to the time of its sale to the Gibson Guitar Company is probably best told by George "Buzz" King. Bringing the Slingerland name back to a position of respect and competitiveness in the drum world was a task that called for more than corporate financing and high-tech marketing. The real key was to give the line a personality, a *heart*. Through these years, Buzz personified Slingerland in the tradition of Don Osborne, Larry Linkin, Spencer Aloisio, and many other great names from Slingerland's past.

The following is a combination of two interviews with Buzz. One interview was done by David Blum of Edelmann Scott Inc. for a 1991 HSS press release. The other was done by Rob Cook in January, 1994, just days before Slingerland reached what would turn out to be yet another turning point in its history.

DB: When did you first discover drums?

BUZZ: My first exposure to drums came from my father, who had been a professional drummer. The first sound I was exposed to, in fact, was the old Slingerland sound. When I was in the second grade, I found this drum set in my parent's basement. (Buzz points to an old Slingerland set in the corner of his office, the kind of drums Buddy Rich or Gene Krupa would have played.) As you can imagine, it was far too big for me. So that Christmas, my parents bought me a toy set.

DB: Did you take lessons?

BUZZ: Yes. Throughout grade school I had private lessons. And I also played percussion with the school band. In seventh grade, I even began playing for money. I had a band that played covers at clubs and local dances. We played songs by the Ventures and the Yardbirds. I kept playing throughout high school, both in the school band and professionally.

DB: At the time, were you interested in playing professionally for the rest of your life?

BUZZ: No. Actually, I was interested in science. So when I went to college I majored in biology and minored in music composition. I did keep playing, though. I supported myself by playing the college club scene. I had a band called Daddy Rabbit. And in 1973 we had a big break when we landed a recording contract. We did record a record, but due to problems I won't go into, it was shelved.

DB: Were you getting fed up with the music business at that point?

BUZZ: Yes. At that point I was ready to give up music, at least professionally, for a life of science. The next logical step for me was graduate school, so I applied to medical schools all over the country. And then I moved to Richmond, Virginia to study Behavioral Pharmacology at the Medical College of Virginia for four years. The whole time, though, I was playing music and working at a music store to pay for school.

DB: How has your scientific background affected your music?

BUZZ: Well, as a laboaratory technician at the hospital and through studying behavioral pharmacology, I learned to plot and design experiments. I learned that everything has a structure. And essentially, that's what music is— structure. In jazz, for instance, you have a basic structure, and improvisation is nothing more than straying from that structure and then coming back to it. Science also helped me in the design of drums. Knowing how to set up experiments to test different variables, such as percussive sound characteristics, was very helpful in designing the Lite.

DB: What caused you to change careers— from being a scientist to being a product manager for a drum company?

BUZZ: Well, I was still undecided about my career choices. I kept asking myself, should I be a scientist or a drummer? I was put in charge of the drum department at a large music store. And I even started my own small company (which, incidentally, is still operating) that makes custom cases for drums and other musical equipment. But I was still working as a lab technician and as a behavioral pharmacologist.

DB: What finally happened that made you decide to go into the music business?

BUZZ: Well, HSS, Inc. contacted me. They'd heard about my equipment cases and wanted some for their Hohner accordians. They needed someone who knew the drum business well. I met with Horst Mucha, HSS's president, and after some interviews he offered me the job. How could I turn it down? I was put in charge of everything from customer service to distribution for their drum products.

RC: When did you join HSS?

BUZZ: I got hired by Hohner after they moved down from Long Island to Richmond, Virginia, in about 1985. They moved out in about 1983. They used to be the Sonor distributor in the '60s- then Sonor distribution went to the Charles Alden company for several years, then Hohner got involved again. They needed somebody to run the Sonor division; product specialist product management, travel with reps, and everything else.

I did that for three or four years, and then Sonor took the distribution away in 1989, and gave it to Korg. At that point we had a percussion-oriented team of reps who were selling Sabian, Sonor, Vic Firth, and other percussion products. Those guys needed a drum line so we looked around at Rogers, at Gretsch. At that point Slingerland was owned by Gretsch and still is. He'd bought the company when it was going out of business, and just sat on it for a few years.

RC: Was all the machinery and stuff taken to Gretsch?

BUZZ: Yes, but the machinery was very old. In fact the Gretsch equipment was much better. He did not plan to make drums with the Slingerland name; the plan was to do like Island Music was doing with Rogers. [Island Music was a general music jobber which for a time licensed the Rogers name and designs. The drums they brought to market were very low quality imports which looked just like the much higher quality American-made Rogers CBS had produced.] He had a set designed- it was the Spirit set only it wasn't refined at all. We got involved at that point as distributors, in a royalty-type agreement. When I got involved, I convinced the people in my company that we wouldn't be able to sell the Slingerland name that way— it was too powerful of a name to bastardize that way. Anyway, we needed something in a hurry, so the first thing we did, we sold the first container that came in that Fred had designed and worked with, the Spirit stuff. Then I changed it. I changed a lot of the fittings, the shell design, the inside of the shells, the coverings, thicknesses, to get them up to standard.

RC: About when would that first container have been?

BUZZ: Late 1989. Then I convinced them we needed a flagship— expensive, quality American-made product. The European countries were looking to the U.S. for American- made drums. I designed the Slingerland Lite shells and the whole concept behind the Slingerland Lite drum set which was a thin, contemporary sound— thin shells, no reinforcement hoops, reduced diameter, isolation on all the lugs and all the parts, premium heads— we were the first company to offer the Evans heads as standard equipment.

RC: How did you design the shells?

BUZZ: Gretsch works through Jasper. We had shell-molds made for certain diameters that they didn't have— we paid for all the shell molds, all the sizes. We [HSS] own those– Fred doesn't own those. Also various other castings and so forth to put the hardware together. I designed the way the spur works on there with the gull-wing type spur similar to the Sonor thing.

RC: So your molds are used by Jasper Wood Products Company only to produce the Slingerland Lite drums and they have other molds that are used for the other drums ?

BUZZ: Right. Only our drums are made with our molds.

RC: Other than the sizes, is there a difference between the Gretsch shells made by Jasper and the Slingerland Lite shells made by Jasper?

BUZZ: Oh yeah! Gretsch isn't pure maple, or hasn't been up to now that I know of. They're still using inner plies of gumwood or something. Gretsch has their own sound and we have our own sound. I began with Slingerland's traditionally thinner shell, six and seven millimeters. And I chose the rock maple wood construction not only because it's plentiful in the country, but because it's stable, dense, and easy to work with. I also wanted the shells to be as solid as possible, with no filler plies. That way there's less vibrational interference.

RC: Did you keep the Spirit Series coming in even after you got the Lite series off the ground?

BUZZ: Oh yes— in fact that's the bulk of our sales, but then the Lite kicked in and at the same time we had the Radio King remade. That took quite a while because Fred had to find somebody to make those shells.

RC: Who makes the solid shells for the reissue Radio Kings?

BUZZ: I know who makes those shells, but I'm not at liberty to say. [aside: but they're made by a furniture company] Fred paid for those molds. They're based on two of my own old Radio Kings; they took them apart and made everything exactly the same diameters. The way the parts fit together is what makes a Radio King sound the way it does— it's not just the shell. In the old days everything fit tightly and you had big overtones. Big band drummers made the sound a standard- since it was what everybody was hearing, it became what everybody *wanted* to hear.

RC: Who lacquers and assembles the Radio Kings?

BUZZ: The Slingerland Lite series and the Radio Kings are finished in the Gretsch factory with Slingerland stains— that red right over there is the original stuff! The white marine pearl we use on the one Radio King and on the Artist Classic series is the original.

RC: What's the story on the disruption in production about a year ago when the word in the industry was that the EPA (U.S. Evironmental Protection Agency) made Gretsch stop lacquering drums?

BUZZ: There was no disruption. There was a disruption in Gretsch shipments— I don't know what he's doing with that, but I know that when I order Radio King product and I order Lite series drums, I get my product, covered or lacquered.

RC: You mentioned the European demand for American drums— who handles that end of things?

BUZZ: The growth has been mainly domestic, but European sales are growing. I'm the one who does all the export sales except for South America, and Fred does Japan. All the export numbers are growing— of course it's easy to be up when you start at zero! The export thing is up about 600% so far this year. The French market has been our big European customer. They bought only Lite and Radio King up until this show [1994 Winter NAMM], they're just now ordering some Spirit series. They didn't even buy the Artist before- they bought a few sets last year in Frankfurt, but mostly high end.

Then last year we got Sonor back at HSS. I released the Artist series which has been a really good product for us. It's a maple-mahogany-maple shell that sounds like the old three-ply thing with maple reinforcement rings— the traditional Slingerland sound. They're made in standard jazz sizes. These are made in Taiwan with American maple and American coverings, American isolation things, little nuts and bolts- all from the United States. Everything is shipped over there and they assemble them and lacquer them or cover them. Ninety percent of our endorsement roster which is mainly jazz guys from up in New York, Boston, the Los Angeles area– they play the Artist Custom series and they rave about the sound.

RC: And that series is a lot less expensive than the Lite?

BUZZ: It sure is. That's why we had to go to the foreign assembly. You see a lot of big-name endorsees for different companies playing very expensive drums. The whole idea of an endorsee program is to set up guys that up-and-coming drummers want to emulate so they'll buy the same kind of equipment. We wanted to make sure that the kids could *afford* to buy the same gear they see our endorsees playing.

RC: You seem to have an interesting endorsee roster...

BUZZ: We're supporting American music. No thrash and metal, but *real* American music forms. I don't want to sound judgemental, but it's just the affinity that we've developed– the traditional jazz and old-time rock, etc. We have '60s and '70s bands coming out of the woodwork; the guy from Canned Heet and a lot of the other guys from the old roster are coming back.

RC: What happened to the old shell-making equipment in Chicago?

BUZZ: If there's anything left, it's down at Fred's warehouse, not being used. I'm trying to bring the whole Slingerland thing back as much as possible. Our marching percussion is made now in the United States- near St Louis, in a different factory.

RC: They're making shells there?

BUZZ: I think those shells are Keller.

RC: The whole marching thing got dropped when Gretsch bought Slingerland?

BUZZ: Probably even before that.But that's right, Fred did not do anything with the marching end of things. Tim Henry helps me with the marketing of that product.

RC: Do you feel stable in that, if you continue on this growth curve, what if Fred were to catch a wild hair and say to himself "gee— this Slingerland thing is really taking off! I think I'll do it myself!"

BUZZ: He certainly could do that. Very easily. He'd be stupid to, though, because he doesn't have the sales force in place at this time to handle the marketing.

DB: Are you glad you made the career choices you did?

BUZZ: I wouldn't change a thing.

Buzz was right that Gretsch did not have the marketing staff to take Slingerland away from HSS. Fred Gretsch *was*, however, able to capitalize on the inroads that Buzz and HSS had made with the line by selling the whole ball of wax. In a stunning development it was announced that a purchase agreement had been signed with the Gibson Guitar company. The agreement was signed in Fred Gretsch's office on February 21, 1994, less than 30 days after the interview Buzz King gave Rob Cook, and, coincidentally, on the 25th anniversary of the death of George Way.

GIBSON ACQUIRES SLINGERLAND

Why would a guitar company buy a drum company? The Gibson connection with drums dates back to the days when as a division of Norlin its sales staff also represented Pearl drums. The sales and marketing staff, advertising budget, trade show presence, etc. were all geared up to do the job not only for Gibson guitars, but for a drum line. There are two sharply differing versions of what exactly caused the Gibson/Pearl split, neither of which have any direct bearing on the Slingerland story. The bottom line is that Pearl left Gibson to set up their own distribution network and to "fill the drum gap" Gibson worked out a distribution deal with Mapex. (For more on the Mapex product developments, see the interview with Sam Bacco.) Owning a drum line was more appealing than simply distributing one in light of the Pearl loss, and with a few discreet inquiries Gibson executives found that Slingerland could be purchased.

The Slingerland acquisition by Gibson placed quite a number of music industry folks in awkward situations. Remember (Buzz King interview) that Fred Gretsch, owner of Slingerland, had a Slingerland licensing and distribution arrangement with HSS. Terms of the acquisition called for Gibson to honor that agreement; they agreed to do for HSS everything that Gretsch had previously done for HSS. It would be an understatement to say that the Mapex company was concerned that their U.S. distributor now owned a competitive drum line. Observors speculated that since nothing much changed in the first year of this arrangement that both distribution deals (Gibson/Mapex and HSS/Slingerland) would continue for the two to three years left on their terms before any major changes would be made. The HSS/Slingerland deal was the first to terminate early. Although HSS had shipped a number of Slingerland outfits to Anaheim for the January 95 NAMM music convention, dealers entering the hall on opening morning found that there were no Slingerland drums at the HSS display. In eleventh-hour negotiations, the HSS/Slingerland arrangement had been terminated. The other shoe was dropped when it was announced just before the Nashville 95 NAMM summer music convention in July that a distribution deal had been arranged between Mapex and Washburn.

Drum manufacturing started up in Nashville, pretty much under the direction of Sam Bacco and Pat Foley. Neither Bacco nor Foley were on the Gibson payroll as employees, choosing the relative independance of working as consultants.

PAT FOLEY,
SLINGERLAND CUSTOM SHOP, 1995

RC: Are you a drummer, Pat?

PF: No. A lot of people assume that, because I've been pretty visable in the drum world since the late '70s when I started doing drum customizing. I'm a guitar player. I always enjoyed tinkering with guitars, repairing and refinishing them, so I finally tracked down a guitar maker who would work out an apprenticeship with me.

RC: Where were you?

PF: Detroit. I was 19 in 1973 when I first got into the guitar apprenticeship program with an excellent Detroit luthier, Jim Riesenberger. I don't know what he's doing today, but he was a great guitar maker. He'd made instruments for Gordon Lightfoot and other artists in the Detroit and Toronto area. I had a little repair shop in Detroit and worked for another shop doing their repairs for them. (Strings 'N' Things, Birmingham, Michigan)

RC: So how did you get into drum work?

PF: In 1977 I went to L.A. just on sort of a whim and ran into a friend of mine who was working for some big name bands; Paul Jameson. He was working for the Eagles at the time, and asked me if I could repair some

Pat Foley in his Slingerland paint shop, 1995

drums. So I repaired some drums for Don Henley, through Paul.
RC: Structural repairs?
PF: Yeah, he wanted to convert some tom mounts which involved plugging some big holes and then touching up the lacquer. I think they were originally Gretsch drums and he was putting a different kind of mount on them. I found that the finish work I'd been doing translated very well to drum repairs. There simply were not many people doing that kind of work at that time. Today there are dozens of drum customizers, but back then you never even heard the term 'bearing edge'.
RC: Did you set up a shop in L.A. to do the work?
PF: Yes. I rented a garage. Paul and I in effect had a business together. He knew a lot of these people so he'd bring the repair and refinish work to me. The drum work got to be a specialty we were noted for. I was always able to distinguish my work through special finishes and special attention to finish work. We reworked a lot of old Slingerland Radio King drums that we sold to session players; Jeff Porcaro, Russ Kunkel, and guys like that.
RC: I've heard that many old Radio King snare drums do need some work. What kind of restoration did you find neccessary?
PF: A lot of them tend to be out of round. You kind of have to make a determination whether the drum can be repaired or not. Sometimes you can coax them back into round and if the hoop is coming loose you can clamp them round and hope they'll stay. From my experience in those days if I got a drum that was dead round, it was sort of rare and today would be a collectable drum. At that time, however, the vintage drum market wasn't what it is today. We were basically using the solid maple shell Radio Kings as raw materials to make custom drums. The were eight-lug drums so we put on Gretsh die-cast 8-lug hoops. We used some Sonor throw-offs, or (Ludwig) P-85s, even an occasional Zoomatic. I have to admit that we somewhat bastardized them.
RC: Did you work on the bearing edges?
PF: Yeah, but we tried to use the same profiles. They tended to change from drum to drum and we found that certain formula that seemed to work for most of the guys. They wanted a pretty shallow bearing edge, not much of a sharp point. Some were sharper than others so we'd rework them so they sounded good.

The Super Radio King that we make now is really a throwback to that kind of drum, even though it's a ten-lug drum. It has die-cast hoops and the shallow profile on the bearing edges like the older drums from the thirties and forties. It seems particularly appropriate and satisfying that I work for Slingerland now building the new Radio Kings and hopefully building and restoring the reputation of the Radio Kings.
RC: I understand that you started getting some studio experience in your L.A. days, also.
PF: I started working as an assistant in drum-related situations; what today you'd call the job of a drum-tech. In those days you were either a roadie or an engineer. I think I was somewhere in between. I'd be called in to supply drums a lot of times, or to tune drums, or just generally be available to help with recording sessions with regard to the drums. That led to producing. I did eventually have some success with some records that I produced and was fortunate enough to spend a year in England recording as a producer. One thing led to another and I spent five years running a recording studio in the Caribbean before moving to Nashville where I started up a small studio recording mainly reggae and hip-hop.
RC: How did you get involved with Slingerland?
PF: Actually it was before Slingerland, when Gibson was distributing Mapex drums. The head of the drum division was Tracey Hoeft. I barely remembered him, but evidently I had been helpful to him in some way back when he was running Paragon Music in Florida. My name kind of stuck with him. He was appointed head of a Mapex project to establish Mapex as a U.S. made brand. He tracked me down, and was surprised to find that I was right here in Nashville. I went down to see him the day after he called, and he offered me a position as a consultant. The position kind of evolved into the current one in which I head up the custom division. At this point we're still a small outfit, so I run the finish department, help oversee production, and assorted other stuff.
RC: What kind of time frame are you looking at now when it comes to catalogued or custom drum orders?
PF: There's really not much difference because we build most everything to order. If you order a set right now in emerald green, Josh will write the order, it'll get initiated within two weeks of the order date, and get shipped within six weeks of the order date. If it was a custom set it wouldn't be much different. It might take an extra week because I'm going to put some orders aside and say "ok, I'm going to do custom finishes next Monday". Really anything we say we can do, we can do in a timely manner.
We have not been encouraging elaborate graphics right now because that takes a lot more time than people realize.

We really have a pretty wide range of finishes available. We have 16 colors and finishes as standard plus we give people the ability to combine colors. I'll have a

guy say he wants purple at the edges, or even just tell me to experiment. I had one guy say he wanted a very subtle blue tint, so I stained a shell blue and stained black over the blue. Then when the clear was put on you could see just enough of the blue coming through that it was a very eery effect. Everybody liked it, so we put it into production and we call it Raven Blue.
RC: You're working with polyurethane finishes?
PF: Right. In the past I've been real accustomed to working with nitrocellulose lacquer. I used it for years and years. When we started out the production facility here I experimented back and forth and came to the conclusion that expecially today, in 1995, you really have to use a catalyzed product. You have to be able to guarantee against weather checking. If I do a beautiful set for you in nitrocellulouse lacquer I can't possible guarantee it against checking. It doesn't matter how well you care for them, they *will* eventually weather-check. Today the standards for drum finishes on the high end stuff are very high. You have to be dead level and properly buffed out. We experimented with a number of finishes and settled on the catalyzed polyurethane. We can do fine finish work with it, tint and shade it, it looks every bit as good, but it's much more resistant to chipping and weather checking.

There isn't really a precedent for the design we're using in the old Slingerland. Soundwise it's different; there's a lot of attack and with the RIMS isolation mount there's a lot of tone generated. It's not for everybody, but these drums record incredibly well.
RC: Are you doing any covered drums?
PF: We do them in small quantities. Our finish work has been a big selling point but I think now that we've established a reputation for fine finish work we can do a little more with the classic finishes. We now offer white marine pearl, black diamond pearl, and champagne sparkle.
RC: How about the sound of the new Slingerland drums as compared to old Slingerland drums?
PF: The new drums have a very contemporary sound. Sam and I have discussed that a lot. We'd like to bring back some of the older Slingerland designs shellwise.
RC: Three-ply shell with a big reinforcement hoop and big round bearing edges?
PF: I would love that! Maybe we can if we're successful enough with what we're doing. What Sam wants to do is the '70s thing; the big thick 5-ply (Unimold) construction. Sam thinks those are very underrated. I really like those old '60s thin shells with the big fat reinforcement hoops. Every time we get one in for repair it calls my attention back to that. It was a different sound. They're a little harder to control, but they just have an ooomph to them that I like.

We decided on the six-ply cross-laminated shell that we've got, going to eight-ply on anything 18" or over, and ten-ply on the snare drums because of the higher tension requirements. All of us insisted on the die-cast hoops, even though they're more expensive. That was part of our vision of what we wanted to do and is one of the things that make our drums a cut above. I see the Studio King as our flagship model even though it's a digression from earlier Slingerland stuff.

JOSH TOUCHTON; DIRECTOR, SLINGERLAND CUSTOMER RELATIONS (1995 Interview)

RC: How long have you been here, Josh?
JT: Two and a half years now. Before that I was on the road with a band and worked for a while in a retail music store. That experience gives me a pretty good feel for where our customers are coming from.
RC: Has your job description changed much as the staff and product line has evolved?
JT: Not really. Technically my job title is director of customer relations but because we're so small and we

Pat Foley (left) and Josh Touchton review the production schedule, 1995

all get along so well, it seems like everybody does everything. Right now I'm doing some marketing, artist relations, and even shipping.

RC: Are you the guy a prospective dealer contacts to discuss getting the Slingerland line?

JT: No, that is arranged through the DSM, or District Sales Manager. I'm the guy everybody calls when they want to order product but can't reach their DSM. I'm kind of the hub for the DSM's; they can call in to find out what the stock situation is, who I've been talking to, and so forth. It's a pretty smooth system.

RC: Have you seen the dealer list growing pretty steadily?

JT: Definitely. We've been adding about two dealers a week and I expect by the end of September 1995 it'll be about five dealers a week. I expect it to taper off a bit later in the fall.

RC: Has production been able to keep up with the increasing dealer base?

JT: Yeah, the production growth has pretty much matched dealer growth. We moved to this new building back in April, and really are still growing into it. Although dealer orders get priority in production, we've still been able to make up a few kits for stock. We've been keeping it at about ten stock kits. If a dealer calls and is a big hurry for something, we can let them know what's in stock and hopefully ship out something right away. I started making up weekly stock lists and faxing them to the DSMs. Now I've got dealers who call in asking for that list.

RC: I noticed the stickers being put inside the shells. Are those serial numbers for dealer and customer identification purposes, for insurance, etc.?

JT: It goes a lot further than that. We log those numbers into a database. Given one of those numbers we can look up all kinds of information on that drum or the outfit it went out with. We'll have the date it was shipped, whether it was a stock outfit or custom, the finish, the other drums that went with it, anything that was different or unique about that production run, and so forth. That will help us match additional pieces later or replace pieces. This information should also be of extreme interest to collectors in years to come.

JOHN ALDRIDGE, contract drum engraver

RC: I understand the first Slingerland drums you engraved were for HSS?

JA: That's right. There are a lot of people out there who would like to have a hand-engraved drum but don't want to pay a thousand bucks for a black beauty. When I saw the relatively inexpensive copper-shell Slingerland drum that HSS was selling, it was just what I was looking for. I started engraving their drums in the fall of 1994. I had engraved a couple of drums that were going to be displayed at the HSS Slingerland display at the January 1995 Anaheim NAMM music convention. Noone knew ahead of time that Slingerland distribution was going to change the day the show opened. So I took the drums over to the Gibson Slingerland display and they decided to continue with the engraving. They wanted to do just the 7x12 and 7x14 in copper and brass. They asked for some specific pattern information, so I drew up a very close replica of the original Slingerland engraving pattern from the 1920s. I think there may be plans to do a black beauty at some point in the future.

RC: Are these drums going to be collectable?

JA: I think they'll be fairly collectable almost immediately. Although the shells so far have been Taiwanese and not the best of shells in terms of quality, these are still numbered limited editions with hand engraving. There will be only twenty of the first series, and these are the very first metal drums made by Slingerland since being bought by Gibson. Historically this kind of thing has come to mean something to the value of the drum even if the quality is not the greatest. Look at '60s Ludwig drums. A lot of them are really dogs, but they're all really hot simply because of when they were made and what was happening at the time.

RC: I notice that you're engraving "Slingerland, Nashville". I presume the earlier ones just said "Slingerland, U.S.A."?

JA: Right. From the very first drum that I engraved specifically at the request of Gibson, I put Nashville in. This was in large part for myself so I could determine which was which. Three or four of them say "Nashville, USA", or "Nashville, TN". I was kind of flying by the seat of my pants since noone really ever told me specifically what they wanted. There are some where the logo goes straight across, some where the logo curves upward. I sign everything I engrave and I put a little number inside that helps me identify it. I keep a database to record anything unique about the drum.

SAM BACCO: Independant consultant to Slingerland

Bacco in his Slingerland office, 1995

RC: Fill us in on your early drum background.

SB: I'm 41 now, and I've really been involved with drums about as long as I can remember. I was born in Pittsburgh to two Italians; I was the oldest son of an oldest son. I knew from the time I watched the big parades from my dad's shoulders that drums were my thing. The power and excitement of all those big drums thundering down the street; I just knew drums were going to be a big part of my life. I started studying formally at age six with local legend Babe Fabrizi. He had an amazing operation; a big store with a tremendous collection of old drums. He had five or six studios where his top students taught the beginners. He controlled my development all the way through school up until my college days.

RC: Any particular styles of music that shaped your development as a kid in Pittsburgh?

SB: The jazz scene was great. George Benson was from Pittsburgh, and Horace Silver. Max Roach was there so much that I thought he lived there. Really, though, I grew up in the Pittsburgh Symphony. Every Saturday I was literally there all day. In the morning we'd have a Youth Symphony concert. By the time that was over the players would be coming in for the afternoon matinee and they'd spend some time coaching us. I'd stay for the matinee and go back for the evening concert. I toured Europe with the Youth Symphony and started subbing in the regular Symphony when I was 17. I went to Duquesne University in Pittsburgh, graduating in 1975. In 1976 I successfully auditioned for the Mexico City Symphony. It was quite a culture shock going to work in a city where I didn't speak the language, didn't know anyone, etc., but overall it was a wonderful experience. I was able to work with some of the world's top conductors and played on what are considered to be definitive recordings of works by certain Mexican composers. The problem that developed with that job was that we were paid in pesos, and devaluation started to hit in a big way. My salary seemed to drop to nothing in just a few months, and I had to find something in the States. I met my wife, a violinist, while I was in Mexico City, and her sister was in Nashville. We came to check it out, and were told that there was no way I could get my foot in the door at the Nashville Symphony, although they did have openings for violin subs. We moved here and my wife started playing right away, although it took me a little longer. I eventually moved up the list and became principal percussionist and associate tympanist, my current position. In the meantime my repair business grew, and I did some teaching at Belmont College. They have a strong music business program; a number of people I had as students went on to become producers and artists– people like Vince Gill and Trisha Yearwood. Partly because of that I started getting studio calls, and before long I found myself playing on some pretty big records.

RC: At what point did you hook up with Slingerland?

SB: I hooked up with Gibson before they bought Slingerland. Tracey Hoeft called me at about the same time he called Pat Foley, when he was trying to assemble a team to design the Mapex U.S. Maple series. There was no shop to speak of here, so I did some of the first actual drum building at my shop. I made custom Mapex kits for Terry Bozzio, Billy Cobham, and Mike Portnoy at my shop. The problem that developed was that orders were being taken for this new series before production was really set up. It got to a point where there were hundreds of drum sets on order with no way to deliver them. At the same time Mapex was working on their new high-end Orion series and there were long discussions within Gibson about possible acquisitions. As you can see, today's situation was already developing.

RC: I understand the Slingerland acquisition involved quite a bit of negotiating?

SB: Tracey did a lot of the haggling. That's what he is really best at. We didn't actually buy Slingerland lock, stock, and barrel. The reality was that most of Slingerland that survived was in really bad shape and basically was a bunch of very dated machines that were engineered for a certain period that wouldn't really meet the criteria of today's production schedules. There was shellmaking equipment that had been laying dormant for years, probably never to work again. Certain parts were rusted and other parts were warped. There were untold amounts of piles that we had to dig through trying to sort out what was useful and what was not. In the end Gibson bought the rights to the Slingerland name and all of the trademarks, all of the patents and archives, X dollars worth of hard tooling, and X dollars worth of parts that were useful to us. There were Radio King shells, some American-made lugs and hoops, etc. My involvement was to counsel Tracey and assist him in what we really needed. I was there the day the deal was finalized; the papers were signed in Fred Gretsch's office on February 21st, 1994. That date, ironically, was the twenty-fifth anniversary of the death of drum pioneer George Way.

RC: So now the Nashville facility became home to not only the Mapex U.S. Maple series, but also to Slingerland.

SB: Right. By this time some equipment had been installed, such as a shaver table for doing edges, and spray booths. They finally decided to drop the U.S. Maple line. The feeling was that they had accomplished what they set out to do, which was give the Mapex name some credibility. In the meantime Mapex had completed development of their high-end Orion series. We added that line to our Mapex distribution, and used our production facilities for making Slingerland exclusively. Everybody on the floor, the main nucleus of guys, has all stuck together and we've really come along way on a personal level. We're all pulling together in a family/team kind of thing and really starting to roll. As it grows everyone has to kind of take on more responsibility in narrower areas.

RC: The Studio King name seems ideal to describe the updating of the venerated Radio King.

SB: Our thinking exactly. I had been making custom sets for studio players here for years, and had specs that worked. Strangely enough, they were real similar to the specs that Pat had kind of come up with; they were basically like a real modern version of the Gretsch drum. It just works in the studio, the guys love it.

RC: I'm sure you've picked up on the sentiment in the vintage drum community that the Radio King reissue didn't come close enough to the original?

SB: I would consider that drum, which we inherited from HSS and Gretsch, to be a reintroduction. What we really want to do, and I think we *need* to do, is a true reissue of the Radio King.

RC: With the original strainer and everything?

SB: That's right. One problem you run into is inconsistency. I brought in the three Radio Kings I own, borrowed a couple of others, and had Pat bring his in. We examined them and found that they're very different. It almost seems that about every two weeks they had a different kind of version! There are Radio Kings with thicker shells and thinner shells, rounder edges and flatter edges and sharper edges. It almost looks like they were doing a lot of the edge work by just rough cutting it on the shaver table and finishing it with some kind of spinner by hand. Some of them are quirky at best. Because the heads being put on the drums were skin, it didn't matter as much. Also because they were often using green wood, the shells often warped. The outside diameter of some old Radio Kings which were made for skin heads can make plastic head mounting rather tedious. Naturally we want to make a reissue that is as close to the original as possible, but we don't want to take it so far that we're deliberately making a bad drum. We're using the same glues they used, we try to use the same lap they used, and we took an average of what we felt was the best representative model of thickness and reinforcement hoop size. There really was no other way to do it unless we were to pick out one specific drum and say "Ok- this was Gene Krupa's personal Radio King from 1939 and we're going to duplicate it." We *could* do that, but won't. We examined representative samples of 30's, 40's, 50's, and even 60's before arriving at the reissue shell being used now. We have reworked the hoop, copying the original brass hoop. In reality it's a much better hoop because there's more attention to detail, and it's just dripping with chrome. We've continued to stamp the gate out of the bottom hoop as a cost concession. We may in the future cast the hoop and rivet the gate on like the old ones. I'm working right now on drawing the modernistic lug which we're preparing to reissue. I've got the original drawings for the super lugs and super throw-off.

Mid 1990s production, Nashville

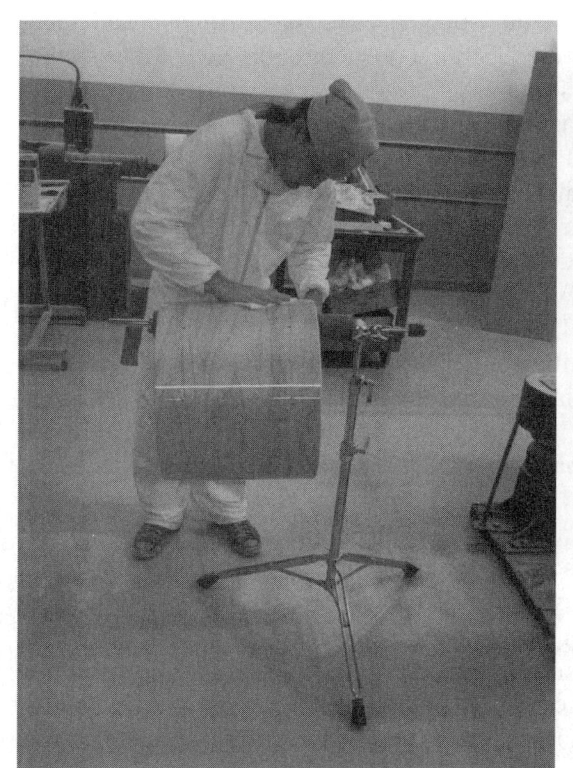

Slingerland as a Gibson division 1995–2003

I had been working on The Slingerland Book for several years when I heard a rumor in 1994 that Gretsch had sold Slingerland to Gibson. Knowing that Gibson was based in Nashville, I immediately reached for the phone and called my best drum contact in Nashville to see if he had heard anything about it. Sam Bacco was the best possible person to call; it turned out he not only knew about the transaction, he had helped engineer and facilitate it. He explained that the truckloads of Slingerland "stuff" had already been unloaded in Nashville and they were gearing up to make Slingerland drums. I was anxious to visit as soon as possible to see what sort of historical documents were included with the purchase, but Sam explained that such a visit would need approval from higher-ups and should wait a couple months until things settled down a bit. As soon as I got the go-ahead, I flew to Nashville and spent a couple days pawing through boxes and file cabinets. My findings were rather disappointing considering that there were something like 15 filing cabinets and maybe a couple dozen cardboard cartons. I was hoping for business records, catalogs, and photos from Slingerland's earliest days to the present. Nearly everything there dated from the 1980s and much of it was very mundane; employee performance evaluations, time sheets, etc. There were a few endorser photos, files with endorser contracts, a (very) few patent files, and files of correspondence related to patents and litigation of the 1930s.

The upside of the visit was the incredible vibe of the Slingerland facility. They were already producing beautiful drums for some top endorsers, and everybody in the shop was excited to be a part of the time-honored marque's revival. I felt a little bad for Buzz King at HSS, who had apparently had the rug pulled out from under himself by Fred Gretsch, but it certainly appeared that this was going to be a good thing for the Slingerland name. After all, look at the astonishing turnaround of the Gibson guitar line!

It certainly appeared to be a good thing for Fred Gretsch. I have not been privvy to the details of the transaction, but more than one source informed me off the record that Gretsch paid $200,000.00 for Slingerland, collected $800,000.00 in royalty payments from HSS, then sold it for $1,000,000.00. There was a certain amount of miscommunication at the time of the transaction, and Gibson personnel were surprised to learn that per the terms of the "fine print" in the purchase agreement, quite a bit of Slingerland-related stuff remained at the Gretsch warehouses; some finished drums,

The Slingerland "Archives" several months after they were unpacked in Nashville. While these file cabinets and boxes held the promise of a treasure trove of Slingerland historical information, there were hardly any documents prior to 1980, no product catalogs, and few endorser files.

Slingerland's "Snappy Snare" maker

part, and manufacturing equipment. One such piece that Sam Bacco was particularly disappointed to learn was not included was the machine that for decades had been used by Slingerland to stretch springs into snappy snares for snare drums. Although it would never be economically feasable to refurbish the machine and actually use it to produce snares again, Bacco felt strongly that as a significant historical piece it should remain a part of Slingerland. He convinced the higher-ups to negotiate the machine's purchase from Gretsch, and it was eventually moved to Nashville.

There was, understandably, a certain amount of confusion surrounding many of my questions related to marketing and distribution of Slingerland drums. For instance, when I asked about the status of HSS Slingerland endorsers, I learned that not only was there not a plan yet, but no one seemed to even know who those people were. I was asked to send them a list of their endorsers!

Slingerland drum production continued in Nashville until 1998. There was notable turnover in the executive staff, and it was clear that the division was not producing the kind of return on investment that was expected. Nor surprisingly, Gibson suddenly announced in 1998 that they were closing the Nashville facility. At the time it was stated that the equipment was being moved to Memphis where a new factory would be built, but the trucks never got unloaded in Memphis.

The Slingerland name was not completely removed from the marketplace; an internet presence was established, with a firm named MusicYo distributing inexpensive imported gear online.

The owners of Gibson concentrated on other facets of the empire for several years. One of the new developments was the purchase of the floundering Baldwin Piano Company with several manufacturing facilities in Arkansas. With an abundance of idle manufacturing space and the dot-com business waning, Gibson decided to take another stab at making Slingerland drums in the U.S.A.. The first drums to be assembled at the Conway, Arkansas, plant were exhibited at the summer, 2003, NAMM show.

The author (right) with Mike Hassell; President of Slingerland from June of 1997 to March of 1998; longer than any of his 8 predecessors over the preceding 3 years.

SLINGERLAND ENDORSEES

. This list started with artists whose names and/or photos appeared in ads and/or catalogs as users of Slingerland, Deagan, and/or Leedy equipment and/or as clinicians for (or advisors to) the Slingerland company.

There were plenty of variables which resulted in a wide variety of endorsee agreements; over 500 endorsees are listed here, spanning 70+ years. Even in specific eras there was a wide range of endorsee arrangments which ranged from no compensation except publicity to discounts on equipment, to custom-made equipment, to outright cash payments. (Gene Krupa was in a class all by himself, with a royalty on every drum Slingerland sold and an option to turn these royalties into an interest in the company!) With the exception of Gene Krupa, the endorsees of the '30s, '40s, and '50s received little or no compensation except customized, discounted and sometimes free equipment.

In the '60s and '70s, the situation heated up. Artist contracts included free gear and annual guarantees for travel expenses, paid personal appearances, guaranteed numbers of paid dealer clinics, and even outright cash payments in the tens of thousands of dollars.

These artists were all Slingerland endorsees unless identified as Deagan (D) or Leedy (L). S,L = they were at various times listed as both Leedy and Slingerland endorsees.

Name	Years		photo, page
Abts, Matt	1995–1999		
Adam, Biff	1994		
Adler, Henry	1939–1940		90,92
Agello, Andy	1941–1957		95
Agren, Morgen	1994		
Albrecht, Rudy	1929		
Alcorn, Cy C.	1934		
Alexander, Mousey	1979		99
Alias, Don	1979–1983		99
Allison, Joe	1983		
Altmiller, Jess	1934		
Anton, Artie	1951-1955		
Anunciacao, Luiz Almeida	1983		
Appice, Carmine	1983		114
Appice, Vinnie	1983		
Appleyard, Peter	1983		
Arabia, Phil	1951–1955		
Aronoff, Kenny	1982		
Artese, Joe	1941–1953		86
Atkinson, Fin	1929		
Austin, Ernie	1940		91
Ayers, Roy	1979–1983		
Babcock, Scott	1994		
Bachman, John	1940–1941		93
Bailey, Dave	1960–1970		97
Baron, Butch	1982		
Baron, Ron	1983		
Bartee, Ellis	1951–1957		
Bean, Ralph	1956–1960	(L)	
Beecher, Mark	1994		94
Beerheide, Al	1940		
Bellamy Brothers	1983		
Bellson, Louis	1941–1979		99,106,107
Bellson, Tony	1979–1983		100
Bennett, Phil	1982		
Benson, Ed	1939		
Benson, Fred	1937–1940		89,92
Best, Pete	1995–1999		
Berk, Dick	1982		
Bevan, Bev	1977–1983		100
Biery, Tim	1982		
Bissonnette, Gregg	1993–1995		116
Blowers, John	1937–1940		89,92
Booker, Maruga	1994		
Bower, Chas. M.	1929		
Bradley, James Jr.	1979–1983		100
Brewer, Steve	1995–1999		
Brokensha, Jack	1983		
Brown, Chas	1940		94
Brown, Ollie	1979		99
Browning, Bill	1965–1976		
Brun, Henry	1994		
Bruno, Howard	1941– 1953		87,92
Bulkin, Sidney	1951– 1957		
Burghoff, Gary	1982		
Burne, Jimmy	1940–1941		93
Burns, Roy	1959		105
Burrid, Jay	1982		
Butch	1995–1999		
Calarco, Dave	1983, 1995–1999		
Callahan, Brian	1979		99
Callahan, Larry	1951–1953		
Callas, Charlie	1979–1983		99
Calire, Mario	1995–1999		
Callios, Charles	1955– 1957		
Campbell, Jimmy	1957–1983		97
Campbell, Victor	1994		115
Capp, Frank	1965	(L)	96
Carlson, Frankie	1953		87
Carrington, Terri Lynn	1979–1983		99
Carson, Rob	1983		
Casanova, Alber	1994		
Casey, Dave	1995–1999		
Cassidy, Ed	1983		

Name	Years		photo, page
Catlett, Sid	1941–1953		95
Chalifaux, M.P.	1929		
Chapin, Jim	1951–1957		
Chisholm, Claude	1934		
Christian, Bobby	1941–1960	(S,L)	95
Christie, Jim	1995–1999		
Christine, Lily	1957		
Clare, Kenny	1979–1983		100
Clark, Bill	1956	(L)	
Clemens, Eddie	1929		
Cobb, Jimmy	1994		
Cole, Cozy	1937–1957	(S,L)	89
Collins, Myron	1959–1965		
Collura, Angelo	1995–1999		
Cool, Tre	1995–1999		
Coomer, Ken	1995–1999		
Combine, Bud	1941		95
Conner, Jack	1979–1983		
Conte, Luis	1979		100
Cooper, Jackie	1937–1953		89,91
Cotter, Robt. H.	1934		
Cottler, Irving	1941–1965	(S,L)	96
Crawford, Harvey	1940		94
Currier, Dave	1994		
Cusatis, Joe	1967–1973		
Cyr, Johnny	1940		92
D'Imperio, Danny	1976		
Dadey, Kwaku	1983		
De Oliveria, Geraldo	1982		
Davis, Ron	1982		
Davis, Tom	1979–1983		100
Davis, Troy	1994		115
De La Parra, Adolfo "Fito"	1994		
De Los Reyes, W. Jr.	1979–1983		99
De Los Reyes, W. Sr.	1979–1983		99
DeLucia, Dennis	1983		
De Nicola, Tony	1957–1967		97
Deakin, Paul	1995–1999		116
Deems, Barrett	1960–1983		91,97,99
Deery, Arthur	1929		
DeLorenzo, Victor	1995–1999		
DeMerle, Les	1979–1983		99
Dengler, Carl	1940–1941		93
DePont, Nei	1983		
DeVito, Frank	1955–1983		
Dhooghe, Chas. J.	1934		
Dickerson, Walt	1983		
Dinkins, Fred	1994		
Doucette, Paul	1995–1999		
Downing, Reggie	1929		
Drummond, Billy	1994		
Duncan, Roy	1934		
Duncan, Steve	1979–1983		99
Dunlop, Frankie	1962–1970		97
Dunn, Harry C.	1929		
Durawa, Ernie	1983		
Durrett, Ward	1983		
Economou, Bobby	1979–1983		99
Edie, Jack	1955–1957		
Ehart, Phil	1977–1979		100
Ehrlich, Bill	1956–1960	(L)	
Elliott, Dick	1940–1953		94
Elliott, Don	1983		
Engel, Fred	1929		
Erskine, Peter	1976–1979		113
Eschert, Louis	1929		
Escolies, Antoniano	1956–1965	(L)	
Fabrizi, "Babe"	1940		91
Fancher, Frank S.	1929		
Fankell, Randy	1994		
Fatool, Nick	1956	(L)	
Feld, Morey	1951–1970		
Feldman, Victor	1983		
Ferraro, John	1982		
Finger, Paul E.	1929		
Fitzsimmons, Jim	1957–1960		
Fleck, Stanley	1929		
Flynn, Frank	1940–1941		88,93
Fontana, D.J.	1995–1999		
Foster, Marquis	1951–1953		
Francis, Stanley	1929		
Franks, Eddie	1929		
Freeman, Archie	1941–1961	(L,S)	95
Friesen, John	1968		
Fryefield, Rick	1994		
Fuller, Charles	1934		
Gaber, George	1983		
Garcia, Richard	1983		
Gartner, Kurt	1994		
Garwig, Chet	1929		
Gay, Dick	1995–1999		
Geary, Hal	1941–1953		
Genther, Hal	1960		
Genther, Phil	1956–1958	(L)	
Genuario, Gerry	1979–1983		100
George, Marvin	1940		94
George, Peewee	1941–1953		86
Geston, Louis	1929		
Gibbs, Terry	1979–1983	(D)	
Gibbins, Mike	1994		
Gibson, Dave	1994		
Golden, Gary	1941		
Goldenberg, Morris	1968		
Goodman, Wm "Chick"	1929		
Gordon, Wally	1937–1939		89
Gore, Doug	1983		
Goslee, Adrian L.	1929		
Grady, Eddie	1957		
Grah, Bill	1983		
Graham, Eddie	1983		99
Graham, Roy	1929–1940		94
Gratton, Rick	1994		
Gray, Davie	1940		92
Graziano, Lee	1994		
Green, Henry	1970–1973		
Greer, Sonny	1956	(L)	

Name	Years		Page
Guaglianone, Hank	1983		107
Guerrero, Chico	1956–1965	(L)	
Gully, Terreon DeAutri	1994		
Gwaltney, Tommy	1983		
Hagaman, F.W.	1934		
Hager, Chic	1940		94
Hahn, Harold	1941–1953		
Hale, Owen	1995–1999		
Hall, Willie	1983		
Hampel, Gunter	1983		
Hampton, Lionel	1941– 1977		95
Hanna, Jake	1962–1983		97,99
Hanson, Bill	1940		91
Hanson, Roy	1929		
Hardy, Hagood	1983		
Harner, Bud	1979–1983		99
Harper, Wynard	1994		115
Harr, Haskell W	1959–1976		
James Harris	1994		
Harris, Joe	1960–1965	(L)	96
Harte, Roy	1941–1951	(S,L)	
Harty, Bill	1951–1953		
Hass, Steve	1994		
Hatfield, Steve	1994		
Hawkins, Ralph	1940–1941		93
Hawthorne, Harry	1983		
Hayes, Carl C.	1929		
Hayes, Louis	1959–1994		115
Haynes, Roy	1960–1964		97
Helfelbein, Joe	1929		
Herndon, John	1995–1999		
Herstoff, Charlie	1940		91
Hiraoka, Yoicha	1983		
Hess, Derek	1982		
Hobbs, Gary	1979		99
Hoggard, Jay	1983		
Hong, Sherman	1983		
Hooff, Sam	1994		
Hornbaker, Wayne	1929		
Hulsey, Phil	1976–1979		100
Humphries, Lex	1959–1960	(L)	
Hunt, Roy	1934		
Hutcherson, Bobby	1979–1982	(D)	
Huttlin, Joseph	1929		
Hylander, Mark	1994		
Igoe, Sonny	1941–1983		95,97
Israel, Yuron	1994		115
Jackson, John	1929		
Jackson, Duffy	1994		115
Jackson, Milt	1979–1983	(D)	
Jackson, Oliver	1968–1983		
Jacobs, Malcom	1994		
James, Bob	1994		
Jason, Liam	1994		
Jefferson, Ron	1962–1967		97
Jerger, Jake	1957–1994		97,109–112
Johnson, King	1940		91
Jones, Rufus	1964–1973		
Jones, Spike	1951–1957		
Julian, Eddie	1941– 1957		95
Kalt, Vern	1929		
Katz, Debbie	1983		
Keane, Brothers (Tom and John)	1979–1983		100
Kennedy, Chas. "Pop"	1929		
Kiffe, Karl	1941–1953		
Keith, Howard	1940		91
Kimker, Bud	1941		
King, Walter	1940		92
Kirkland, Rick	1983		
Klemm, William E.	1929		
Kluger, Irv	1956	(L)	
Knobel, Howard	1934		
Koss, Don	1968–1970		
Krell, Stanley	1951–1959		
Kozak, Eddie	1983		
Kroner, Billy	1940		93
Krupa, Gene	1936– 1977		86,95,97
Kurtz, Harry "Whitey"	1929		
La Monaca, Caesar	1934		
La Towsky, Waldo	1995–1999		
Lamond, Don	1941		
Landham, Byron	1994		
Lanin, Howard	1929		
Larson, Randy	1983		
Lavorgna, Bill	1970		
Lavorgna, Joe	1968		
Laylan, Rollo	1937–1939		90
Lee, Lance	1995–1999		
Leeman, Cliff	1940–1957		92
Lehman, Gene	1941		
Lent, Jimmy	1929		
Lewis, Mel	1982		
Lewis, Tony	1994		
Lloyd, Joe	1929		
Lodice, Charlie	1979–1983		100
Lofrano, Tony	1940		91
Long, Sam	1929		
Longo, Pee Wee	1941 - 1953		87
Lovett, George	1957		
Lucarelli, Mark	1982		
Lyman, Abe	1929		
Lynchau, Jack	1929		
MacKenzie, Jerry	1983		
Mainieri, Mike	1979-1983	(D)	
Mancini, Dave	1983		
Manne, Shelley	1958 - 1956	(L)	96
Marsh, George	1983		
Marshall, Walter	1929		
Martin, Chet	1956-1960	(L)	
Marty, Bill	1941		
Maslach, Rick	1994		
Mason, James	1934		
Maurizio, Nat	1929		
May, Rick	1995–1999		
Mazzei, Tony	1929		
McBride, Elmer	1940		94

McCarthy, Bob	1940		94
McClintock, Poley	1941-1953		95
McCullas, Jas.	1940		91
McCurdy, J.E.	1934		
McEntire, John	1995–1999		
McFay, "Monk"	1940		91
McHugh, Chris	1995–1999		
McKinley, Ray	1937-1957		90,92
McLean, Don	1951-1955		
McNamara, Ken			93
McPherson, Chuck	1994		
Metz, Ben B.	1929-1940		94
Michaels, Eric	1994		
Michaels, Ray	1940		94
Miles, Butch	1973		
Mill, Jackie	1951-1953		
Millar, Chris	1994		
Miller, Ben	1979-1983		99
Moffitt, Jack	1951-1953		
Moffitt, Jonathan	1983		
Molenhof, Bill	1979	(D)	
Monk, Thelonius Jr.	1994		
Moore, Robert F.	1956-1960	(L)	
Moore, Stanton	1994		
Morales, Humberto	1956-1965	(L)	
Moreira, Airto	1979		99
Morey, Brad	1940-1941		93
Moriya, Jun	1979		99
Morrow, Greg	1995–1999		
Morris, Bobby	1960 - 1970		97
Mosca, Ray	1959 - 1960	(L)	
Mosello, Joe	1979-1983		99
Moynahan, Fred	1934		
Moynihan, Clifford	1934		
Musquiz, Roland	1994		
Murphy, C.R.	1934		
Murphy, James	1929		
Nash,Lewis	1994		93,115
Nash, Louie	1940		
Nathan, Morty	1941-1953		
Naviera, Jimmy	1956		
Nicholson, Harry	1940		93
Nieto, Ubaldo	1956-1965	(L)	
North, T.W.	1934		
Norvo, Red	1979-1983	(D)	
Oliveira, Geraldo de	1979-1983		99
Olson, John	1994		
Olsson, Nigel	1973-1983		100
Osborne, Don	1955-1967		97
Osborne, Don Jr.	1970-1977		
Owen, Charles E	1956-1960	(L)	
Paddock, Sean	1995–1999		
Parker, Don	1994		
Parks, Les	1968-1973		
Patten, George	1929		
Payton, Walter	1979-83		100
Pellici, Gene	1941-1953		

Perkins, Walter	1965	(L)	96
Perrone, Salvatore	1956-1960	(L)	
Peterson, Dan	1983		
Pfeiffer, Chris	1994		
Phyfe, Eddie	1951-1961		
Poole, Charlie	1983		
Porello, Ray	1982		
Porello, Rick	1982		
Potter, Gregg	1983		108
Powell, "Specs"	1956	(L)	
Previte, Bobby	1994		
Price, Jessie	1940-1957		92,95
Price, Mark	1995–1999		
Puente, Tito	1956-1968	(S,L)	97
Purdie, Bernard	1995–1999		116
Purtill, Maurice	1937-1953		88,90
Rader, Abbey	1994		
Rae, John	1967-1983		100
Rager, Chad	1994		
Raiche, Joe	1960-1967		97
Rale, Phil	1937-1953		89,92
Rasnur, Joan	1982		
Ratazcjak, Dave	1982		
Reed, Jerry	1982		
Reedus, Tony	1995–1999		
Reyes, Walfredo Jr.	1983		
Reyes, Walfredo Sr.	1983		
Rice, Joseph	1929		
Rich, Buddy	1937-1940 & 1968-1977		86,90,92
Rich, Dave E.	1940		94
Richards, Emil	1983		
Richmond, Danny	1962-1967		97
Rickey, Bobby	1941-1953		95
Robyn, Chris	1994		
Robinson, Jack	1940		92
nson, John	1982		
Robinson, Scott	1983		
Rongo, Tony	1941		
Rose, Adonis	1994		
Rosen, Sam	1940		88,92
Rosenfeld, Jason	1994		
Rosengarden, Bobby	1968-1983		99
Rosenzweig, Al	1929		
Rowland, Sam	1934-1936		
Rudisill, Ernie	1941-1953		
Rundell, Tommy	1959-1961		
Rupp, Jim	1983		
Rushakoff, Harry	1994		
Rutherford, Bruce	1995–1999		116
Saidon, Ed	1983		
St John, Dennis	1994		
Salmon, Jim	1959–1962		
Saltzman, Jack	1940		91
Sanders, Red	1940		94
Sandler, George	1994		
Sanford, Fred	1979		94
Sauer, Warren	1929		

Name	Years		Pages
Saulter, John	1929		
Savage, Ron	1994		
Schar, O.	1929		
Schinstine, Bill	1970–1976		
Schwomeyer, Dedee	1979–1983	(D)	
Scrima, Mickey	1940–1953		87,93
Sehrer, Frank	1940–1941		87,93
Seraphine, Danny	1973–1983		100
Shanahan, Dick	1941		
Shaughnessy, Ed	1941–1965		95,97,103,104
Shears, Sidney	1929		
Sheen, Mickey	1970–1983		
Shendal, Adam	1979–1983		100
Sheppard, Harry	1983		
Sherman, O.B.	1929		
Showker, Bunny	1953		87
Shurtleff, Bob	1959		
Silbaugh, David	1994		
Sinder, Josh	1994		
Sinnett, Jae	1994		
Skowba, Arthur W.	1929		
Slosberg, Jerry	1941–1951		
Smadback, Paul	1983		
Smith, Arthur	1940		94
Smith, Bill	1955–1957		
Smith, Neal (Alice Cooper)	1970's (?)		
Smith, P.L.	1934		
Smith, Reggie	1979–1983		
Sneed, Floyd	1982		
Snitzer, Martin	1929		
Snyder, Frank	1940		
Snyder, Terry	1956	(L)	
Sodergren, Kurt	1995–1999		
Sommer, Ted	1962–1967		97
Sonship	1979		100
Spangler, Bob	1940–1953		88,92
Sparks, Marvin	1994		
Spencer, Joel	1983		
Sperling, Jack	1956–1983	(S,L)	
Stanley, Bruce	1940		94
Steele, Carol	1983		
Stefko, Joe	1979–1994		100
St John, Dennis	1976–1983		100
Steinhauser, Frank "Heinie"	1929		
Stewart, Teddy	1941–1953		
Stocki, Greg	1995–1999		116
Stout, Gordon	1979	(D)	
Stover, C. Oscar	1959–1965		
Stover, Harold	1941–1953		95
Strauu, Ike	1929		
Street, Bill	1956–1960	(L)	
Stuverud, Richard	1995–1999		
Sullivan, Floyd	1941–1957		95
Sussewell, John	1983		
Sutherland, Chris	1994		
Suttell, Lee	1934		
Tana, Akira	1979–1983		100

Name	Years		Pages
Tate, Grady	1982		
Theckston, Norman	1929		
Thigpen, Ed	1983		
Thomas, Terry	1995–1999		116
Thomas, Tommy	1951–1957		95
Thommes, Billy	1995–1999		
Thompson, Eric	1979–1983		100
Thompson, Ron	1983		
Tilken, Ralph	1941		
Tjader, Cal	1979	(D)	
Todd, H.R.	1934		
Tomkins, Tom	1994		
Tormanen, Sami	1995–1999		
Torme, Mel	1951–1983		102
Toscarelli, Mario	1955–1957		
Tough, Dave	1937–1953		86,89,91
Treviano, Roel	1983		
Tucker, Ray	1994		
Tuthill, George	1983		
Ulano, Sam	1964		
Unwin, Kenny	1940		93
Vale, Evie	1941–1953		95
VanLeer, Henry	1940		91
Varney, Bob	1941–1957		
Ven Der Zeeuw, Bart	1995–1999		
Vernon, Joe	1940–1941		93,97
Vig, Tommy	1979–1983	(D)	
Vincent, Jimmy	1951–1963		95
Vincent, Johnny	1948		102
Von Blomberg, Arthur	1994		
Wackerman, Chad	1979–1983		113
Wagner, Bo	?		
Wagner, Charles	1929		88,91
Washington, Kenny	1994		115
Wajler, Zig	1994		
Walsh, Steve	1983		
Wannamaker, Jay	1983		
Ward, Nelson	1929		
Webster, Al	1994		
Wechter, Julius	1983		
Weiner, Ray	1983		
Wendt, Freddie	1929		
White, Charles M	1956–1960	(L)	
White, Jack	1983		
Whiteman, Paul Jr.	1940		91
Wilber, Charles	1940–1941		93
Willard, Adam	1995–1999		
Williams, John	1968		
Winston, Fred	1983		
Wohl, A.A.	1929		
Wood, Bud	1929		
Zaremba, Buzz	1940–1941		93
Zembruski, Victor	1941–1957		
Zigmund, Elliott	1994		
Zoob, Andy	1983		
Zuger, Ben	1929		
Zupnick, Brian	1982		

Gene Krupa

Buddy Rich

Davie Tough

"Pee Wee" George

Frank Sehrer

Howard Bruno

Joe Artese

"Pee Wee" Longo

Frankie Carlson

Bunny Showker

Mickey Scrima

Frank Flynn

Bob Spangler

Maurice Purtill

Bo Wagner

Sam Rosen

1937

JOHN BLOWERS, DRUMMER STARRING WITH BUNNY BERIGAN'S ORCHESTRA. 100% SLINGERLAND EQUIPPED.

PHIL RALE, STARRING WITH EMIL COLEMAN AND HIS "SOCIETY BAND." 100% SLINGERLAND EQUIPPED.

WALLY GORDON, STARRING WITH BENNY MEROFF'S ORCHESTRA. 100% SLINGERLAND RADIO KINGS.

JACKIE COOPER, THE HOLLYWOOD MOVIE STAR. A GREAT DRUMMER. EQUIPPED 100% SLINGERLAND RADIO KINGS.

FRED BENSON, DRUMMER STARRING WITH ART KASSEL AND HIS "CASTLES IN THE AIR." 100% SLINGERLAND EQUIPPED.

COZY COLE, A GREAT DRUMMER AND "KING OF THE SEPIA'S." 100% SLINGERLAND RADIO KINGS.

1937

ROLLO LAYLAN, STARRING WITH THAT GREAT LEADER, PAUL WHITEMAN, THE "DEAN OF MODERN AMERICAN MUSIC." 100% SLINGERLAND.

DAVEY TOUGH, THE GREAT SENSATIONAL DRUMMER WITH BENNY GOODMAN. EQUIPPED 100% WITH SLINGERLAND RADIO KINGS.

MAURICE PURTILL, A BIG-TIME DRUMMER, STARRING WITH TOMMY DORSEY. EQUIPPED 100% WITH SLINGERLAND RADIO KINGS.

RAY McKINLEY, THE GREAT GENIUS STARRING WITH JIMMY DORSEY. EQUIPPED 100% WITH SLINGERLAND RADIO KINGS.

BUDDY RICH, THE NEW, GREAT SENSATION WHO HAS CLIMBED RIGHT UP WITH THE BIG BOYS. EQUIPPED 100% WITH SLINGERLAND RADIO KINGS.

HENRY ADLER IS GOING PLACES, STARRING WITH LARRY CLINTON. EQUIPPED 100% WITH SLINGERLAND RADIO KINGS.

Charlie Herstoff with Jack Denny

"Babe" Fabrizi with Happy Felton

Davie Tough with Benny Goodman

Tony Lofrano with Jimmy Jackson

King Johnson with Ramona

Jack Saltzman with Al Jolson Show

Billy Hanson back from Brazil

Howard Keith with Gary Nottingham

Jackie Cooper Movie Star

Charley Wagner Chicago Theatre

Barrett Deems with Joe Venuti

Jos. McCullas with the New Yorkers

Ernie Austin with Jack Teagarden

Henry van Leer Amsterdam, Holland

Paul Jr., son of Paul Whiteman

"Monk" McFay "Krupa" of Honolulu

1940

Ray McKinley with Will Bradley

Maurice Purtill with Glenn Miller

Buddy Rich with Tommy Dorsey

Cliff Leeman with Charlie Barnett

Phil Rale with Emil Coleman

Howard Bruno with Ozzie Nelson

Johnny Blowers with Bunny Berigan

Jessie Price with Harlan Leonard

Johnny Cyr with Hal Kemp

Bob Spangler with Vincent Lopez

Fred Benson with Bernie Cummins

Jack Robinson with Don Bestor

Henry Adler with Larry Clinton

Sam Rosen with Charles Baum

Davie Gray with Clyde McCoy

Walter King with Griff Williams

1940

Ralph Hawkins with Artie Shaw

Buzz Zaremba with Blue Barron

John Bachman with Baron Elliott

Frank Sehrer with Dick Jurgens

Frank Flynn with Ted Fio Rito

Brad Morey with Harold Menning

Louie Nash with Tony Cabot

Mickey Scrima with Harold James

Ken McNamara with Chuck Liedman

Carl Dengler NBC, Rochester, N. Y.

Harry Nicholson with Percy Faith

Jimmy Burne 12 year old sensation

Joe Vernon with Bob Dade

Kenny Unwin with Isham Jones

Billy Kroner with Ruby Newman

Chas. Wilber Kalamazoo Symphony

1940

Bruce Stanley with Tommy Tucker

Chic Hager with Fernando

Roy Graham WGN Chicago

Arthur Smith with Jack McLean

Dick Elliott with Dick Shelton

Benny Metz Oriental Theatre Chicago

Marvin George with Gus Arnheim

Harvey Crawford with Art Kassel

Frank Snyder with his Rhythm Kings

Elmer McBride with Johnie Haws

Ray Michaels with Abe Lyman

Red Sanders with his Serenaders

Bob McCarthy Kentucky Serenaders

Chas. Brown with his Brown Buddies

Al Beerheide All American Band

Dave E. Rich KWK St. Louis

1941

NATION'S TOP
DRUM STARS SHINE
WITH SLINGERLAND
GENE KRUPA
ED SHAUGHNESSY WITH CHARLIE VENTURA
SONNY IGOE WITH BENNY GOODMAN
LIONEL HAMPTON
EDDIE JULIAN WITH VAUGHN MONROE
POLEY McCLINTOCK WITH FRED WARING
BOBBY CHRISTIAN N.B.C. CHICAGO
JIMMY VINCENT WITH LOUIS PRIMO
SID CATLETT
BUD COMBINE WITH HARRY JAMES
JESSE PRICE JAZZ SEXTET
TOMMY THOMAS A.B.C. CHICAGO
BOBBY RICKEY WITH CHARLIE SPIVAK
SMOKEY STOVER WITH ORRIN TUCKER
ANDY AGELLO WITH CARMEN CAVALLERO
EVIE
EVIE VALE WITH FRANKIE CARLE
FLOYD SULLIVAN WITH JOHNNY LONG
ARCHIE FREEMAN WITH TONY PASTOR
SEND FOR
FREE NEW CATALOG
10¢ (IN U.S.A.) EACH FOR DRUMMER PHOTO PICTURED ABOVE
OR SINGLE PICTURE OF ANY DRUMMER SHOWN ABOVE
SLINGERLAND DRUM CO.
1325 BELDEN AVENUE · CHICAGO 14, ILLINOIS

1960s Leedy

Shelly Manne and his Leedy Drums

I LOVE MY Leedy DRUMS
MORE THAN "ANYTHING"
SHELLY MANNE
IF YOU WANT THE BEST
BUY Leedy
send for our latest catalog
LEEDY DRUM CO.
2249 WAYNE AVE., CHICAGO, ILL.

IRV COTTLER

WALTER PERKINS

JOE HARRIS

FRANK CAPP

Leedy
Jack Sperling

1963

The nation's finest Drummers use Slingerland!
JIMMY VINCENT
BOBBY MORRIS
TITO PUENTE
BARRETT DEEMS
SLINGERLAND
DAVE BAILEY
GENE KRUPA
JAKE HANNA
Jake Hanna
ROY HAYNES
JIMMY CAMPBELL
DANNY RICHMOND
DON OSBORNE
JOE RAICHE
FRANKIE DUNLOP
SONNY IGOE
ED SHAUGHNESSY
JAKE JERGER
RON JEFFERSON

1967

MOST TOP ROCK N' ROLL GROUPS PLAY *Slingerland*

THE FOREMOST IN DRUMS

YARD BIRDS

HERMAN'S HERMITS

The Guillotines

The Mamas & Papas

The Association

The Standells

Paul Revere and the Raiders

TURTLES

THE LEFT BANK

JOHN'S CHILDREN

THE BUCKINGHAMS

GARY & THE HORNETS

SHADOWS OF KNIGHT

Slingerland

AIRTO
MOUSEY ALEXANDER
DON ALIAS
LOUIE BELLSON
OLLIE BROWN
BRIAN CALLAHAN
CHARLIE CALLAS
TERRI LYNE CARRINGTON
BARRETT DEEMS
LES De MERLE
STEVE DUNCAN
BOBBY ECONOMOU
EDDIE GRAHAM
JAKE HANNA
BUD HARNER
GARY HOBBS
BEN MILLER
JUN MORIYA
JOE MOSELLO
GERALDO de OLIVEIRA
W. DE LOS REYES, SR.
W. DE LOS REYES, JR.
BOBBY ROSENGARDEN
FRED SANFORD

1979

AKIRA TANA
TONY BELLSON
BEV BEVAN
JAMES BRADLEY, JR.
JOE STEFKO
KENNY CLARE
LUIS CONTE
TOM DAVIS
DENNIS ST. JOHN
PHIL EHART
PETER ERSKINE
GERRY GENUARIO
JACK SPERLING
PHIL HULSEY
KEANE BROS.
CHARLIE LODICE
ERIC THOMPSON
NIGEL OLSSON
WALTER PAYTON
JOHN RAE
REGGIE SMITH
DANNY SERAPHINE
ADAM SHENDAL
SONSHIP

1979

MAX ROACH

A Slingerland endorsee?

Even before the rock craze of the '60s, endorsee scene was becoming something of a battleground for the drum companies.

The photos here are from a series of unreleased endorsee photos that Slingerland commissioned in Chicago in the summer of 1957.

The next day after receiving Roach's notice that he had changed his mind about endorsing Slingerland drums (below left), Bud received a chastisement from Phil Grant of Gretsch (below).

SEP 30 1957

Blue Note ×

Phila

27 September 1957

Slingerland Drum Company
1325 Belden Avenue
Chicago 14, Ill.

Attention: Bud Slingerland

Max phone Triangle 5-2357

Dear Bud:

I regret to say that I have changed my mind and will not be able to go through with your proposition to play and endorse Slingerland drums.

The Tympani which you sent me will be returned very shortly.

I am sorry if this decision has caused you any inconvenience but I hope you will understand my position in this matter.

Sincerely,

Max Roach
Max Roach

P.S. I will be very happy to pay for the pictures you took of me in Chicago if you will let me know what the cost is.

THE FRED. GRETSCH MFG. CO
Musical Instrument Makers since 1883
BROOKLYN • CHICAGO
EVERGREEN 7-5200 · CABLE ADDRESS: DRUMJOLIN, NEW YORK
EASTERN BRANCH AND FACTORY
60 BROADWAY, BROOKLYN 11, N. Y.

30 September 1957

Slingerland Drum Company
1325 Belden Avenue
Chicago, Ill.

Attention: Bud Slingerland

Dear Bud.

Perhaps we should feel pleased you think so highly of the Drummers who play and endorse Gretsch Drums.

The Drummers to whom you made those flattering offers all have bought their own Gretsch equipment. In addition their prominence in the drumming field is due in a large degree to the continued advertising we have given them for a long period of time. It has taken plenty of Gretsch advertising dollars to build them up to their present prominence.

For our part, we're proud to advertise these Gretsch users but we don't think they should be subsidized. Don't you think that, in the long run, it would be better for all of us to build up our own featured Drummers rather than making a wholesale raid on a competitor?

Cordially,

THE FRED. GRETSCH MFG. CO.

Phil Grant
Phil Grant
Vice President

PG:gh

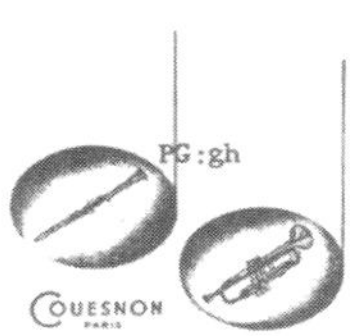

Mel Torme
1940
JAZZ CONCERT
Johnny Vincent
1948

Ed Shaughnessy, early NYC days

Ed Shaughnessy presented something of a marketing challenge to Slingerland as an endorsee. He was the "drummer's drummer"; talented, innovative, and charismatic. His outfits, however, were rather out of the mainstream. He used tiny bass drums with the double-bass set utilized at CBS in the mid '50s (below).

The set shown at the left consisted of a 10"x22" bass drum, 7"x10" and 10"x12" mounted toms, and a 14"x14" floor tom. The color was also a concern for Slingerland. Bud asked Ed to use a different color, worried that this photo would boost sales of a "silver waffle" that Slingerland was afraid was not very durable and would lead to complaints.

Another hold-up in Slingerland's release of Shaughnessy promotional material was confusion over what exactly to say about Ed. While well-known in the pro drumming community, he was not exactly a household name to the general public. In response to Bud Slingerland's inquiry as to what could be said about his activities, Shaughnessy asked that he be referred to as "free-lancing on the NY jazz scene".

Slingerland finally got the kind of Shaughnessy photo they'd been after with this 1961 shot. This stained maple outfit had a 14"x24" bass drum, 9"x13" mounted tom, 16"x16" and 14"x16" floor toms.

Roy Burns:"I wnted a drum set solid black pearl covering from the time I saw my first one, which belonged to Sonny Igoe. Sonny recommended me for the job with Woody Herman, a gig I had for about three months before it led to the offer to join Benny Goodman in 1957. The Slingerland kit I used then was far and away the best set of drums I ever owned, and the Radio King 5"x14"solid maple shell snare with it was the best snare drum I ever owned. When I hear some of the recordings that are being reissued now from that band, it makes me almost want to cry that I don't have that snare now. The set in this picture was my next set *after* that one."

OCTOBER, 1941: Slingerland announces the Gene Krupa National Amateur Swing Drummers Contest

Drummers! **ENTER GENE KRUPA'S NATIONAL AMATEUR SWING DRUMMERS' CONTEST!**

(18 years old or under)

HERE'S a golden opportunity for the young drummers of America. The nation's No. 1 drummer, Gene Krupa, offers you:

1. A chance to win the National Amateur Swing Drummers' contest.

2. Any one of scores of fine prizes, including complete sets of the famous Slingerland "Radio King" drums.

3. A trip to New York City, with all expenses paid, for the winners who compete in the finals.

4. National publicity for you and a real chance to get started on the road to success!

It's Easy

. . . to enter Gene Krupa's National Amateur Swing Drum Contest, and it costs you nothing. The only requisite is that you are an amateur swing drummer, 18 years old or under.

There will be a local, regional, and a final national contest where the King of young swing drummers will be crowned! Literally thousands of dollars worth of the finest SLINGERLAND drums will be given as prizes. Who knows—this may mean a national championship, a wonderful prize, and a flying start on a professional career for you!

So don't delay a moment. The contest starts immediately. Take the coupon to your nearest Slingerland dealer today.

"4 out of 5 of the world's greatest drummers play Slingerlands!"

Sponsored by:

SLINGERLAND DRUM CO.
1335 Belden Ave. Chicago, Ill.

Take this to your nearest Slingerland dealer who will give you complete information.

Mr. Dealer:

Please enter the bearer in Gene Krupa's National Amateur Swing Drummers' Contest, which is sponsored by the Slingerland Drum Company.

Name ....

Address ....

City .... State ....

I am .... years old.

Winner of the Gene Krupa National Amateur Swing Drummers' Contest

LOUIS BELLSON

Success did not come automatically to Louis Bellson; he'd been driving the width of Illinois weekly from his home in Moline to Chicago to study with Roy Knapp.

The Krupa contest, however, immediately focused national attention on him. He landed a road gig with Ted Fio Rito's Orchestra, and has been busy ever since. Big bands, festivals, recordings, clinics, etc.— a remarkable career which in many ways paralleled those of Buddy Rich and Gene Krupa. Bellson endorsed Slingerland drums upon winning the contest, up until he joined Benny Goodman's band. Goodman's manager told Bellson that Benny had a contract with Gretsch. Louis did not feel that it would work for the new teenage drummer to announce that he played Slingerland drums, so he switched to Gretsch. (In retrospect, Bellson does not feel Goodman would have had a problem with his Slingerland affiliation.)

When Slingerland terminated their relationship with Buddy Rich in the late '70s (and Krupa having died in 1973), they needed an endorsee of this stature and once again arranged an endorsee agreement with Bellson. "Louis was a perfect fit for Slingerland at the time," says former Slingerland president Larry Linkin. "he had an excellent reputation, fantastic chops, and was great to work with!"

38 years after Bellson's career was jump-started by winning the Krupa contest, Slingerland sponsored another national competition, this time in Bellson's name. Most of the logistics and event details were coordinated by Sam Geati. The event attracted 600 participants in 23 states. Louie's band played at the finals in Las Vegas on December 2, 1979.

In addition to an appearance on "The Tonight Show", winner Hank Guaglianone from Rolling Meadows, Illinois, received an $8,000.00 scholarship, a set of drums, and was featured in ads.

Slingerland delivers percussion.

Chicagoan Gregg Potter found that it was not neccessary to win "the whole enchilada" to realize the benefits of national exposure resulting from his success in the Louis Bellson Drum Contest. Potter won the regional competition held at Franks Drum Shop. Slingerland featured Potter (left, seated at the drum set) in a national ad campaign.

While still a teenager, Potter found himself living every garage-band drummer's dream; playing the big venue. This 1984 Slingerland promotional picture was taken onstage at Chicago's Soldier Field.

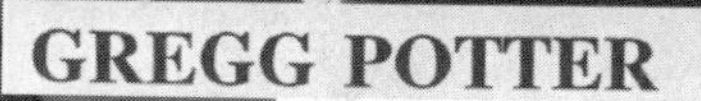

photo by Steven Arazmus

Gregg Potter, 1995

(Firth endorsee photo) Potter went on from the Bellson Contest to do recordings, television and radio, and a lot of live work. His performance resume includes work with Joe Walsh, Rick Nielson and Robin Zander, Steve Stevens, Adrian Smith, Vivian Campbell and Rudy Sarzo, and others.

JAKE JERGER

The following interview is excerpted from an interview conducted by David Anfuso in 2003. For the full interview as well as more photos and other Jerger material, go to: http://www.vintagesnaredrums.com/other_stuff/jake_jerger/jake_index.html#

DA: Jake, how did you start playing the drums?

JJ: A customer of my dad's business was playing with the Edison Drum and Bugle Corps of Chicago. He showed me how to hold the sticks in a traditional grip. He then took an orange crate upended and began teaching me how to do a drum roll. I was seven years old at the time– 1934. I would then go home and beat on pots and pans while my brother Steve played along on the accordion. After hearing me play those pots and pans for weeks my dad realized it was time for me to get some real drums and take lessons from a drum teacher.

DA: Who was your first teacher?

JJ: My godfather Michael worked for a manufacturer of jukeboxes and he serviced them all over the city of Chicago. He knew all the spots where the musicians would hang out. "I know a good drummer playing at the Club Laurel on Ashland in Chicago," he said. His name was Jimmy Russell and he had a five-piece combo. He also played trombone; which flipped me out because he would keep his feet going, pick up the trombone, play a chorus, then go back to playing drums. He'd come to my house and the lessons were $1.50 per lesson in 1936. We studied out of Eddy B. Straights book, which was "THE" book at that time. We went through the book in about a year and he suggested to my dad that I get another teacher. Mr. Russell suggested the number one teacher in Chicago, Roy C. Knapp.

DA:What was it like auditioning for Roy at the age of 9 and how much did lessons cost?

JJ: Roy Knapp was the staff percussionist for the WLS radio live broadcasts. He did that for most of his life. He also was a teacher for at least that long but when I started he was about 45 years old. If I wanted an audition I would have to go WLS and meet him there. Another friend of my dad's who worked at WLS arranged the audition. My brother came with his accordion and I sat on Roy's drums. I could barely reach the pedals. We played some type of ragtime number. Roy said that's enough I'll take you on. He looked straight at me and said, "You have to practice or I won't teach you". He scared me on the spot! We arranged the lessons at $4.00 a ½ hour. The lessons usually ended up being an hour because he really liked me. We started on the snare because he thought I had good instruction and continued from where my last teacher left off with the snare drum. He knew I really wanted to learn the drum set, so he would teach me Rumba beats, the samba, the tango and syncopation. When he picked up sticks he was marvelous, though it was rare for him to pick up sticks in a lesson.

Roy also taught me mallets and tympani. He would be able to sit across the room at his desk and tell me I was a little flat or sharp on the tympani, I think he had perfect pitch. He loaned me a marimba so I could learn the instrument. I had that marimba until the 60s, when he finally asked for it back. This just shows how kind he was. We were good friends all of my life.

I took lessons from age 9 until I was 18. When I left he had about six other teachers on staff on the sixth floor of the Kimball Hall building at Jackson and Wabash.

DA: When did you play your first paying gig?

JJ: My brother Steve and I would play at family restaurants owned by friends of my parents. The little money we made went towards our music lessons.

DA: What was your first Slingerland set?

JJ: At that time I was playing a made up set of WFL drums and Slingerlands. The toms had the old Zephyr lugs. They were purchased from Frank Gault at Frank's drum shop. Frank was always nice to me and gave me good prices on drums because I was a Roy C Knapp student. At that time I think I was Roy's youngest student.

Jake Jerger with brother Steve (at right) and his parents

DA: Why and when did you join the Military Band?
In high school at the age of 16 I joined the Musicians union. There was plenty of work, because many drummers had joined the service. I was playing at the club *Alabama* with Boyce Brown, a well-known blind saxophone player. These gigs were union scale. At 18 I was starting to get draft notices, so Roy and my dad had a talk about my future. They both thought this was the best thing for my future.

I enlisted in the Navy in September, 1945.After completing boot camp, I waited six weeks before a percussionist was needed, then was placed with the 154th band which was sent to London to replace the Arty Shaw band. It was a 38-piece band that entertained dignitaries– an "Admiral Band", and the only Navy band not stationed on a ship.

It was "cream" duty. There were no facilities to house the band, so we lived in hotels, boarding houses and private homes. This band was the third priority band in the country, so we had everything we needed. Over the next three years we played in 29 different countries. We played every event and military service in London. We were always gigging– from a three piece to a big band to a marching band. It was the best education I could have gotten without going to college.

After two years, I was the only guy in the band that was offered a 30-day leave if I would agree to come back and stay with the 154th Navy Band. I had become Third-Class Petty officer by taking exams, and they were going to make me Second-Class Petty Officer without taking an exam. Basically the Admiral's staff liked me and wanted me to spend my fourth year with the 154th Navy Band. So I did.

After my discharge from the Navy, I returned to the Knapp School of Percussion, which by this time was a AAA college accredited school.

DA: When did you start teaching?

JJ: Roy asked me to take a teaching job in the Winnetka, Illinois, school system in April, 1951. Roy gave me the confidence to teach, and told me I could do it. His teaching method stuck with me; I rarely played in lessons when I became a teacher. If I couldn't explain it to a student, I did not want to play it for them because they would just copy me instead of reading the music.

I also started writing drum set music. I taught at New Trier High School and Winnetka schools until 1981. I also worked with other Chicago suburban high school band directors to improve their percussion programs.

I started teaching at Oakton Community College in 1974 as a part-time percussion teacher, and created an entire percussion ensemble and jazz band program from the bottom up. The ensembles from Oakton played all over the area, including all of the events at the college. We had a variety of guest artists and near the end of my tenure we were invited to play Carnegie Hall. We were also fortunate that same year to have Louis Bellson as our guest artist for our spring concert in May, 1991. Bellson also came back to Oakton College for our last concert in May 1995.

I taught at North Park College from 1980 to 1987. I have taught thousands of students and over 60 thousand lessons from 1951 to 1981, developing some world-class players. It has made me a very proud teacher.

Seaman Jerger

DA: When did you first meet Bud Slingerland and become associated with him?

JJ: Roy Knapp was a Ludwig endorser, and recommended Ludwig Drums. I paid $300 for a Ludwig drum set with hardware and Zildjian cymbals in 1949. I did not like the snare drum because the strainer was choking the drum. In 1952, I told Roy about my problem and explained that I wanted to change drums. Roy suggested that I take the snare to the Ludwig factory. He said, "Tell Bill Ludwig Jr. that I sent you, and you're not happy with the snare drum." I went to the factory and sat with Ludwig Jr. in his office. I told him, "Roy Knapp told me to see you because I don't like the snare strainer. It chokes the snare. What can we do about it?" He basically told me I did not know what I was talking about. "We sell thousands of these drums and no one else is complaining," he said. I left the Ludwig factory. Much to Roy's dismay, I started looking at Slingerland.

One of the musicians in the band I was playing in at the time had a music store. I went to him and he gave me a great deal; I traded in the Ludwigs for Slingerlands, which I never thought I would do. He also arranged for me to go to the Slingerland factory and get the drums set up with the clamps and holders positioned the same as my Ludwig drum set.

I went to the factory, and while I was telling an employee where I wanted everything, Bud Slingerland approached. He stopped to ask my name and what I was doing at Slingerland. I explained that I was fed up with my Ludwig drums, especially the snare drum.

The Slingerland set was a Black Diamond Pearl kit with a Chrome Krupa Snare. The snare drum from that kit now belongs to Billy Jeansonne at Vintage Drummer Magazine.

Bud and I started talking, and I told him I was a former Roy Knapp student, teaching in Winnetka. He said, "You are? I live in Wilmette!" It was a warm reception and he asked me to come to his office when I was finished there. I went to his office and he said, "We have to do some things together. I can help you, and you can help me. You're young, ambitious and doing great things." At that time I was playing live television at NBC, teaching at New Trier High School, and the Winnetka School System. That black diamond drum set was the last set of Slingerland drums I had to pay for; I had carte blanche with Slingerland Drum Company from that point on.

Bud and I met a few more times after that. He said he wanted me to grow with the company; to become an endorsee, clinician and number one tester for sticks, heads, hardware and drums. He wanted someone outside of the plant to offer advice on products.

This was the start of a long relationship with Bud Slingerland and Slingerland Drums.

DA: What was the first agreement and what did it entail?

JJ: A talk and a handshake! There was nothing in writing. Each gig for Bud was on a pay-for-time-spent basis. Bud never took advantage of me and it showed when he paid me for my time. If I had to take a few days to travel, he would compensate me for my lost lesson money; pay me for working the event, plus expenses. When it came time to pay, he would say, "How much, Jake?" I would say, "$250.00." He would chuckle and say, "That's more than Marilyn Monroe!" He would write the check without complaint. I really felt he was proud of me. He realized that I was a team player, and he liked that kind of person.

Jake Jerger with his Dlack Diamond Pearl Radio King kit

DA: What drums did you play at that time?

JJ: Bud had me trying every drum in every finish to see the reaction from people in the audience. Bud helped me publish my first book, and I even created a group of ensembles for multiple set players. The biggest was 54 heads for 6 drum sets. When I needed six sets for my groups, Bud would send them. He was a very generous man and let the students keep them at factory cost if they wanted them.

DA:How easy was it to get drums from Slingerland?

JJ: They were just a phone call away. I would just call Bud and he'd say, "Whatever you want, Jake." In the late 60s to early 70s, Bud asked me to go to three tom toms. I told him, "I'm finally learning how to play two toms on the bass drum, and you want me to play three?" I used the swivomatic tom holder turned to the other side, and added 8" and 10" toms on a stand. I loved it so much that I wanted to bring more drums on gigs but I did not want the extra weight. I also switched to match grip when playing the extra toms. It was natural, because I was using the same grip on tympani and mallet instruments.

I went to Bud with an idea to create a drum set that had nesting drums. The drums are actually longer and single headed. If you look at the Slingerland catalogs in the 60s, you'll see this set with my picture and my drum book in front of the floor tom.

So when I went on a gig, I carried three cases; one for the bass drum, one for all of my toms, and one trap case. I played that white marine pearl set for many years and eventually had it re-covered in black diamond pearl. Slingerland catalogued those drums for many years.

DA: How did the relationship develop with Bud Slingerland and what was your role?

JJ: I had immediate access to Bud. Periodically he

Jake Jerger, 1967

would call me the night before, and ask me to stop by after work at 5:30. He would say he wanted me to see a new product. As soon as I walked in the door, he handed me a scotch on the rocks. He really made me feel like he needed me. He appreciated my opinion because I never skated around the topic when looking at new products. I would just tell him straight out– it does not work, or it is a great product. I think since our first talk he realized I was this way and that's why he wanted me around. I turned out to be a guinea pig for different finishes, from all of the sparkles to an all-chrome set. Sometimes he would take the set back, sometimes he'd just tell me to keep the set for research. He was a very generous man, and I never sold Slingerland drums that I'd been given.

DA:What was the factory like?

JJ: Everytime I went to the factory I would walk around and talk to the people working the line. I got along with everybody. I even found factory jobs for a few students.

When my books came out I found myself doing more clinics for Slingerland at colleges, high schools, and conventions all over the Midwest. In 1966 I did a big clinic at Franks Drum Shop in Chicago and met Louis Bellson. Earlier that year, Louis had done a huge "Rogers Day" at Franks Drum Shop. He picked my students as "best ensemble" and "best soloist" that day. After the event, Louis asked my students who their teacher was. He made them call me up from the drum shop and I met him over the phone. He wanted to tell me I was doing a great job teaching these young "cats" how to play the drums!

In 1972 Slingerland sponsored my Maine West High School ensemble to the first "International Hall of Fame Day" at the Sherman Hotel. All of the players were in college or professionals, and I had the only high school group. I had a talk with Bud that day, and he told me he was selling Slingerland because he had cancer.

In 1974 the Percussive Arts Society invited me to perform at the 2nd International Percussion Day. I went with the New Trier High School Jazz Band and featured the 3 drum battles, 18, 36, & 54 Heads. Slingerland sent six new sets to the event.

I stayed with Slingerland for two more years, but it was not the same after Bud sold. President Don Osborne treated me nice, but did not use me as much. If I needed anything I could still get it... I was just there. From 1952 to 1976 I had all of the percussion equipment I ever needed at no cost.

Jake Jerger *Slingerland*

CHAD WACKERMAN

Became a Slingerland endorsee while still a youngster with the family group "Wackerman and Company". Chad went on to become Frank Zappa's drummer, a solo artist, and in-demand clinician.

Peter Erskine was another artist who established an affiliation with Slingerland while still virtually a youngster, then went on to carve himself a tremendous reputation. In his early career, Erskine played with Stan Kenton, Maynard Ferguson, and Weather Report.

In the 1960s, Rock and Roll began to sell lots of drums. Rock drummers were quite aware of what their endorsements could demand, and tried to negotiate the best possible endorsee contracts. Carmine Appice (who made his name with such power rock groups as Vanilla Fudge, Jeff Beck, Ted Nugent, and Rod Stewart) was one of the most successful endorsement negotiators. His 1983 endorsement agreement with Slingerland called for:

1. A Slingerland "Carmine Appice advertising budget" of $25,000.00. The ads were to be evenly split throughout the year, had to incorporate Carmine's concert tour and personal appearance itineraries, promote his LP's and books, and were subject to Carmine's approval.
2. A clinic program booking Carmine for ten clinics at $1,000.00 to $1,750.00 (plus expenses) each.
3. Three complete drum outfits.
4. Two trade show appearances per year at $1,250.00 per day, with a $5,000.00 annual guarantee.

Commenting on his endorsement decision for the press release, Carmine stated "The reason for my playing Slingerland Drums is they have the capability of building specific types of custom drum outfits that my style of playing demands. It's a great sounding drum and together we have designed a custom outfit that I will be playing on the Ted Nugent tour. I am very proud to be endorsing the same company that Gene Krupa also proudly endorsed for so many years, and I sincerely look forward to a long and successful association with my new family at Slingerland."

The association did not turn out to be nearly as successful as Krupa's; Carmine notified Slingerland (through his L.A.-based agent) several weeks before the scheduled expiration of the first year's agreement that he would not be renewing the agreement and that no further advertising should be placed. The agent explained that Carmine had chosen to make "a new and long term association with another drum company."

Slingerland officials were embarrassed by this photo of endorsee Appice which ran in Circus magazine. The drum outfit is obviously a Ludwig outfit, with a couple Syndrums in the small tom-toms.

HSS Era Endorsers

1990s Gibson Era Endorsers

Terry Thomas
(The Screamin Cheetah Wheelies)

photo by Bill Thorup

Gregg Stocki
(Marty Stuart)

Bruce Rutherford
(Alan Jackson)

Paul Deakin (The Mavericks)

Bernard Purdie

SLINGERLAND PERSONNEL

The folks on the next few pages are some of Slingerland's executive, sales, administrative, and supervisory personnel. This is by no means a comprehensive list, and the dates listed for the most part represent only the dates these folks are pictured in Slingerland catalogs. Many no doubt were actually employed by Slingerland over a much longer time frame.

None of the Slingerland family members were really musicians. They were, however *very* sharp business people who could appreciate the value of having lots of drummers in a drum factory. This is what developed the bond between the Slingerland staff and the Slingerland product. Working together and with their endorsees, the folks at Slingerland knew they were producing world-famous products that were making music history. It would have been impossible for the Slingerland family to simply hire a bunch of production workers and create the Slingerland mystique that these folks created. These are the people who were the real *heart* of the company.

The role of the field sales reps was important to Slingerland, particularly from the late '50s through the late '70s. (A fact underscored by the inclusion of regional rep photos in a number of catalogs of this era.) The reps were not required to devote their time exclusively to Slingerland— they were free to rep other lines at the same time. Bud Slingerland even helped arrange for John Clark to represent Getzen band instruments.

Bud monitored the movements of his reps by recording in a journal the dates and postmarks of the reports they were required to regularly send in. Since Slingerland had an in-house floor planning program set up, it was important that the reps regularly visit floor-planned dealers to check the stock. (Any gear which was not in stock when the floor check was made had to be paid for immediately.) By logging the movements of the reps Bud was able to keep tabs on the floor-planned merchandise. The reps were not enthused about all the extra work it took to send in post-card reports regarding their whereabouts, and some deliberately sent in their reports from obscure towns with very long names, causing extra work for Bud as he entered the data in his journal— an effort to discourage him from requiring this extra work altogether.

Don Osborne, on a personal level, was much closer to the sales reps than Bud Slingerland had been. They found him much easier to get along with, and as soon as he had the authority he immediately stopped requiring postmarked activity reports.

Larry Linkin was also good friends with his field sales force. He depended heavily on them to communicate the new product and program news to dealers, and they seldom let him down.

JOHN M. CLARK

John Clark was the only sales rep to work for Slingerland under every president from Bud Slingerland (1963) through Larry Rasp (1984).

The owner of a large music store in Atlanta, Georgia, suggested to Bud Slingerland that John would be a good sales rep for him. Bud had John come to Chicago to "audition". At the time every Slingerland rep had to be a player, so it wasn't until after passing the audition with Don Osborne that John was hired on as a rep.

"I wasn't with Slingerland continuously the whole time," John says. "there were a couple times I was doing other things. And a couple times they had bright young MBA business types fresh out of school, determined to set the business on fire and make millions of dollars. I usually got a phone call in about six months, asking if I'd take the territory back."

Aloisio, Spencer
Sales Manager, V.P.
1970–1986

Dibella, Richard
Purchasing
Agent

Gary Beckner
Sales Manager
1973–1976

Dvorak, Joe M.
Chicago Area Sales
1934–1955

Browning, Bill
Central Eastern
Sales
1965

Elkins, Jim
Southern
Sales
1955–1957

Elliott, John
Office Manager
1955–1965

Engdahl,Charles
Controller
1973–1976

Haar, Jimmy
Western Sales
1955–1961

Havlicek, Gerry
Mid-Western Sales
1955–1965

Hickle, Lee
Sales for IL, IN,
MI, & WI
1963–1965

Hollerich, John
Chief engineer
& designer
1973

Hoult, Jim
Cost Accountant
1976

Johnson, Art
Plant Manager
1973–1976

Kelley, Bill
Plant Manager
1955–1962

Lofdahl, Bill
South-Eastern Sales
1963

Meyers, Warren
Plant Manager
1963–1965

Moffatt, Al
Marketing
Supervisor
1973–1976

Morey, Brad
Marketing
Supervisor
1973–1976

Osborne, Don
Sales & Service
1955–1963
Sales Manager
1964–1965
President 1973–1976

Perkins, Smokey
South-Western Sales
1962–1967

Phillips, Jack
CO., NV., AZ. Sales
1962–1964

Raiche, Joe
Eastern Sales
1960–1964

Vorback, Charlie
Eastern Sales
1955–1959

Drawing Board Snare Drums, 1973

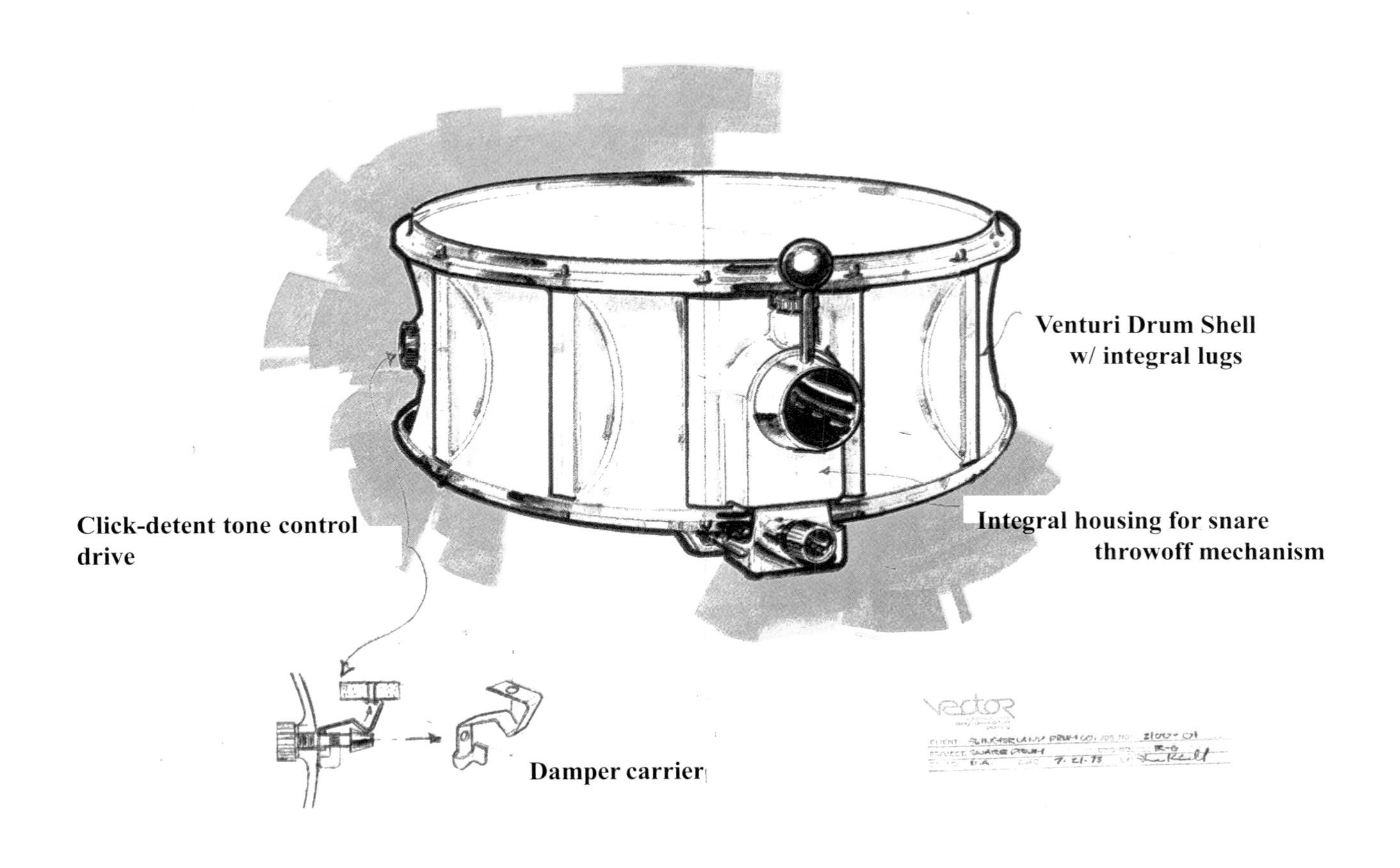

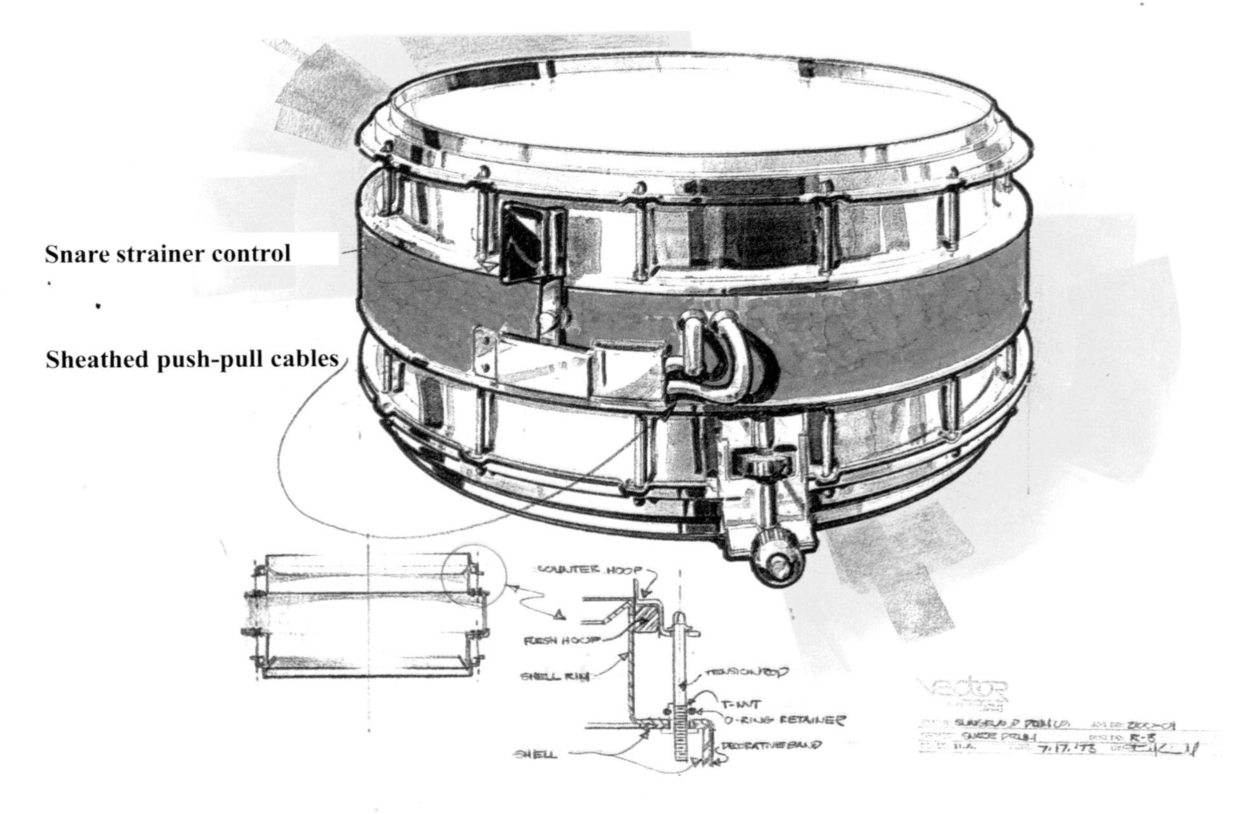

Drawing Board Snare Drums, 1973

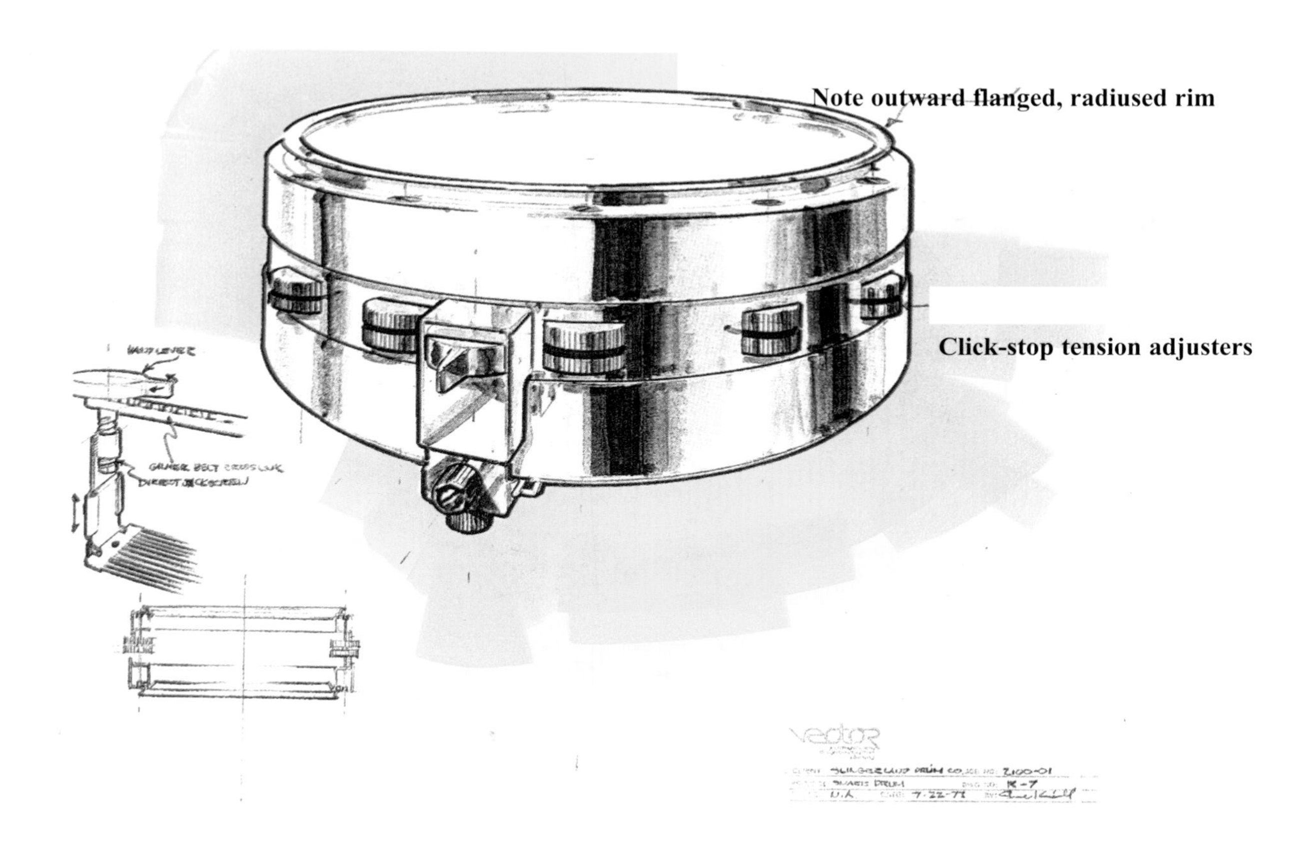

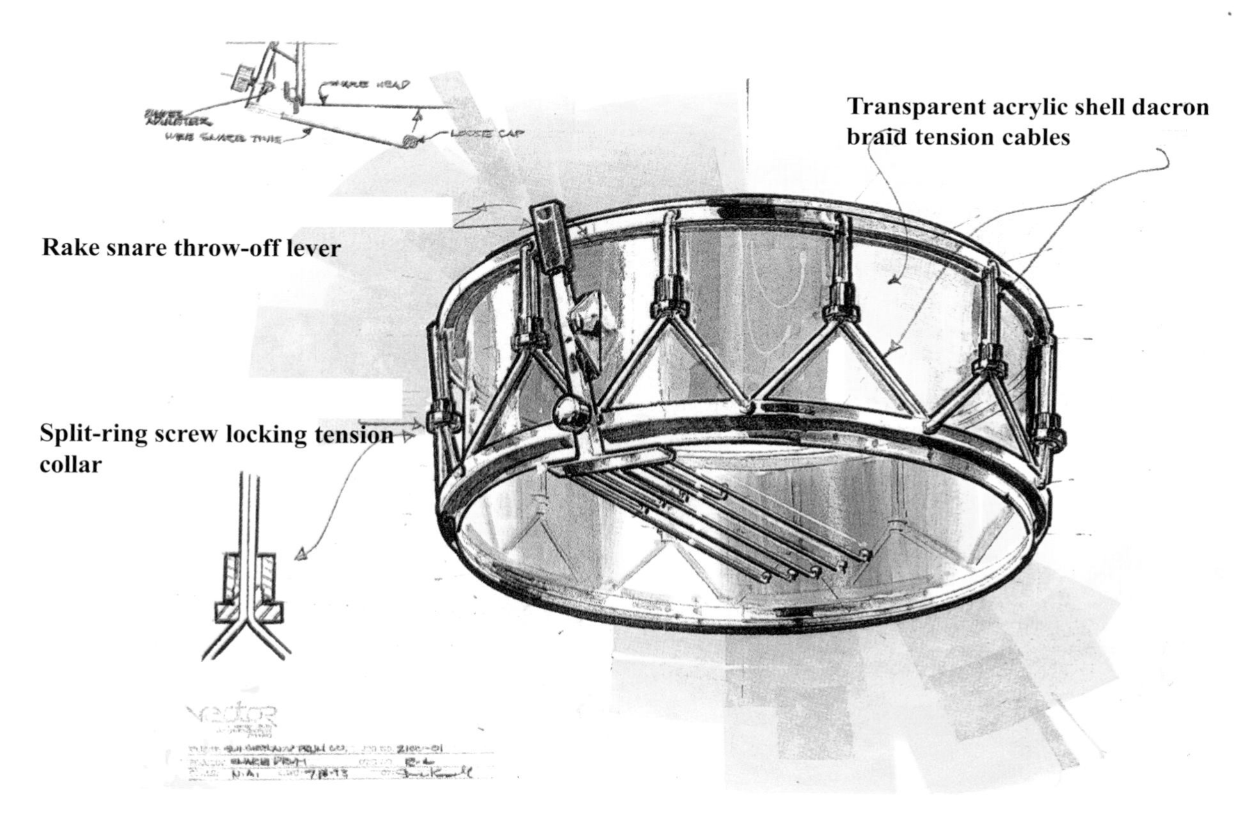

Uncatalogued Engraved Models

Little is known at this writing about the Broadcaster, an uncatalogued model apparently from the 1930s. The author is aware of only a couple Broadcasters in existence; one is a wooden-shell 5x14, the other is this "Black Beauty". This drum is *very* unusual; Radio King strainer, 6 lugs, and a 6.5x13 shell size!

Lipskin: 8-lug 6.5 x 14

Lipskin photos courtesy of Nathan Moy

DAVE BROWN COLLECTION

British collector Dave Brown is a familiar figure on the American vintage drum show circuit. The exceptional outfits shown on this page are typical of the pieces Brown's collection is famous for– clean, rare outfits from the 1920s and 1930s. The "Full Dress" Duall kit at lower right is particularly rare. Dave Brown can be contacted at diddle@audiophile.com.

STEVE MAXWELL COLLECTION

The drums on this page are on display at *Steve Maxwell Vintage and Custom Drums,* located at 410 S. Michigan Ave. (Suite 914) in Chicago. Steve can be contacted by phone at 630-865-6849 or by email drummermax@aol.com.

Mel Tormè's favorite Slingerland kit, made for him by Don Osborne who used 1970s era shells with 1940s era hardware.

Johnny Karoly was the runnerup to Louis Bellson in the 1941 Gene Krupa contest. His prize was this snare drum. It is a 7x14 Gene Krupa model Radio King with solid maple shell, 16 lugs, "clamshell" strainer and brass lower rim. As catalogued, the top rim was brass also, but Johnny requested that his be built with a wooden top hoop and claw hooks, mirroring the earlier Ray McKinley model. Karoly went on to build a successful drumming career, including a stint with Tommy Dorsey's band.

Buddy Rich's last Slingerland kit as an endorser. He switched from this kit to Ludwig. Rich finished out his life playing Slingerland, but not as an endorser; his last kit was a Radio King kit, customized by Joe MacSweeney.

all photos this page courtesy Steve Maxwell

DONN BENNETT COLLECTION

The Donn Bennett Drum Studio in Seattle is world-famous not only for the many clinics and special events, but also for the steadily expanding museum which features famous drummers' gear. The shop is at 13212 NE 16th #7, Bellevue, Washington. 425-747-6145. www.bennettdrums.com

John "J.R." Robinson's Black chrome over maple snare drum that he used with Rufus in 1981.

Buddy Rich Trap Case

This Slingerland kit is not part of the museum; it belongs to Matt Chamberlain and was at Bennett's shop for refurbishing.

Gene Krupa 9x13 tom tom

all photos this page courtesy Donn Bennett

photos by Timothy Meinig

DONN BENNETT COLLECTION

photo by Timothy Meinig

late 1990s Slingerland ad featuring Tre Cool (photo by Paul Haggard)

One of Tre Cool's signature outfits, after a 2001 Cleveland *Green Day* show that finished with a flaming finale.

photo by Timothy Meinig

photo by Timothy Meinig

Carmine Appice's Slingerland kit from the Ozzy Osbourne 1983 *Bark At The Moon* tour and video. The snare drum (at left) features gold-plated hardware.

EDDIE MOSQUEDA COLLECTION

Eddie Mosqueda has been collecting Slingerland and Slingerland Radio King outfits and snare drums since around 1970. He also has an extensive collection of Ludwig 60s "Ringo" finish outfits and snares. He can be contacted at designbyed@yahoo.com.

photo courtesy Eddie Mosqueda

Blue Diamond Pearl (an uncatalogued color) 7x14 Radio King snare, probably from the early to mid 1940s; note the aluminum cloud badge

photo courtesy Eddie Mosqueda

Chrome-over-brass Radio King snare drum. This very unusual (and uncatalogued) snare drum was acquired by Eddie from original owner Roy Harte, who with Remo Belli founded Hollywood drum shop Drum Paradise.

MIKE CUROTTO COLLECTION

1928 5x14 Black Beauty

1930s 5x14 Rose Marine Pearl Duall

MIKE CUROTTO COLLECTION

1920s–1930s 5x14 red/green/blue "Speckle" (uncatalogued finish) Tone Flange Model

1920s or 30s 5x14
Sea Green Pearl, Tone Flange

1920s or 30s 5x14
Sea Green Pearl /Artgold
Fancher Model (Tone Flange)

1920s or 30s 6.5x14
Sea Green Pearl Fancher Model
(Tone Flange)

1920s–1930s 5x14 Solid Maple
Peacock Pearl 8-lug Professional Model

1930s 5x14 Black Diamond Pearl/Artgold Duall

MIKE CUROTTO COLLECTION

Very rare 1920s–1930s 4x14 Gold Sparkle/Artgold Tone Flange Model

Lavender Pearl/Artgold 5x14 Tone Flange Fancher Model

MIKE CUROTTO COLLECTION

1930s–1940s 5x14 Black Enamel (Brass shell) Radio King

1940s Chrome-over-wood Radio King. Inside shell is inscribed "okay Chrome"

1930s–1940s 8x14 White Marine Pearl, Bernie Mattison Model Radio King

1930s Black Diamond Pearl/Artgold sold maple Broadcaster

1940s–1950s 4.5x13, Solid maple piccolo Radio King

1930s–1940s 4.5x13 Solid Maple Gold Sparkle piccolo Radio King

1940s White Marine Pearl 4x14 Solid Maple Radio King

1930s–1940s 6.5x14 Solid Maple Radio King

MIKE CUROTTO

Mike Curotto has at this writing been playing drums for 44 years and teaching for 40. (He currently teaches at Gelb Music, of Redwood City, California.) In about 1995 Mike began to develop an interest in vintage drums. He read up on the subject and started with a dual-strainer WMP WFL snare. Curotto's collection today numbers over 250 snare drums as well as outfits and original catalogs.

Where did Mike find all the incredibly rare drums? He regularly monitors Ebay and has become adept at auction tactics, but says a great deal of credit must be given to the vintage drum community network. For many of the country's top vintage drum dealers and collectors, Mike is the first number called when they come across something extremely rare.

The two tone flanges at the left of the page are original brass and aluminum tone flanges from the collection of Mike Curotto. The aluminum and brass tone flanges shown at the right side of the page are exact reproduction tone flanges that Curotto has had commissioned. Curotto makes these available to collectors; he can be contacted at 650-595-2022, or email mike@curottodrums.com.

Original Tone Flanges | **Curotto Reproduction Tone Flanges**

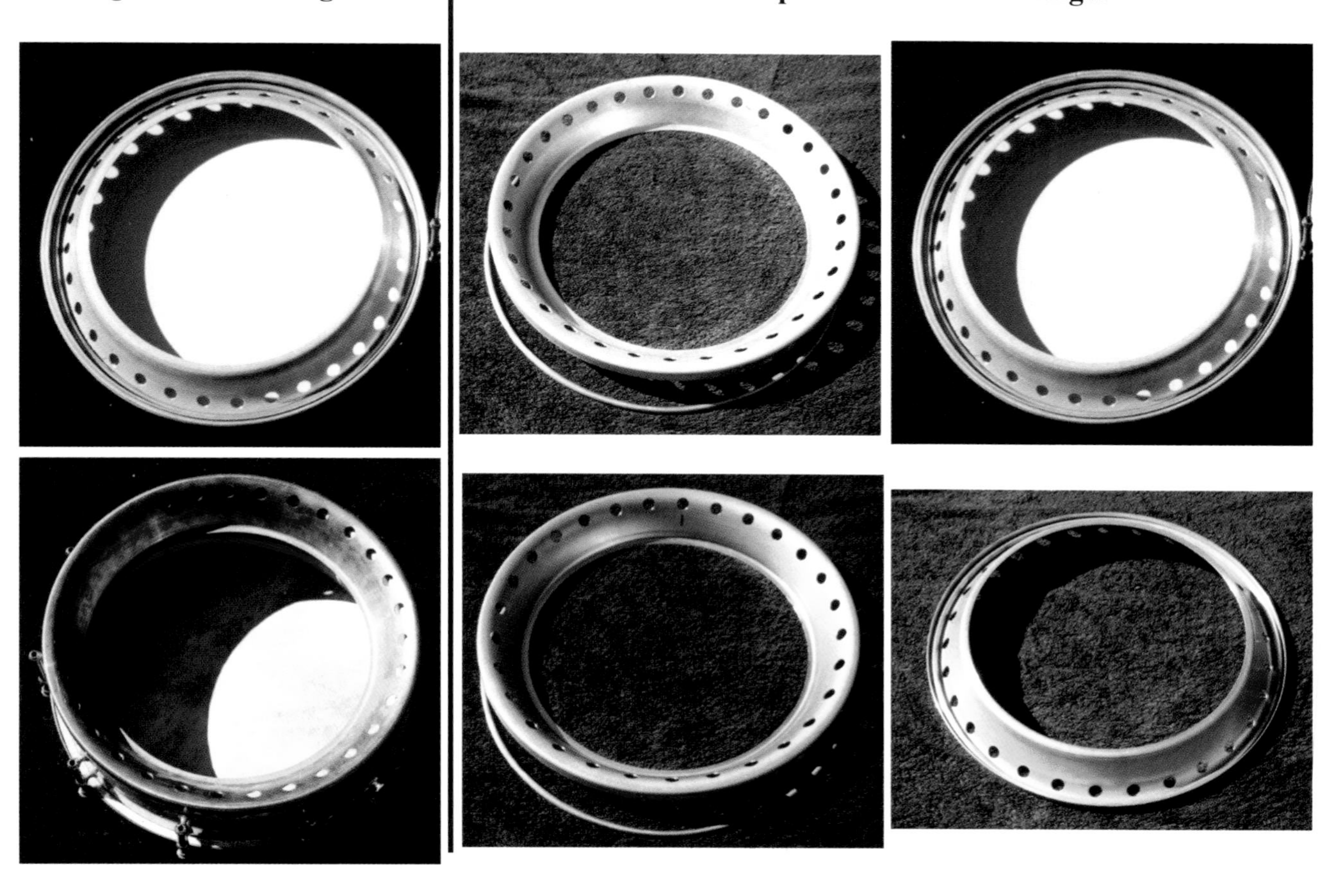

Slingerland's first catalog of 1928 followed the lead of competitors Leedy and Ludwig in offering hand-painted bass drum scenes. The offerings were expanded slightly in the 1934 catalog, shown here. This was the last catalog to offer such scenes.

Slingerland Catalogs

For more information on these catalogs,see Appendix 2

1928
5.5x8.5, 80 pages

Catalog B 1930
5.5x8.5, 64 pages

1934
5.5x8.5, 96 pages

1936
5.5x8.5, 96 pages

1937
5.5x8.5, 20 pages

1938
5.5x8.5, 96 pages

1939
5.5x8.5,42 pages

1940
5.5x8.5, 80 pages

1941
5.5x8.5, 32 pages

1947
8x11, 22 pages

1948
8.5x11, 24 pages

#51, 1949
8.5x11", 30 pages

1951
8.5x11, 32 pages

#54 1953
8.5x11, 32 pages

#55 1955
8.5x11, 36 pages

#555 1955
8.5x11, 22 pages

#57 1957
8.5x11, 36 pages

LEEDY 1956
8.5x11, 24 pages

LEEDY 1958
8.5x11, 28 pages

LEEDY #60, 1959
8.5x11, 32 pages

LEEDY #62, 1962
8.5x11, 32 pages

#59 1958, #60 1959,
#61 1960, #61A 1961
8.5x11, 40 pages

#63 1962
8.5x11, 56 pages

#63A 1963
8.5x11, 56 pages

LEEDY #70 1965
8.5x11, 36 pages

#65 1964
8.5x11, 64 pages

#67 1965
8.5x11, 64 pages

#68 1967
8.5x11, 72 pages

#69 1968
8.5x11, 72 pages

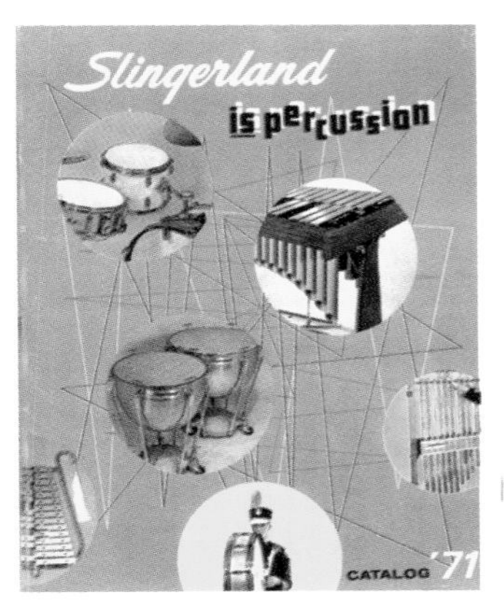

#71 1970
8.5x11, 80 pages

1973
8.5x11, 80 pages

1976
8.5x11, 84 pages

1977-1978
8.5x11, 72 pages

1979
8.5x11, 90 pages

1983
8.5x11, 34 pages

Slingerland
THE DRUMMERS' CATALOG

1985
8.5x11, 22 pages

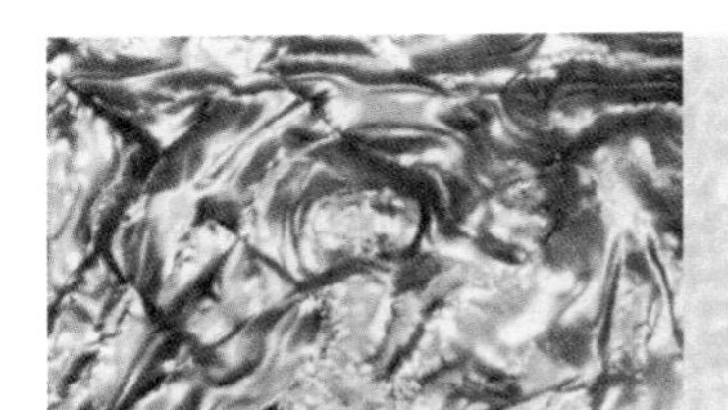

Black Diamond Pearl
1928–1995

Marine Pearl
1928– 1994

Sparkling Red
1934–1986

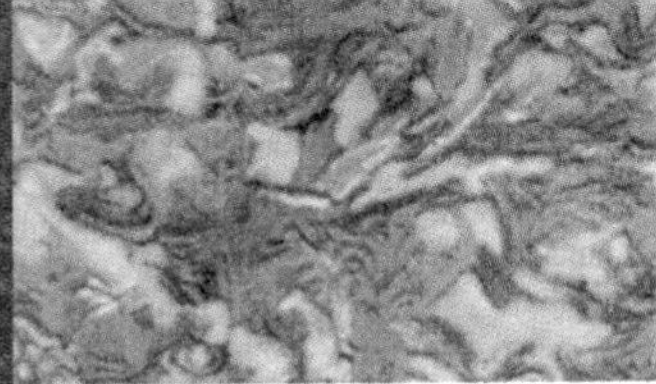

Opal Pearl
1929–1938
Also referred to as Peacock Pearl

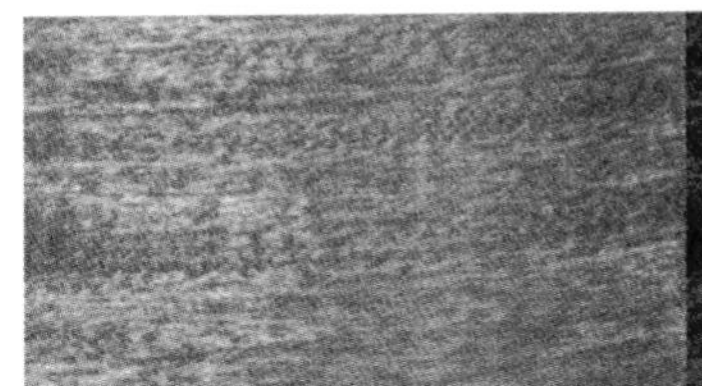

Mahogany
1928–1986

Walnut
1928–1939 1976–1986

Brilliant Gold
Called sparkling gold after 1929.
1928–1979

Sea Green
1928–1938

Lavender
1929

Rose Pearl
1929

Coral Pearl
1934–1938

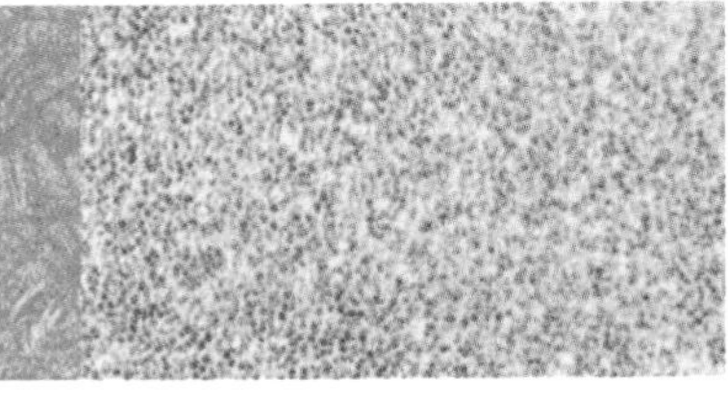

Sparkling Silver
1934–1986

The finish at left can probably best be described as a "Brown Abalone." This was not a catalogued finish and to date the author is unaware of any other example of the finish. This drum belongs to (and photo supplied by) Mike Curotto.

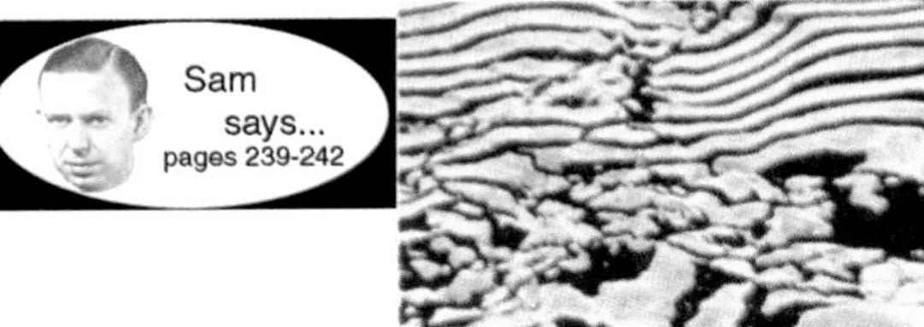

Abalone Pearl
1936

Antique

1934–1938

Two colors of lacquer are actually used for each Antique finish. In 1936 the following color combinations were available at no additional charge from the regular prices: Silver & Blue or Gold & Blue, Silver & Black or Gold & Black. Other colors (sometimes more than two per drum) were certainly applied, and this technique continued through the late 1960s, though the term "Antique finish" appears in Slingerland catalogs only until 1938.

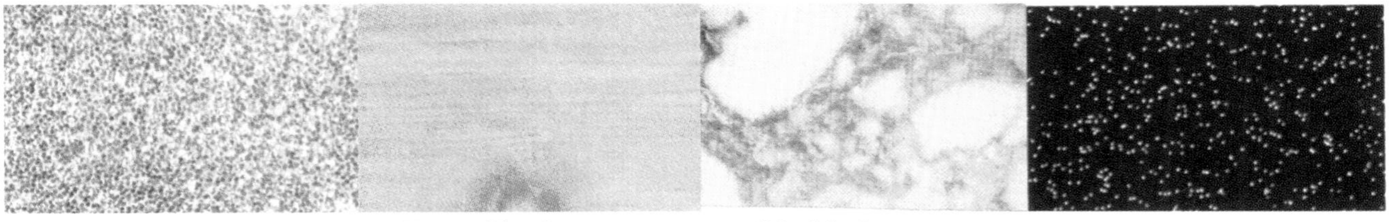

Aqua Sparkle Pearl
1959

Knotty Pine Lacquer
1955–1957

Marble Lacquer
1955 - 1957

Black Sparkle
1958–1967

Outfits were catalogued until 1962 (Knotty Pine) and 1963 (Marble), but neither was listed in color swatch charts after 1957. Knotty Pine was reportedly developed specficically for Krupa, to match his basement paneling.

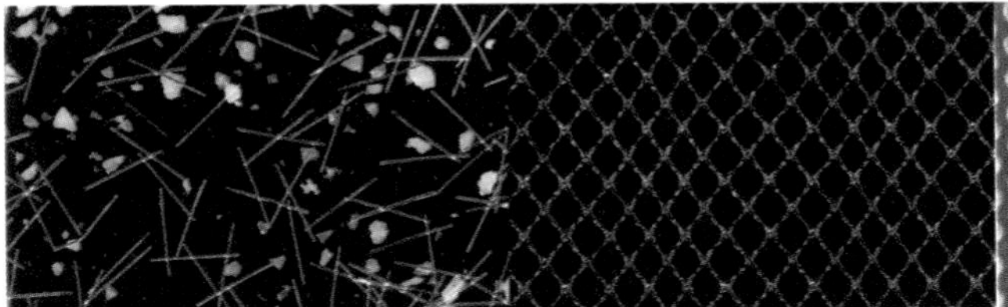

Capri Pearl
1958–1963

Gold Veiled Ebony Pearl
1958–1963

Silver Veil Pearl
1958–1960

Turquoise Veil Pearl
1958–1960

Smokey (Sparkling) Pearl
1958–1960

Light Blue Pearl
1958–1979

Sparkling Pink
1959–1967

Blue Ripple
1961–1967

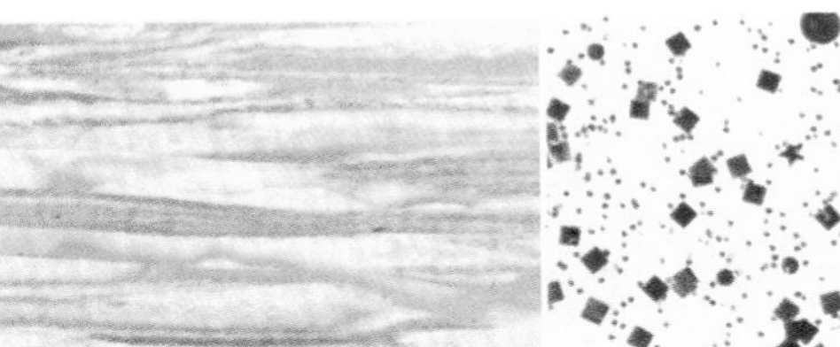

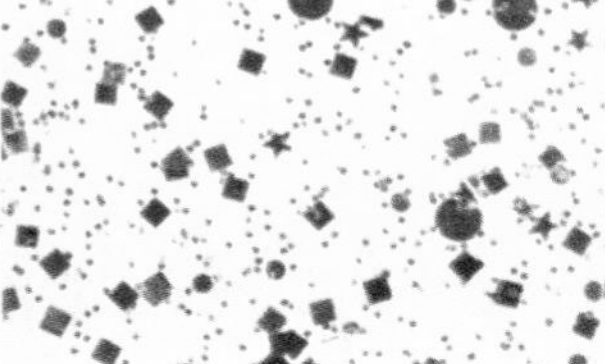

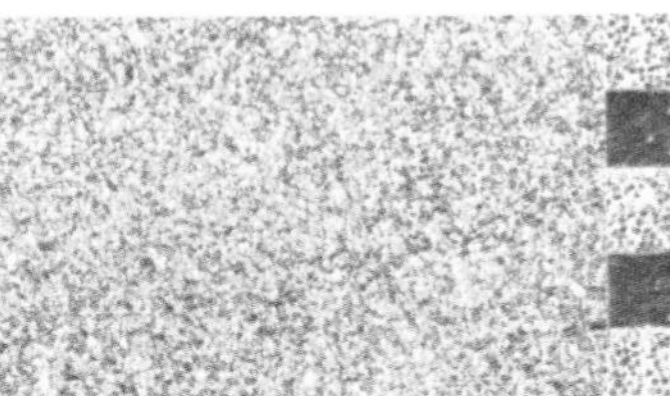

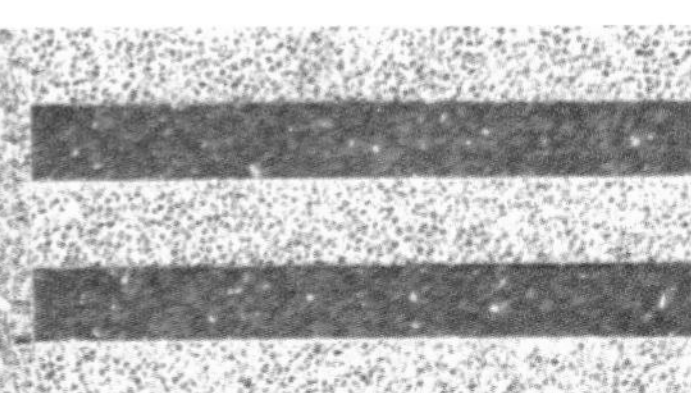

Oyster Pink
1961–1967

Fiesta
1961–1967

Sparkling Pink Champagne
1961–1973

Combination Pearl finishes
1961–1973
(any two of the seven sparkles)

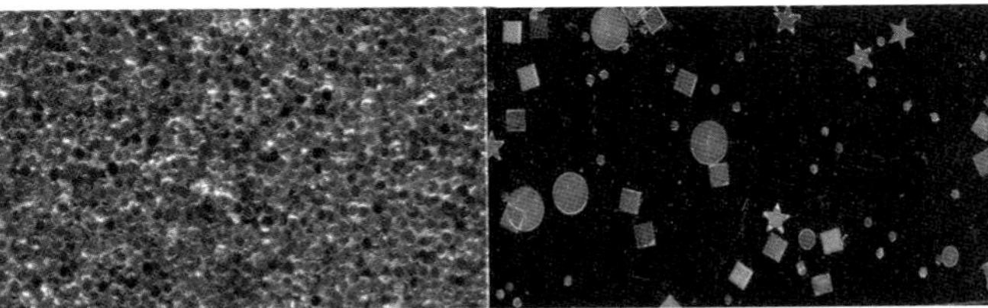

Sparkling Peacock
1961–1963

Mardi Gras Pearl
1961–1963

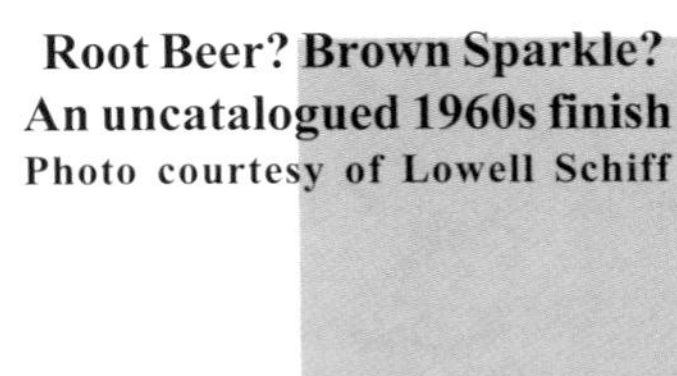

Root Beer? Brown Sparkle?
An uncatalogued 1960s finish
Photo courtesy of Lowell Schiff

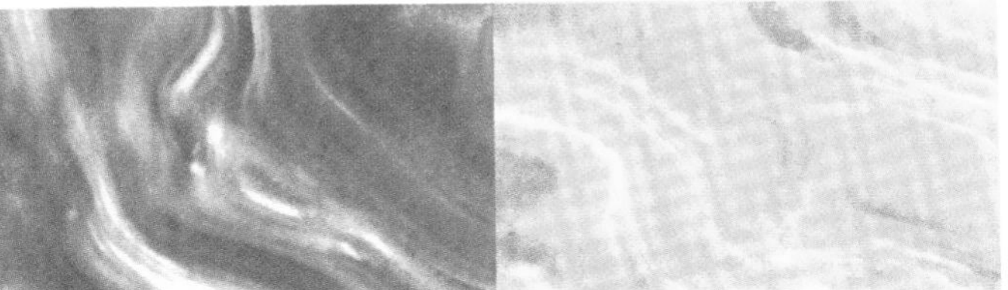

Blue Satin Flame
1964–1977

Gold Satin Flame
1964–1977

Green Satin Flame
1964–1973

Red Satin Flame
1964–1977

Red Ripple
1965–1967

White Satin Flame
1967

Blue Agate Pearl
1965–1977

Black Sparkle
1960–1968

Grey Agate Pearl
1956–1967

Yellow Tiger
1968

Copper
1973

Lavendar Satin Flame Pearl
1970–1973

Red Gloss
1976–1986

Red Tiger Pearl
1970–1973

White Tiger Pearl
1973 - 1977

Sparkling Maroon Pearl
1973

Sparkling OrangePearl
1970–1973

Sparkling Purple Pearl
1970–1973

Tangerine Satin Flame Pearl
1973

Brown Aztec
1976

Green Aztec
1976

Red Aztec
1976

Yellow Aztec
1976

White Aztec
1976

Sparkling Green
1934–1986

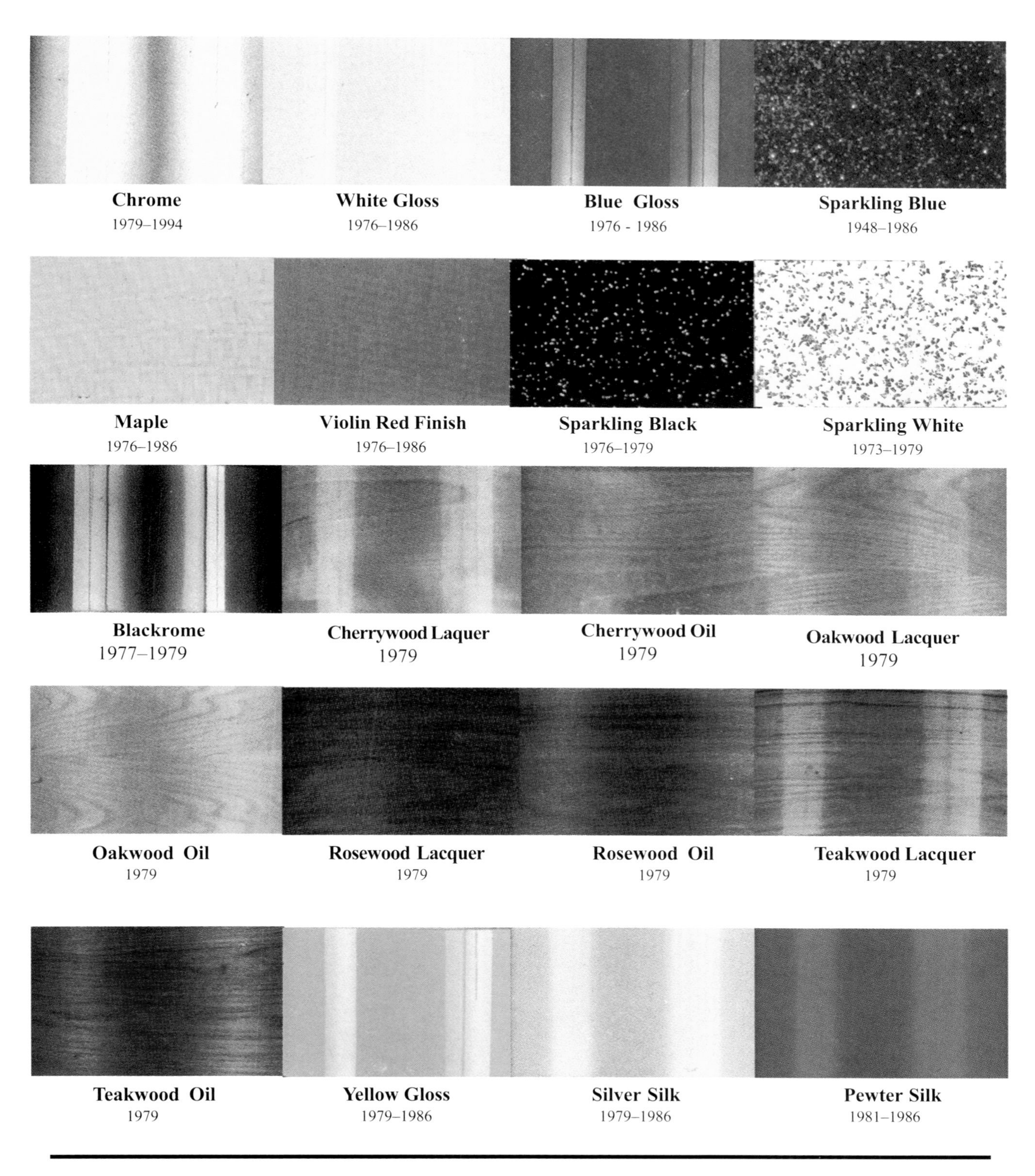

SLINGERLAND-LEEDY COLORS

From 1955 through 1958, the color options for Slingerland's Leedy drums were the same as they'd been in the last Leedy & Ludwig catalog; White Pearl, Black Pearl, Red Sparkle, Blue Sparkle, Gold Sparkle, Silver Sparkle, and Green Sparkle.

In catalog #62 the following colors were added: Black Beauty (solid black pearl), Capri Pearl, Fiesta, Light Blue Pearl, Mardi Gras Pearl, Sparkling Peacock Pearl, Sparkling Pink.

The color swatch page for the Leedy #70 catalog was exactly the same as Slingerland catalog #67.

In the 1970s, the drum finishes Slingerland offered were literally limitless. The acrylic and denim on this page as well as the cordova finishes on the next page were standard finishes. Slingerland even offered to cover drums with artwork of the drummer's choice. To demonstrate and dramatize the possibilities, they showed an outfit at the annual NAMM show which was covered with the Coca-Cola trade-mark.

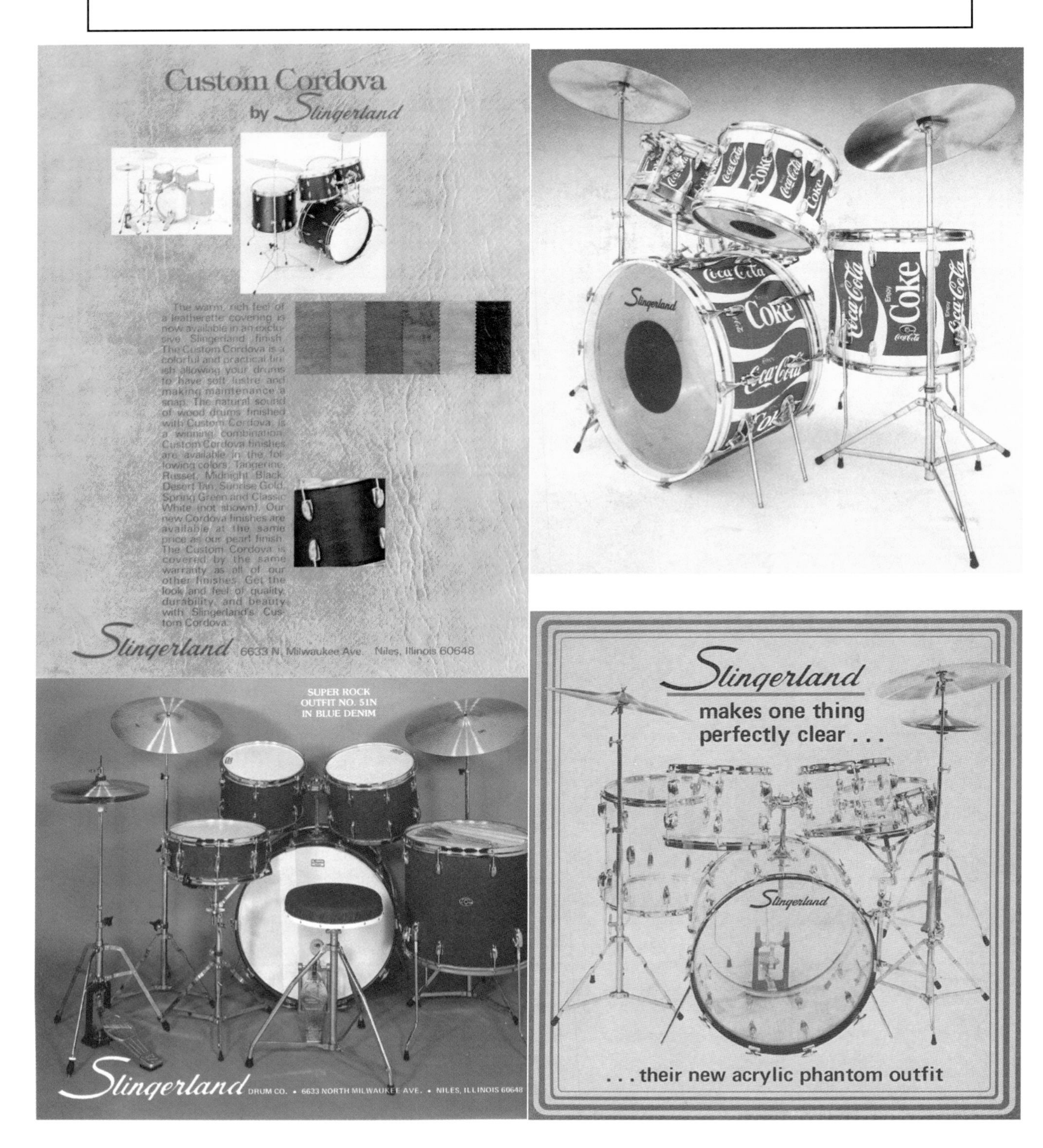

GREGG POTTER

Slingerland

"This was from when I was doing a lot of stuff with Steve Dahl. He always wore really loud Hawaiian shirts, and Spencer [Aloisio] told me "We can make you a drum that'll be as loud as his shirts!" They only had enough of this material to do this snare for me and a floor tom. I wanted a whole outfit, but it couldn't be done."

Gregg Potter

This unique Slingerland outfit was made in 1979. According to Larry Linkin, who was president at the time, the idea originated with West Coast sales representative Phil Hulsey. Helsey told Link about a guy out in California who was doing remarkable inlay work on custom surfboards. The next time Link was in California they went to the surf shop and Link was equally impressed with the craftsmanship of the wood inlay work. He commissioned enough inlaid veneer to cover a complete set of drums. The drums turned out beautifully, but the cost of producing this prototype outfit was too high to consider making this a regular production item. The outfit remained on the shelf until Link was leaving Slingerland. Shortly before his departure, he called Brian Callahan to his office. Callahan had worked in quality control and product development, working on projects such as the TDR, the marching vibes, and cutaways. Link explained that he was leaving and wanted to give a few key people an opportunity to speak up if there was anything in the way of equipment that he could help them with before he left. Callahan immediately asked about the custom inlaid outfit which he had been impressed with when it was being made. Link let Callahan purchase the outfit for the cost of materials and labor.

BRIAN CALLAHAN

BLACK GOLD

Black Gold was a gold-tone brass plating for stands and hardware developed in the early '80s. Black Gold was not around long enough to make it into a regular Slingerland catalog; this art is from the flier sent to dealers.

A huge product roll-out was presented at a NAMM show, complete with beautiful models in sexy black and gold tuxedo outfits. The hoopla only served to call attention to the rather spectacular flop.

HSS ERA FINISHES

SA-3008C-WR (Wine Red) withSH3000

SA-3062C-BB (Bright Blue) with SH3000 hardware pack.

SA-3000C-NM (Natural Maple) with SH1000 hardware pack.

Artist Series: Shown– Wine Red Maple, Bright Blue, Emerald Green, Natural Maple. Also; Graphite Metallic, White Gloss, Black Gloss. Also, in 1993–1994, Black Diamond Pearl, White Marine Pearl

Spirit Series

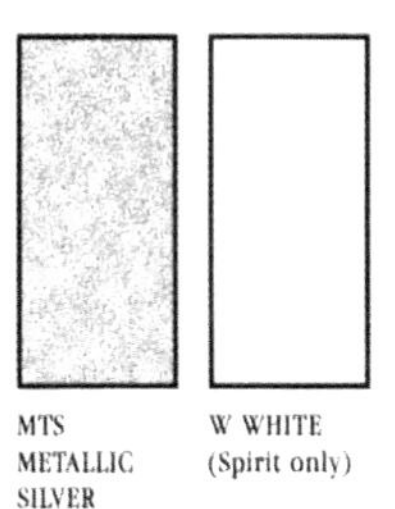

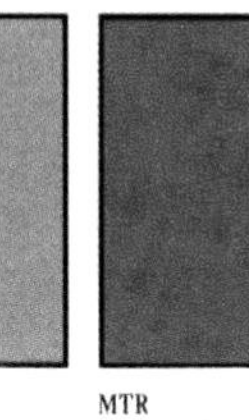

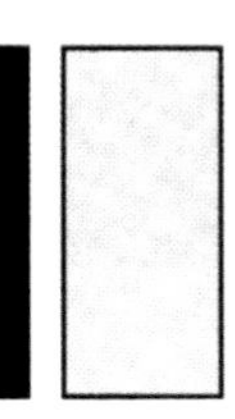

MTS METALLIC SILVER (Spirit only)

W WHITE (Spirit only)

MTB METALLIC BLUE (Spirit only)

MTR METALLIC RED (Spirit & Spirit Plus)

B BLACK (Spirit & Spirit Plus)

CH CHROME (Spirit Plus only)

DKB DARK BLUE (Spirit Plus only)

GIBSON 1990s FINISHES

For the somewhat limited time period that Gibson distributed the Spirit and Artist Custom drums, they supplied them in the same colors as HSS plus added Dark Walnut and Antique Maple to the Artist Custom. Finishes included coverings, classic urethanes, basic classic colors, and grain-enhanced options. Many of the grain-enhanced finishes and sunburst finishes were the direct result of the efforts of ace drum finisher Pat Foley.

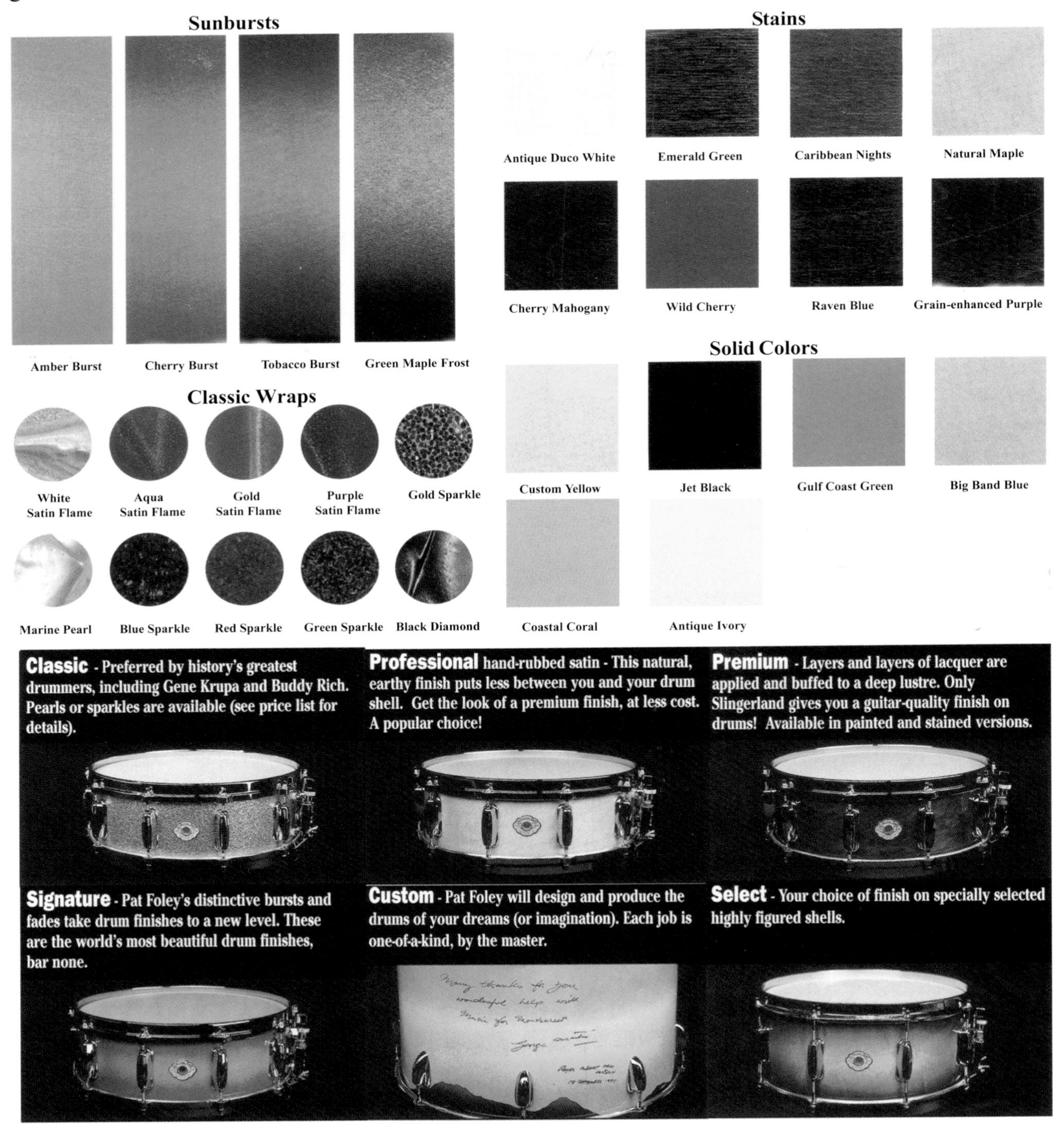

Pat Foley's Studio King Finishes. The drum shown with the Custom finish was part of the outfit Foley made for Gibson to benefit victims of Montseraat's volcanic disaster. The kit, signed by George Martin, was auctioned off at London's Hard Rock Cafe.

2003 Conway, Arkansas, Slingerland

Tour King Series Classic V, Black Marine Pearl wrap

Tour King Series Classic V, Champagne Sparkle wrap

Tour King Series New Standard, Black Marine Pearl wrap

Tour King Series Modern Jazz, Green Glitter wrap

Tour King Series Modern Jazz, Red Glitter wrap

Studio King Series Rolling Thunder, Translucent Violet High Gloss Lacquer

photos courtesy Gibson

SLINGERLAND BADGES

Like their major competitor Ludwig, Slingerland did not always stop the use of older badges when a new badge was introduced.

THE SQUARE BADGE
c. 1927

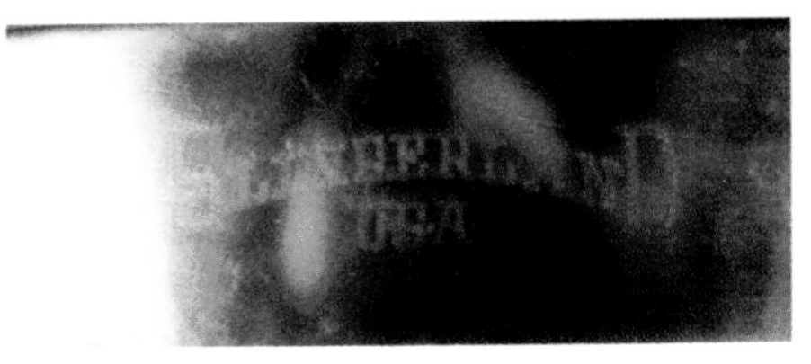

Earliest metal-shell drums had no badge; Slingerland was engraved in the shell

The square badge was probably the first badge Slingerland used on a drum. To date it has only been spotted on the "Geisler drum"; a cast aluminum drum strikingly similar to the banjo. (See page XX.) Badges of identical size and lettering style were used on versions of this drum sold by the Liberty Musical Instrument Company as well as Geisler, the manufacturer.

SLINGERLAND BRASS CLOUD BADGE 1928–1941

This is the badge used on nearly every Slingerland drum which had a badge from 1928 to about 1941. On earlier versions (left) the lettering is etched into the surface; letter space is lower than the surface. These areas were sometimes painted (center). On later badges (right), it's the *rest* of the surface that is etched.

FANCHER MODEL

The "Fancher Model" drum was only catalogued as a field drum but the badge was installed on some tone-flange concert drums as well.

MUSIC STORE BADGES

Slingerland evidently provided OEM drums for at least two music stores (Hager Music of Grand Rapids, Dorn & Kirschner of Newark,) and possibly others. The drums sporting these badges look exactly like the Slingerland Artist model of 1929.

LIPSKIN SPECIAL MODELS

There were no catalogued drums with the designation Lipskin, so it is presumed that these drums were produced for a dealer. The engraving at right is from an engraved black-nickel plated brass snare drum. The cloud badge below is from the "bearing-edge ring" drum shown on page XX. The cloud badge at lower right is from a Artist Model-type drum. All three appear to have been made in the late 1920s.

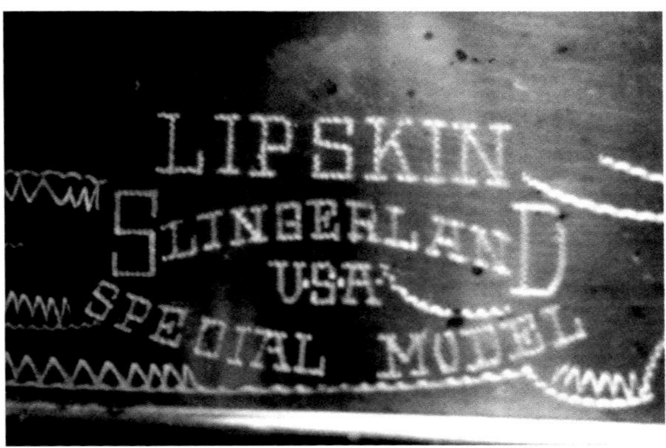

Photo courtesy Nathan Moy

Photo courtesy Les Rutledge

Photo courtesy Frank Vilardi

KRUPA'S DRUMS

Krupa's equipment was often identified; Zildjian stamped his cymbals with a GK. All three of these badges are mounted on one of Krupa's snare drums.

WARTIME CLOUD BADGE
1942–1947

Restrictions on the use of brass forced Slingerland to make their early '40s cloud badges out of aluminum. These badges show up on postwar drums as well.

MEDIUM OVAL, 1951
About the same as the 1948 oval, but smaller. (lacquered brass).

LARGE OVAL c. 1948–1950
This was the first badge Slingerland used which was not square or a cloud. First used in about 1948, it's a brass badge with raised letters and a lacquered finish.

SMALL OVAL, 1955–1959
First used in about 1955, this brass badge was not painted. It *was* lacquered with clear lacquer to prevent tarnishing.

LEEDY BRASS 1955–1959
The first Leedy badge that Slingerland produced, 1955. Quite similar to the Slingerland small oval.

LEEDY BLUE OVAL
c. 1960–1963

SHELBYVILLE
c.1965–1966

BRASS & BLACK CHICAGO
1960

BRASS & BLACK NILES
The first badge produced after Slingerland's 1960 move to Niles. For the first year or two there were no serial numbers on these badges.

MARCHING PERCUSSION 1970s

SILVER & BLACK NILES
Mid 1960s through early 1980s

FOIL NILES
1985, cardboard shell drums

HSS ERA BADGES: The brass "Ridgeland, S.C." oval badge was used on the American-made Lite series. (late '80s to early '90s). The "Ridgeland, S.C." cloud badge was used on the HSS Radio Kings. All of the rest of the badges below were used on imported drums such as the Spirit series and Artist Custom drums. The badges below which have no serial numbers were the "second badges" on snare drums and toms which had two badges. Though this marks the first time that regular production-model drums were fitted with two badges, they are not the first Slingerland drums known to have been made that way. Snare drums as early as 1962 and some tom-toms of the '70s were made with two badges (on a special-order basis).

HSS ERA
late 1980s–early 1990s

NASHVILLE CLOUD
1994–1998

Studio King

Radio King

Conway, AR
2003–

For the most part, Slingerland's product offerings in the first catalog were very similar to those of the competitors'; tube lugs, engraved black-nickel snare drums, oil-painted scenes on the bass drums, the relatively new "pearl" drum coverings, stands, effects, accessories, and the usual assortment of cymbals (Zildjian, Italian, Ajaha, and American brass.)

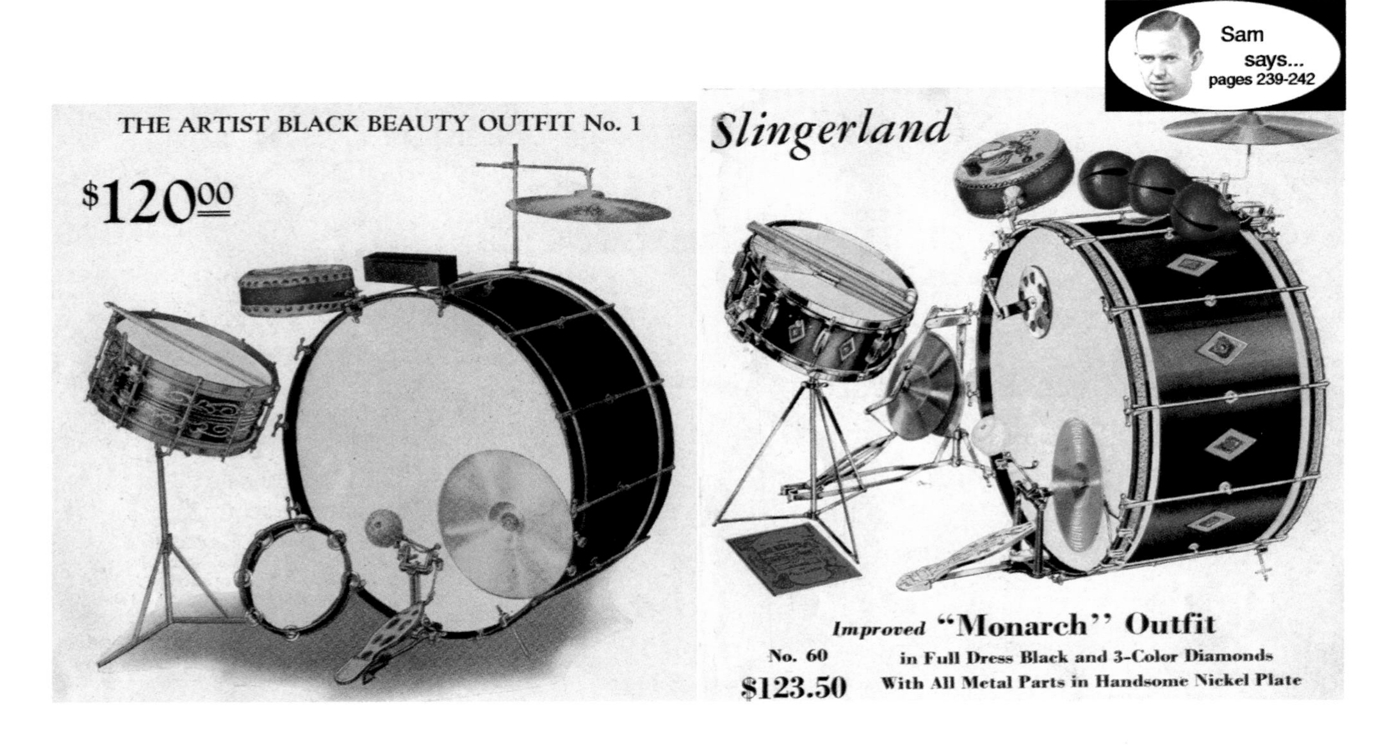

Cymbal Stands

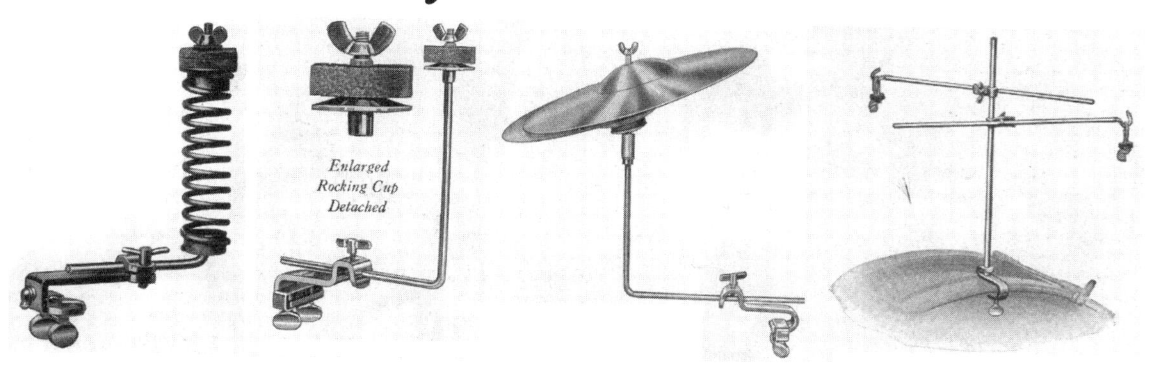

From the company's first catalog which featured the cymbal holders shown above, all cymbal holders were designed to fasten to the bass drum hoop until postwar days.

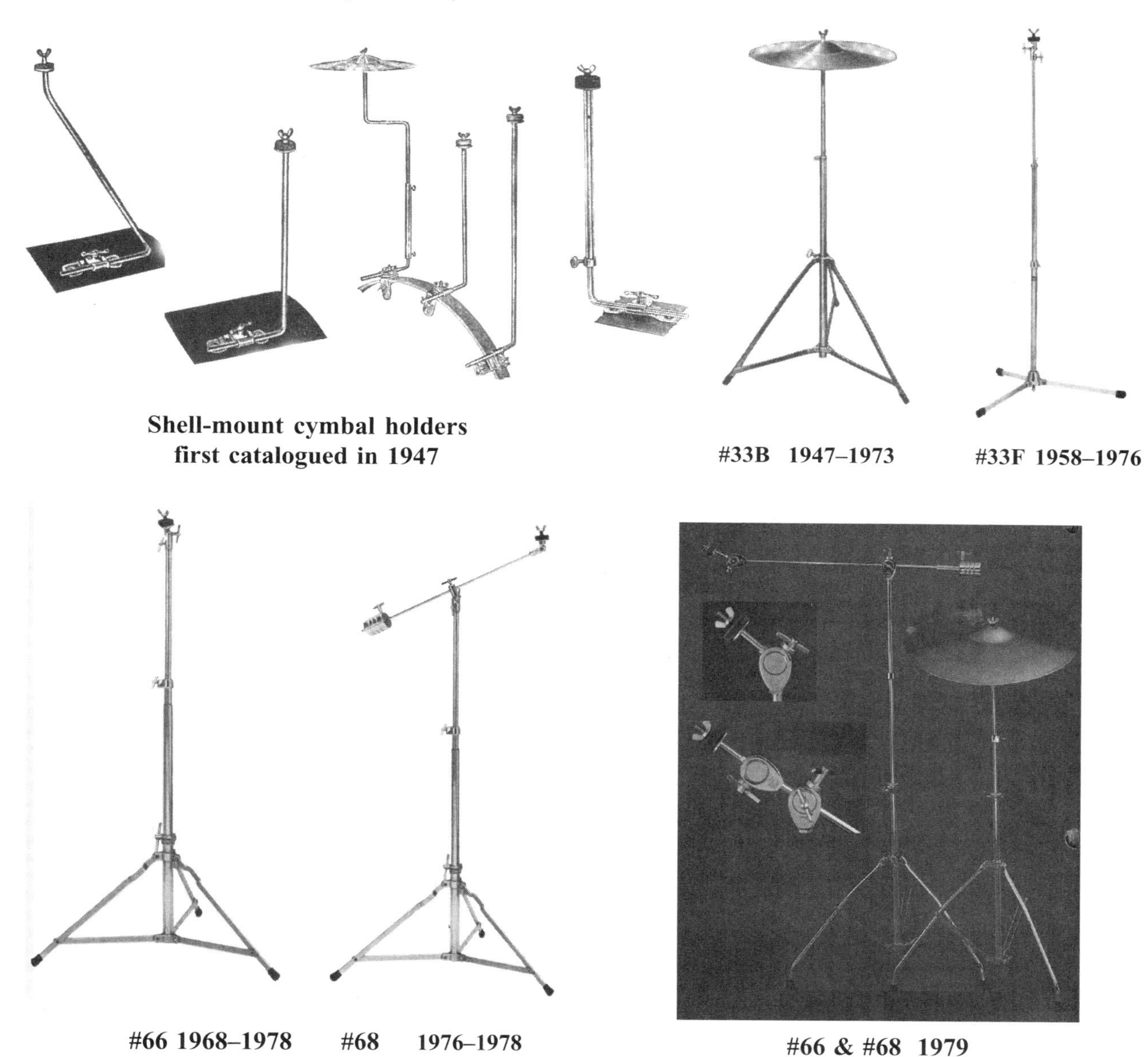

Shell-mount cymbal holders first catalogued in 1947

#33B 1947–1973

#33F 1958–1976

#66 1968–1978

#68 1976–1978

#66 & #68 1979

Not shown: Other designs of shell-mount holders (retractable, etc.), '80s imported (Magnum) hardware.

Hi-hats

#805 Sock Cymbal Pedal
1928–1938

#944 "Wow" Cymbal Pedal
1930–1932

#839 Holmes Afterbeat Attachment
1936 only

#835 Featherweight
1936 only
(2 lbs. 15 ounces)

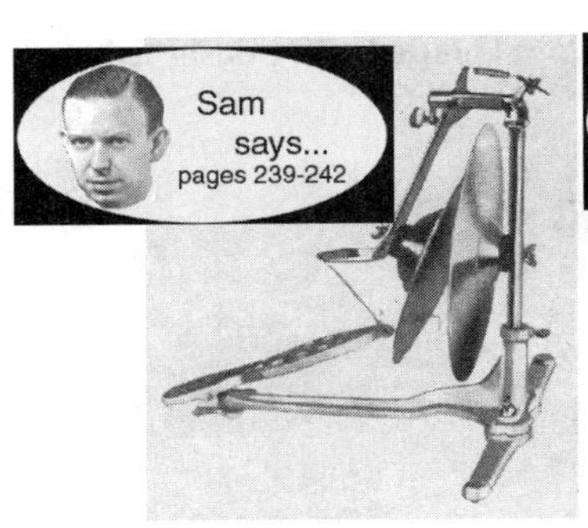

#1468 "Duncan" Sock Cymbal Pedal
1932–1936

#1114 Duncan Pressed-Steel Pedal
1934–1938

#837 Wowsok Cymbal Pedal 1936 only

#837 Professional
1939–1968
(height 30" to 33")

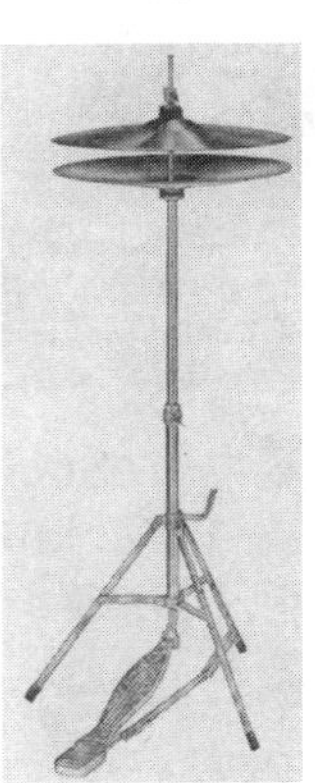

#836 Krupa
1949–1973
(height 24" to 36")

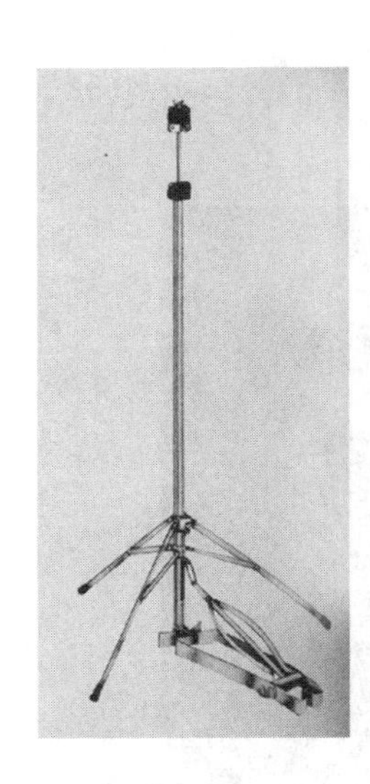

#804
1930–1939
1962–1973 as #835

#804 (Direct Pull)
1962–1979
A design improvement of the first flush base hi-hat, the 803, introduced in 1958.

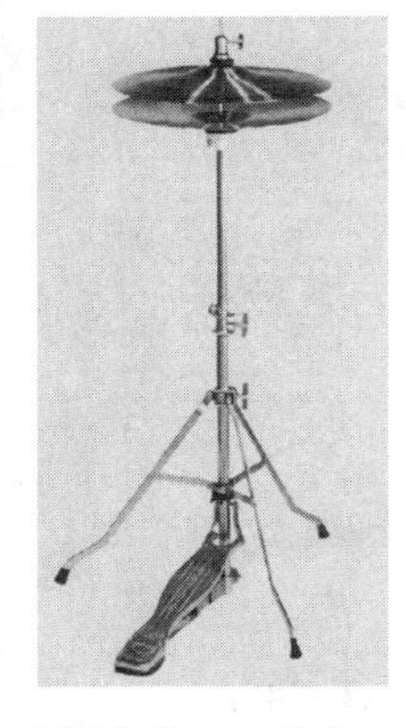

#808 Smoothie
1969–1973

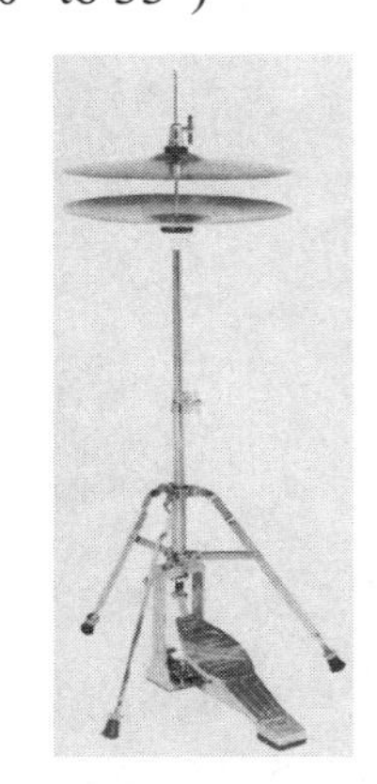

#806 Dynamo
1969–1979

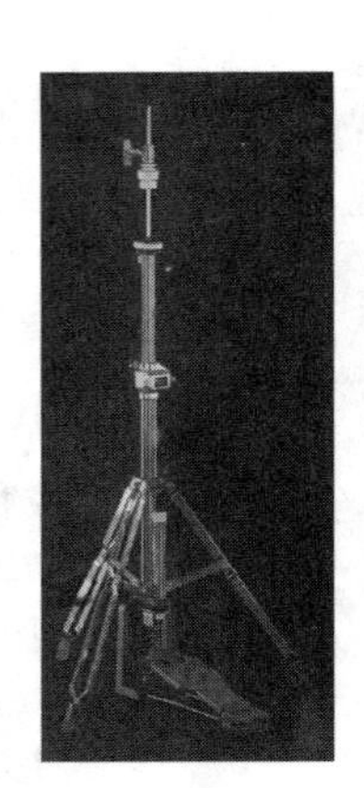

#1965 Magnum
1983-1985

Slingerland and cymbals

Slingerland's first drum catalog featured two brands of "Slingerland Oriental Cymbals": K. Zildjian cymbals made in Constantinople and Italian-made Ajaha cymbals at about half the price. (Cheaper brass cymbals were also listed.)

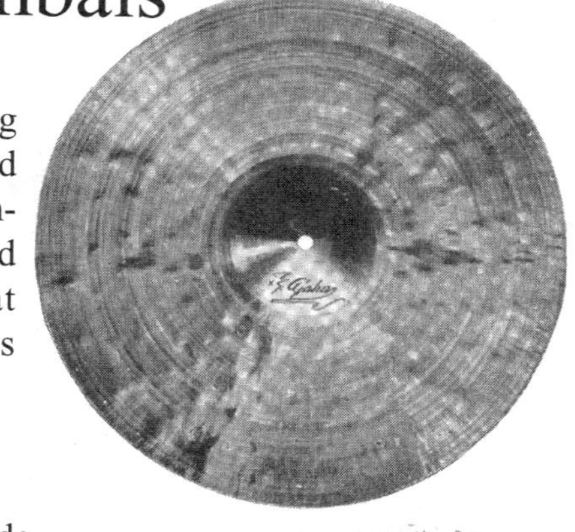

Alejian (a private-label brand made for Slingerland by Zildjian) replaced Ajaha in 1930 and Avedis Zildjian replaced K Zildjian in 1934. These two lines were the only cymbals listed by Slingerland until 1947 when they added a third line. "Genuine Tuscanese" cymbals were imported from Europe and were a little cheaper than the Alejian cymbals. This was the lineup through 1967.

From 1968 through 1971 the three cymbal lines Slingerland catalogued were the Avedis Zildjian cymbals, Genuine Zilco Cymbals (about 40% cheaper than Avedis Zildjian), and Slingerland Deluxe Cymbals (about 24% less than Avedis Zildjian cymbals). The Zilco cymbals were made in Meductic, New Brunswick, Canada from the same alloy as Avedis Zildjian cymbals, but with a shortened manufacturing process. In 1973 the Zilco line was replaced by the Alejian brand which, again, was a private-label line manufactured by Zildjian specifically for Slingerland.

In 1976 Slingerland printed the first catalog in the company's 48-year history which did not include Zildjian cymbals. The only cymbals included were the Italian-made Kashian cymbals. Zildjian distribution resumed in 1977 and continued along with Kashian through the early '80s.

A rift in the Zildjian family resulted in a division of assets in 1981. Armand got the Avedis Zildjian Company in Massachusetts, while brother Robert got the Canadian manufacturing facility which he developed into Sabian. The 1983 Slingerland catalog listed only Sabian cymbals, and was the last Slingerland catalog to include cymbals.

Bass Drum Pedals

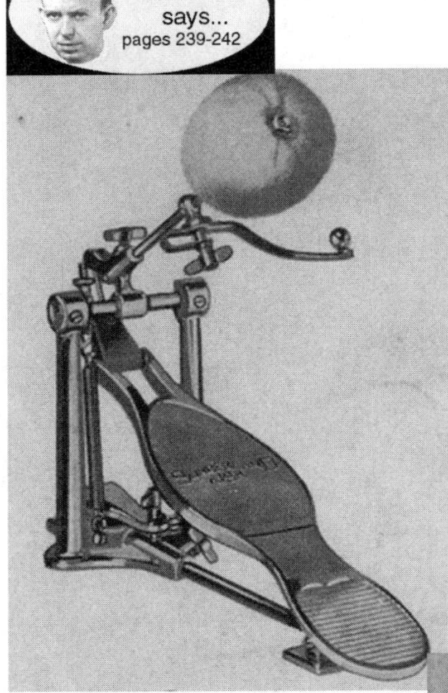

#724 Speed Pedal
1928–1949
1930 only– holes in footboard
(part # changed to 725 in '47)

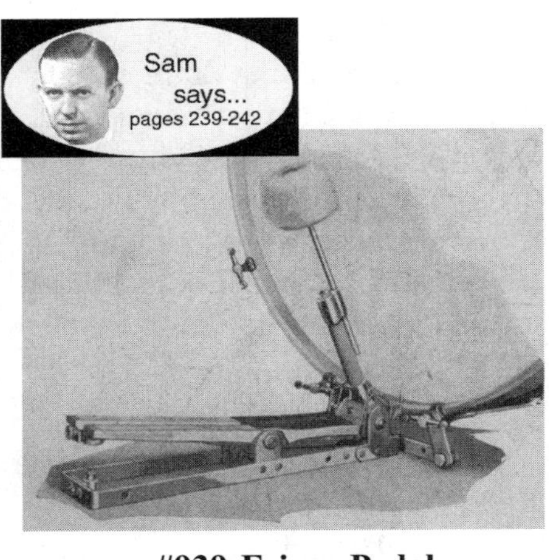

#939 Frisco Pedal
1934–1936

#726 Junior Pedal
1928–1941
(1928's version featured a swiveling footboard)

HH
1947-1949

#940 Epic
1934–1971
Changed to #939 in 1947.
Black until 1963, then red.

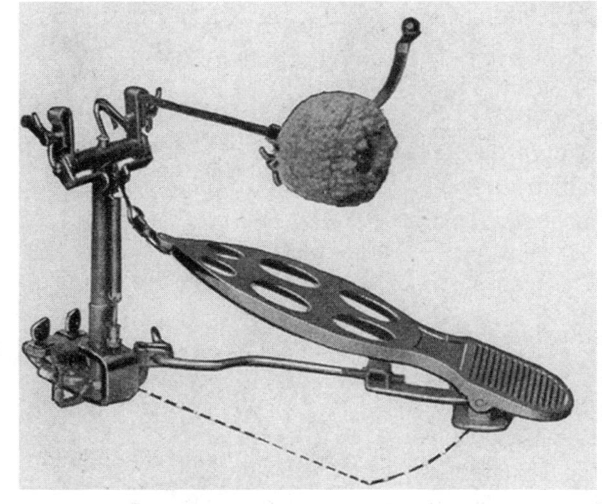

#725 Perfection Universal
1928–1932

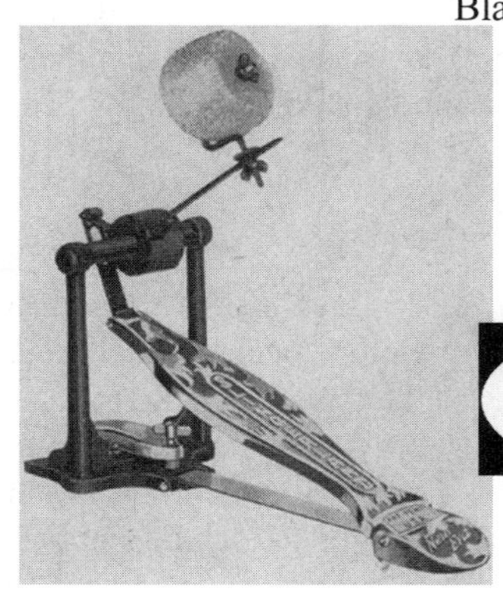

#1550 New Era
1934–1936

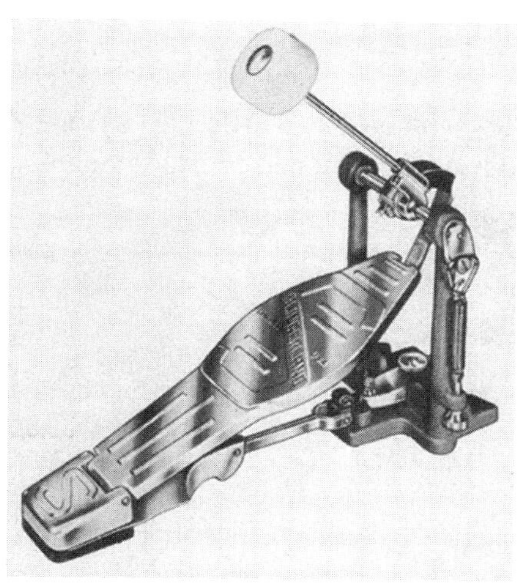

#938 Tempo King
1963–1979
"Snap-On" 940W (wood rims)
& 940M (metal rims) '65–'70

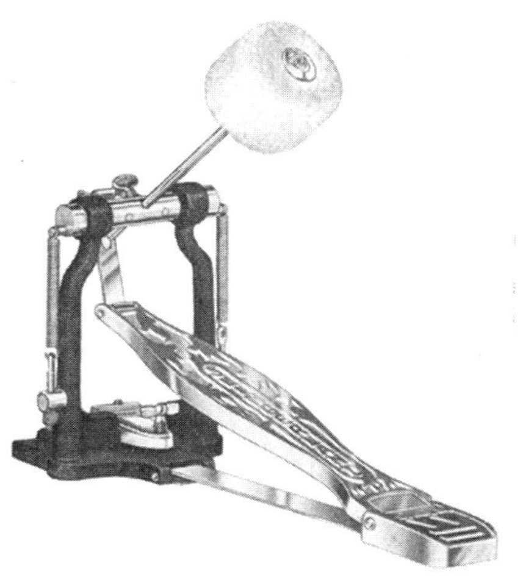

AA
1953–1967
Black 1953–1957
Blue 1958–1967

Leedy XL
1956–1965

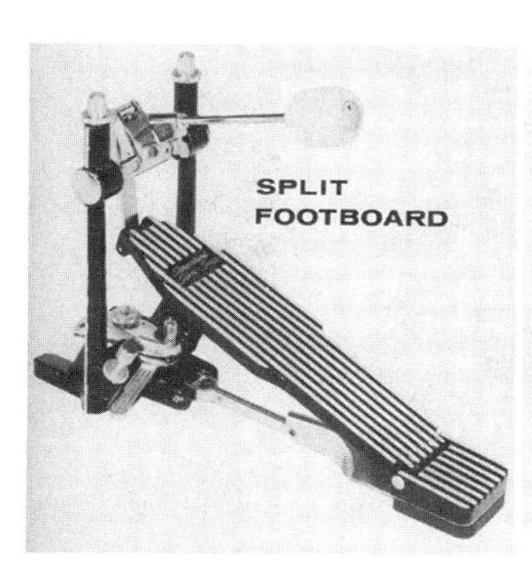

#942 Super Speed
1973–1978

#941 Super Speed
1971–1978

#944
1979–1983
(Also yellow #943 in 1979)

Leedy #1938
Shelly Manne Pedal
1965

Leedy #1940M,W
1965
wood (W) or metal (M) hoops

Snare Drum Stands

Through the years there were numerous variations on the snare drum stands shown here. The differences from the models shown here, however, were slight such as height differences and models designed to accomodate drums larger than 14".

From the first catalog through 1954 all catalogued Slingerland snare drum stands were close variations of the 801 and 897. The 801 was supplied with higher-end outfits, the 897 with cheaper outfits. First appearing in the 1930 catalog, these two stands were in the Slingerland line for decades. The 897 was discontinued in 1965, while the 801 was still in the line in 1979!

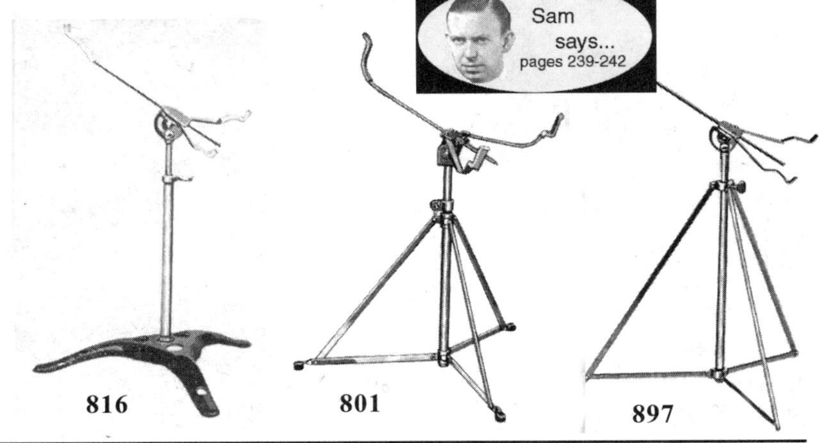

816 **801** **897**

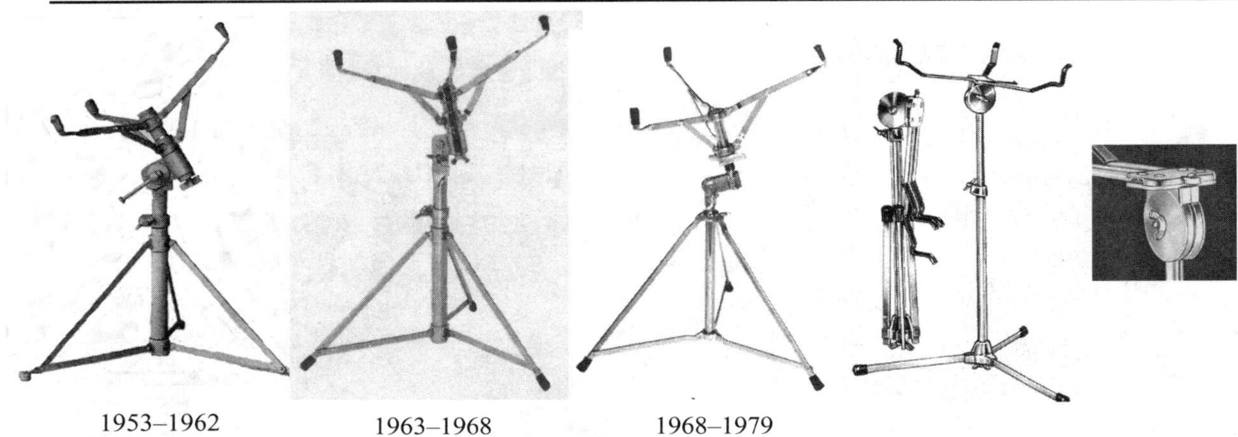

1953–1962 1963–1968 1968–1979

#1382 Super-Grip
1953–1979
Introduced in 1953, this stand was renamed the Rocket in 1968 when Slingerland made it standard equipment on higher-end outfits.

#802 Flush Base
1958–1979
When introduced in 1958, this became standard equipment with all outfits. The ratchet allowed angle adjustment at one-degree intervals.

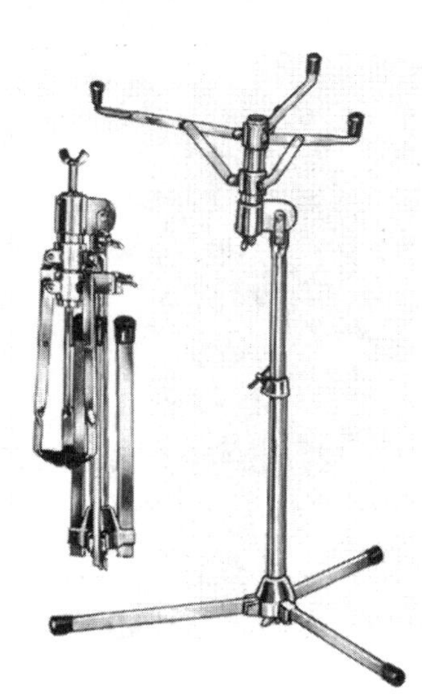

#805 Buck Rogers
1958–1976
The Buck Rogers drum stand was produced by Walberg & Auge. (The stand was named by Hollywood drumming legend Andy Florio in the '40s when he ordered the stand that "looks like a Buck Rogers ray pistol".

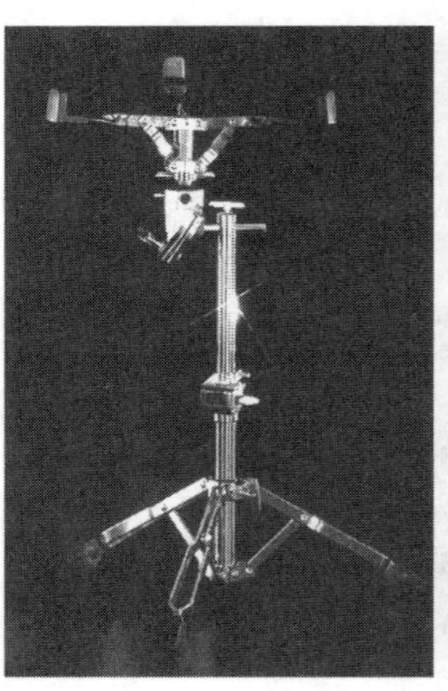

Magnum (left) and Spirit stands
1983-1985 (imported)

SLINGERLAND'S STRAINER STORY

The 813 JUNIOR THROW-OFF

Used on Slingerlands first bottom-of-the-line models. This strainer was discontinued some time before 1934.

The 674 SHUR-GRIP

Replaced the Junior Throw-Off on the Universal models in 1934.

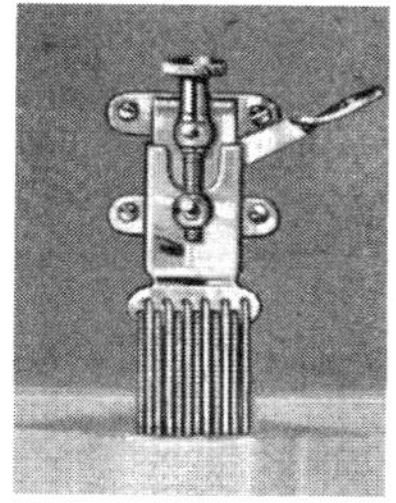

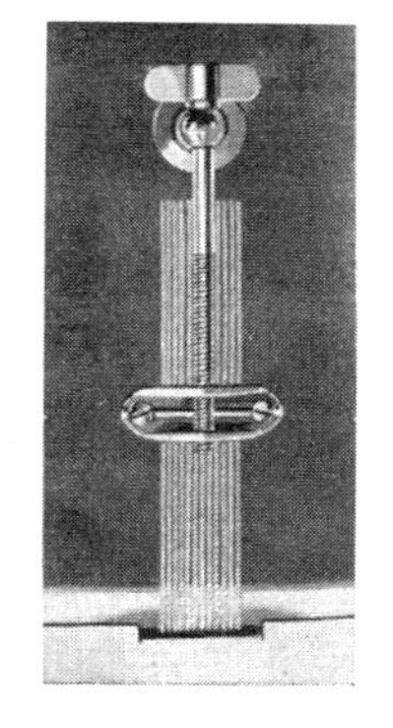

672 POST STRAINER

Replaced the Junior Throw-Off on the Juvenile snare models in 1934. This strainer was sold on all parade drums in 1928. From 1934 on it was sold only on the lower-priced parade drums. This strainer was discontinued in the early '40's (wartime).

673 POST STRAINER

The 673 Parade drum strainer remained pretty much unchanged from its introduction in 1934 until 1958 when is was finally replaced by the Rapid Steet Drum Strainer The stock number was not changed; the Rapid Street Drum Strainer was also given stock #673.

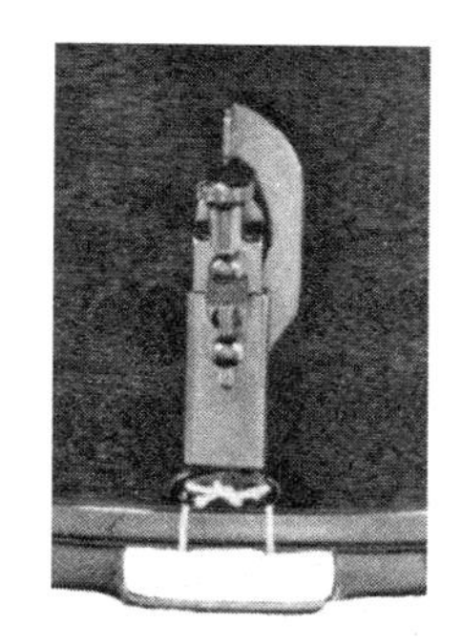

673 RAPID STRAINER

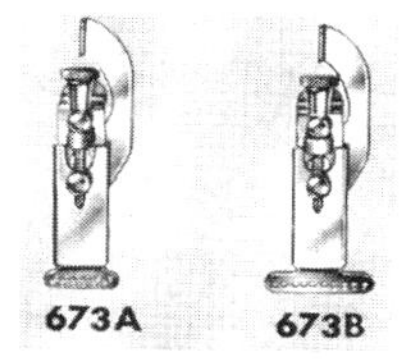

From 1947 to 1957 there were two versions of the 673 post strainer; regular and the wide-gate model. These were replaced by two versions of the Rapid Strainer, above.

The Three-Point Shur-Grip

This strainer was used on Junior model drums from 1934 to 1941. (Junior models were discontinued during the war, and brought back in 1953. This strainer was used again then, until 1957.)

Small Post Strainer

The Junior Model was equipped with this small post strainer from 1958 to 1964 when it was discontinued.

The DUALL Strainer

(For more on the Duall drum, see page XX.)

A solid shaft passed through the drum, an early "parallel" mechanism

The Duall drum did not stay in the Slingerland line long because of patent difficulties. There are relatively few of these drums around today.

This snare setup was ahead of its time in that the snares were permanently fastened in plated brass end-plates and arranged so that they could not touch each other. It took less than a minute for the player to change from one set of snares to another by simply loosening screws in plates at both ends of the strainer. The three available snare options were coiled wire, gut, and wire-wound silk.

The "Three-Point" Strainer

Slingerland never actually referred to any of their strainers as "three-point" strainers; this is a term that collectors in recent years have coined, and often use interchangeably with the term "Krupa Strainer" to refer to a number of Slingerland strainers, all of which attach to the shell at three points. The first of the "Three-point" strainers was in Slingerland's first catalog (1928) and was referred to by Slingerland as both The Professional Throw-Off, and The Speedy Sure Hold Snare Strainer.

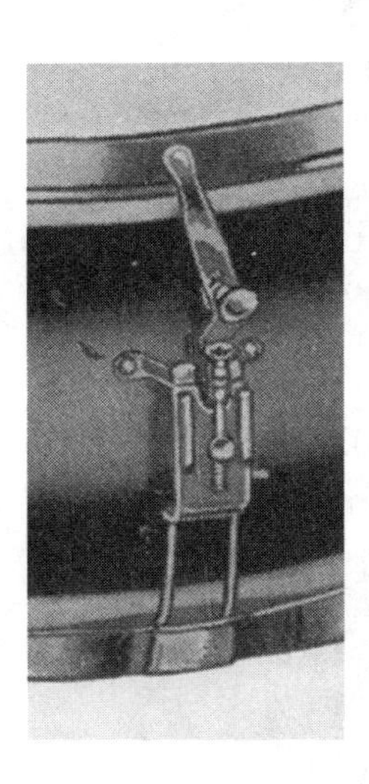

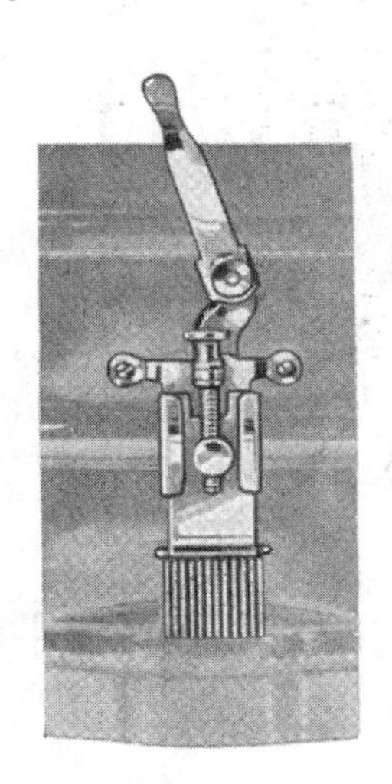

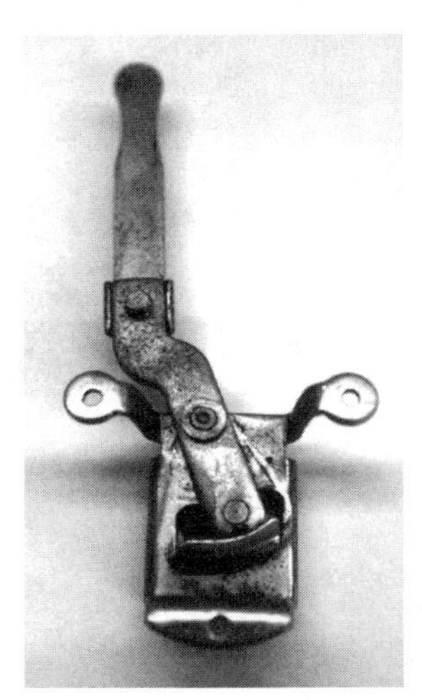

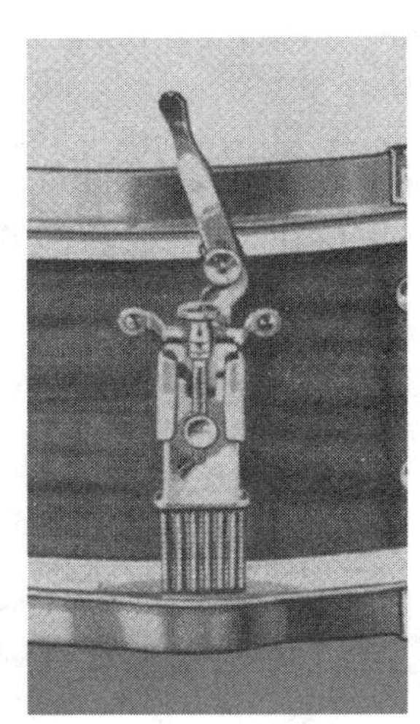

The 1934 catalog refers to this strainer not only as the Instant Throw-Off Lever but also as the Rapid Throw-Off Muffler Strainer.

The 1936 catalog refers to this strainer as the "Professional Throw-Off Muffler Strainer" and (on the parts page) as the "Speedy Snare Strainer".

While this strainer has had many names, the stock number remained constant; it was the 967. The original 967 strainer flanged in toward the drum at the bottom. This flange had holes through which the snares were looped, to be secured with the butt on the other side of the drum.

The strainer release lever extended above the rim of the drum, so the drummer could quickly and easily release the snares. The earlier levers extended further above the edge of the drum (above, right; pre-WWII) while post-WWII models were shorter (above left; cut from the 1948 catalog).

The RADIO KING Strainer

It has unfortunately become the custom among vintage drum dealers and collectors to refer to all Slingerland solid-shell wood drums as Radio Kings and to *not* consider any drum a Radio King *unless* it has a one-piece (as opposed to plied) shell. What *really* distinguished the Radio King models from other Slingerland drums were the "Radio King Brackets" which drew the tension on the snares *outward* rather than *upward.*

When the Radio King drums were introduced in 1936, the "brackets" called for a modification of the 967 strainer. The strainer shown here, with the flange *out* away from the drum shell for Radio King use was identified as the 967B, while the old-style 967 became known as the 967A.

From 1941 to 1974 the 967B had just one single screw hole rather than multiple holes for the snares. This was because the Radio King snare sets were secured with aluminum straps which had single holes to align with the strainer hole.

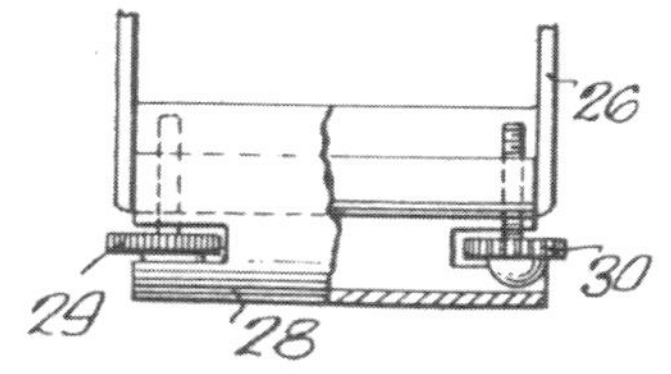

From their introduction until 1938, little leveling knobs provided fine tuning on both the snare and butt side. (Parts 29 and 30 in patent drawings.)

The 967A would in 1948 be renamed the Rapid strainer. (It remained unchanged except the name.) It retained that name until the #673 (see previous page) was introduced. (To further confuse the issue, the 1955 catalog refers to a 967A as a Radio King strainer (though it's mounted on a drum without the RK brackets) and to the 967B as a Rapid Strainer.)

The upper section of the three-point strainers, which originally had been a separate piece secured by a thumbscrew so it could be swiveled down out of the way for transporting (and some playing situations), was eventually made an integral part of the strainer. The first catalog parts page to show this change was 1963, though the change was certainly made much earlier— possibly as early as the late '40s. These strainers were referred to (in the parts section of the 1963 catalog) as Radio King Strainers; the 967B was identified for use with the metal strap snares, while the 967A had 12 holes for gut, silk, or wire snares.

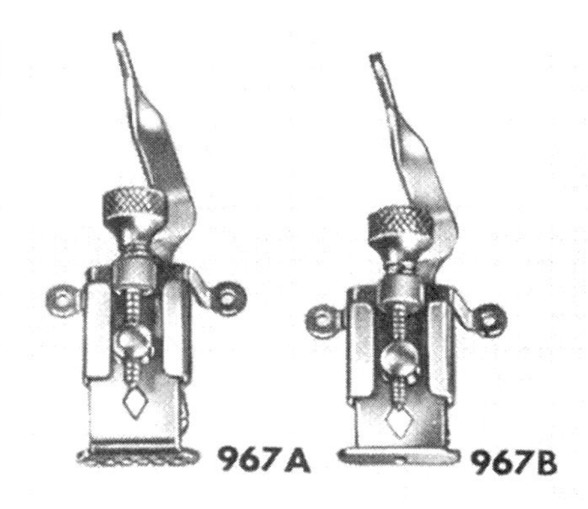

Radio King Patent

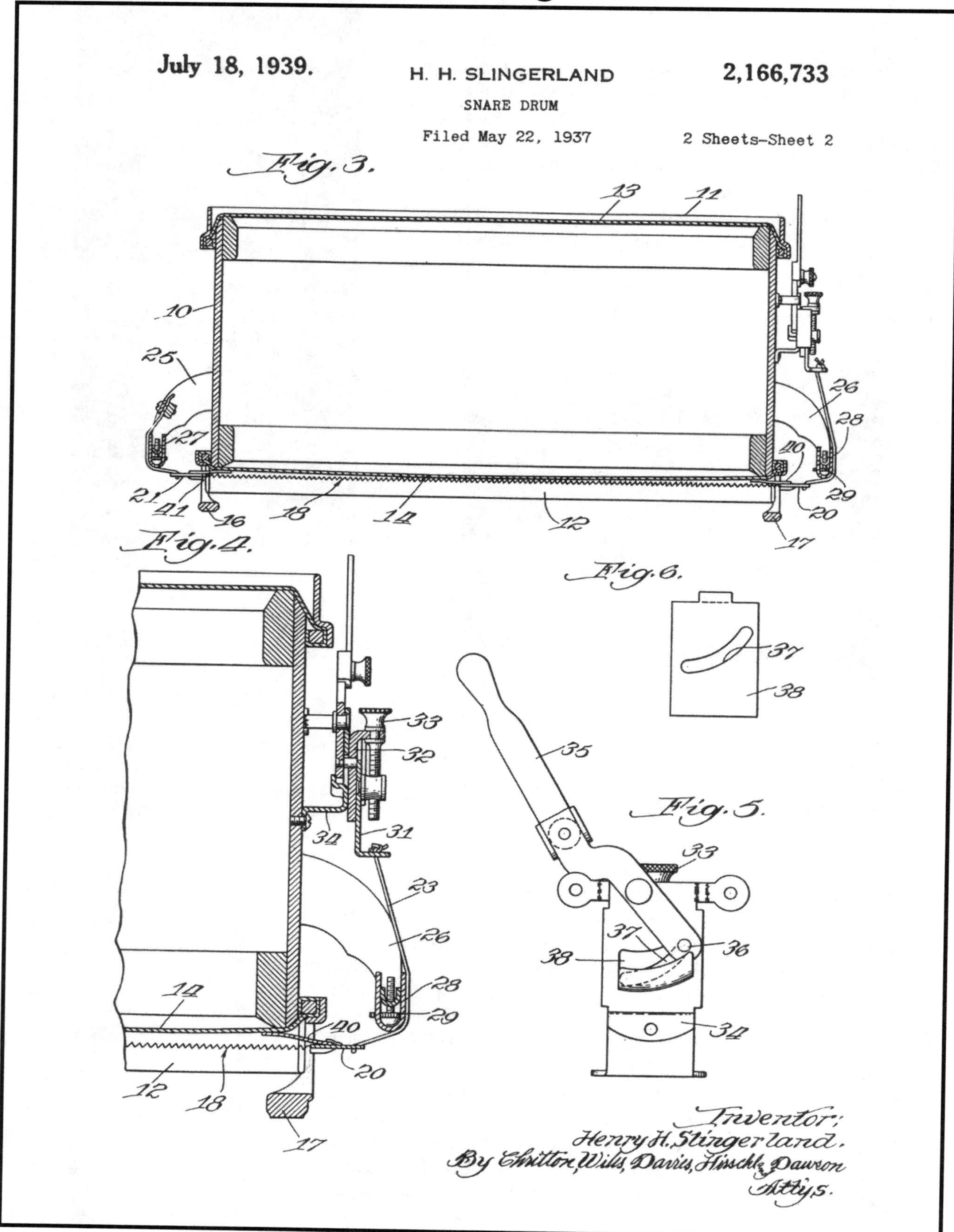

The Super Strainer (Clamshell)

The Super Strainer is commonly known as the clamshell strainer among today's collectors and dealers. This strainer was introduced in 1940. It seemed like a good idea at the time, but the telescoping levers generally have not weathered the years well; most found today have been broken off. (At this writing, no after-market replacement levers are being produced.)

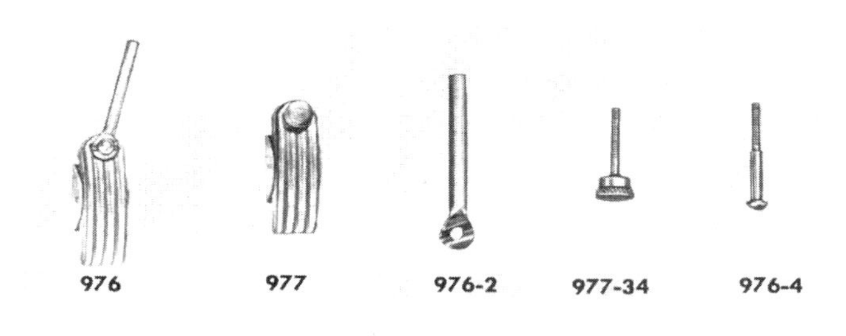

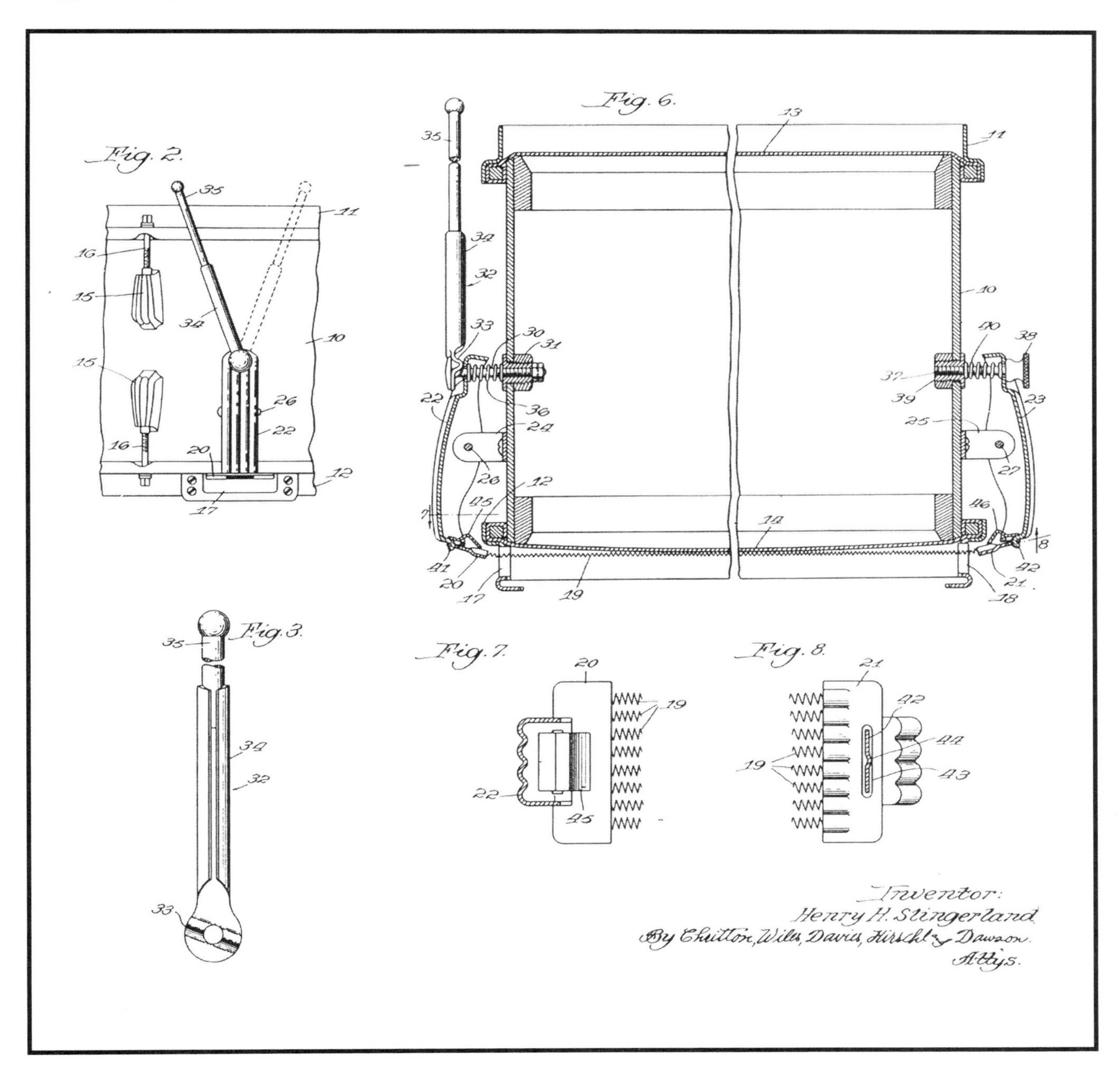

A unique aspect of the clamshell strainer is that tension adjustment was located on one side, while the throw-off mechanism was on the other.

The Dual Super Snare Strainer

Super Sound King with Dual Strainer

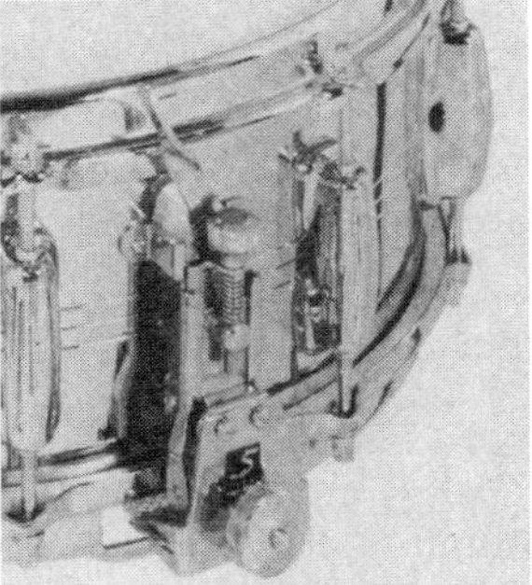

Dual Throwoff

Dual Butt

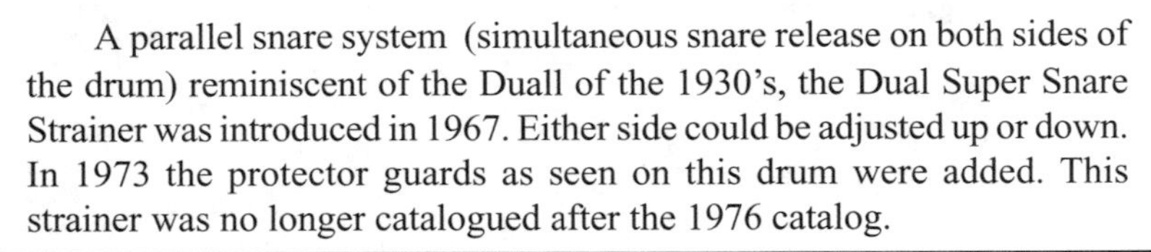

A parallel snare system (simultaneous snare release on both sides of the drum) reminiscent of the Duall of the 1930's, the Dual Super Snare Strainer was introduced in 1967. Either side could be adjusted up or down. In 1973 the protector guards as seen on this drum were added. This strainer was no longer catalogued after the 1976 catalog.

The Zoomatic Strainer

In about 1964 the Zoomatic strainer replaced the clamshell strainer. This strainer remains in the Slingerland line to the time of this writing— over 30 years.

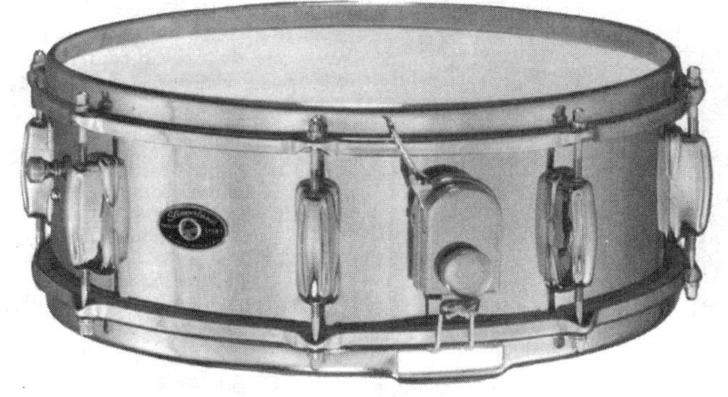

1964 Gene Krupa Sound King (brass shell) snare drum with the then-new Zoomatic strainer.

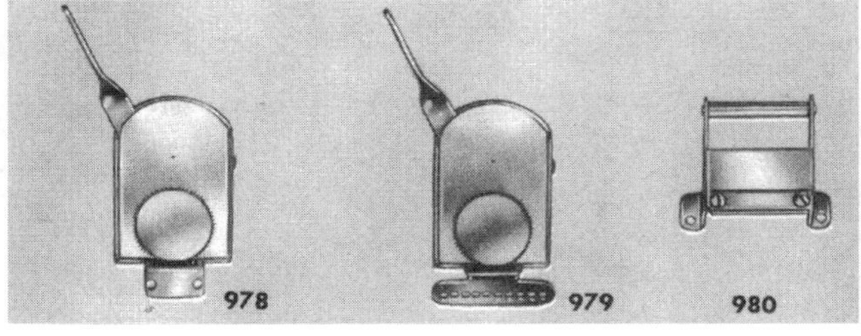

By 1965 the knob was reduced in size and a large "Slingerland" was stamped on the strainer.

The TDR Snare Strainer

The TDR strainer first showed up in the 1973 catalog referred to only as a "completely new strainer." It was introduced as the TDR in the 1976 catalog. It combined the simplicity of the 673 Rapid strainer with the Radio King bracket design that carries the snares all the way off the head. This design remained in the Slingerland line through the mid 1990s.

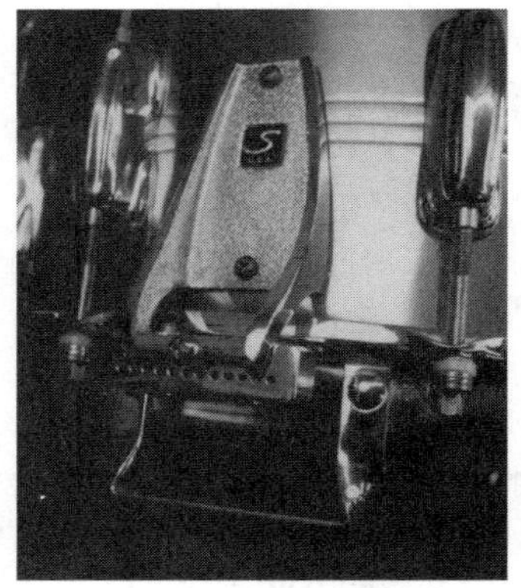

TDR Strainer, Cont'd.

The TDR came in two "flavors": the standard unit as seen in the parts diagram here, and a gut-snare version which had individually adjustable snares similar to Ludwig's super-sensitive. By 1983 only the standard version was catalogued.

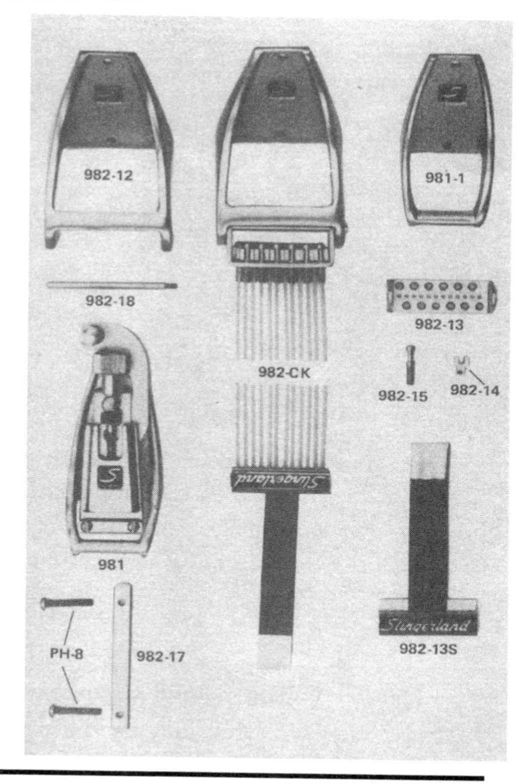

No. 981 "TDR™" Strainer:

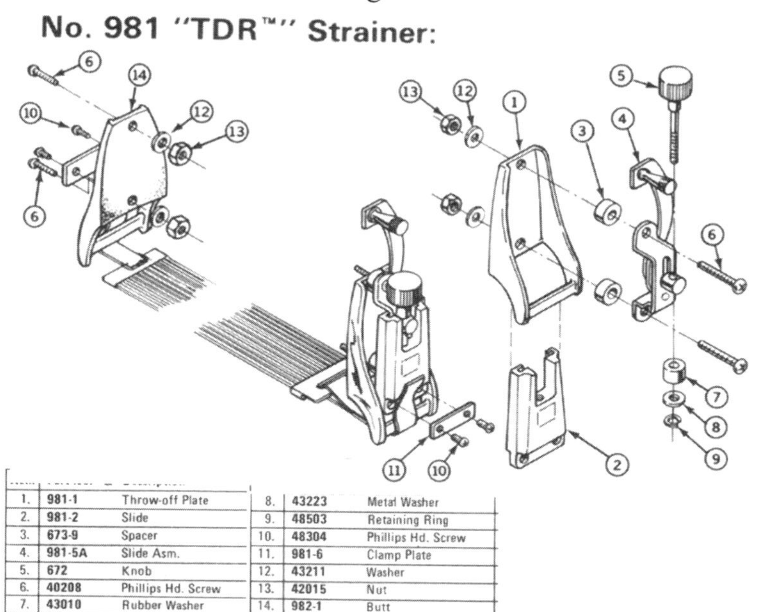

1.	981-1	Throw-off Plate	8.	43223	Metal Washer
2.	981-2	Slide	9.	48503	Retaining Ring
3.	673-9	Spacer	10.	48304	Phillips Hd. Screw
4.	981-5A	Slide Asm.	11.	981-6	Clamp Plate
5.	672	Knob	12.	43211	Washer
6.	40208	Phillips Hd. Screw	13.	42015	Nut
7.	43010	Rubber Washer	14.	982-1	Butt

Slapshot Snare Strainer

The Slapshot snare strainer was introduced in the early 80's. The snares remained under tension even when the strainer is thrown off, like the parallel mechanisms of the Duall and Dual. Individual snares could be tuned on the gut snare version which, like the TDR, used a different butt. The name for the strainer came from the large throw-off handle which worked so smoothly that Slingerland purported all it took to throw the strainer off or on was a slap of the hand. The Slapshot became standard equipment on all TDR snare series snare drums and remained in the line until 1986.

No. 982 "Slap-Shot™" Strainer:

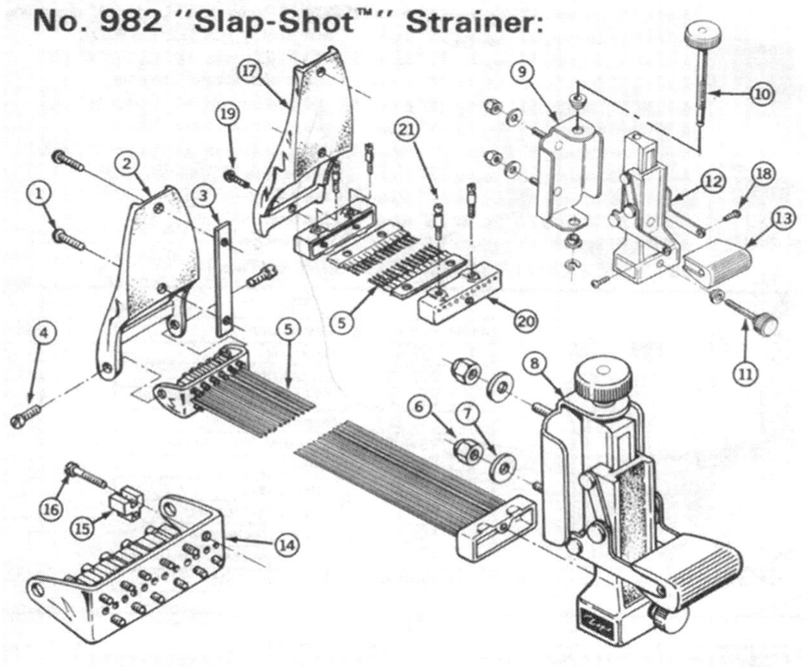

Item	Part No. &	Description	Qty.
1.	40208	Phillips Hd. Screw	2
2.	982-12	Butt (for Gut Snares)	1
3.	982-17	Strap Nut	1
4.	983-9	Screw	2
5.	Snare Units - See Price List		
6.	42018	Nut	2
7.	43215	Washer	2
8.	983	Slap Shot Strainer Asm.	1
9.	983-104	Base Asembly	1
10.	983-105	Adjustment Screw	1
11.	983-106	Tension Screw, Bushing & "E" Ring	1
12.	983-200	Slide Sub-Assembly	1
13.	983-4	Handle	1
14.	982-13	Snare Bar	1
15.	982-14	Adjusting Block	12
16.	982-15	Adjusting Screw	12
17.	981-12	Butt (for Wire Snares)	1
18.	40224	Handle Screw	2
19.	40203	Phillips Hd. Screw	1
20.	983-1	Snare Bar	2
21.	985-3	Adjusting Post	4

(Slingerland Era) Leedy Strainers

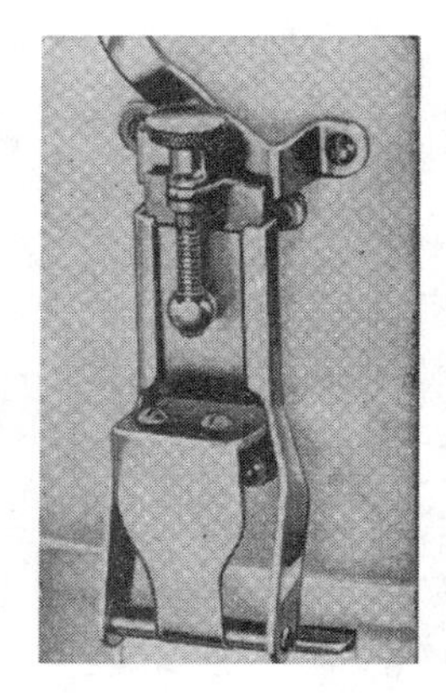

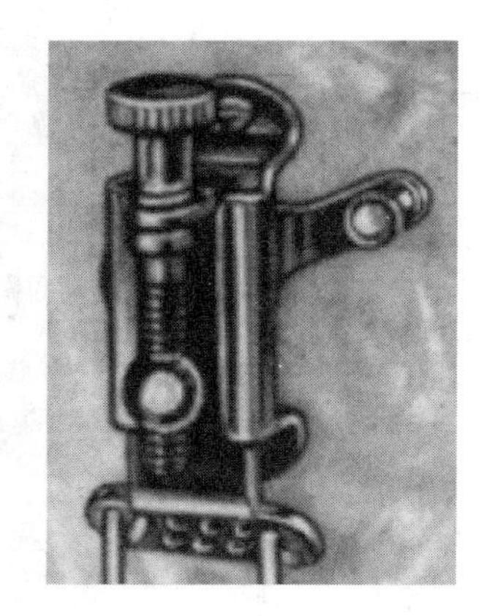

The Broadway Extension snare strainer (left) was an older Leedy design that Slingerland kept in the line. The Pioneer snare strainer (center, which was a Ludwig design) was replaced by a Leedy version (right, #1673) of the Slingerland Rapid strainer (#673).

The Leedy Three-Point strainer was similar enough to the Slingerland #967 that they used the Slingerland #967 art for catalog depiction of the Leedy #1967.

Our tip-off that the strainer at right is a #1967 Leedy strainer (other than the fact that it's on a Leedy drum) is the diamond-shaped hole in the lower section. Most key parts for these two strainers are not interchangable.

The patent on the Slingerland strainer was granted to H.H. Slingerland Sr., while a patent on the Leedy strainer was granted to Conn engineer Leroy Jeffries (a former Leedy, Indianapolis, employee).

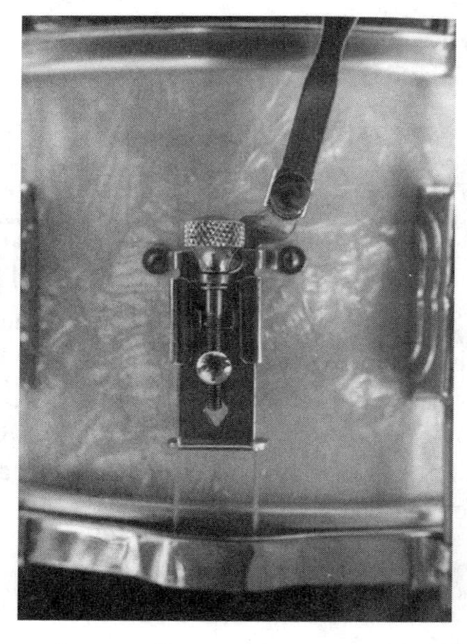

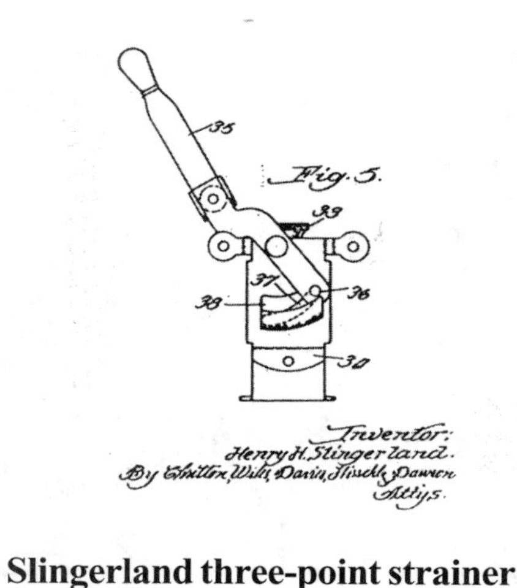

Slingerland three-point strainer

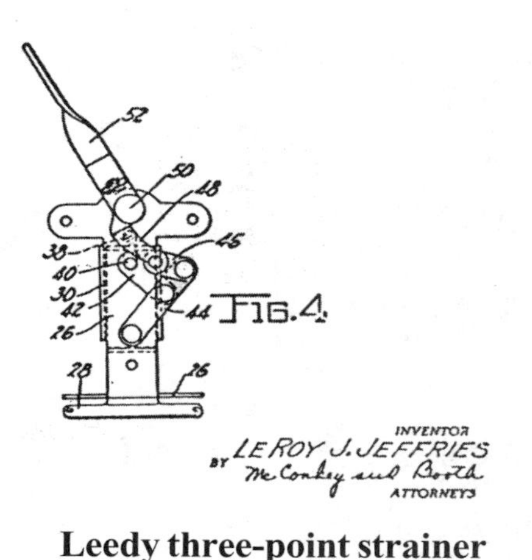

Leedy three-point strainer

HOOPS

Belly Slim

Slingerland offered flat metal counterhoops (#669), single-flanged counter hoops (#670), and double flanged (#671, described in the catalog as "Metal counterhoops with protective apron") from the beginning. Through 1936 the 669 flat counterhoop was available only in nickel. The other two hoops were available in nickel, chrome, or art-gold. Art-gold was discontinued by 1936.

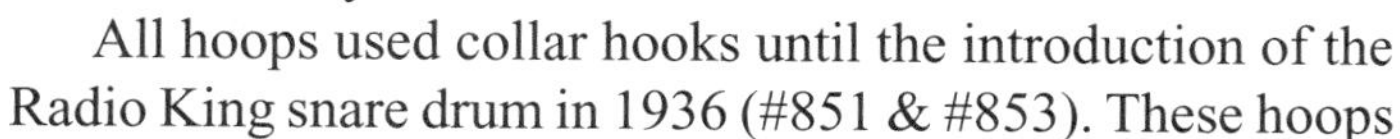

All hoops used collar hooks until the introduction of the Radio King snare drum in 1936 (#851 & #853). These hoops were called the “Radio King Full-flanged metal counterhoops.” Tom-tom hoops were not produced in this style until about 1948. Gradually the hoops requiring collar hooks were supplied on fewer and fewer models, but remained in the catalogs through the late 1960’s.

At least two types of collar hooks have been sold by Slingerland, though never at the same time: parts sections of catalogs always list only one and identify it as the #974 collar hook. Some collectors refer to the two styles below as the “belly” (left; stamped from one piece of metal and kind of “cheesy”) and the “slim” (right; a brazed assembly).

HARDWARE PLATING

NICKEL– It is fairly easy to distinguish between chrome and nickel on older drums, particularly if the drums have not been very recently polished; the nickel is far more tarnished. Highly polished nickel can be nearly as shiny as chrome, but is closer to a yellowish tint than the bluish tint of chrome.

BLACK BEAUTY– The “Black Beauty” drums made by Slingerland and Ludwig in the ’20s and ’30s were actually brass shells dipped in an oxidizing bath. Newer re-issue drums were actually plated with a black finish.

ARTGOLD– A simulated gold plating. (Lacquered copper plating.) This was an option on most models in the first catalog (1928), but soon became available on fewer and fewer models. By 1936 it was offered only on the Patrician outfit— a top-of-the-line outfit. By 1937 it had disappeared from the catalogs altogether.

TUTONE– In the late 1920s, Tutone referred to solid finish drums with Artgold plated hardware. The Artist model bass drums were offered in 1928 in a highly polished walnut finish with all fittings Artgold plated. Artist Tutone model snare drums were offered in Walnut, Mahogany, White Enamel, and Black Ebonized shells.

GENUINE GOLD– While Slingerland may well have custom-made an odd drum here and there through the years with genuine gold plating, the Artist Model listing in the 1928 catalog was the only gold-plated catalog offering.

CHROME– Slingerland began chrome plating in 1934. At first a slightly more expensive optional substitute for nickel on only a few models, chrome eventually was available on everything in the line. Nickel was not totally discontinued until 1959.

The Radio King snare mechanism dictated that Slingerland bring back the snare gate they first introduced on the Duall drum.

The 1936 Artist Model snare drums also sported full-flanged hoops with tension rod ears, but did not need the snare gate. The snare-side hoop instead was simply bent back away from the drum a bit (below left).

The Radio King hoops were engraved. Up until 1948, the Radio King (and all other) tom hoops were single-flanged hoops requiring collar clips.

Radio King Hoop Engraving

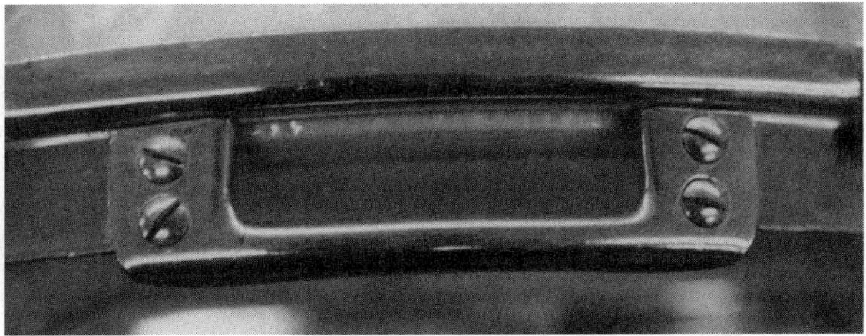

The snare gate on the earliest Radio King models (like the gate on the Duall) was about the same width as the snare set and was fastened to the hoop with machine bolts (above left). After 1942 the gate was wider and secured with machine bolts for a brief time (above right), then rivets (below left). Snare-side hoops with a simple cutout for the snare (below right) were introduced in 1955 and were standard equipment on mid-priced snare drums and parade drums.

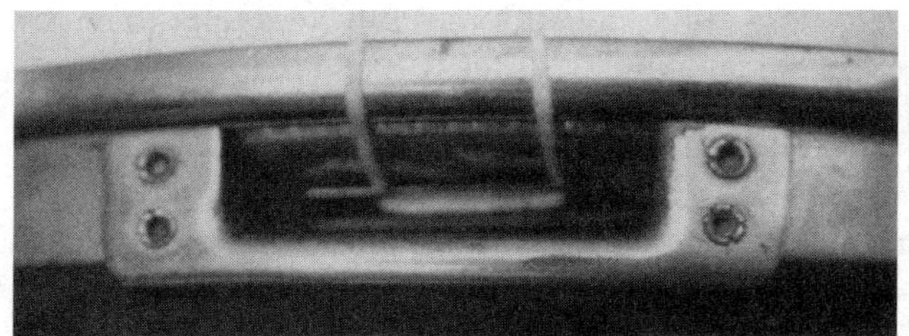

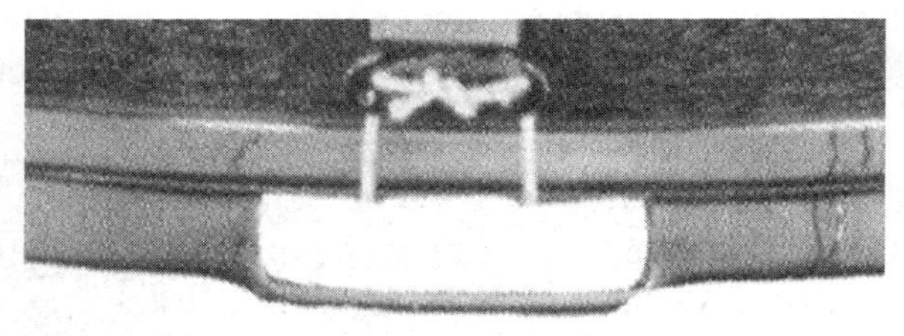

The triple-flanged hoop....

Slingerlands triple-flanged hoops have always been distinctive from their competitors because theirs are the only ones which flange inward toward the middle of the drum rather than outward. Introduced in 1955, these patented hoops were made of brass until 1973 except for a brief, almost experimental, batch of aluminum hoops in the late 50's. The drums equipped with these hoops were very light, and the hoops required no plating. They were not, however, attractive enought to catch on. All drum hoops were steel from 1973 forward until 1993 when the reissue Radio King snare drums were once again fitted with brass hoops.

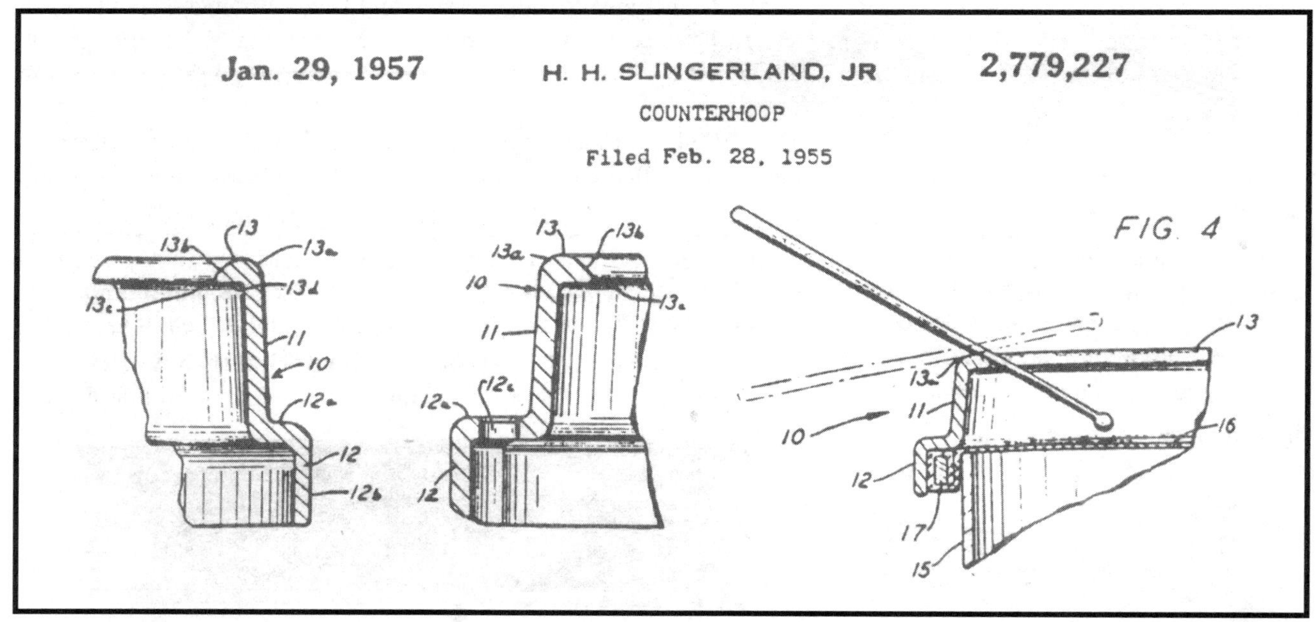

A letter dated July 25th, 1958 was sent with the first mailing of the 1959 catalog, announcing that the height of the hoop represented by "11" in the above diagram had been reduced and that the width of the hoop represented by "12c" had been enlarged, to provide additional support of the flesh hoop.

Mufflers

Slingerland snare drums were not equipped with internal mufflers the first couple years, but by 1934 the catalog art indicated mufflers were being installed on the drums. The muffler was undoubtedly the single-pad version of the Harold R. Dodd muffler which got its name from its inventor. This muffler first appeared in the catalog as an accessory in 1934.

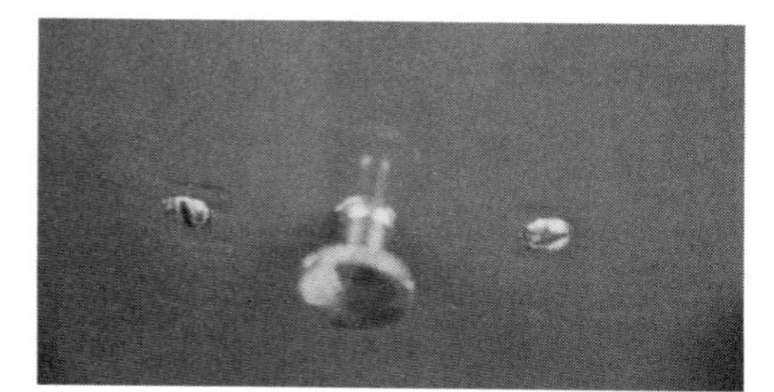

The Shur-Grip muffler #1465, catalogued from 1934 to 1940, was way ahead of its time. Rogers "reinvented" this muffler in the 1980s and their lead was followed by Yamaha, Tama, Pearl, and others. Besides not requiring holes in the drum shell, the muffler allows for a natural downward movement of the head as the drum is played, muffling the head on the "upswing."

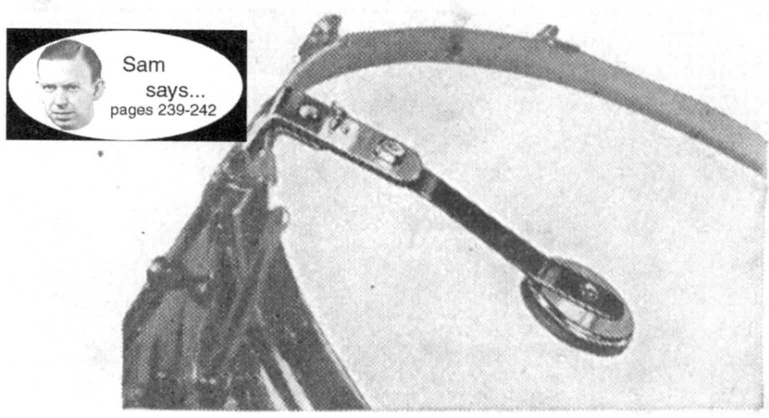

No. 1080

By 1936 the Harold R. Dodd muffler had two pads and was available in chrome (#1081) and nickel (stock #1080). Like the earlier single-pad version, each pad had a cup washer stamped "Slingerland, Chicago, ILL." The felt color was usually yellow, red, or green. Around 1942 the cup washers were eliminated and felt color was usually grey. The size of the knurled adjustment knob was also expanded; the newer ones were $^{5}/_{8}$", the older ones slightly smaller. The first (nickel) $^{5}/_{8}$" knobs had a flat-top (below, left), while newer (chrome) knobs were peaked. (below, right)

The 943 Shur-Grip bass drum muffler (left) was catalogued from 1934 to 1938. The 935 Deluxe Shur-Grip (right) remained in the line from its introduction in 1936 all the way to 1979.

The 1115 Epic bass drum muffler was only catalogued from 1934 to 1940.

The 933 Ray McKinley internal bass drum muffler was in the line from 1940 through 1978.

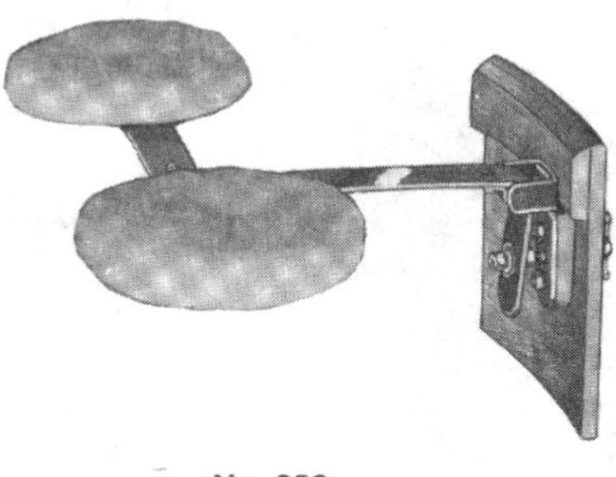

No. 933

Maybe they made it, maybe they didn't. When the Slingerland Double Pressure Tone Controls were announced in a early '50s sales flier they may have been "vapor-ware;" today's term for products which are introduced in prototype form, and brought into production only if the reception merits it. The blurb below is from George Way's copy of the introductory flier, to which he had added a note "Some of these items look pretty good— expect to make any of them?

SLINGERLAND DOUBLE PRESSURE TONE CONTROL

This is a new tone modulator which is available for snare drums in 5½", 6½", 7", and 8" shell depth sizes. It features INSTANTANEOUS throw off or on of the double pads with a clever lever flip. Thus the drummer can change with tremendous speed from open rolls, solos, etc. to a soft whisper. Modulating both heads gives drum a fine tone—follows sample principle as matching the heads. Simple installation diagrams and instruction shipped with the double modulator. When ordering be sure to indicate the exact SHELL DEPTH of the drum (not overall measurements). Simply measure between both head surfaces. In Chrome only.

No. **1085½** Double Flip Off Modulator, chrome 5½" shell.................**$10.50**
No. **1086½** Same for 6½" shell depth.................**10.50**
No. **1087** Same for 7" shell depth.................**10.50**
No. **1088** Same for 8" shell depth.................**10.50**

THE MODERN TONE CONTROL

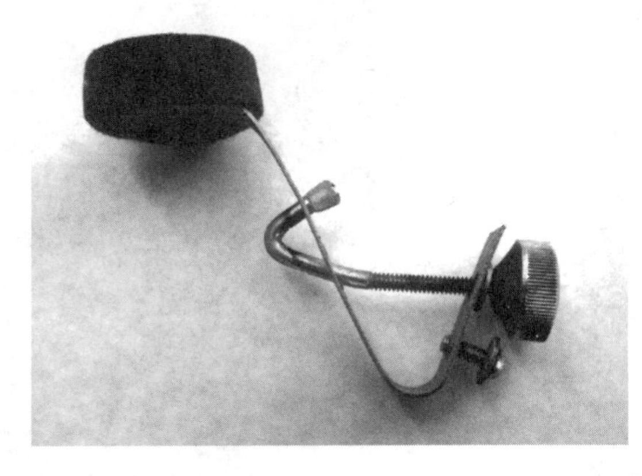

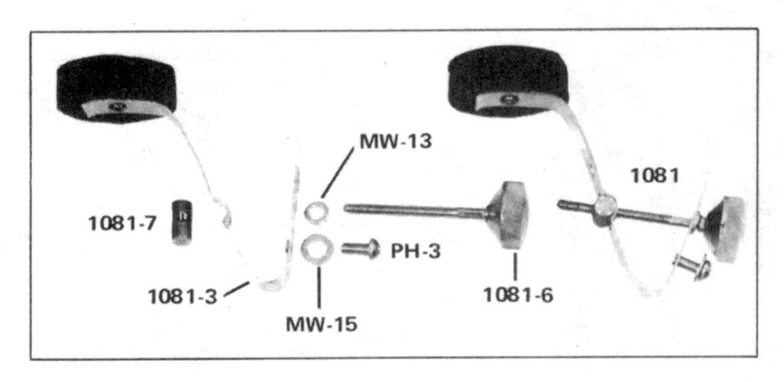

Introduced in the early 1960s as illustrated on the left. Changed to the post assembly shown in the parts cut on the right in about 1975.

Tunable tom 1936

Separate tension tom 1936
Designed by Krupa and Rowland

Chinese type toms 1940

Tenor Tymp tom 1936-41 (metal bottom)
This concept was revived on marching drums in the 1960s.

Single headed toms, 1941

Slingerland Lugs

Lugs as listed in the 1934 Slingerland catalog. From 1928 through 1934, all Slingerland drums were shipped with tube lugs.

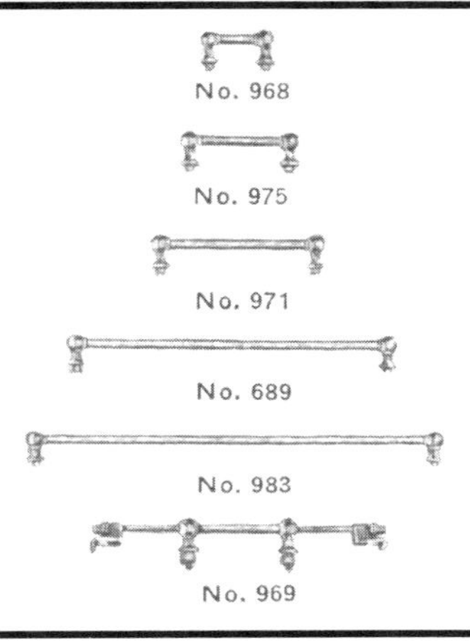

Collar Hooks. For metal counterhoop drums.
No. **974** —Nickel **$0.20**
No. **974C**—Chrome .... **.30**

Square Head Collar Screws (Rods)
No. **972** —Nickel **$0.15**
No. **972C**—Chrome .... **.25**

Separate Tension Double Post Tubular Lugs
No. **968** —4 " drum, Nickel........ **$0.60**
No. **968C**—4 " drum, Chrome....... **.90**
No. **975** —5 " drum, Nickel........ **.60**
No. **975C**—5 " drum, Chrome....... **.90**
No. **971** —6½" drum, Nickel........ **.60**
No. **971C**—6½" drum, Chrome....... **.90**
No. **689** —Parade Drums, Nickel..... **.70**
No. **689C**—Parade Drums, Chrome.... **1.05**
No. **983** —Bass Drums, Nickel....... **.70**
No. **983C**—Bass Drums, Chrome...... **1.05**

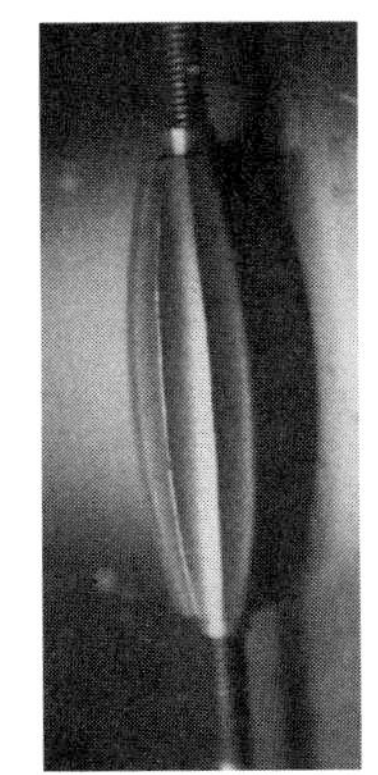

Streamlined lugs were introduced around 1936, described in the catalog under the heading "Streamlined lugs for Radio King Drum" and " # 846— for all size orch. drums" The first versions of this lug did not utilize threaded inserts; the tension rods threaded directly into the casting itself.

By 1938, Slingerland began using single-ended Streamlined lugs on tom-toms (right). The next catalog which shows the change in the parts section indicates that the lug above (#846) was changed to part #547-S. For most of the tom-toms, they used a single-ended version of the same lug, identified as #547. (Some small tom-toms used a 547-S mounted in the middle of the shell, with extra long tension rods; see Davie Tough's set in the endorsee section.)

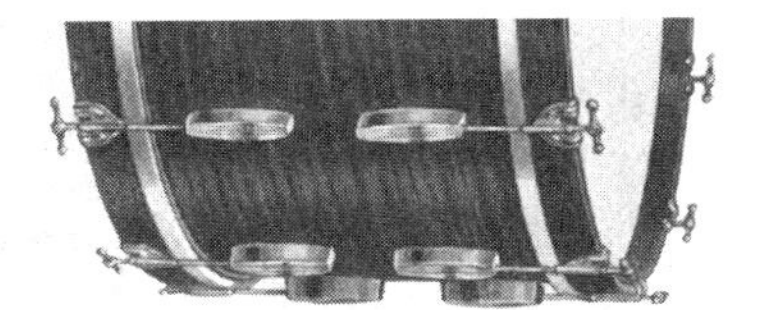

Single End #548

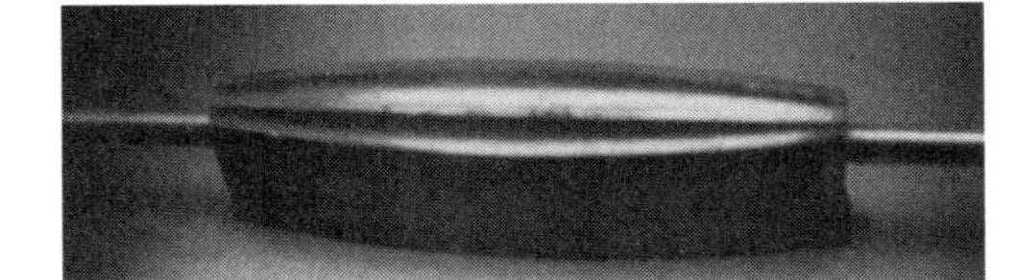

Open (Single Tension) #549

At the same time the 547 showed up on the tom-toms, a larger streamlined lug was introduced on the bass drums. For single tension bass drums, this lug was #548 which was hollow and open at both ends. A single-ended version, #549, (similar to the tom-tom 547) was used for double-tension bass drums. The distance between mounting screws on the 547 is 2 ¼". The distance between mounting screws on the 548 and 549 is 3".

ROLLING BOMBER LUG

The rosewood Rolling Bomber, or wartime lug, was made for just a few years during WWII when the War Production Board dictated that drums could be made of no more than 10% (by weight) of metal. The carved wooden lug had a metal insert for the tension rod to thread into.

BEAVERTAIL LUGS (1940)

In about 1940, the #564 small beavertail lug was introduced on some models of snare drums. After the war, a larger version of the beavertail lug, the #561, was made for larger toms and bass drums.

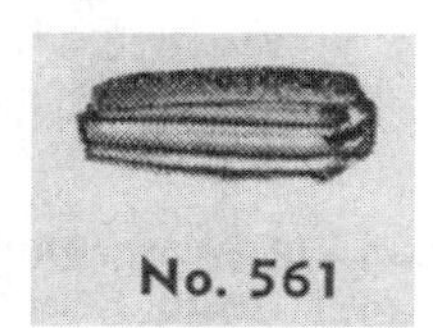

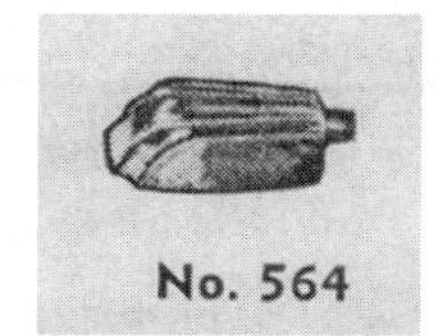

LUG-SCREW WASHER

Although early bass drums used large cup washers on the screws that secured the lugs (below), most snare drums used star lock washers until the late '40s when they too got this washer.

THE "1955" LUG

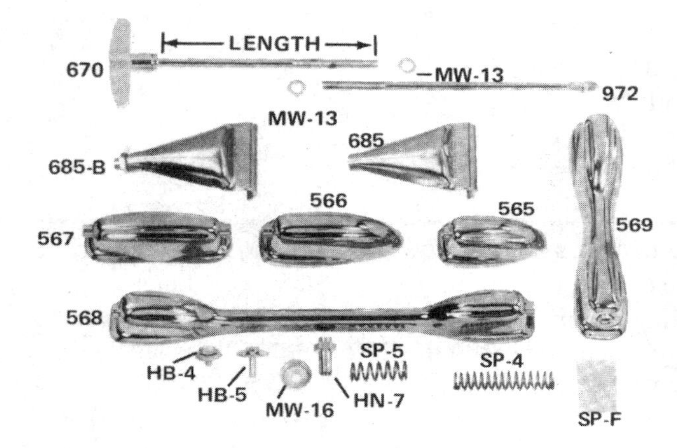

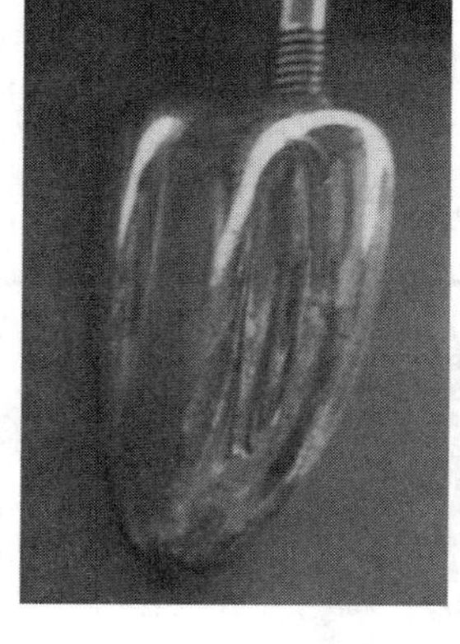

#566 for large toms and bass drums,
#565 for snare drums and parade drums,
#567 separate tension double end lug.
#'s568,569 introduced in 1970s

SLINGER-LEEDY LUGS

In the Leedy & Ludwig days, drums which had separate lugs for top and bottom used the lug shown at left. Drums of that era which utilized one double-ended lug in the middle of the shell utilized Ludwig's Imperial lug, below. Slingerland came up with a new lug (right) to replace the Imperial . (1956–1965)

Pictured: 1564 for snare drums and small toms. The slightly larger 1561 was used for large toms and bass drums.

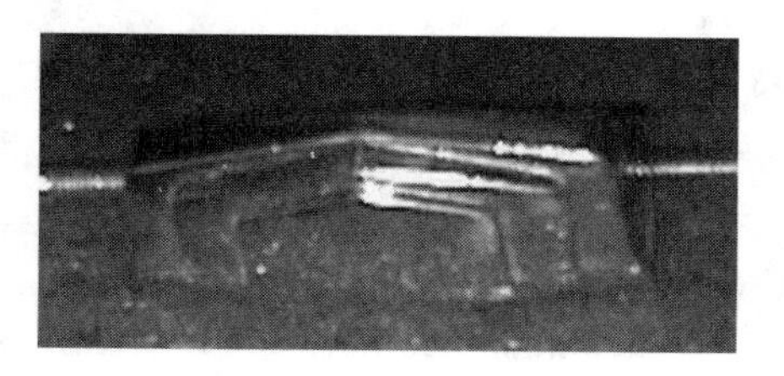

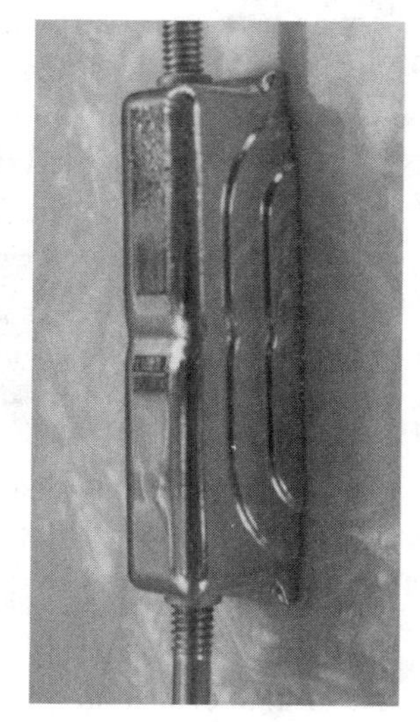

Sam says... pages 239-242

Slingerland Tom Holders

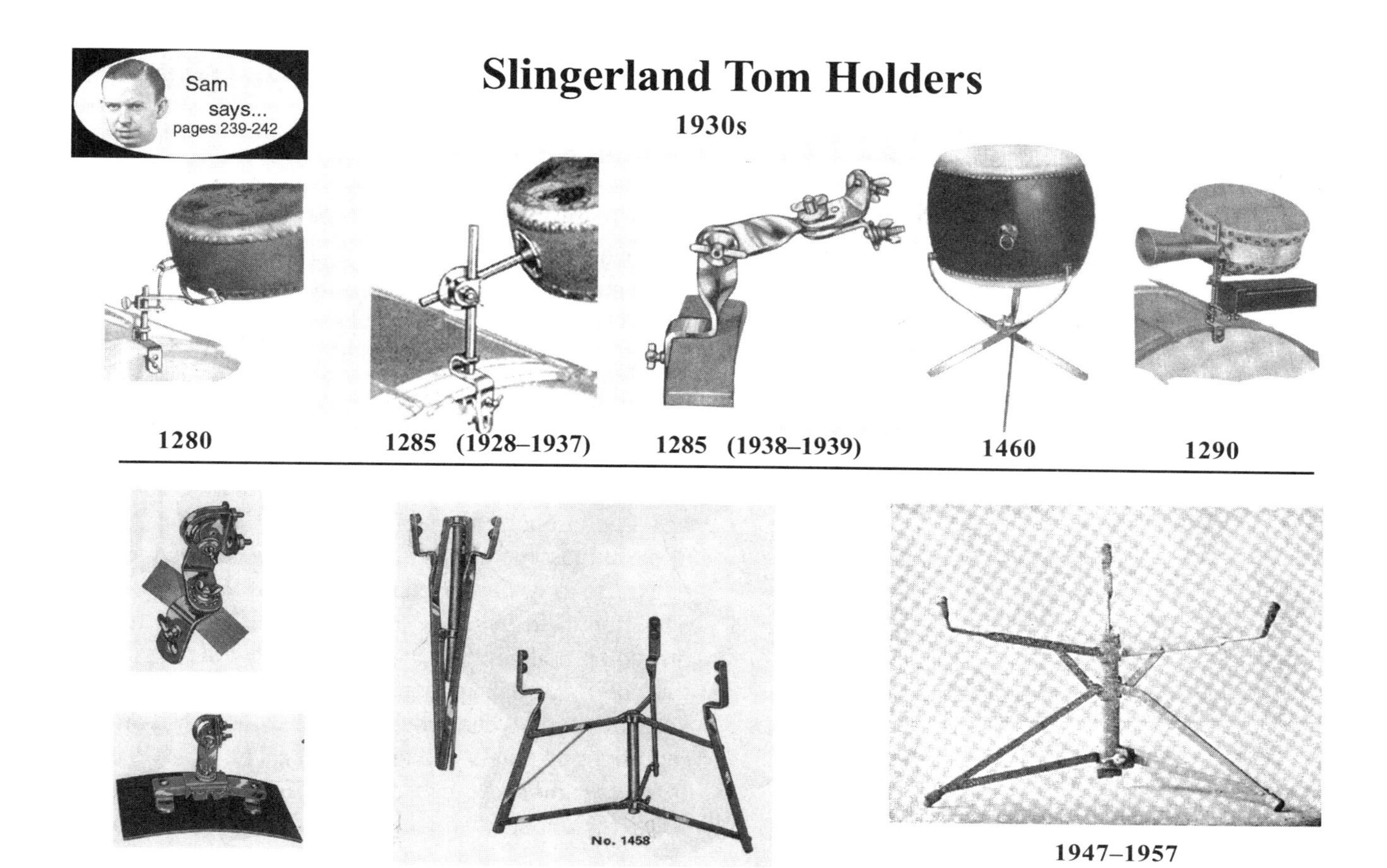

1930s

1280 | 1285 (1928–1937) | 1285 (1938–1939) | 1460 | 1290

1940s–1950s

1940–1946

1947–1957

1955

Ray McKinley tom holder

#171

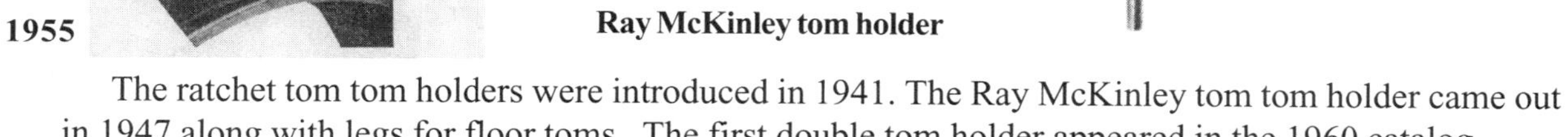

The ratchet tom tom holders were introduced in 1941. The Ray McKinley tom tom holder came out in 1947 along with legs for floor toms. The first double tom holder appeared in the 1960 catalog.

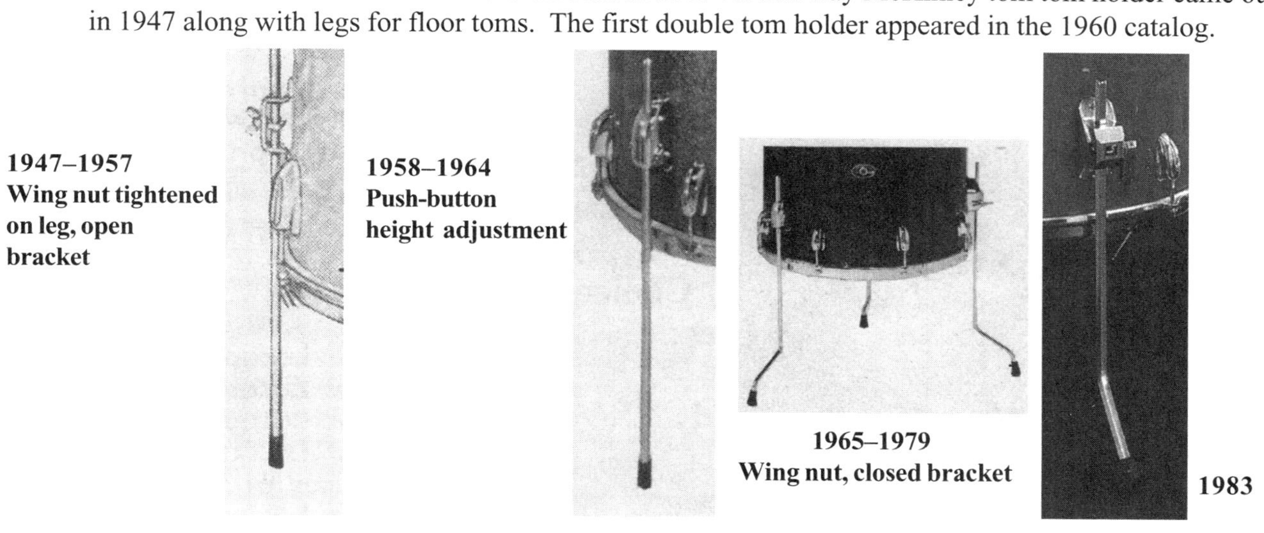

1947–1957
Wing nut tightened on leg, open bracket

1958–1964
Push-button height adjustment

1965–1979
Wing nut, closed bracket

1983

Pax-All Trap Console; An Early Rack System

It seems likely that Slingerland purchased the Pax-All from another manufacturer such as Premier. It was catalogued by Slingerland only in their first drum catalog of 1928 while Premier and several other manufacturers (primarily English) had already been selling nearly identical systems for several years.

1928 catalog copy:

"The most modern of all trap consoles. Built to meet every requirement of the drummer. Comes equipped with wheels and brakes so that entire outfit, including snare and bass drum, can be moved quickly if desired or locked in place on the band stand. The temple block rail (part of the standard equipment) is assembled with special clamps for the blocks; thus, additional clamps are not neccessary. The new rail assembly is the modern means of holding the temple blocks. The trap rail is the new DeLuxe Model, covered with any color pearl at no additional cost. Consoles in the past were large and troublesome affairs and drummers complained because the trays destroyed the beauty of the best drums. The New Slingerland Console, with it's pearl tray in any color, will now enhance the beauty of the bass drum and augment the appearance of the entire outfit. Be sure to specify when ordering what color pearl you will require on the table and table edges. The console itself is a very rigid and sturdy device. It is constructed of the finest tubular steel which gives maximum strength."

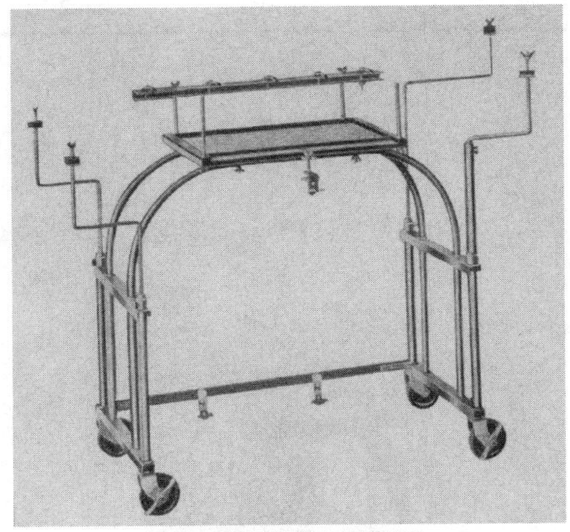

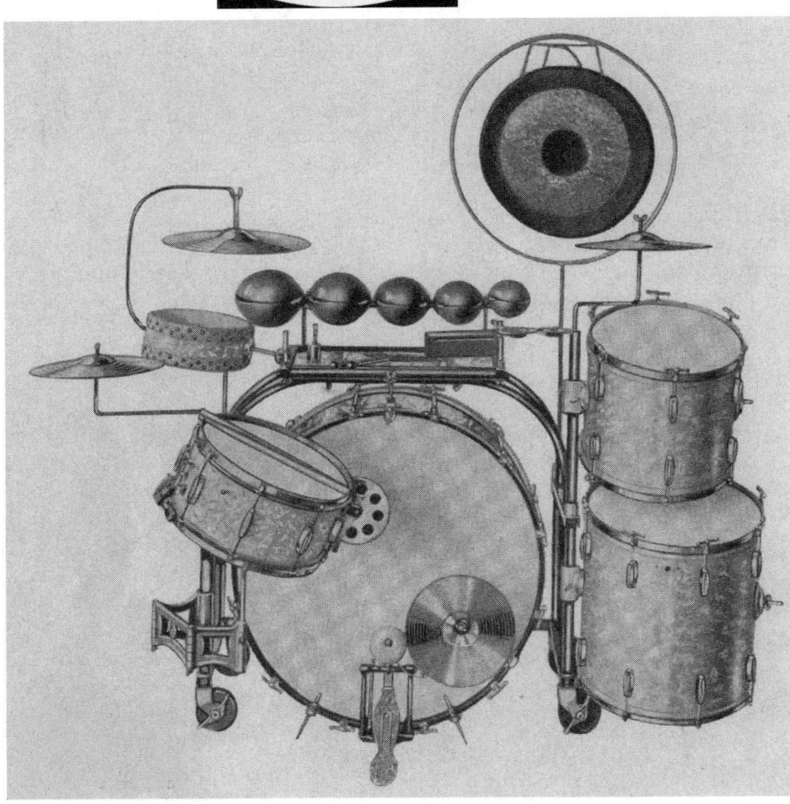

1755 1757

Goose-Neck Cymbal Holders

Snare Drum Holder

The first tom holder unique to Slingerland was 1968's set-o-matic. The patent for the set-o-matic was issued to Bud Slingerland. Although it was a big improvement over what had been available previously, the double-tom set-o-matic severely restricted the range of settings available to the drummer. This situation was not remedied until 1976 with the Super Set-O-Matic.

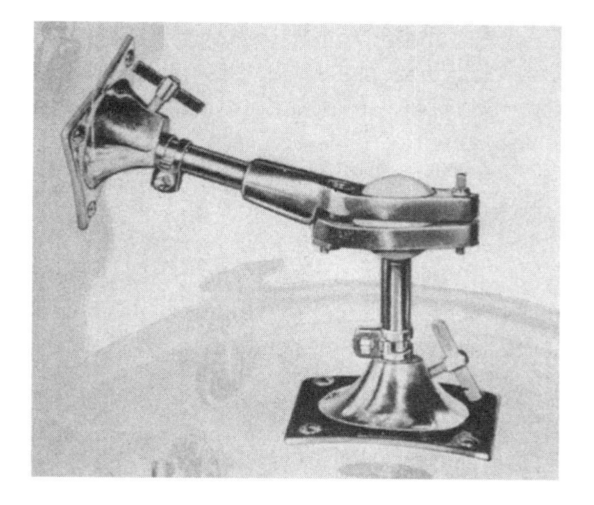

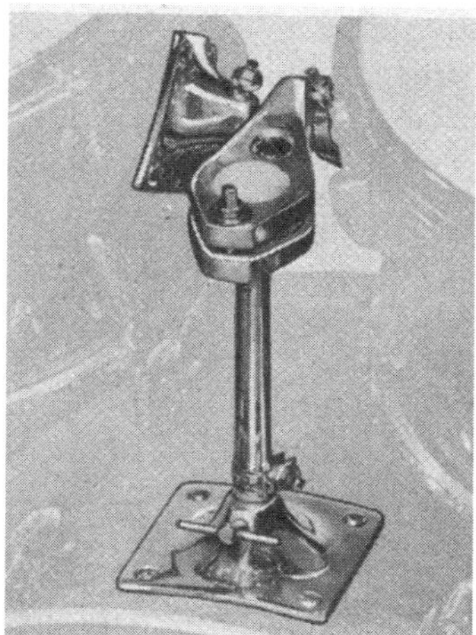

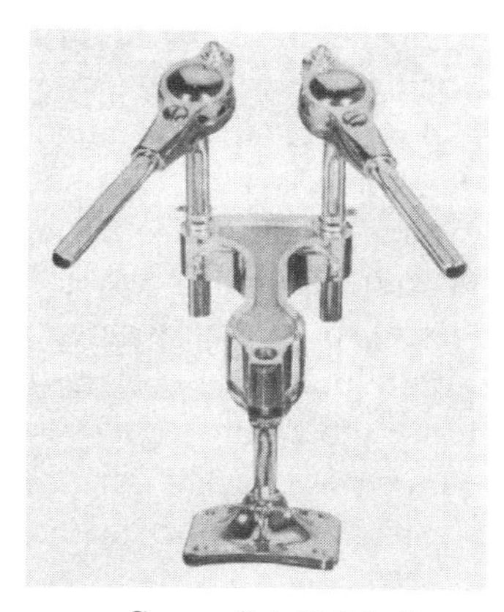

Super Set-O-Matic

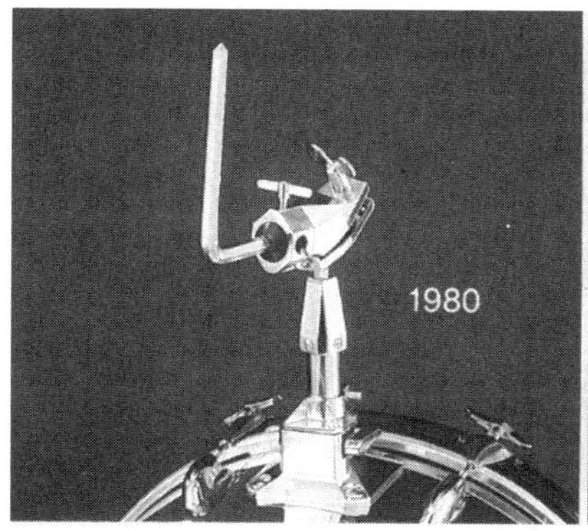

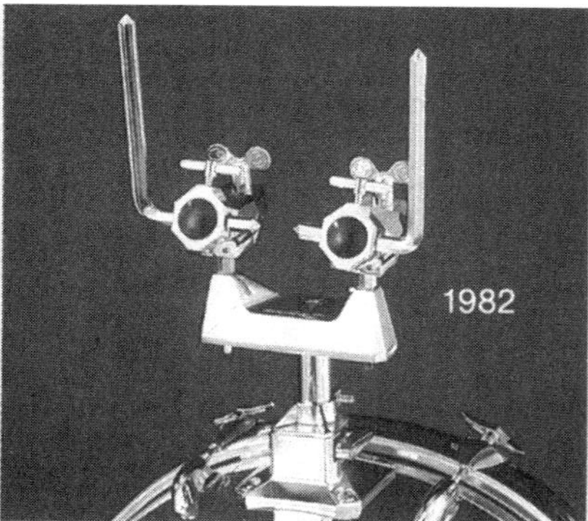

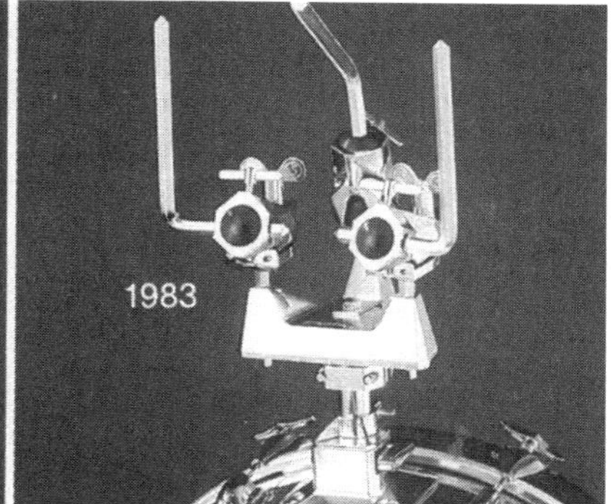

The imported Magnum series hardware of 1983 finally brought Slingerland up to speed with the competition.

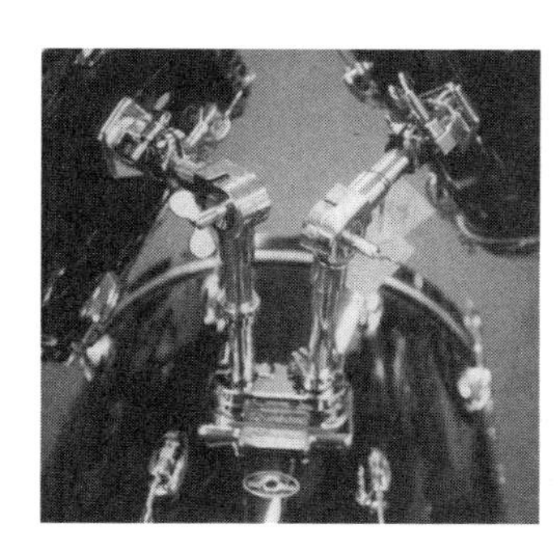

HSS Era Artist, Spirit Series

Early HSS Era Lite Series

Late HSS Era Lite Series

Gibson Era

The Slingerland Shell Story

The range of materials from which Slingerland drum shells were made includes cast aluminum, solid wood, plied wood, brass, steel, acrylic, phenolic, "masonite", and even cardboard. For the most part, the drums that were the most successful from an acoustic standpoint ended up being the most rewarding business decisions. The drums which were conceptually ridiculous in terms of acoustics ended up flopping in the marketplace. The truth of the matter is that most Slingerland product development decisions were very bottom-line oriented. While this orientation resulted in the most spectacularly successful drum company in America while the firm was family-owned, spectacular success did not always translate to superior quality. This fact is more evident in Slingerland drum shells than anywhere else in the product line. Jon Cohan (Boston drummaker and vintage drum expert) sums it up this way: "I don't think that I have ever come across an older Slingerland wood-shell drum that has no problems whatsoever with the shell. Even the choicest Radio Kings which have been carefully stored and look great in terms of finish and plating always seem to be a little out of round, or the reinforcement hoops are separating, or some other structural problem. I think they were in a hurry to make drums and bent a lot of green wood. On the other hand, I've never come across a Leedy or Stone drum that, even after 70 or 80 years, isn't still right on the money."

ALUMINUM SHELL DRUMS

It is believed that the first drum to be sold with a Slingerland name badge was the aluminum-shell Geisler drum, see page 18. Since this drum was not manufactured by Slingerland and was apparently never catalogued, we start our shell discussion with the first catalog, 1928.

METAL SHELL DRUMS

The first metal-shell Slingerland drums to be catalogued were one-piece brass shells. Slingerland emphasized this feature, as well as the fact that no solder was used. (Ludwig's brass shells of the day were two-piece soldered shells.)

WOOD SHELL DRUMS

The first Slingerland snare drums were solid wood (mostly mahogany or walnut with an occasional maple). Bass drums of the same era were either solid wood or laminated. By 1934 solid-shell bass drums were no longer available. The laminated-shell drums were described as being either "improved 3-ply" or "new 5-ply".

Cut from 1936 catalog

REINFORCEMENT HOOPS

Reinforcement hoops are the bands of wood fastened to the inside of the shell. The primary reason for these was to strengthen the shell and keep it in round. Sizes of reinforcement hoops varied widely during the years. Some floor toms and bass drums from the 1930s had very wide reinforcement hoops (2 1/4" wide, often with not only reinforcement hoops at the top and bottom, but also one in the middle of the shell.) By the '60s, the hoop size had been reduced to 1" on the toms and 1 1/4" on the bass drums. Most reinforcement hoops were made from maple; those installed in the Shelbyville, Tennessee, drums of the early '60s were oak.

RADIO KING SHELLS, 1930s–1950s

Radio King toms and bass drums covered with a pearl covering are three-ply shells. Mahogany inside, mahogany outside, and poplar in the middle. If it was a duco finish, it was a two-ply shell; mahogany inside, maple outside. The reason for that was maple took paint well. Plied snare drums have an outer ply of maple, a thick middle ply of poplar, and a third (very thin) inner ply of mahogany.

A GAP IN METAL-SHELL PRODUCTION 1942–1957

There was a gap in the production of metal-shelled drums during the war years when the war production restricted the use of metals; no more than 10% of a drums weight could be attributed to metal components. Thought the war was over by the late 1940s, steel and brass remained in short supply. The next catalogued metal shell model did not appear until 1958. In another veiled reference to Ludwig, Slingerland at that time pointed out that their drum was built without "a sound-distorting center bead".

MASONITE SHELL

An uncatalogued series of drums made from a masonite material were sold from approximately 1954 to 1958. Most models which have surfaced have been lacquered single-tension drums, though the drum in this photo is a 5x14 double tension snare drum. (Thanks to Ryland Fitchett for bringing this drum to the author's attention.)

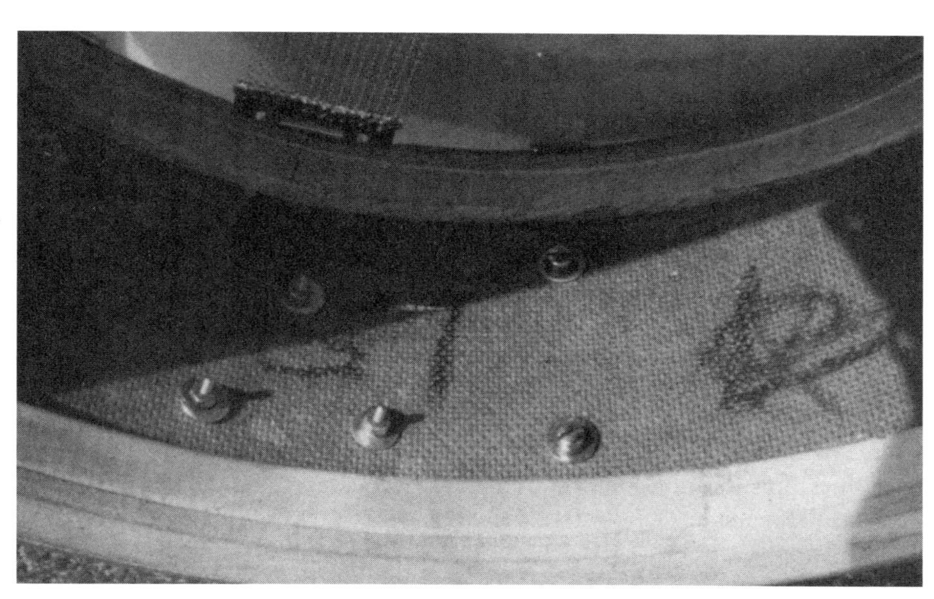

SOLID-WOOD SHELL DRUMS

While nearly all the major drum companies originally made solid-wood snare drums in the '20s and into the '30s (and even made a number of solid-shell bass drums), more and more turned to plywood until Slingerland finally claimed (in 1950) to to be the only drummaker still making a solid snare drum shell.

The solid snare drum shell is exclusive
The solid snare drum shell is an exclusive Slingerland feature. Each SOLID snare drum shell is hand turned for exact sizing to a perfect circle. It is the strongest and most durable shell made. Makes for easier playing, greater sensitivity of snares, and easily controlled power and volume.

c. 1963 UNIMOLD

Sometime around 1960 (possibly several years earlier, though not mentioned in the catalogs until 1963), Slingerland began to make their laminated shell models utilizing the "unimold" construction technique. Rather than dry-bending or steam-bending a flat piece of laminated plywood, the unimold process utilized a mold. A piece of veneer was put in, then a layer of glue, then the middle layer of wood, more glue, a third layer of wood, then some glue top and bottom, and, lastly, the reinforcing rings. The mold was heated while a large inflatable bladder was lowered into the middle and inflated. This put the layers of glue and wood under extreme pressure and heat simultaneously.

Shells were being made this way in Chicago before the same type of process was developed by William Connor for shell production in Shelbyville, Tennessee. The Shelbyville shells were three-ply shells with the outer and inner plies of mahogany and the middle ply of poplar. The reinforcement rings were maple in the Chicago drums, oak in the Shelbyville drums. The process remained pretty much unchanged when Slingerland shifted from three-ply to five-ply shell production in the late 1970s. According to Slingerland factory records from 1981, the five-ply shells were maple/poplar/maple/poplar/maple with 1/26" maple plies and 1/8" poplar plies. (When mahogany was applied as an outer ply, it was 1/16". The oil based resin used to fuse the shells was custom to Slingerland. The 1979 catalog offered five-ply drums as standard, with a three-ply option at no extra charge.

Shell Dating Tips

Most early 1960s drums had an inner ply of mahogany (a dark, reddish wood.)

Beginning in the mid 1960s, the inner ply was more often maple, a blonde wood.

From the late 1960s into the mid 1970s, the inside of the shell was painted a tannish beige color. They went back to a natural maple inner ply at the same time they stopped putting in reinforcement rings, in the 1970s.

Tom-toms did not have vent holes or badges until the early 1960s. (This includes the early Niles toms.)

Brushing glue on plies about to be put into the mold.

If not uniformly & tightly clamped, pearl drum covering material buckles and separates because it shrinks as it ages. Slingerland used clamp assemblies made up of burlap, wood, and clamps.

1983

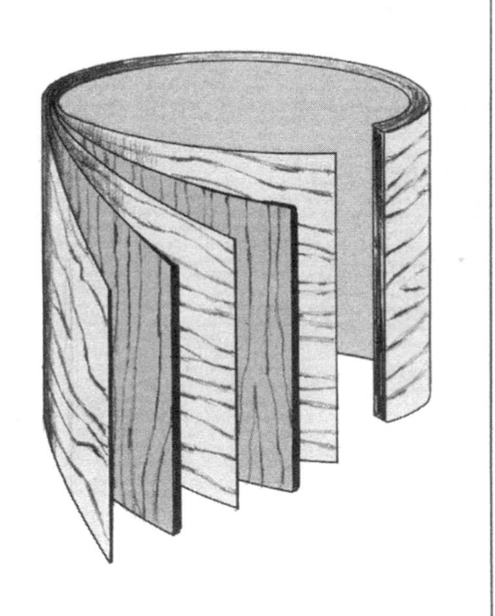

LEFT. The five plies of Slingerland's premium wood shells are hand-shaped, molded into a perfect cylinder, then laminated simultaneously under heat and pressure. This process uses less glue than others, permitting full tonal resonance through the wood, resulting in maximum strength and sound. **RIGHT.** Every Slingerland drum shell is checked to micro-tolerances to assure a uniform bearing edge for clean, distortion-free sound.

THE SLINGERLAND "ODYSSEY"

"Odyssey" drums were made by Remo. These PTS drums were inexpensive phenolic tubes fitted with clips to secure the Pre-Tuned Series drum heads. These heads were self-tensioned and pretty much untunable. (You could increase the tension, but not decrease it beyond the head's self-tensioned tuning. The series of PTS drums that Remo made for Rogers, the R-340 line, did not even have lugs; just inexpensive clips to sort of hold the heads in place. Spencer Aloisio recalls the Odyssey as sort of a test-marketing experiment with Remo; the company never really made these a regular part of the line.

Slingerland Pres. Dick Richardson presents a savings bond to Susan Kramp of Downers Grove, winner of the Name-The-Drum-Set competition.

ACRYLIC SHELLS

(photo, page 140)

During the transparent drum craze of the mid-1970s, Slingerland made a few acrylic outfits and field drums. Like the other clear drums on the market, the look was striking, but the sound was rather unremarkable

CARDBOARD SHELLS

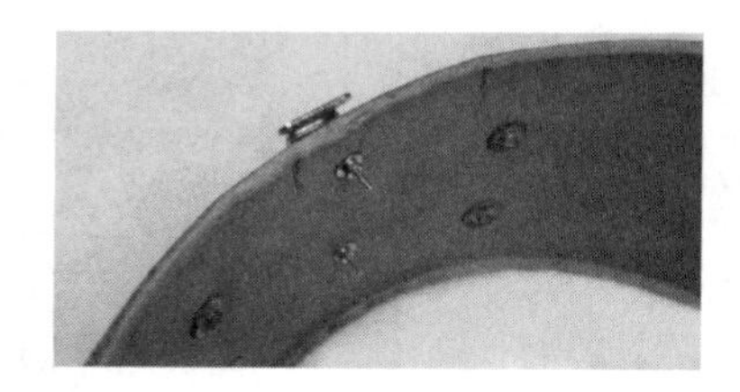

Slingerland drum quality reached a new low in the early 1980s when they actually sold drums which were little more than large cardboard tubes with pearl covering and some drum hardware slapped on. The tubes were sturdier than the mailing-tube type, as they were actually made from Sonatube. (Sonatube is used for telescopes and as forms for casting concrete pillars.) The basic material was nevertheless cardboard, and the bearing edges quickly lost their integrity.

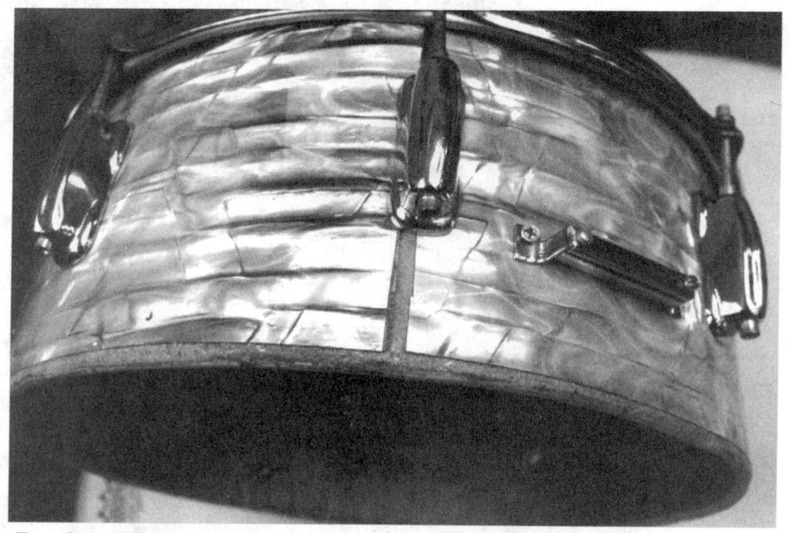

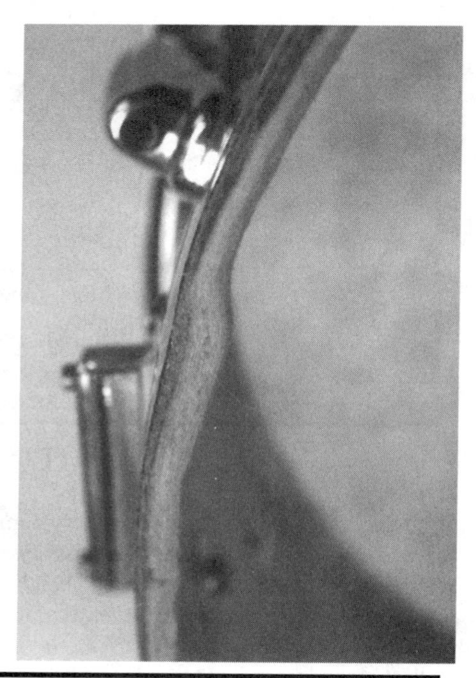

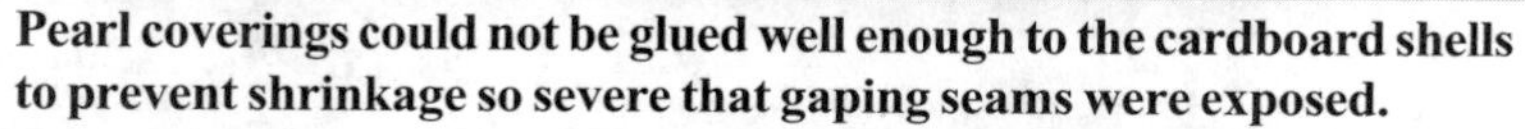

Pearl coverings could not be glued well enough to the cardboard shells to prevent shrinkage so severe that gaping seams were exposed.

SHELLS IN THE GRETSCH/HSS ERA

Shells for the Lite series were six plies of North American rock maple; 6mm tom thickness, 7 mm snare thickness.(No reinforcement rings.) These shells were produced by Jasper Wood Products in Jasper, Indiana, using molds which were designed and owned by HSS. (The shells were shipped to Gretsch for final assembly and finish work, then to HSS for distribution.)

The HSS Artist Series drums were five-ply North American maple and mahogany. The wood was shipped to Korea where the shells were made and assembled.

HSS Spirit Series drums (Taiwanese) were made with nine-ply all-mahogany shells.

GIBSON ERA SHELLS

The Lite, Artist Custom, and Spirit series were all discontinued in January of 1995 when Gibson terminated their distribution arrangement with HSS. One Gibson official at the time stated that the product left in stock was simply warehoused because they were embarassed by the poor quality. The HSS molds at Jasper were pulled by Gibson and the plan was to have them modified and shipped to New Hampshire shell manufacturer Keller. In the meantime Gibson used fairly standard Keller shells for the Studio King series; all-maple six-ply tom-toms, eight-ply bass drums, and ten-ply snare drums.

Radio King solid maple shell snare drums were designated as “Original” and “Select”. “Select” shells were made from maple with unique grain characteristics such as flame and birdseye grains.

Snare Drums

The following is a listing of all snare drums (excluding juvenile, junior, and parade drums) Slingerland is known to have catalogued, plus a few uncatalogued models. Since most of this information is based on Slingerland catalogs, a certain margin of error is built in. (Slingerland's first production snare drum, the "Geisler" drum featured in the opening chapters, was never catalogued.) Model changes were often not reflected in catalogs which for decades depended wherever possible on artwork retained from prior catalogs. (It's not unusual to see four or five catalogs in a row listing the same "new" product.)

ENGRAVED MODELS

In its early years, Slingerland produced three series of hand-engraved drums: the gold-plated and Black Beauty Artist Models shown here, and "black metal" versions of the Duall. These are probably the rarest and most valuable production model drums produced by Slingerland. (Other Slingerland drums may rival the rarity and value of these models, but primarily because they were unique prototype models or endorsee drums.) At this writing, there are no known gold-plated Artist models or engraved Dualls in existence, and only a few Black Beauties.

Art Gold Trimming
124–4x14   134–5x14
126– 6.5x14

Nickel Plated Trimming
165–4x14   166–5x14
167– 6.5x14

Unlike Ludwig's Black Beauty which was made from two pieces of brass soldered together at the bead and soldered again where the bearing edge met the shell, the Slingerland drum was made from one piece of brass. It was much heavier brass than the Ludwig Black Beauty. A 5"x14" Ludwig Black Beauty (with heads and all hardware) weighs in at 7 lb. 13 oz., while the Slingerland drum shown here weighs 9 lb. 11 oz.

ENGRAVED GOLD-PLATED ARTIST MODEL 1928 only.

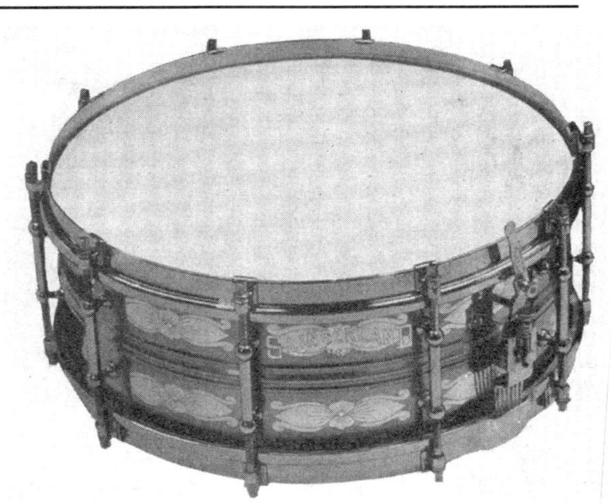

Since this model was discontinued by 1929, these model numbers were reassigned to Art gold hardware versions of standard brass-shell Artist models of the same sizes.

133–4x14   134–5x14   135–6.5x14

THE FANCHER MODEL

The Fancher model street drum was a tone-flange model catalogued in 1928. While an orchestra snare drum was never catalogued, several are known to exist, and are very similar to the earliest Artist models: 10 tube lugs, solid shell, tone ring, and #967 strainer.

A small article in a suburban Chicago paper (*North West Ledger*) reported a personal appearance by Fancher in the late '20s: *The World's Champion rudimental drummer, Frank S. Fancher, demonstrated his skill on the snare drum at the Humboldt Lions club Tuesday. Mr. Fancher has participated in contests all over the world, winning more than two hundred first prizes, cups, and medals. He is now connected with the Slingerland Banjo and Drum Company. "There's only one way to play a drum," says the champion, "and that is the right way." The Humboldt Lions were a unit in declaring Mr Fancher master of the drum.*

THE DUALL MODEL

The Duall model drums were tone-flange models featuring the Duall strainer. The series was short-lived; probably because of patent litigation problems, see page 34.

In the end, the Slingerland Duall snare drum was included in only one Slingerland catalog, in 1934. A special fold-out flier was also printed, from which the copy below is reprinted. The Duall snare drums were made only in 5x14 and 6.5x14 shell sizes, but with many options; metal or wood shells, pearl coverings, etc.

BEN WEINBERG, drummer with Al Jolson, says: "I have purchased the beautiful Slingerland outfit shown in the photo and I must say it surely is the finest set I have ever owned or played upon. The snare drum, your new DUALL Model, has the most perfect muffler I have ever used. So far I have used the outfit in combinations of from four to forty men and there hasn't been a time when the drum failed to cut through. I can safely say that it has everything a real drummer needs."

THREE NEW TYPES OF SNARES FOR DUALL MODELS

Snares for all Slingerland "DUALL" Model Drums are manufactured in units consisting of: Snares and end-plates. Snares are permanently fastened in plated brass end-plates, and are so arranged that they cannot touch each other. This insures a maximum snare action at all times.

The change from one set of snares to another requires less than one minute. Simply loosen screws in plates at both ends of strainer, remove snares, insert new set, replace screws, and tighten.

The New Slingerland "DUALL SENSITIVE" Coiled Wire Snares are standard equipment on all DUALL Drums. Gut or Wire-Wound Silk Snares may be had at no additional charge.

Prices include snares mounted in End-Plates for DUALL Model Drums.

No. 1500—DUALL SENSITIVE Coiled Wire........	$3.00 Each
No. 1501—Gut Snares for DUALL Models	
No. 1502—Wire-Wound Silk Snares	

THE *Newest* IN SPARKLING THREE-COLOR DIAMONDS

While Slingerland continued to make thumb-rod parade drums and junior models, the thumb-rod orchestra snare drums were catalogued only in 1928.

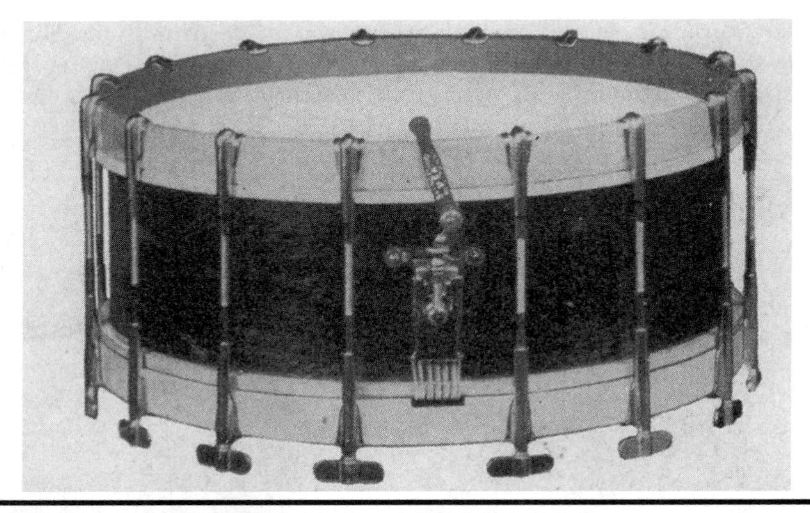

THE PROFESSIONAL SERIES 1928-1941

These drums were very similar to the Artist series, but were eight-lug models offered in fewer finishes. (Nickel, brown mahogany, and walnut.) These drums had single-flanged hoops and were not equipped with the tone flange or internal muffler. The triple bead on the metal-shell models was replaced by a single bead beginning in 1934. In 1940 the wood models appeared with streamlined lugs (the model designations were changed to #151 for the 6 1/2", #157 for the 7"), though the metal shell models still had tube lugs.

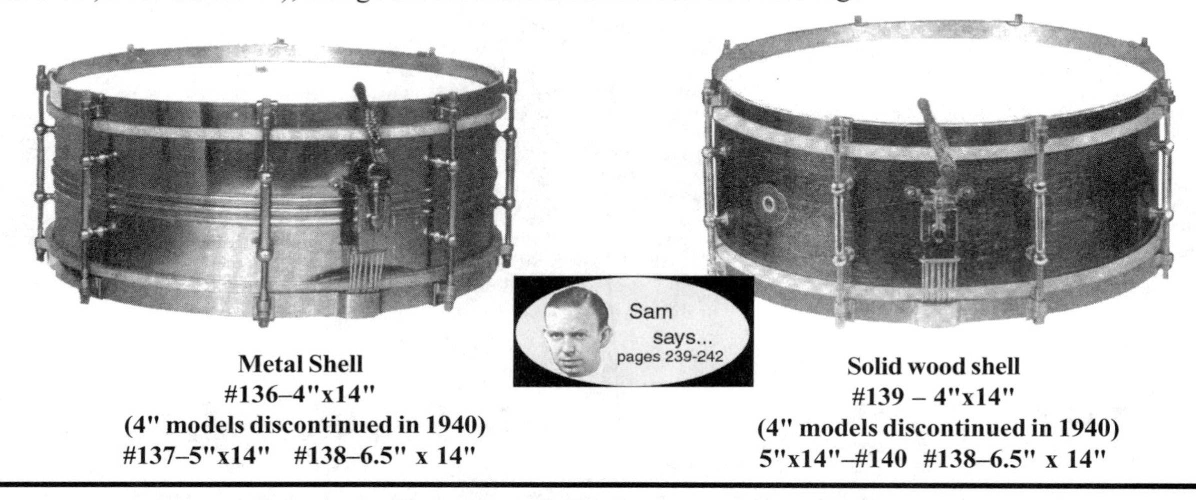

Metal Shell
#136–4"x14"
(4" models discontinued in 1940)
#137–5"x14" #138–6.5" x 14"

Solid wood shell
#139 – 4"x14"
(4" models discontinued in 1940)
5"x14"–#140 #138–6.5" x 14"

UNIVERSAL MODELS 1928-1941

he Universal models had six lugs, the Junior Snare Throw-Off, and were offered in fewer sizes and finishes (Nickel and mahogany only). In 1934 the strainer was changed to the #674 Shur-Grip. Other 1934 changes included discontinuation of the metal 4"x14" and a switch of model numbers on the metal 5"x14" from #143 (triple bead as seen below) #05 (single bead) In 1940 the 4"x14" wood shell was replaced by the #146 6.5"x14".

THE ARTIST SERIES

1928–1938

The Artist series snare drums were Slingerland's premium snare drums when they published their first catalog in 1928. All the drums in this series were equipped with the tone flange (see p. 24), the #967 strainer (see p. 184), and 10 tube lugs. Wood models had solid shells, metal models were one-piece brass. Hoops were "semi-floating," or double-flanged.

Chart of Artist series (wood shell) model #'s, 1928–1929:

		Marine Pearl	Sea Green Pearl	Blk Diamond Pearl	Tutone	Brilliant Gold	Lavender Pearl	Rose Pearl	Opal Pearl
4"x14"	Art gold	100	121	115	112	106	171	-	-
5"x14"	"	101	122	116	113	107	172	157	154
6 1/2"x14"	"	102	123	117	114	108	173	-	-
4"x14"	Nickel	103	162	118	127	109	168	-	-
5"x14"	"	104	163	119	128	110	169	156	152
6 1/2"x14"	"	105	164	120	129	111	170	-	-

Notes: In addition to the wood-shell models charted here, there were nickel-plated brass-shell artist models (photo above right); #130 4" x 14", #131 5" x 14", and #132 6 1/2" x 14".

The Tutone models were also offered in Mahogany, white enamel, and black "ebonized." Lavender and Rose Pearl finishes were 1929 only. Opal Pearl was introduced in 1929, and in later years was also referred to as Peacock Pearl. The Rose and Opal Pearl models were available only in 5"x14" in 1929.

1934 CHANGES:

Tone flanges were discontinued by 1934. Upper line snare drums now were fitted with internal mufflers. Different model numbers were no longer assigned to the same drums with different finishes; only the shaded model #'s above were used.

1936 CHANGES:

4"x14" wood-shell models were discontinued. Wood models were fitted with the Streamlined lugs. Chromium plating was introduced, and separate model numbers assigned; 4"x14" metal #133, 5"x14" metal #134, and 6 1/2"x14" metal #135. Artgold was discontinued, and the #'s 113 and 114 were reassigned to chromium wood-shell models 5"x14" and 6 1/2"x14" respectively.

THE RADIO KING

The successor to the Duall as Slingerland's top-of-the-line snare drum was the Radio King. To many of today's vintage drum dealers and collectors, any Slingerland snare drum that has a solid maple shell is considered a Radio King. This is technically incorrect, as Slingerland produced other models with solid maple shells which were never marketed as Radio Kings, and sold Radio King snare drums with plied shells. (Tom toms supplied with Radio King drum outfits sported hoops engraved "Radio King", though tom toms were never made with solid shells.) A better way to identify a true Radio King snare drum is the presence of the snare support brackets on both the strainer and butt ends; these are part of the basis of the patent. In the patent application of 1937, H.H. Slingerland claimed as new and unique the fact that the snares remained active over the entire width of the drum head, though this certainly was not the first drum to see snares extend off both sides of the snare head. Ludwig's Super (late '20s), Leedy's Broadway Parallel (1930), and even Slingerland's own Duall accomplished this.

The same catalog (1936) that introduced Gene Krupa as an endorsee introduced the Radio King snare drum, though the patent was not applied for until 1937 and granted in 1939.

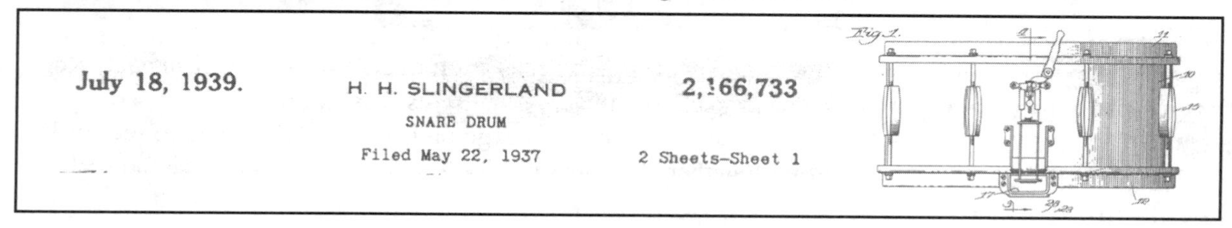
July 18, 1939. H. H. SLINGERLAND 2,166,733
SNARE DRUM
Filed May 22, 1937 2 Sheets-Sheet 1

THE FIRST RADIO KINGS

It is rumored that the very first Radio Kings were actually tube-lug drums. If there were such drums, they are probably the rarest of the Radio Kings. The earliest catalogued Radio King models appeared in 1936 as shown here: streamlined lugs without inserts (rods threaded directly into the lugs), engraved brass hoops, and the distinctive Radio King snare brackets.

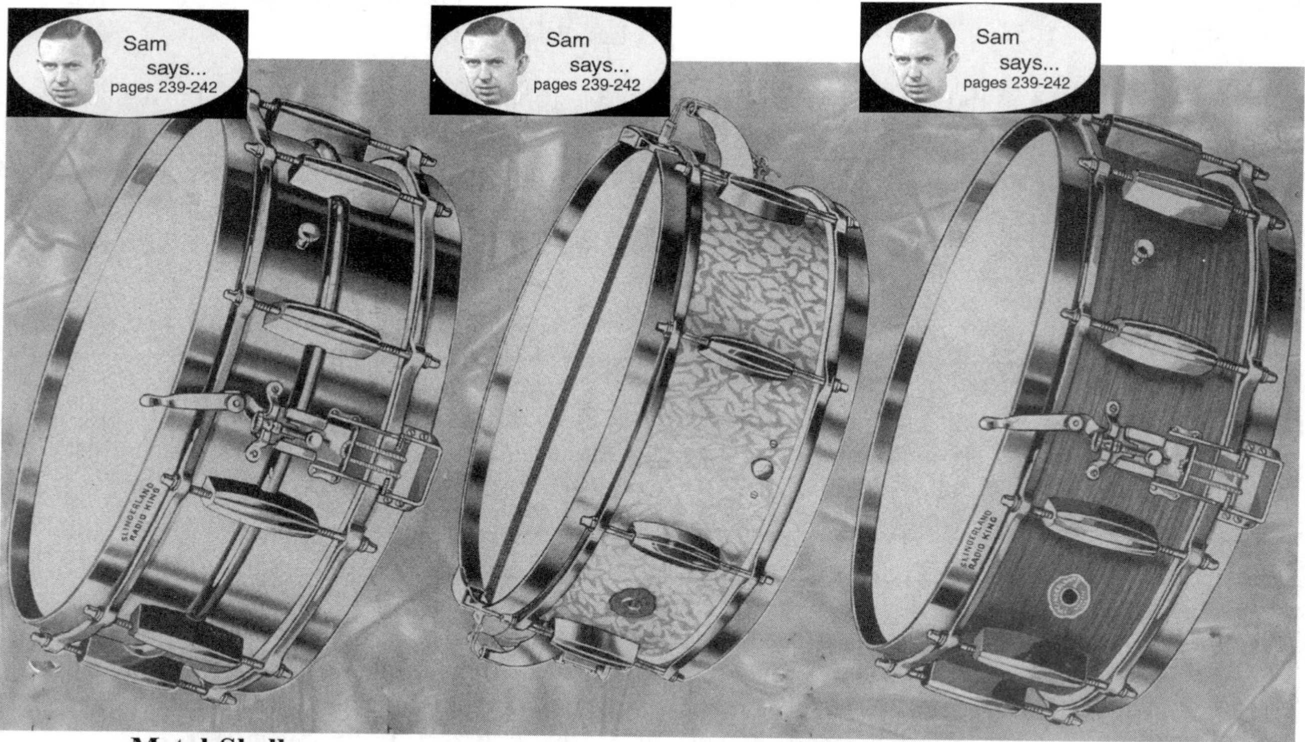

Metal Shell
132-RK 6.5x14 Nickel
135-RK 6.5x14 Chromium

Wood Shell
128-RK 5x14 Nickel 113-RK 5x14 Chromium
129-RK 6.5x14 Nickel 114-RK 6.5x14 Chromium

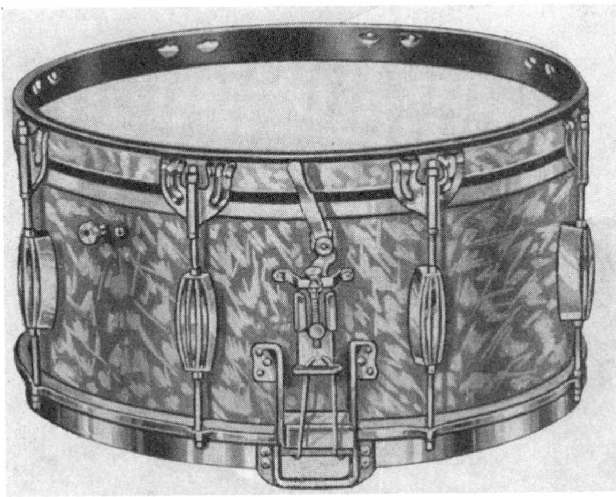

RAY McKINLEY RADIO KING 1937–1941

6.5x14, 8x14 Pearl or Duco, nickel or chrome
1940, 1941
In 1940, the 6.5 models replaced by 7"

BUDDY RICH ARTISTS' MODEL RADIO KING SWINGSTER 1940 - 1941

In addition to the change from six lugs to 12 lugs, the 6.5" models were discontinued in 1940. This is one of the very few drums known as a Radio King model which did not feature the Radio King snare brackets.

BUDDY RICH ARTISTS' MODEL RADIO KING SWINGSTER 1939

6.5x14, 7x14, 8x14 Duco or Pearl, Chrome or Nickel

SUPER GENE KRUPA RADIO KING 1940–1953

7x14, 8x14 Duco or Pearl, nickel or chrome
Added in 1948: 5 1/2"x14" Pearl and Lacquer

GENE KRUPA RADIO KING 1936–1953

In 1936, this model was offered only in the 6 1/2"x14" size WMP, with chrome hardware (#115).

In 1937 & '38, the #116 (choice of Duco finishes) was added. Beginning in 1939, both models were offered in nickel as well as chrome. In 1940 7" and 8" models were added, though the 8" was catalogued for only one year. In 1941 5" models were added.

BEN POLLACK RADIO KING 1936–1937

6.5x14, Pearl or Duco finishes, Nickel or Chrome

BAND MASTER RADIO KING
1936 only

6.5x15, 8x15 Nickel or Chrome, Wood or metal shell. Lacquer or antiqued standard, extra charge for pearl.

BERNIE MATTISON RADIO KING
1936–1939
(1937–1939 catalogued as the Band Model Radio King)

8x14 Nickel or Chrome, Pearl or Duco

ARTISTS' MODEL METAL SHELL RADIO KING
1940–1941

#148 6.5x14 Nickel, #149 6.5x14 Chrome

STUDENT MODEL RADIO KING
1948–1953

This was a rather unusual model in that it has none of the usual Radio King attributes; three-ply shell rather than solid, no RK snare brackets, no engraved hoops. Nickel hardware only, in polished mahogany or lacquered. #151 5.5x14, #157 7x14

BOP SNARE DRUM
1948–1962

4"x13", Pearl, Lacquer

"PICCOLO" NOTE:

Although this is the only 13" snare drum catalogued except for juvenile models, others were produced. The author is aware of 3-ply and solid-shell 13" drums with and without the RK engraved hoops. These drums were evidently special-order instruments.

CONCERT KING 1948–1953

Radio King strainer, but no engraved hoops & not called a Radio King. (three-ply laminated shell)

CONCERT KING 1955–1962

Listed in 1960 as Haskell Harr models

In 1963 Pearl versions were discontinued and zoomatic strainer became standard.

8x15, 6.5x15, 6.5x14 Mahogany, lacquer, or Pearl

HOLLYWOOD ACE SWING MODEL RADIO KING
1939–1954

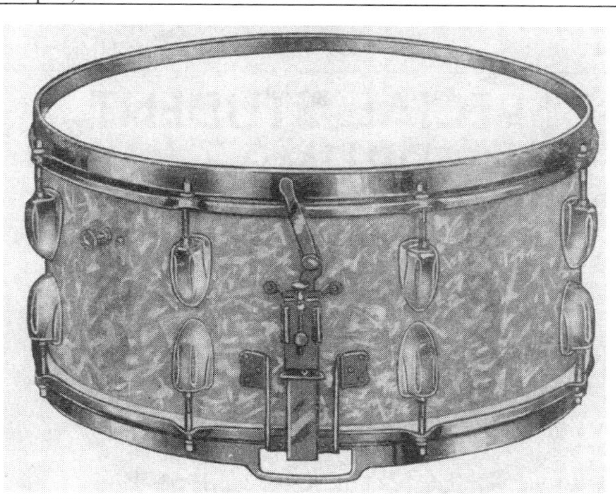

HOLLYWOOD ACE SWING MODEL RADIO KING
1955–1957

7x14, 8x14 Pearl, Duco, Nickel or chrome. In 1955 the lugs were updated and triple-flange hoops were added.

8-lug

STUDENT MODEL RADIO KING 1955–1967

(From 1960 on, this drum named the Student Model Snare Drum)

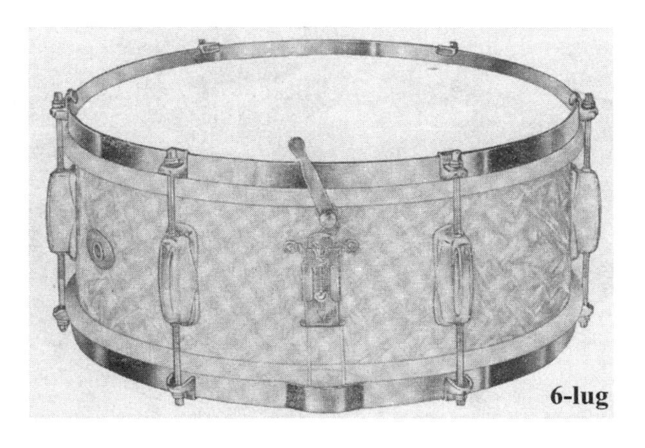

6-lug

SPECIAL STUDENT DRUM 1955–1967

Both drums 5.5x14, 7x14. These three-ply shell drums initially offered only in lacquer or mahogany finishes, nickel-plated hardware. Beginning in 1958, the hardware was chrome and all models were equipped with the rapid strainer. Pearl finishes added in 1963.

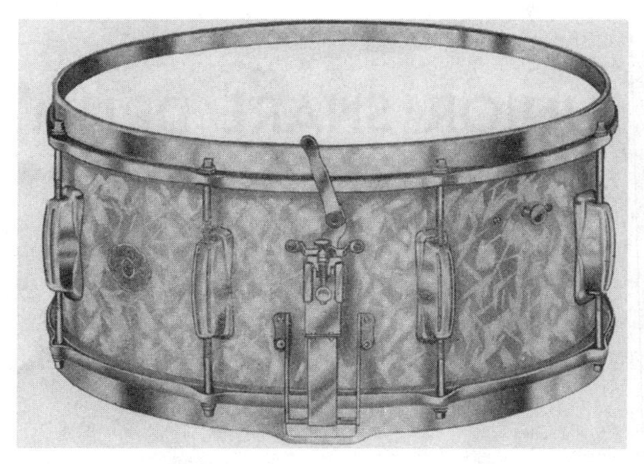

GENE KRUPA RADIO KING 1955–1962

(From 1957 on, the words "Radio King" are dropped and these models are simply the Gene Krupa Snare Drum)

Similar to the 1936–1953 models, but with the new style "1955" lugs and the "steel ribbon" strainer. Solid maple shells.
5.5x14, 6.5x14 (discontinued 1958), 7x14, 8x14 (discontinued 1958), Pearl, Lacquer

SUPER GENE KRUPA RADIO KING 1955–1962

(From 1957 on, the words "Radio King" are dropped and these models are simply the Super Gene Krupa Snare Drum)

Similar to the 1940-1953 models, with new "1955" lugs. (8 lugs on 5" models, 16 lugs on taller models.) Among these models are also the first premium-series 13" snare drums. Solid maple shells. 7x14, 8x14, 5.5x14, 5.5x13, Pearl, Lacquer

All models choice of nickel or chrome until 1958,then only chrome.

BRASS SHELL SNARE DRUM 1958–1962

5x14. In 1962 a 6.5x14 chromed version was added and these drums were listed as the Barrett Deems models. Supplies in lacquered brass or chrome finish.

HOLLYWOOD ACE 1958–1976

After years as a solid shell drum, in 1958 this drum is listed as a three-ply shell model. The other major change is the switch from the Radio King to the Rapid strainer. 5.5x14, 7x14, Pearl or lacquer.

RADIO KING MODEL 1963–1976

The first Slingerland models to be called Radio Kings since the student Radio King in 1958. One of only 2 models in the Slingerland line to have a solid shell in 1963. In 1976 the shell was a unimold shell. 5.5x14, 7x14 Pearl, Lacquer

DELUXE STUDENT MODEL 1963–1976

This 3-ply shell drum was made only in a 5.5x14. The pearl-covered drum was #161, the lacquered #162. The model designation 162 was discontinued in 1976 because all finishes were the same price.

CONCERT HALL
1963–1976

3-ply shell. 6.5x14, 6.5x15, 8x15. Originally the standard finishes were mahogany and lacquers only, with an extra charge for pearl covering. In 1976 all finishes were the same price.

STANDARD CONCERT MODEL
1963–1977

3-ply shell, 6.5x14, 6.5x15, 8x15. Mahogany and lacquers were standard finishes; extra charge for pearl. Shell changed in 1977 to 5-ply.

ARTIST MODEL 1963–1979

5.5x14, 7x14. Solid maple shell.Originally supplied with a calf batter head and plastic snare side head unless otherwise specified.

In 1964 a 10-lug version was introduced. In 1968 "Buddy Rich" was added to the name. By 1970 the name was back to simply "Artist Model". In 1976 the 7x14 was discontinued.

STUDENT ALUMINUM SHELL
1965–1979

#140 5x14. In 1977 2 wood-shell models joined the #140, listed as student models. Both had five-ply shells and 8 lugs. #146 was a 5.5 shell, the #148 was a 7" shell.

FESTIVAL MODEL CHROME SNARE DRUM
1963–1970

brass shell
1963: 8-lug 5x14 & 6.5x14
1964–1972: 8-lug and 10-lug 5x14 & 6.5x14
1973–1979: steel shell 8-lug & 10-lug 5x14

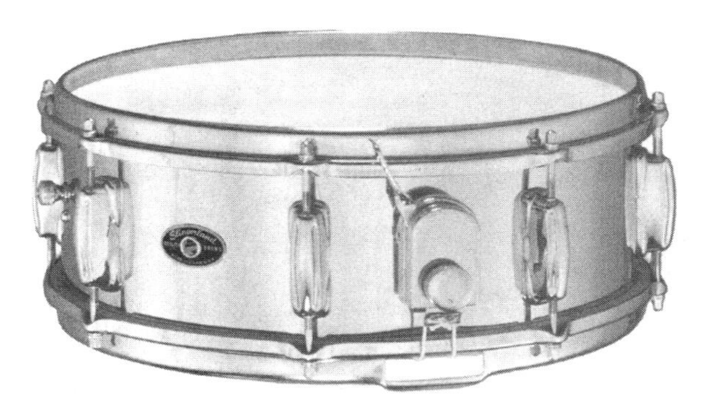

GENE KRUPA SOUND KING
1963–1977

8-lug and 10-lug 5x14 and 6.5x14
Chrome plated brass shell which was smooth until 1965, then the shells had three lines around the middle. Catalog blurbs boasted that these models had “no sound-distorting center bead”.

RADIO KING CHROME SHELL
1963–1967

Brass shell, "with no sound-distorting center bead"
1963: 8-lug 5x14 & 6.5x14, 1964: 10-lug versions added
1965: three grooves added around the center of the shell.

DELUXE CONCERT KING 1963–1972

3-ply shell 8x15,6.5x15, 6.5x14
Very similar to Concert King models of 1955–1962, but with zoomatic strainer.Mahogany and lacquers standard, pearl available for an extra charge. (Gut snares optional.)

SUPER SOUND KING 1967–1976

Brass shell

#120 5x14 #121 6.5x14

DELUXE CONCERT KING
1973–1977

5x14, 6x14, 6.5x15. In 1973, The Deluxe Concert King shell was changed from three-ply to five-ply, the strainer was changed to the new TDR strainer which took the snares all the way off the head on both sides, and hot lacquer was applied to the inside of the shell.

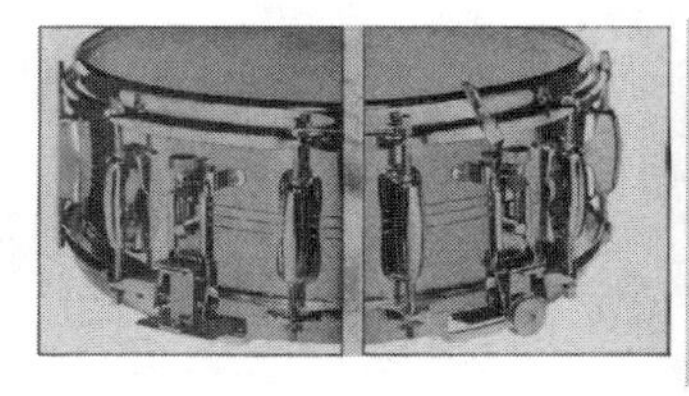

Before 1973 (left), After 1973 (right). Post-1973 models also had a protective bracket over the strainer.

BUDDY RICH SNARE DRUM
1970–1973

4x14

BUDDY RICH SNARE DRUM
1976–1977

Three air vents, including badge grommet.
5x14, 6x14 5-ply wood shell, 5x14, 6.5x14 chrome over brass

TWO-TO-ONE MODELS
1979

5-ply shell 5.5x14, 6.5x14 gut or wire snares
Chromed brass shell 5x14, 6.5x14, wire snares
Lacquered brass shell 5x14, 6.5x14, wire snares

TDR MODELS 1979

5-ply shell 5.5x14, 6.5x14
Chromed or lacquered brass 5x14, 6.5x14

SPITFIRE (12-lug) Models 1979

Same options as TDR with addition of gut snares and combination gut and wire snares. Four air vents, including badge grommet. Reportedly inspired and/or influenced by Louis Bellson, and unofficially referred to as the "Louis Bellson" model.

RADIO KING
1979

One of the first "reissue" drums made by Slingerland, the Radio King series brought out in 1979 featured solid maple shells, the Radio King strainer system, and double-flanged hoops at a time when all other drums in the line had triple flanged hoops.
5.5x14, 6.5x14 10 lug, Radio King strainer
5.5x14, 6.5x14 10 or 12 lug, TDR strainer

100 SERIES SNARE DRUMS
1981–1985

5-ply shell, 5.5x14, 8-lug, rapid strainer
5-ply shell, 5.5x14, 6.5x14, 10-lug, slapshot strainer
Chromed steel, 5x14, 6.5x14, 8 or 10 lug, rapid strainer
Chromed or lacquered brass, 5.5 or 6.5x14, 10-lug, slapshot
A few foil-badged cardboard shell 100 series drums were produced by Slingerland in 1985.

200 SERIES SNARE DRUMS
1981–1985

Chromed or lacquered brass, 5.5 or 6.5x14, 12-lug, slapshot strainer
This series, along with the 100 and 700 series, were the last Slingerland drums to be manufactured in Chicago.

700 SERIES, OR MAGNUM SERIES
1981–1985

5-ply 7x14 10-lug,
8x14, 9x14 10 or 12 lug
Chromed or lacquered brass 8x14, 10 or 12 lug

Slingerland Leedy Snare Drums

Most available in mahogany, lacquer, or pearl at different price points. Hardware was nickel with a chrome option until 1958 when chrome hardware became standard.

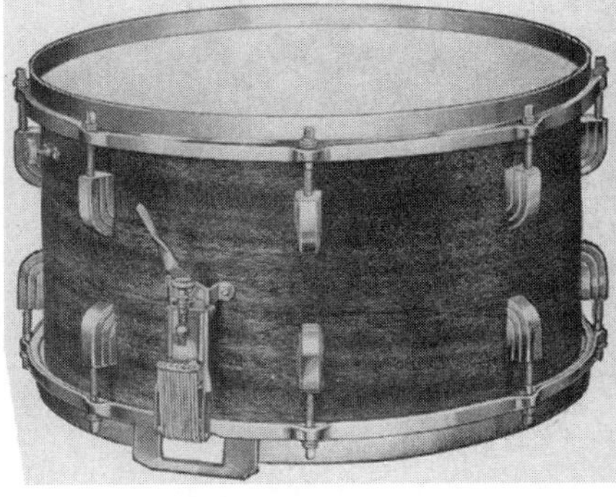

CONCERT KING 1956–1965

1956–1965: 6.5x14, 8x14
1959–1965: 6.5x15, 8x15

THE UTILITY 1956–1960

5.5x14, 6.5x14

RELIANCE 1956–1960

5.5x14, 6.5x14

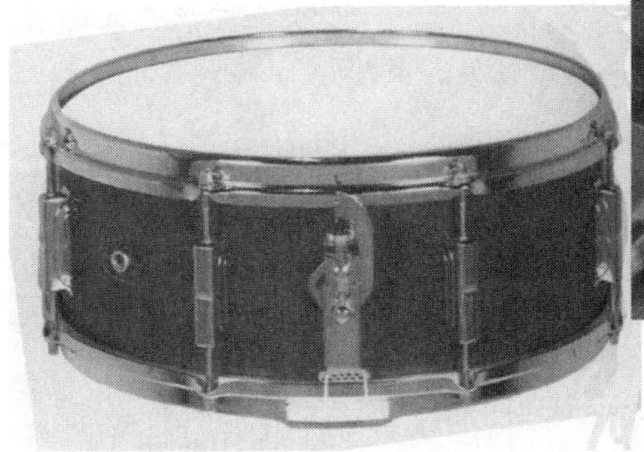

RAY MOSCA MODEL 1959–1964
FRANK CAPP MODEL 1965

5.5x14, 6 or 8 lug, Pearl or Lacquer

SHELLY MANNE CHROME SHELL 1965

5x14, 6.5x14, 8-lug or 10-lug

ALUMINUM SHELL MODEL 1965

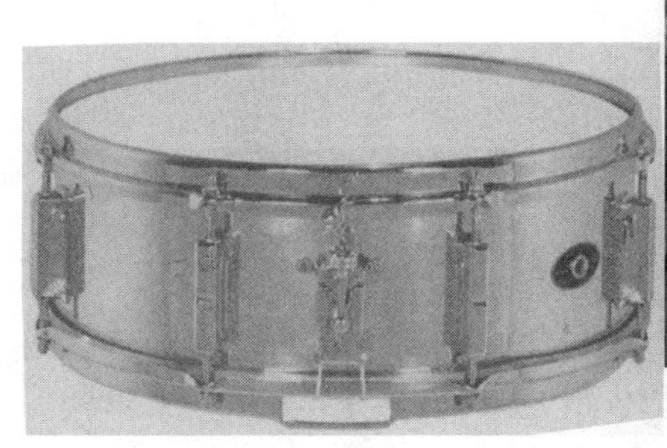

1959: JACK SPERLING MODEL
1960–63: JOE HARRIS MODEL

5x14 Chromed or lacquered brass shell

IRV COTTLER CHROME SHELL 1965

5x14, 6.5x14 8 or 10 lug. Similar to the Shelly Manne metal-shell model, but with a solid brass shell and "Instant" throw-off.

BROADWAY 1956–1965

1956–1958: 5.5x14
1956–1965: 6.5x14, 8x14

SHELLY MANNE MODEL 1958–1965

4.5x14, 5.5x14 lacquer or pearl
New "stick-saver" triple flanged hoops. Similar to the New Era, but in 1958 Slingerland introduced the double-ended snare drum lugs.

NEW ERA 1956

4.5x14

HSS ERA SNARE DRUMS 1989–1994

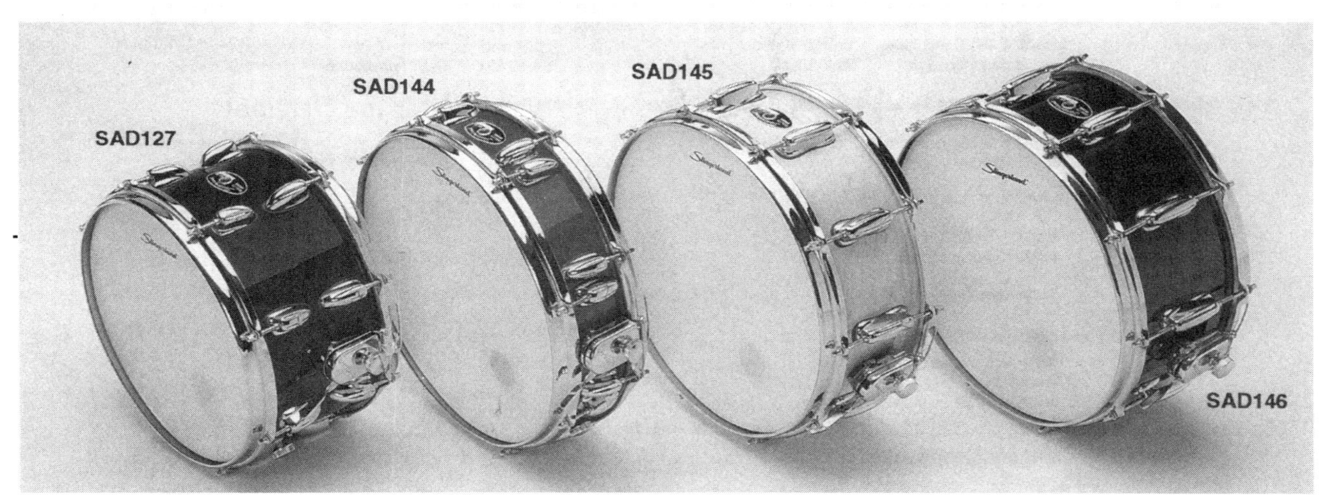

Spirit Series: Imported. SD14 6.5x14 chromed steel, SD145 5.5x14 chromed steel, SBP14 4x14 lacquered brass, SBS145 5.5x14 Lacquered Brass, SBS146 6.5x14 Lacquered Brass. (All 10-lug) Not pictured: SKS127 Solid copper shell 7x12, SKS147 solid copper shell 7x14, SBCS127 Chromed brass shell 7x12, SBCS147 Chromed brass shell 7x14

Gibson in 1994 added some hand-engraved models with the original 1928 floral pattern. Copper: SCB0712 7x12, SCB0714 7x14, and Brass SBB0712 7x12, SBB0714 7x14.

Artist Series: The Artist Custom series was developed by Buzz King of HSS. Shells were 5-ply Maple (outer and inner) and mahogany (middle). Made of American wood, the drums were actually made and assembled offshore. 7mm with 45-degree bearing edge) SAD127 16-lug 7x12, SAD144 10-lug 4x14, SAD145 10-lug 5.5x14, SAD146 10-lug 6.5x14, SAD148 10-lug 8x14 Under Gibson (late 1994) the shell was changed to 9-ply, still maple and mahogany. (Another change at that time was that the SAD144 went from 10 lug to 16 lug.)

Lite Series: With a 6-ply maple shell made by Jasper to Buzz King's (HSS) specs, this series brought the manufacture of Slingerland snare drums back to the U.S.. The shells were finished and hardware was assembled by Gretsch for HSS. This snare was fitted with the TDR snare strainer system.American made. 6-ply rock maple 7mm with 45-degree bearing edge. SLD14 7x14

Radio King Series: American made, 1-ply steam-bent rock maple with reinforcement hoops With Vintage hoops: SRK110 5.5x14, SRK111 6.5x14. With triple-flange hoops: SRK210 5.5x14, SRK211 6.5x14

GIBSON ERA SNARE DRUMS 1994–

Radio King Standard
triple-flanged hoops, solid shell
RKS-5514 5x14, RKS-6514 6.5x14

Radio King Original
engraved hoops, solid shell
RKO-6515 6.5x14, RKO-5514 5x14

Super Radio King
die-cast hoops, solid shell
SRK-5514 5x14, SRK-6514 6.5x14

Studio King 4x14
SKS-0414 10-ply shell

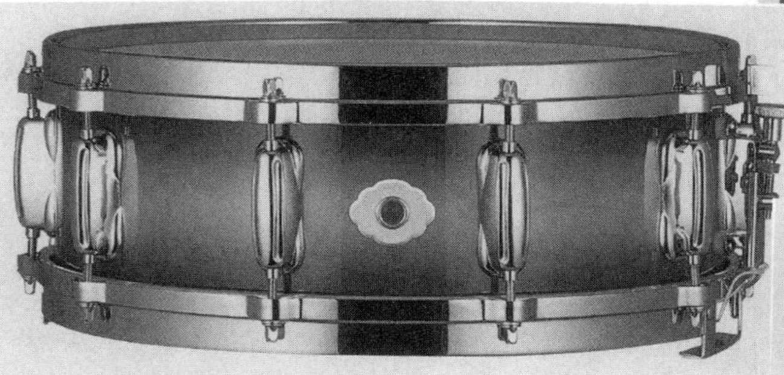

Studio King 5x14
SKS-0514 10-ply shell

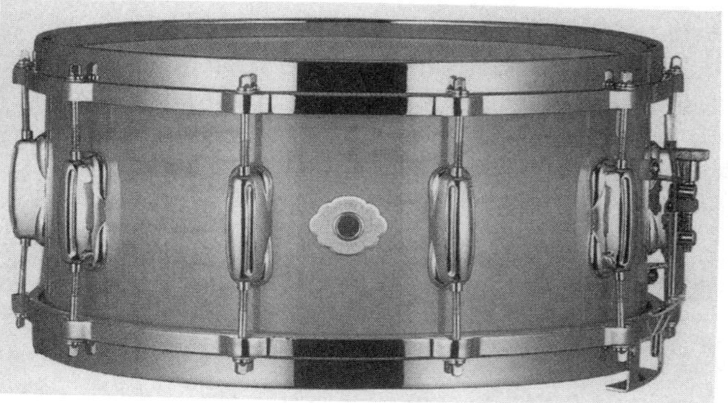

Studio King 6.5x14
SKS-6514 10-ply shell

SLINGERLAND DRUM OUTFITS

ARTIST BLACK BEAUTY OUTFIT
1928 Only.
5x14, 14x28

DAISY DRUM OUTFIT
1928–1929
4x14, 10x24

HONEY BOY DRUM OUTFIT
1928–1929
3x13, 8x24

MAJESTIC DRUM OUTFIT
1928–1929
5x14, 14x26

SNAPPY PARTNER OUTFIT
1928–1929
4x14, 12x26

THEATRICAL DRUM OUTFIT
1928–1929
5x14, 14x28

Radio
1928
5x14, 12x26

Patrician
1928
5x14, 14x28, 10

Monarch
1928
5x14, 14x28, 10"chinese

Metropolitan
1928
5x14,14x28,10

AMERICAN BOY OUTFIT
1934–1940
3x12,6x22

BROADWAY OUTFIT
1934–1938
5x14,12x26

The bass drum was a 12x26 when the outfit was introduced in 1934, changed to a 14x24 in 1937 when a sock cymbal and chinese tom were added. (1938 catalog picture here.)

RADIO OUTFIT
1934–1938
5x14,12x26

PREMIER OUTFIT
1928–1936
5x14,14x28

The Premier outfit is pictured here as t appeared in 1928. In 1934 a trap table was added, which was removed again in 1936.

JUNIOR OUTFIT
1934–1938
4x14,8x24

SCHOOL OUTFIT

Listed from 1934 to 1936 with a 4"x13" wood shell snare drum, 8"x24" Universal bass drum and china cymbal as pictured below, the School Outfit from 1937 to 1938 included a 5"x14" professional wood OR metal snare and a 12"x26" bass drum. (The tambourine was also dropped in 1937.)

SPECIAL JOBBING OUTFIT
1936
5x14,14x28

HOLLYWOOD OUTFIT
1934–1936
HOLLYWOOD BOULEVARD OUTFIT
1937
6.5x14,14x28

RADIO KING FULL DRESS STREAMLINED OUTFIT
1937–1939
5x14, 4x10, 14x28

Catalogued with tambourine instead of hi-hat and 26-inch bass drum from 1934–1936 as the "Epic". The 28-inch bass drum was offered as an option in 1936.

RADIO KING FULL DRESS MARINE PEARL DELUXE SWING OUTFIT
1937–1939
6.5x14, 9x13, 12x14, 16x16, 14x28
hold-all trap rail addd in 1938

AIRWAY SPECIAL SWING OUTFIT #4
1939–1941
6.5x14, 6x10, 12x26

RADIO KING FULL DRESS SWING OUTFIT
1937–1939
6.5x14, 9x13, 12x14, 14x28

SUPER SWING KRUPA RADIO KING FULL DRESS STREAMLINED ENSEMBLE #1
1939–1941
6.5x14,9x13,12x14,14x28

GENE KRUPA SUPER RADIO KING DELUXE ENSEMBLE
1941
7x14, 9x13, 12x14, 16x16, 14x28

SUPER RADIO KING "WINDSOR" ENSEMBLE
1941
7x14, 9x13, 10x14, 14x28

GENE KRUPA OUTFIT #92
1937–1939
6.5x14, 9x13, 12x14, 14x28

MARBLE FINISH BALLROOM RADIO KING OUTFIT
1941
7x14, 9x13, 12x14, 14x28

AIRWAY SPECIAL SWING OUTFIT #3
1939–1941
6.5x14,6x10,8x12,12x26

MARBLE FINISH KRUPA JUNIOR OUTFIT
1941
7x14,7x10, 9x13, 14x26

SWING-MASTER OUTFIT
1941
6.5x14, 7x11, 9x13, 14x26

RADIO KING
1941
7x14, 9x13, 12x14, 14x28

SLINGERLAND NEW SWING SPECIAL OUTFIT
1941
7x14, 7x10, 14x26

ROLLING BOMBER
1942
6.5x14, 9x13, 12x14, 16x16, 14x26 or 28

2-N JOBBING OUTFIT
1955–1962
5.5x13, 8x12, 12x20

GENE KRUPA DELUXE RADIO KING ENSEMBLE 1-N
1948–1955
5.5x14, 9x13, 16x16, 14x24 or 26

GENE KRUPA JUNIOR ENSEMBLE 7-N
1948–1962
5.5x14, 7x10, 8x12

SLINGERLAND ERA LEEDY OUTFITS

NEW ERA OUTFIT

1956–1958

Only the first Slingerland Leedy catalog (1956) showed the "doubled up" beavertail lugs on the snare. By 1958 Slingerland had introduced the Leedy double-ended tension casing . A 14x22 bass drum was offered at no extra charge.

8x12
14"x20"
4.5x14

NITE CLUB OUTFIT #1

1956

6 1/2" x14", 14"x24" offered at no extra charge. From 1958 through 1965 this configuration was known as the Shelly Manne Outfit #11.

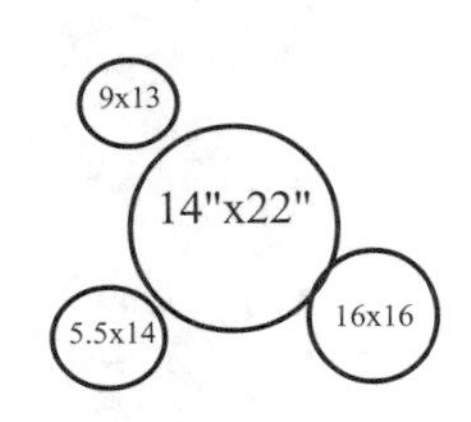

ARAGON OUTFIT

1956–1962

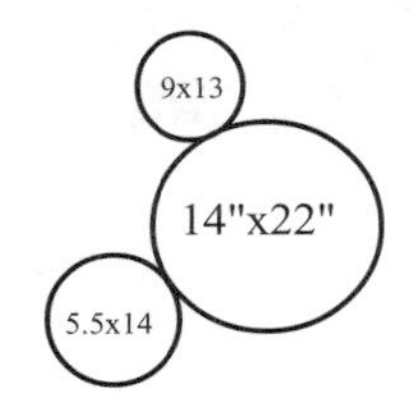

ILLUSTRATED IN BLACK DIAMOND PEARL

THE COMBO OUTFIT #5

1956–1962

The 1956 catalog showed a snare drum with streamlined Slingerland lugs. In 1958 the catalog # was changed to #15 and the snare had the new double-ended Leedy lugs.

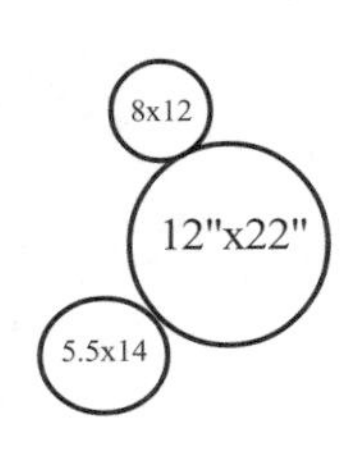

LEEDY
THE "CASUAL" OUTFIT #8
1956–1965
5.5x14, 12x22

Catalog # changed to #18 in 1958 when the double-ended Leedy lugs replaced the Slingerland streamlined lugs on the snare.

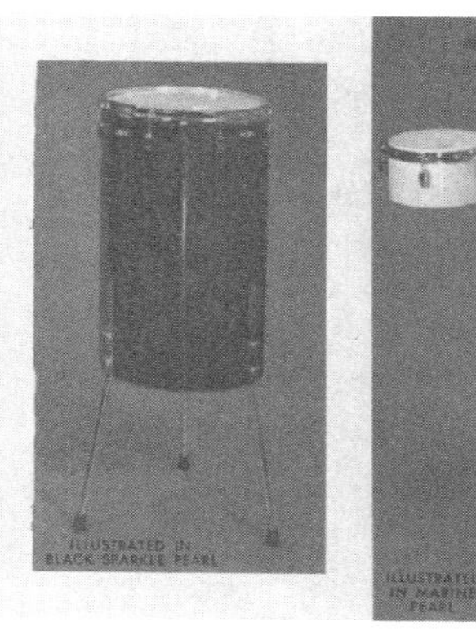

LEEDY COCKTAIL DRUMS
1956–1965 1962–1965

LEEDY RAY MOSCA OUTFIT #12
1962
5.5x14, 8x12, 8x12, 16x16, 14x20
Renamed Drum Solo Outfit in 1965

LEEDY NEW JAZZ OUTFIT #14
1962
5.5x14, 8x12, 14x14, 14x18
Renamed Frank Capp Outfit in 1965 when the bass drum was changed from 18" to 20".

LEEDY COMBO OUTFIT #163
1965
5.5x14, 8x12, 14x20

LEEDY CAMPUS OUTFIT #173
1965
5.5x14, 8x12, 14x20

JAM SESSION 3-N
1955–1970
5.5x14, 14x22

The bass drum muffler and nickel option were both dropped in 1958. In 1963 a hi-hat was added and the snare drum had a new (zoomatic) strainer. Catalogued in 1955 as the Radio King Jam Session 3-N.

SWINGSTER ENSEMBLE 8-N
1948–1967
5.5x14, 12x20 or 22 or 24

Catalogued from 1948 to 1951 with a 24" bass drum, from 1953 to 1964 with a 22" bass drum. From 1964 through 1967, the bass drum was 20".

SWING-MASTER ENSEMBLE 5-N
1948–1962
5.5x14, 12x22 or 24

Catalogued from 1948 to 1951 with a 24" bass drum, from 1953 to 1962 with a 22" bass drum.

MODERN JAZZ OUTFIT
1960–1976
5.5x14, 8x12, 14x20

Zoomatic strainer replaced the Super, or "clamshell" in 1962. Set-o-matic holder replaced the consolette tom holder in 1968.

RADIO KING WINDSOR ENSEMBLE 6-N
1948–1973
5.5x14, 9x13, 14x22 to 26

Originally the bass drum options were either 14x24 or 14x26. By 1953 the options were 14x22 or 14x24. In 1963 and 1964 only a 22" bass drum was offered, then only a 20" bass drum through 1973.
The words Radio King were dropped from the name of this outfit in 1957.

DUET OUTFIT 14N
1960–1976
5x14, (2) 8x12, 16x16, (2) 14x20

The Duet was Slingerland's first catalogued double-bass drum outfit. In 1970 the hardware was beefed up and the rack toms were changed to 8x12 and 9x13. In 1976 the standard bass drum size was increased to 14x22.

The Little Pro outfit, below left, appeared in only one catalog, 1958's catalog #59. It was probably inspired by the junior-size kit that Don Osborne made in 1957 at home in his basement for son Donnie to learn on (left). This "Slinger-Leedy" outfit has a 13" snare drum, 10"x8" and 12"x14" tom-toms, and a 14"x16" bass drum.

Little Pro Snare Drum 5.5x10

Little Pro Outfit
1958
5x6, 5.5x10, 5x10, 16x18

GENE KRUPA DELUXE ENSEMBLE 1-N
1955–1973
5.5x14, 9x13, 16x16, 14x22

With a few updates in hardware and sizes, this outfit remained in the Slingerland line from 1955 through 1973. Nickel was no longer an option in 1960, and the set-o-matic holder was introduced in 1968. In 1976 this outfit was renamed the Deluxe Outfit 1-N and in 1977 the name was changed again to the GK.

The 18"x20" drum with the Combo Be-Bop kit was equipped with one wood hoop and one metal hoop so it could easily be converted from a large tom-tom (with a bass drum pedal striking the bottom head) to a small bass drum.

COMBO BE-BOP
1952–1962
4x13, 18x20

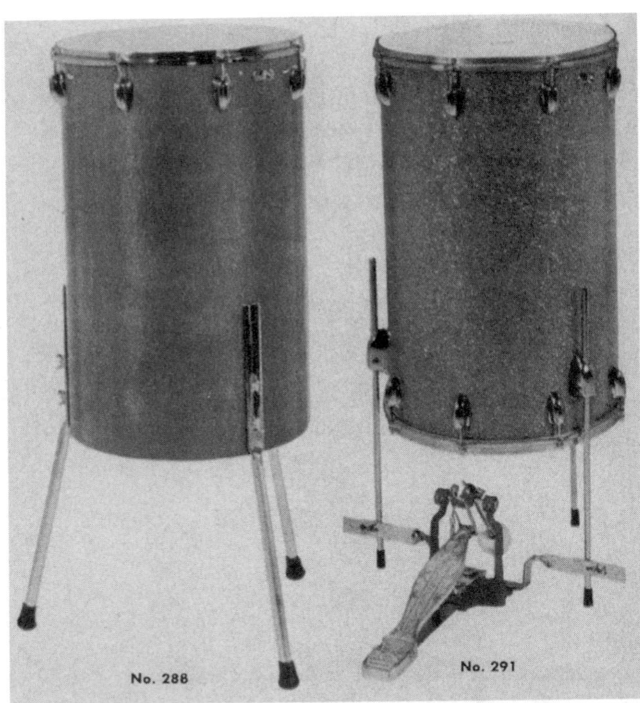

COCKTAIL DRUMS
1953–1976
Single head '53–'76
Double head '55–'76

COCKTAIL OUTFIT
1963–1973
5.5x14,16x16

MODERN SOLO OUTFIT 2-R
1963–1977
5x14,(2) 8x12, 16x16,14x20
First catalogued with 2 8x12 rack toms and the 171 tom holder. In 1968 the outfit was listed with 8x12 and 9x13 toms and the double set-o-matic holder. In 1976 the bass drum was changed from 20" to 22".

STAGE BAND 74N
1963–1973
5.5x14, 9x13, 12x15, 14x22

SWING MASTER 63N
1963–1968
5.5x14, 8x12, 14x22

BE BOP OUTFIT 62N
1963–1968
5.5x14,14x20

GENE KRUPA JUNIOR 17-N
1963–1964
5.5x14,8x12,14x22

JET OUTFIT 20N 1965–1970
Flush-base tom stand standard from 1965 to 1967, set-o-matic tom holder from 1968-1970.

MODERN COMBO 75N
1965–1973
5.5x14, 9x13, 9x10, 14x16, 14x18

ROCK OUTFIT 50N
1968–1978
5x14, 8x12, 9x13, 16x16, 14x20

BUDDY RICH OUTFIT 80N
1968–1977
5.5x14, 9x13, 16x16, 16x16, 14x22

SAN JUAN OUTFIT 65N
1970–1976
5x14, 7x13, 7x14, 16x16, 14x20

AVANTE 60N
1970–1977
5x14, 8x12, 9x13, 10x14, 16x16, 14x22

POP OUTFIT 58N
1968–1977
5x14, 8x12, 9x13, 14x16, 14x20

JOE CUSATIS OUTFIT 4N
1968–1973
5.5x14, 8x12, 16x16, 14x20

PHANTOM 50N-P
1973
5x14, 8x12, 9x13, 16x16, 14x22

CONCORDE OUTFIT 11N 1973–1976
6.5x14, deep bongos, 8x12, 9x13, 10x14, 10x15, 16x16, 18x20, (2) 14x24

DENNIS ST. JOHN 4N 1976–1977
5x14, 9x13, 16x16, 14x22

JAZZ ROCK 57N 1970–1977
6.5x14, 10x14, 10x15, 16x16, 18x20, (2) 14x24

JUPITER OUTFIT 90N 1976–1977
6.5x14, 6.5x10, 8x12, 9x13, 10x14, 12x15, 14x16, 16x18, 14x22

RJB 70N 1976–1977
6.5x14, 8x12, 9x13, 10x14, 10x15, 16x18, 14x24

SUPER ROCK 51N 1976–1977
6.5x14, 9x13, 10x14, 16x18, 14x14

CLASSIC ROCK 61N
1977
6.5x14, 9x13, 10x14, 16x16, 16x18, 14x24

MARQUIS 99N
1977
6.5x14, 8x12, 9x13, 10x14, 12x15, 16x16, 16x18, (2) 14x24

EXPLOSION 610T
1979
5.5x14, 5.5x6, 5.5x8, 6.5x10, 8x12, 9x13, (2) 16x16, (2) 14x24

POWERPLAY
11CW CUT-A-WAY
1979
6.5x14, 6, 8, 10, 12, 13, 14, 15, 16, 16x18, 14x22

DOUBLE HEADER 699T
1979
6.5x14, 8x12, 9x13, 10x14, 12x15, 16x16, 16x18, (2) 14x24

DOUBLE TIME 657T
1979
6.5x14, 10x14, 10x15, 16x16, 18x20, (2) 14x24

ENERGIZER 690T
1979
6.5x14, 6.5x10, 8x12, 9x13, 10x14, 12x15, 14x16, 16x18, 14x22

BLUES TIME 670T
1979
6.5x14, 8x12, 9x13, 10x14, 12x15, 16x18, 14x24

COUNTRY ROAD 671T
1979
6.5x14, 9x13, 10x14, 12x15, 14x16, 16x18, 14x24

A CUT ABOVE 695T
1979
6.5x14, Cutaways 6, 8, 10, 12, 9x13, 10x14, 16x16, 14x22

ON TOUR 658T
1979
5x14, 8x12, 9x13, 14x16, 14x22

THE TRAVELER #2R
1979
5x14, 8x12, 9x13, 16x16, 14x22

FREELANCE 4R
1979
5x14, 9x13, 16x16, 14x22

ROADIE 9R
1979
5x14, 8x12, 14x14, 14x20

NEW HORIZONS 661T
1979
6.5x14, 9x13, 10x14, 16x16, 16x18, 14x24

TIME MACHINE 651T
1979
6.5x14, 9x13, 10x14, 16x18, 14x24

UPBEAT 650T
1979
5x14, 8x12, 9x13, 16x16, 14x22

FUSION 680T
1979
5x14, 9x13, (2) 16x16, 14x22

1983

The Slingerland line was reworked again for the 1983 catalog. Magnum hardware was introduced and the outfits were all reconfigured. The outfits on this page were discontinued before the 1985 catalog was published.

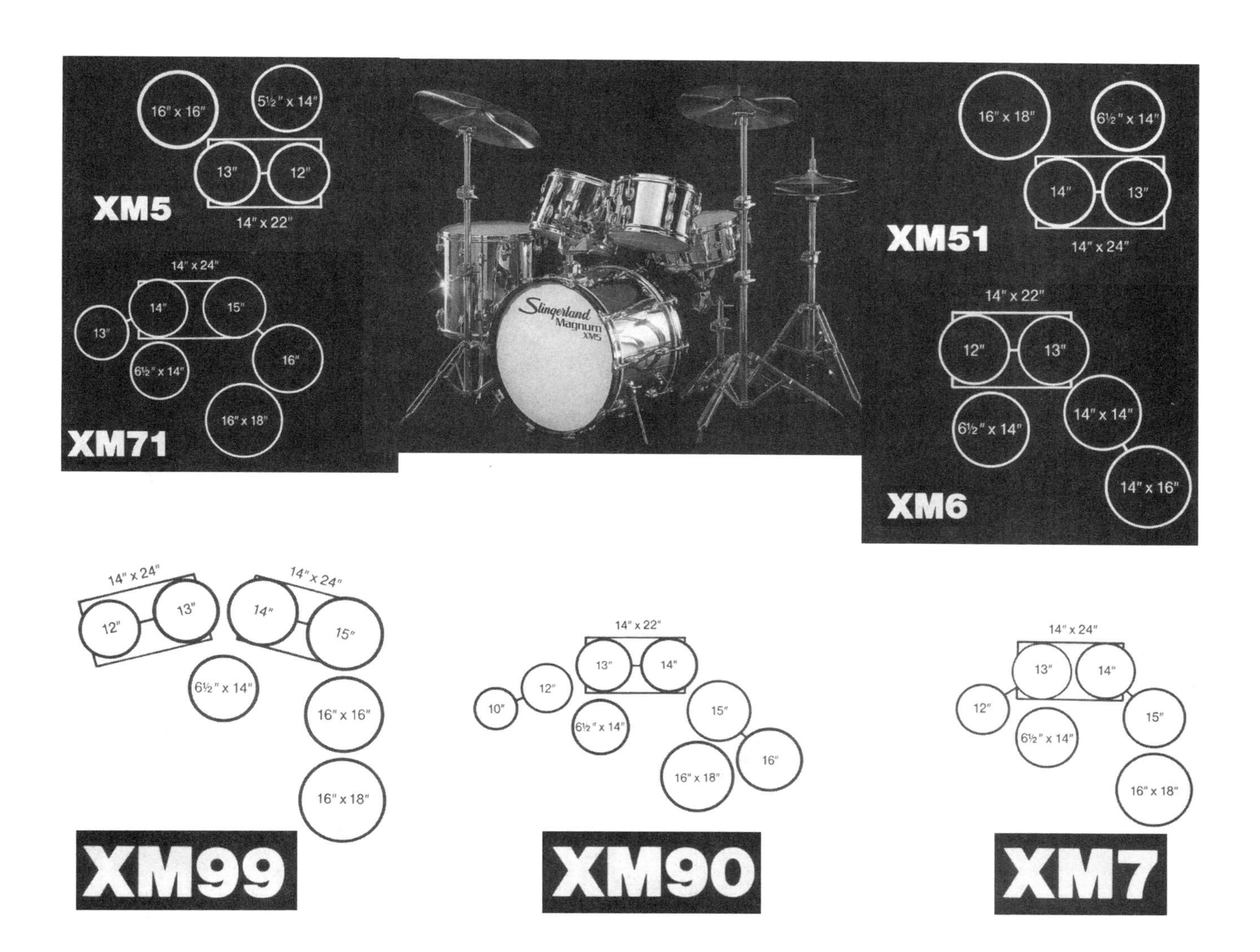

The Artist Series catalogued in 1983 were Spirit series drum outfits packaged with lightweight hardware.

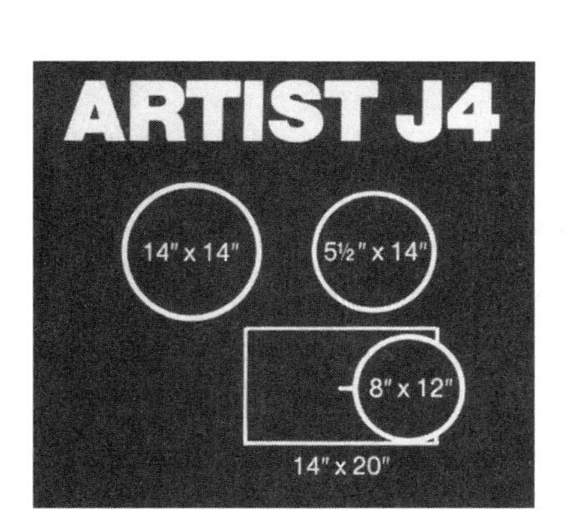

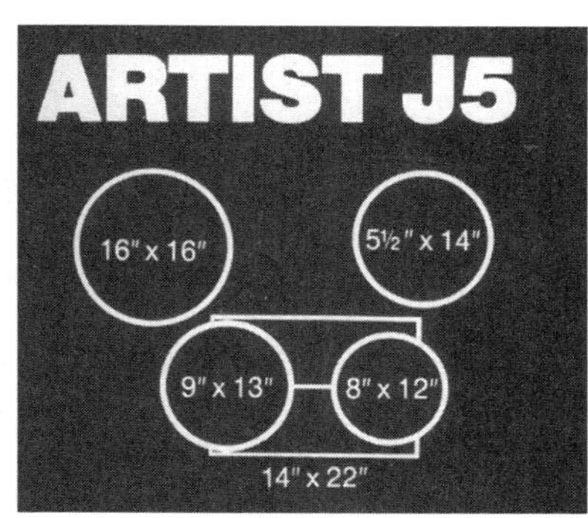

1983–1986

The Magnum and Spirit outfits on this page first appeared in the 1983 catalog, and were still in the 1985 catalog which was the last catalog published while Slingerland was based in Chicago. After purchasing Slingerland in 1986 and moving all Slingerland assets to South Carolina, Gretsch used this catalog until their supply of catalogs and drums was depleted.

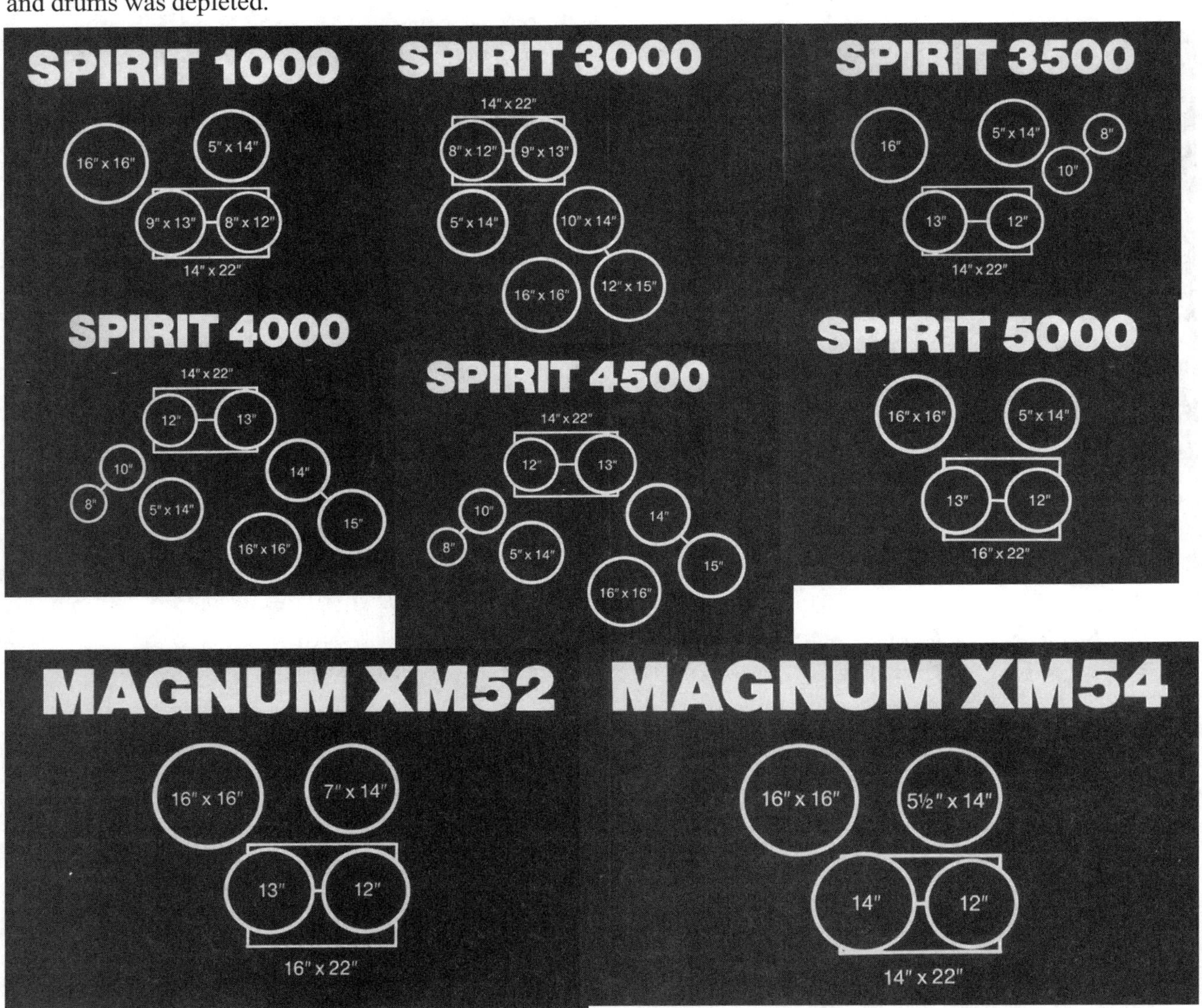

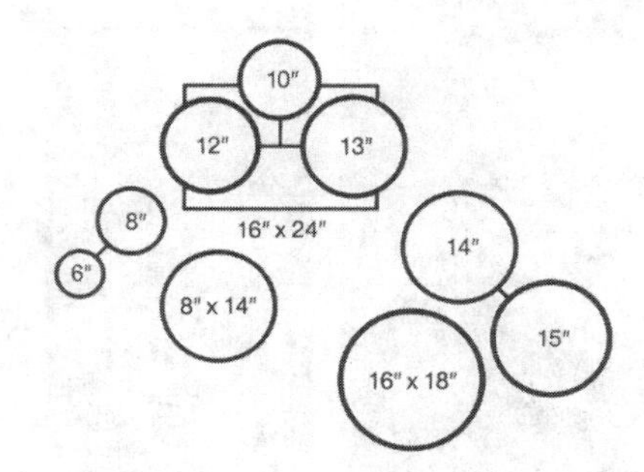

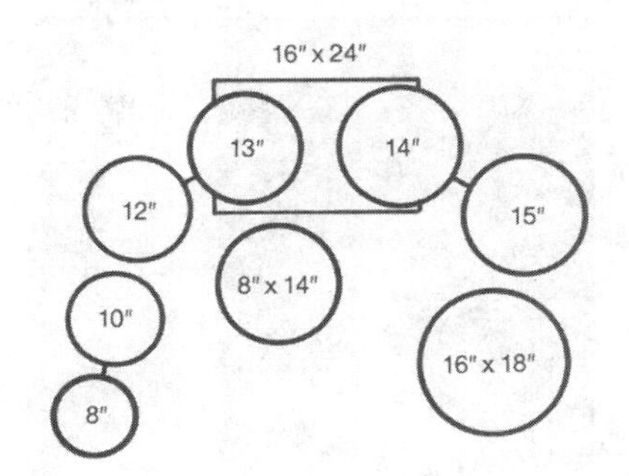

HSS-Era Slingerland 1990–1994

The Slingerland drums distributed by HSS fall into three basic groups: The Spirit series of imported drums were five-ply mahogany shells. The Artist series drums were also made offshore, but with American wood. The shells were five-ply maple (inner and outer plies) and mahogany (three middle plies). The Lite series drums were all-maple shells made by Jasper Wood Products in Indiana. They were made to HSS specs which called for six-ply 6mm shells for toms and six-ply 7mm shells for snare and bass drums.

ARTIST CUSTOM SERIES SETS

SA3008C	14x18, 8x10, 8x12, 14x14, 4x14
SA3000C	14x20, 8x12, 14x14, 5-1/2x14
SA3002C	14x22, 8x12, 9x13, 16x16, 5-1/2x14
SA3060C	14x20, 8x10, 8x12, 9x13, 10x14, 4x14, S35570
SA3062C	14x22, 8x12, 9x13, 10x14, 11x15, 4x14, S35570

FEATURES:

- Traditional Jazz drum sizes-from 8" to 22"
- Traditional felt-loaded lugs
- 5 ply Maple-Mahogany-Maple shell (North American Maple)
- Traditional white coated medium heads standard
- All mounts, leg brackets, and lugs equipped with isolators
- 7 High-gloss lacquer finishes
- Traditional and Studio configurations available
- Custom sizes available on request with or without mounts
- Wide variety of hardware configurations available
- All drums equipped with Slingerland "Stick-Saver" hoops
- Standard tom holder assembly
- Folding adjustable spurs
- Snare drums from 4" to 8" depths
- All snare drums equipped with "Zoomatic" throw-off

POWER CUSTOM SERIES SETS

S3002C	16x22, 10x12, 11x13, 16x16, 6-1/2x14 metal

FEATURES:

- Standard power tom sizes and extended bass drum sizes from 8 x 8 to 18 x 18 and 16 x 20 to 18 x 24
- Traditional felt-loaded lugs
- 5-ply Maple-Mahogany-Maple shell (North American Maple)
- 2-ply heavy clear batter and 1-ply medium clear resonators
- All mounts, leg brackets, and lugs equipped with isolators
- 7 High-gloss lacquer finishes
- Standard 5 piece configurations available
- Custom sizes available on request with or without mounts
- Wide variety of hardware configurations available
- All drums equipped with Slingerland "Stick-Saver" hoops
- Standard tom holder assembly
- Heavy duty folding adjustable spurs

HSS ARTIST SERIES

SA3054C-MP (Marine Pearl) Stands and Cymbals not included

The Artist Classic Series—Traditional *swing* and *be-bop* shell sizes combined with the two most elegant drum finishes in the history of jazz drumming make the artist *classic* series the envy of every aspiring drummer young and old. Slightly larger bass drum sizes allow the drummer full control of the lower register and puts the drummer back into the driver seat of any musical ensemble large or small. But the key to this feeling of power over the music comes not only from the visual appeal of the classic series. It is directly related to the raw materials used in the fabrication of such a unique instrument and the care and workmanship of a company dedicated to making music come alive. *A classic* look and a *classic* sound-**Slingerland is Percussion.**

SA3000C-BP(Black Diamond Pearl) Stands and Cymbals not included

FEATURES:

- **Traditional jazz drum sizes-from 10" to 26"**
- **Traditional felt-loaded lugs**
- **5 ply Maple-Mahogany Maple shell(North American Maple)**
- **Traditional white coated heads standard**
- **Original vintage Marine Pearl(MP) and Black Pearl(BP) finishes**
- **Big Band and small combo configurations**
- **Three snare drum sizes-4, 5.5, 6.5 x 14**
- **All snare drums equipped with zoomatic throw-off**
- **Wide variety of hardware configurations available**
- **All drums equipped with Slingerland stick-saver hoops**
- **Standard tom holder assembly**
- **Folding adjustable spurs**

HSS LITE SERIES

Classic Rock (SCR) 7x14, 10x12,11x13,17x16,17x22
Classic Jazz (SCK) 7x14, 9x10,10x12,15x14,16x20
Rock, Jazz Blues (SRJB) 7x14,9x10,10x12,12x14,13x15,16x20

Studio Recording (SRS)
7x14,9x10,10x12,12x14,13x15,16x20
Pop-Rock (SPR) 7x14,10x12,11x13,16x15,16x20
Heavy Rock (SHR) 7x14,11x13,12x14,17x16,18x18,17x24

The Shells. Construction of the shells begins by using only the finest select North American rock maple. Our craftsmen employ age-old techniques, combined with modern technology, to ensure throughout the entire process that each and every detail is as near to perfection as is humanly possible.

To achieve strong and uniformly dense six-ply (6mm) tom shells and (7mm) snare and bass drum shells, for instance, all plies are cross-laminated, all joints are staggered, and no reinforcement rings are used to influence stability. Therefore, our shells offer less vibrational interference, increased projection and an uncompromised, pure tone.

Also, our comparably thin shells contribute to the higher proportion of overtones in the Lite's overall sound spectrum and the set's more ambient, brilliant frequency spectrum. Because of the shells' high flexional resistance and greater density, however, this ambience does not overwhelm the Lite's prominent fundamental tone. Instead, the two separate tones blend to create a sound that is unique to the Lite.

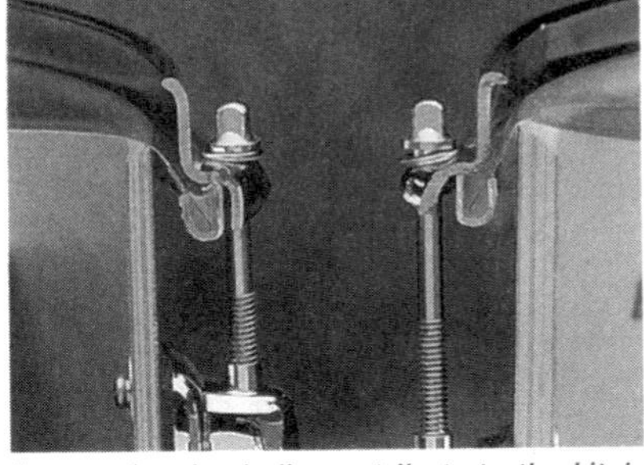

Dense six-ply shells contribute to the Lite's prominent fundamental tone. The Floating Head Principle helps prevent vibrational interference.

The Floating Head Principle. As a general rule, the less contact there is between the head and the shell, the less vibration will be absorbed by the shell. In order to accomplish this, we employed the Floating Head Principle, which creates the "Dresden effect." Although it is traditionally applied to concert timpani, we have used this principle on all our drums. Shells are equipped with precision 45-degree beveled bearing edges, reduced diameter shells, and all drums feature the unique inwardly-flanged Stick-Saver hoops. The drum heads, therefore, extend or "float" over the bearing edge, which results in minimal contact and, consequently, less vibrational interference.

In short, the Floating Head Principle not only maximizes the fundamental tone of the drums, but also aids in decreasing distortion and increasing sustain, allowing a natural decay of the tone.

The Bass Drum. The bass drum comes with the newly designed Evans Genera EQ

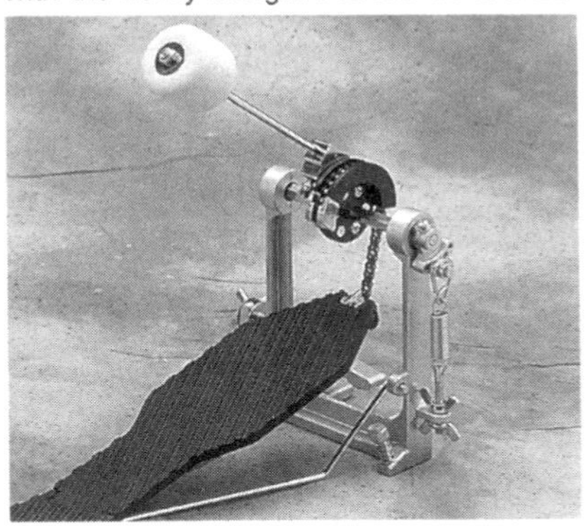

The Genera EQ bass drum system eliminates the need for inferior muffling systems.

bass drum system with a black ambient head that features a Slingerland logo in white. Combined with the new shells, these heads produce a state-of-the-art sound spectrum that eliminates the need to use inferior muffling systems. The EQ Genera drum system also increases the projection of the fundamental tone of the bass drum by allowing the bass drum's bearing edge to properly meet the heads.

The Spurs. Our newly designed bass drum spurs come with memory-locks, large retractable rubber feet and floor spikes. Besides allowing a quicker, more accurate setup, the spurs create a solid suspension of the bass drum shell. This more stationary suspension aids in promoting the fundamental tone of the drum and also helps prevent vibration loss through the floor.

Isolators on the spurs add to the prevention of frequency absorption. And hidden spikes beneath the spurs' large retractable rubber feet permit the option of having a firmer attachment to the floor.

Lite's bass drum spurs provide a solid suspension of the bass drum shell. Notice the original Slingerland-style claw hooks and T-rods.

The Toms. All toms come equipped with Evans CAD/CAM 1000 weight clear batters and resonant bottom heads. The combination of the thicker batter heads, the thinner resonator heads and the dense, very stable shells maximizes the overall tone of the toms. Together they create an ambient, live sound, as well as a strong fundamental tone.

The Snare Drum. The Lite's snare drum features a unique snare strainer assembly that extends across the drum head. The result is two distinct sound possibilities.

1) When struck in the center (a diameter of approximately 4 inches), the snare drum releases a strong, "dry" fundamental tone.

2) When struck off-center, closer to the edge, the snare drum releases a tone composed of a wider variety of overtones, or "color," which is not unlike that of the older Slingerland snare drums from the 30's and 40's. The strainer assembly, combined with a precision bearing edge and snare bed, creates increased sensitivity at the edge of the head.

For ease of adjustment, the snare drum is

adjustable from both sides. And the snare strands are exact replicas of the original Slingerland design. Like the bass drum, the Lite snare is not equipped with a muffling system, and, if properly tuned, does not require one.

The Isolators. All felt-loaded lugs, as well as the holder brackets and the tom tom holder plate, come with extra thick isolators to help prevent frequency absorption throughout the entire drum set.

Plus, improved knurled L-arms come with memory locks to allow exact and versatile placement. Knurled metal L-arms are gripped by the memory locks better and, therefore, attach to the brackets more securely. When the L-arms are combined with the new S5970 isolator bracket, you'll enjoy increased sustain without sacrificing a bright attack.

The tom tom holder comes with a heavy-duty isolator gasket to inhibit tom tom vibrations from reaching the bass drum shell and producing an undesirable sympathetic vibration.

HSS SPIRIT SERIES

S2000-B 5-Piece includes: SBD 22-B 16" x 22" Bass drum, ST 22-B 10" x 12" Tom tom, ST 23-B 11" x 13" Tom tom, SFT 26-B 16" x 16" Floor tom, SD 14 6.5" x 14" Snare drum, Hardware - S35962 - Snare drum stand, S35963 - Cymbal stand, S35966 - Cymbal boom stand, S35964 - Hi hat stand, S1938 - Bass drum pedal

S2000-B 7-Piece Same components as 5-Pc. set plus ST 20-B 9" x 10" Tom tom, S 12" x 14" Tom tom, Hardware - S35570 Double tom stand

S2000-B 8-Piece Same as 7-Pc. set plus SBD 32 - 16" x 22" Bass drum, S1938 - Bass drum pedal

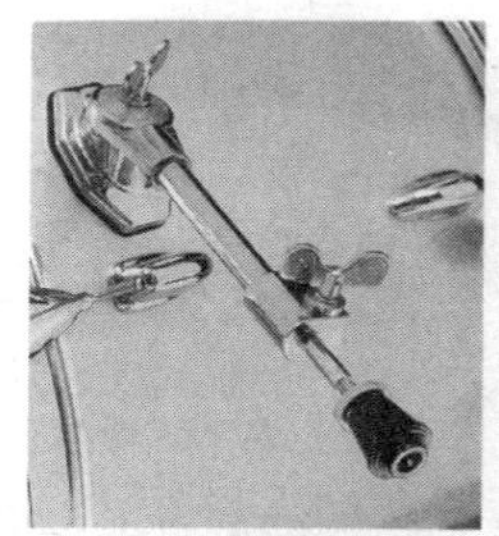

New folding adjustable heavy duty spurs featuring Slingerland "Earnuts". Original Slingerland style clawhooks and T-handles.

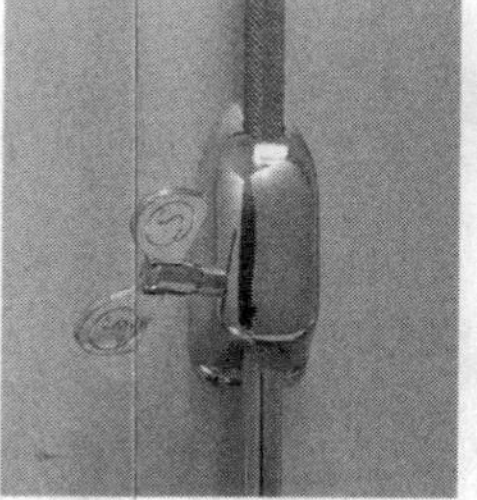

New—original floor tom bracket S590. Heavy duty die cast construction for durability. Slingerland "earscrew" standard for positive set-up.

New Slingerland "earscrew" at all locations on stands for ease of set up.

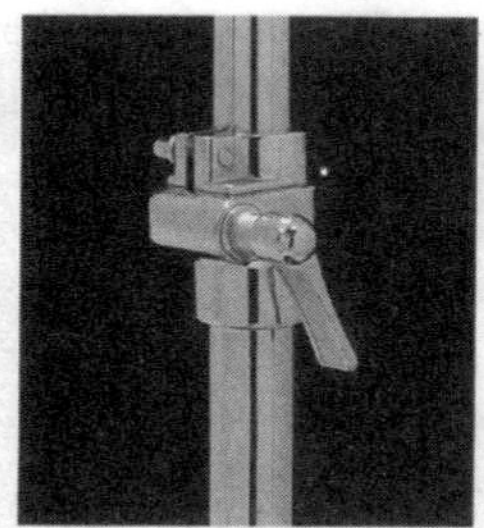

Note ¼ turn quick release height adjustment; adjustable ratchet tilt assembly; memory lock; neoprene sleeve.

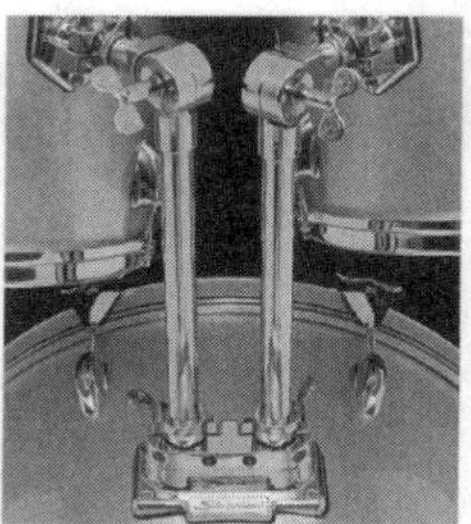

New double tom holder features Slingerland engraved nameplate, isolation gasket, neoprene inserts and "earnuts" at all adjustment locations.

GIBSON SPIRIT SERIES

6-piece Studio kit

- **Classic Slingerland Styling**
- **American Made**
- **Unsurpassed 5 Year Warranty**
- **Double Braced Hardware**
- **Heat and Scratch Resistant Finish**

5-piece Classic kit

4-piece Jazz kit

GIBSON STUDIO KING SERIES, 1998

Modern Jazz SKMJ4 — Broadway SKBW4 — New Standard SKNS4

Classic 5 SKCL5 — Metropolitan SKMP5 — Rolling Thunder SKRT5

Session Master SKSM6 — Performer SKPF6 — Super Studio SKSS7

All of the Studio King kits were also offered in Touring Series versions. The Touring Series drums were fitted with 2.3 millimeter Stick Saver hoops (engraved with the Slingerland name) while regular Studio King series drums had die-cast hoops. The bass drum hoops on Touring Series drums were not inlaid, and finishes were limited to satin stains and classic wraps. They were priced about 25% less than standard Studio King kits.

Classic 5, Touring Series TSCL5

GIBSON SIGNATURE SERIES, 1998

The two kits in the Legends signature series were nearly identical. These B&W photos do not show the main difference; the Krupa kit was covered with a very white White Marine Pearl, while the Rich kit was covered with a White Marine Pearl with a bluish tint.

(Imported) 5.5x14, 11x14, 16x16,16x22
Indica Green with Tre Cool signature badges

SLINGERLAND MALLET INSTRUMENTS 1967–1972

The only early Slingerland drum catalog to include mallet instruments was their second catalog, of 1929. That catalog included three pages of Deagan xylophones, marimbas, bells, and chimes. These instruments were not unique to Slingerland; many drum companies and large music stores catalogued these models.

When Conn sold the Ludwig drum division to the Ludwig family and the Leedy drum division to Slingerland in 1955, the mallet instrument division was sold to Grover Jenkins (The Jenco Company) of Decatur, Illinois. Jenkins was a former small-town clarinet player who got into manufacturing by way of a small repair shop. The mallet instrument line introduced in Slingerland's 1967 catalog was manufactured by Jenco.

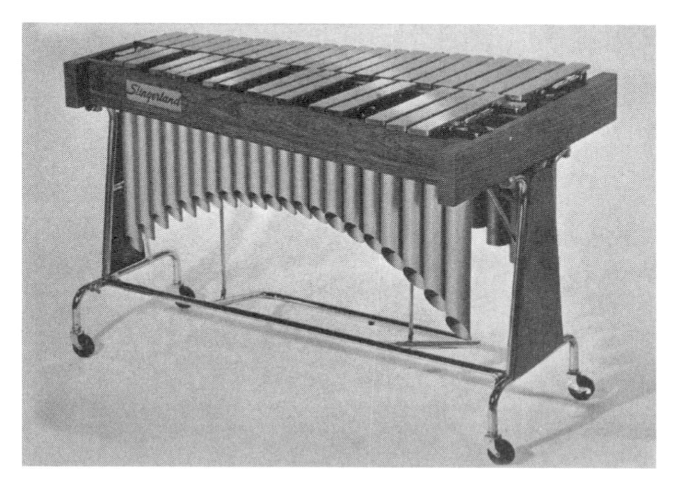

740

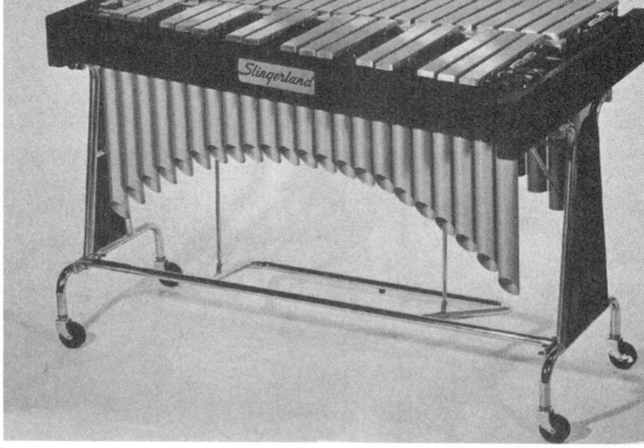

730

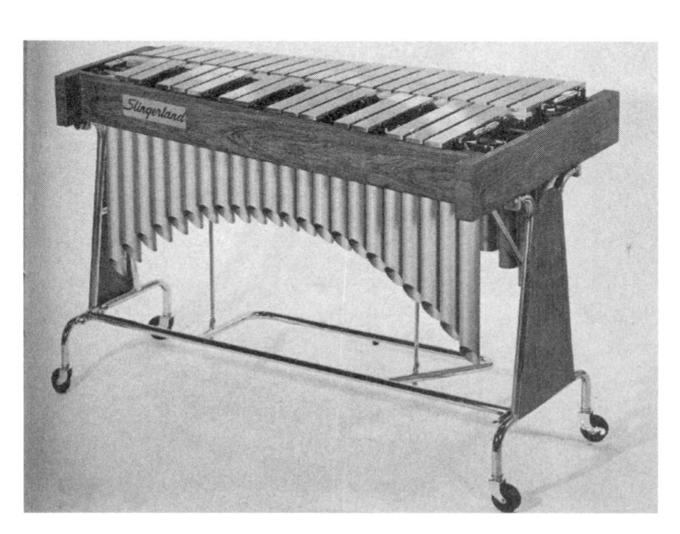

720

700

M802

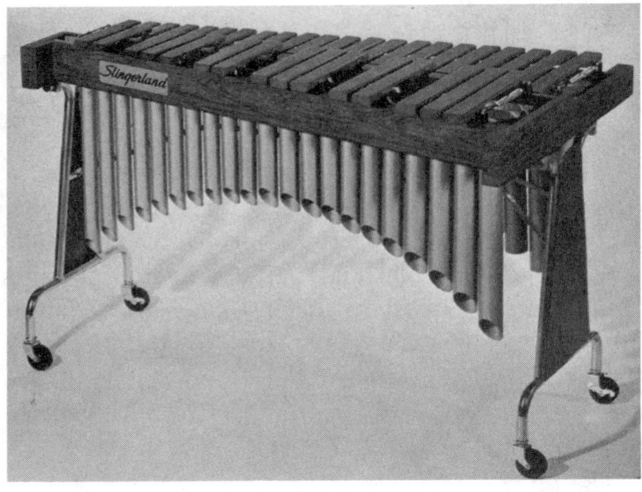

M800

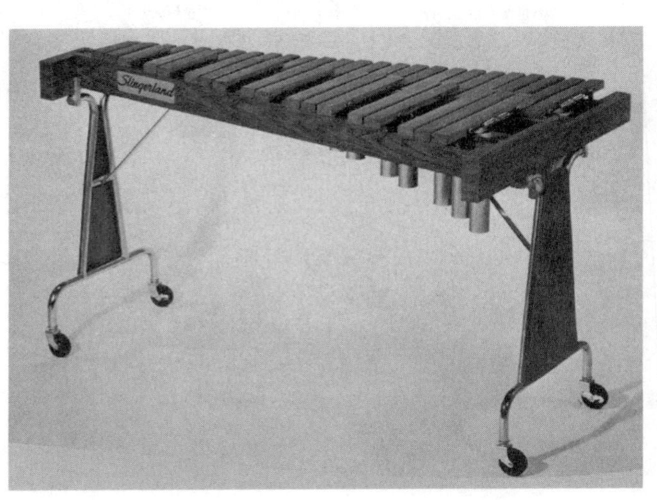

X920

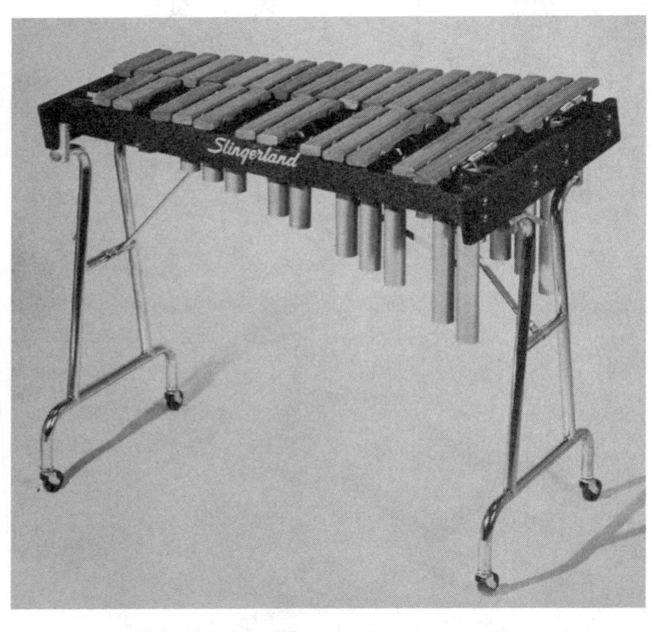

M830 (2.5 Octave)
M840 (3 Octave)

SLINGERLAND 2 1/2 OCTAVES TUNED G59 TO C88 ORCHESTRA BELLS WITH CASE

No. B-600 . . . . $225.00B

Complete with Case & Brass Mallets

Their clear, brilliant tone is unexcelled. Bars are made of alloy steel, 1¼" wide x 5/16" thick, chrome plate. Bars are mounted on rails in a black covered sturdy case, with removable lid.

No. 848 Bell Stand (Pictured on Page 40) $22.00

NEW LITE-WATE ORCHESTRA BELL 2 OCTAVES C TO C

No. B-650 COMPLETE WITH CASE $150.00B

1" x 5/16" Aluminum Bars — Excellent Tone

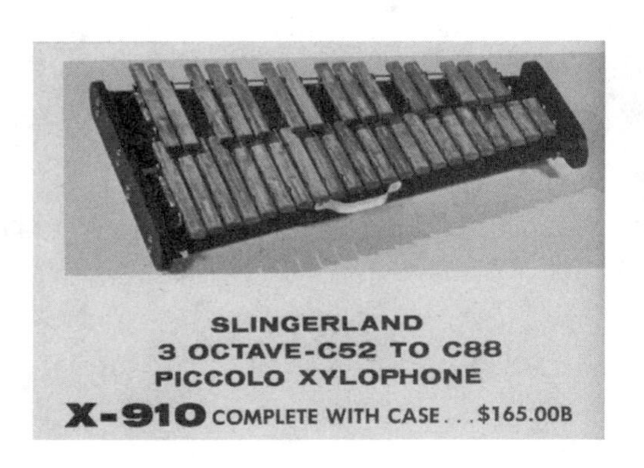

SLINGERLAND 3 OCTAVE-C52 TO C88 PICCOLO XYLOPHONE

X-910 COMPLETE WITH CASE . . . $165.00B

DEAGAN

The Deagan company (dba D.J.C. Corp at the time, previously J.C. Deagan, Inc.) was acquired by Slingerland in 1977 when McMillan owned Slingerland and the Slingerland president was Larry Linkin.

The deal took effect on midnight, October 3. Slingerland paid $250,000.00 at the formal closing, with another $21,000.00 (approximately) to be paid as soon as a final inventory was completed. It appears Deagan was floundering; year-to-date figures from January through the end of June 1977 show an operating loss of over $55,000.00 for the year, and the red ink was nearly deep enough to wipe out the equity which had dwindled to $15,000.00.

So why pay a quarter million dollars for a business with equity of practically nothing? Link was certainly no fool. With the Deagan facility in close proximity to Slingerland, Slingerland's close relationship to Deagan because of the Deagan instruments that had been made for Slingerland, and Link's familiarity with the manufacturing processes and margins, he saw a way this could work.

Deagan had been operating in an older, overcrowded three-story building at 1770 West Berteau. One of the first questions to be addressed was whether to continue operating Deagan there, or relocate it. Slingerland's John Hollerich did a study of the issue for Link. The first thing Hollerich pointed out in the report (which was turned in December 14, 1977) was that the Slingerland plant in Niles was only 65,000 square feet and they were expected to compete with Ludwig, which was operating out of a 280,000-square-foot facility. As Hollerich pointed out, there were four options: A.They could integrate the Deagan operation into the already crowded Niles facility. B.They could add 20,000 square feet on to the Niles facility to house the new division. C.They could rent manufacturing space in a new location. D.They could make some modifications on the present Deagan facility and leave it there. Hollerich, apparently concerned that option A would be chosen, went on to point out that there were compelling reasons to not go in that direction. While it would move the production closer to supervisory personnel and some manufacturing processes such as plating, polishing, and machining could be combined with the drum factory, there were four big drawbacks: A. Deagan would lose its identity. B.All Deagan factory manufacturing and storage space would have to be compressed from the present 20,000 square feet to a maximum of 7,000 square feet. C.This overcrowding would preclude any future growth of either Deagan *or* Slingerland. D.Manufacturing costs would go up due to the increased handling of materials and the need to buy raw materials in smaller quantities due to lack of storage.

The decision was made to leave Deagan where it was and do a little rearranging. In the next three years (Link's last three years with Slingerland) Deagan sales went from $801,000.00 in 1978 to $950,000 in 1979, to $1,265,460 in 1980. In spite of this growth, Link could see that the handwriting was on the wall both for Slingerland and Deagan. He was constantly frustrated at the lack of funds for capital improvements; Slingerland's growth was already being affected. Slingerland sales had grown from $5.2 million the year before Link came to nearly $7 million in 1979, but then began to slip. Just before McMillan sold Slingerland/Deagan to Dan Henkin,Link took advantage of the opportunity to replace Bill Gard who was retiring as the head of NAMM, the National Association of Music Merchants.

The feeling continued to grow at Slingerland that the higher-ups didn't really care about them. Henkin's transition man Tom Burzicki and new Slingerland president Bill Young once again evaluated the Deagan situation. They concluded that maybe a few dollars could be saved by charting a course sort of in between the options Hollerich had listed. In April of 1981 they submitted a joint proposal to Henkin suggesting that Deagan offices be consolidated into the Niles building. Furthermore, they suggested that certain processes (mallet assembly, the wood shop, the machine shop, the paint shop, and the chime/bar polishing) be also "shoehorned" into the Niles building.

By 1982 yet another president was in place at Slingerland: Dick Richardson. Deagan sales were beginning a downward trend, but it wasn't too drastic yet: down from the $1.2 million of 1980 to $1.15 million in 1981. In the first seven months of 1982, sales were $661,000.00. Finally the decision was handed down to move Deagan into the Niles building altogether. "There was no new contruction," says Aloisio, "except for dividing off a couple of rooms for tuning, etc." "That move should never have happened," says Durrett, "it was a big mistake." In addition to the physical compromises that Hollerich had predicted, there were changes in skilled labor. The forced move was the last straw for Deagan veteran Hall Trommer, who resigned. According to Durrett, the real "soul" of Deagan then became Gilberto Serna, who had been with Deagan since the 1960s. By May of 1983 all Deagan materials had been relocated to Niles, but it was nearly two years before production could resume. Finally Spencer Aloisio announced in a May 1985 bulletin to dealers that Deagan would be back in production by June 1st. Gilberto laments that the really crushing blow was that many experienced Deagan workers were terminated and replaced by folks who had no idea what they were doing. Deagan quality plummeted as a result.

The Deagan line within another year became an unprofitable millstone which Slingerland sold to the Yamaha Corporation.

The scale range chart below is from the last Slingerland catalog to include mallet instruments, in 1979. By this time the drum corps arena had expanded to include timp-tom arrays and tuned multiple-tom arrays, so the chart included a scale range for drums.

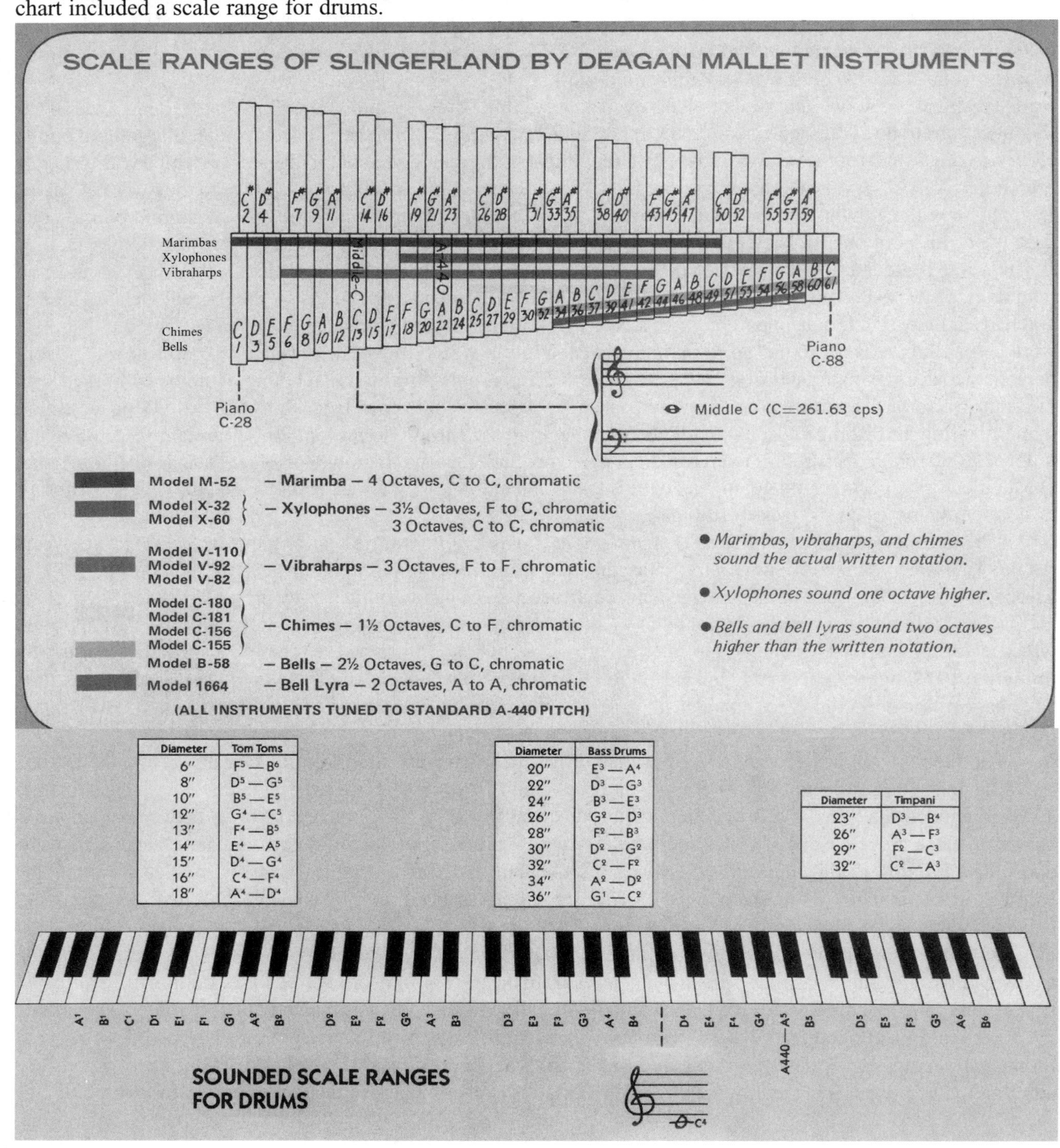

Diameter	Tom Toms
6"	F^5—B^6
8"	D^5—G^5
10"	B^5—E^5
12"	G^4—C^5
13"	F^4—B^5
14"	E^4—A^5
15"	D^4—G^4
16"	C^4—F^4
18"	A^4—D^4

Diameter	Bass Drums
20"	E^3—A^4
22"	D^3—G^3
24"	B^3—E^3
26"	G^2—D^3
28"	F^2—B^3
30"	D^2—G^2
32"	C^2—F^2
34"	A^2—D^2
36"	G^1—C^2

Diameter	Timpani
23"	D^3—B^4
26"	A^3—F^3
29"	F^2—C^3
32"	C^2—A^3

Deagan 1973–1979

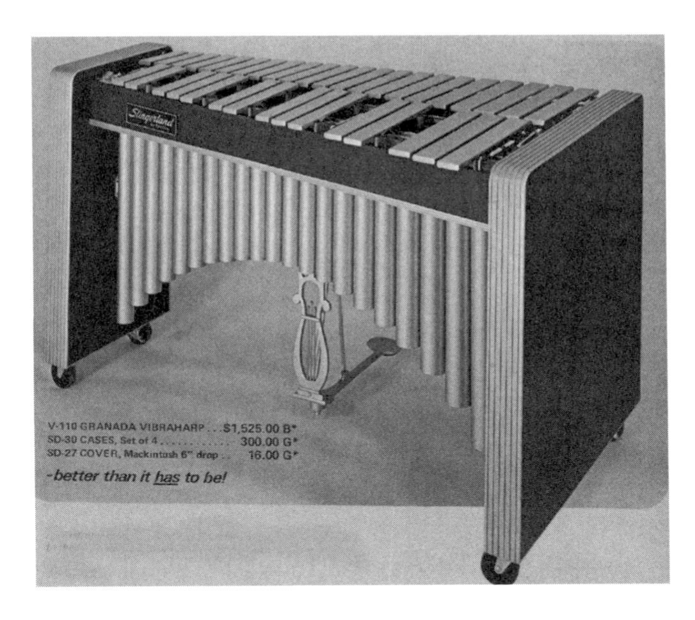

V-110 Vibraharp

Three-octave, F6 to F42

Variable speed motor, 0 to 12 rpm

The catalog number was changed to V113 in 1977 and to Aurora II #1103 in 1979 when the nameplate was changed from Slingerland to Deagan.

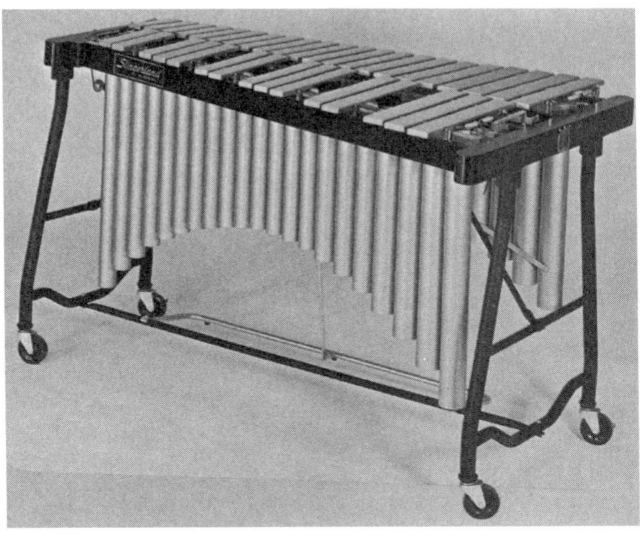

V-92 Vibraharp

Three-octave, F6 to F42, portable

In 1979 the number was changed to #594. There were also a couple cosmetic changes; the nameplate was changed to Deagan and an aluminum trim added to the upper frame. Graduated bar sizes.

A similar model with uniform size 1 1/2" bars was the V-82 which had a three-speed motor rather than continuous. The model number of the V-82 was changed to V-83 in 1977 and 583 in 1979.

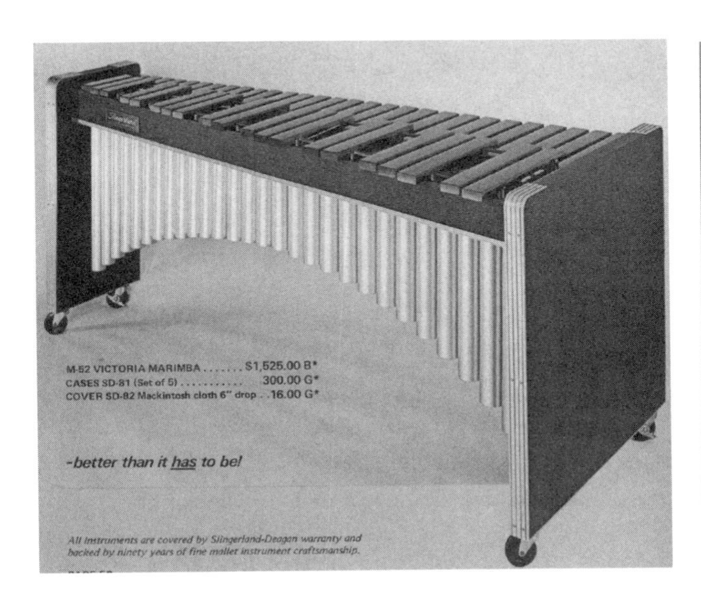

M-52 Marimba

Four-Octave, C-1 to C-49.

Model designation changed to 652 in 1979.

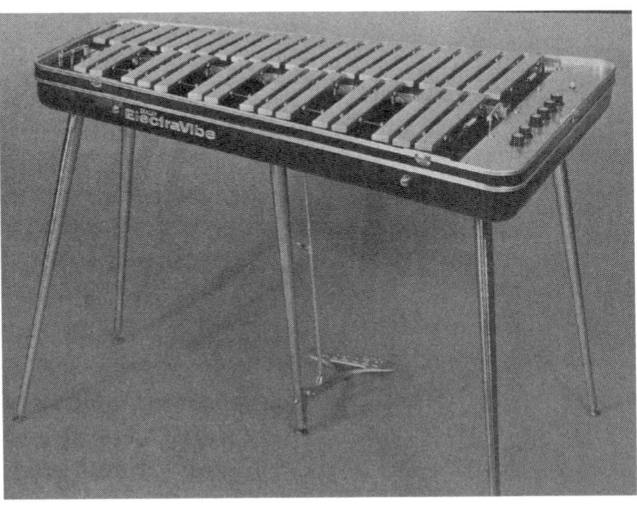

Electravibe 515

Another 1979 reintroduction, the 515 was, according to Deagan, the world's first successful electronic Vibraharp.

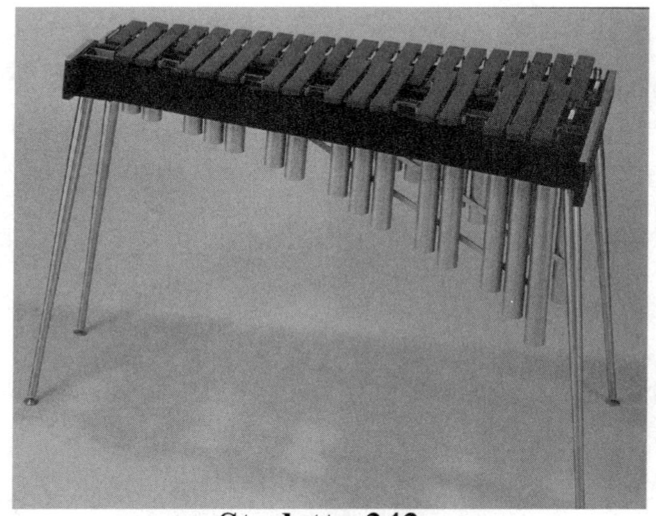

Studette 343

Reintroduction of a portable student model, 3 octaves F-6 to F-42 with rosewood or synthetic bars.

X-32 Concert Xylophone

In 1977 the option of "Klyperon" bars was added, and the # was changed to X-32K (or X-32R for rosewood.) In 1979 the # was changed to 932R,K.)

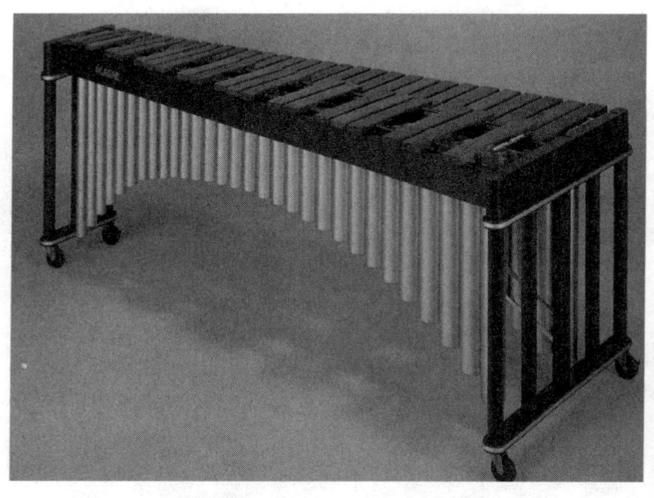

654 Marimba (new 1979)

$4^1/_3$-Octave Economy model

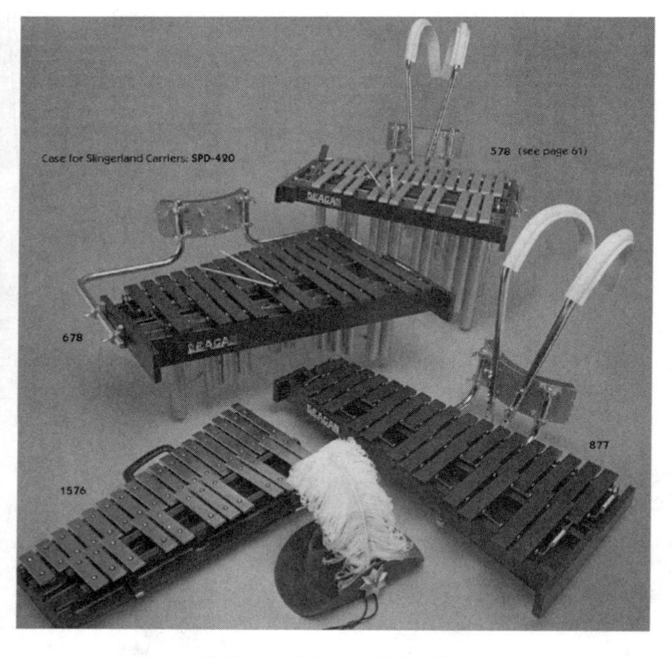

Marching Mallets

The marching mallet instruments were introduced in the late 1970s and included not only the Xylophone, Bells, and Marching Marimba shown here, but also a marching $2^1/_6$-octave Vibe set.

Piccolo Xylophone

#X-60, changed to #860 in 1979 3-Octave C-25 to C-61

Latin Instruments

In 1979 Slingerland introduced a line of professional Latin instruments, shown here. Prior to that, every catalog from 1949 through 1976 included the same pair of Latin Instrument pages shown here on 226 & 227.

Sensational NEW LATIN AM

SLINGERLAND DEEP HAND BONGOS

For the authentic Latin rhythm style of finger playing. Extra deep, with closely set blocks to fit between the knees. Shells are plywood. Made with the new SLINGERLAND heavy duty, non-ferrous FULL FLANGED hoops. Heads are special selected Goat skins tucked and pulled down for hoop clearance to facilitate finger playing. Can be made in any pearl or lacquer finish.

			NICKEL	CHROME
No. **301**	Size 10x8 and 10x6	Pearl finish	$63.00	$70.50
No. **300**	Size 10x8 and 10x6	Lacquer finish	55.50	63.00

(For mounting on bass drum we recommend the shallower Slingerland Bongos No. 302 and 303 as shown herewith.) **Fed. Tax Extra**

WOOD SHELL TIMBALES

Also in 6″ x 10″ and 6″ x 13″ shell sizes, choice of pearl shells or choice of lacquer colors complete with stand. Similar mounting as above, with additional cow-bell holder extra if desired.

		NICKEL	CHROME
No. **308**	Choice of lacquer finishes....	$75.00	$80.00
No. **309**	Choice of Pearl finishes.......	82.50	90.00

PLUS EXCISE TAX

COPPER ALLOY SHELL TIMBALES

New models with the stronger copper alloy shells, (more rigid—greater strength of shell than soft copper or native types). Shell sizes 6″ x 10″ and 6″ x 13″ per pair. Mounted to very sturdy, rigid floor stand, bumper equipped, close, coupled mounting on metal clip plates that enable player to unassemble with ease. Solid—strong—rigid—secure.

		NICKEL	CHROME
No. **311**	Copper Alloy Timbales, pair with stand.................	$82.50	$90.00
No. **361**	Holder attachment for two cowbells	$ 5.25	$ 7.50

PLUS EXCISE TAX

GOURDS
(Cuban Guiro)

Genuine Cuban shell gourds hand painted, in the proper shape and size, thin walled for easy speaking. Evenly notched, and supplied complete with scraper.

No. 1150 Cuban Gourd........ each $6.95

PLUS EXCISE TAX

No. 1150

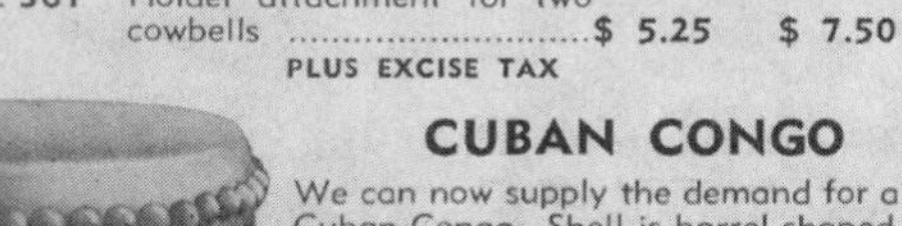

CUBAN CONGO

We can now supply the demand for a true Cuban Conga. Shell is barrel shaped with ten inch head and an eight inch opening at bottom, 32 inches high. Made of ½ inch thick tapered boards that run lengthwise—perfectly fitted. Rawhide tanned, thick mule hide is used for the head. Available in two designs as shown below. This is the drum that Cuban and Be-Bop bands have been demanding.

Cuban design Conga, Yellow shell with black, red and green design.

*No. 284 ....$55.00

NO EXCISE TAX

Be-Bop design Conga, Black shell with yellow design, as illustrated.

*No. 286 ....$55.00

NO EXCISE TAX

MARACAS

The true tone of the genuine Native Cuban maraca cannot be imitated by making the balls of composition. These maracas are perfectly balanced and filled with just the proper quantity of shot.

No. **1129**—Cuban Maracas, per pair................$2.50

PLUS EXCISE TAX

CLAVES

Another native Cuban rhythm accessory of importance. Claves are made in two sizes, to produce the correct native tone. Made from select hickory and stained black.

No. **1149**—Cuban Claves, per pair $1.50

PLUS EXCISE TAX

ERICAN DRUMS by Slingerland

STANDARD DRUM BONGOS

Size 5" x 6" and 5" x 8"

This new Slingerland Cuban instrument is increasing in popularity with the modern drummer. Played either with sticks or by hand. As you will note the counterhoops are pulled below the shell. Truly a fine instrument.

No.	Description	NICKEL	CHROME
No. 302	Choice of Lacquer Finishes	$52.50	$60.00
No. 303	Choice of Pearl Finishes	60.00	67.50
No. 310	Bongo Holder, Fully Adjustable	5.00	7.50

Fed. Tax Extra

No. 298

SINGLE BONGOS

A clever adaption of the single Bongo which fastens to the snare drum or tom tom shell as shown. Shell size is 5"x 6", in choice of pearl or lacquer finishes. Sturdy plate mounting attachment is easily attached to drum shell and lifts out of clip socket quickly and easily for packing. Equipped with Goat head. Features the new Slingerland full flange hoop of heaviest non-ferrous metal, yet cut low for ample head clearance.

No.	Description	NICKEL	CHROME
No. 298	Single 5" x 6" bongo, pearl finish	$30.00	$33.50
No. 299	Single 5" x 6" bongo, lacquer finish	26.25	28.75
No. 304	Bongo shell mount attachment	3.00	4.50

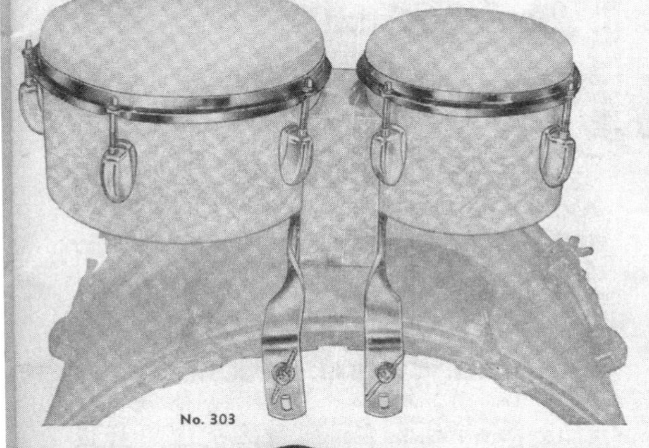

No. 303

See Page 12 For Authentic Cuban Congas

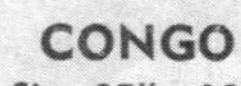

CONGO

Size 27" x 12"

Congas are an instrument which have gained popularity among professional musicians. There are many good bands who are now using the single Conga which is light and easy to handle. There has also been a great demand for them in Oriental bands.

No.	Description	NICKEL	CHROME
No. 280	Choice of Lacquer Finishes	$ 55.00	$ 60.00
No. 281	Choice of Pearl Finishes	65.00	70.00

(COMPLETE WITH SLING)

No.	Description	NICKEL	CHROME
No. 290	Choice of Lacquer Finishes	$115.00	$125.00
No. 289	Choice of Pearl Finishes	135.00	145.00

(COMPLETE WITH STAND)

Fed. Tax Extra

No. 280

THE NEW SLINGERLAND HAND-MADE DELUXE MEXICAN MARACAS

The most artistic hand-made production of Old Mexico. Made of native woods, light, strong, properly weighted and balanced. Each pair is different; hand carvings, designs, scenes, and flowers in gay and artistic hand coloring. 9 inches long overall, ball is 4½ inches long, and 3½ inches in diameter. Excellent for musical use with the true Latin-American tone color.

No. 1114 Slingerland De Luxe, Mexican Maracas, pair............$4.50

No. 1114

TUNED COW BELLS, HOLDERS, AND CLAMPS

Cow Bells Only

No. 1376—3½"	$1.75
No. 1377—4½"	2.00
No. 1378—5"	2.20
No. 1379—6½"	2.50
For Chrome add	1.50

No. 290

SLINGERLAND TYMPANI

1934 - 1940

Slingerland's first tympani were shown in the 1934 catalog as pictured here. They remained unchanged until the last year these models were catalogued, 1940.

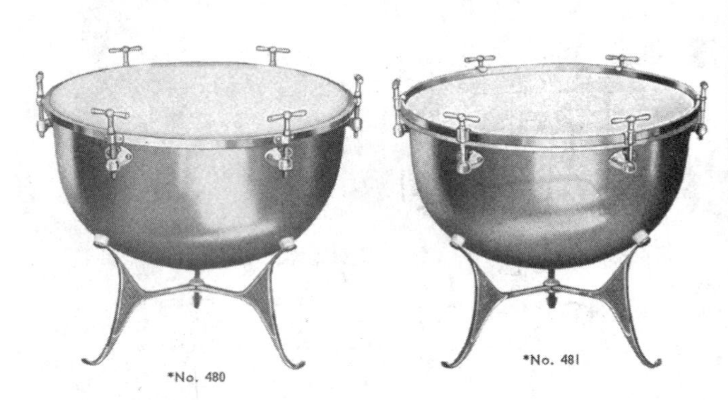

Author's note:

TYMPANI or TIMPANI?

My good friend Deborah Gillaspie pointed out in her proofreaders' notes of the first printing that I was inconsistent in my spelling. I did a little research and found that not only Slingerland but also Ludwig and Rogers switched from tympani to timpani in 1963. The story behind that (if there is one) will have to wait for another day. Please, dear readers, allow me the indulgence of considering both spellings correct.

1949–1961 The Philharmonic Grand Pedal Tympani

According to his cousin Robert Slingerland who was working with him at the time, Bud Slingerland based his pedal mechanism on the auto emergency brake used by Buick. This new timpani line was largely responsible for the tremendous sales increases Slingerland realized in the early fifties.

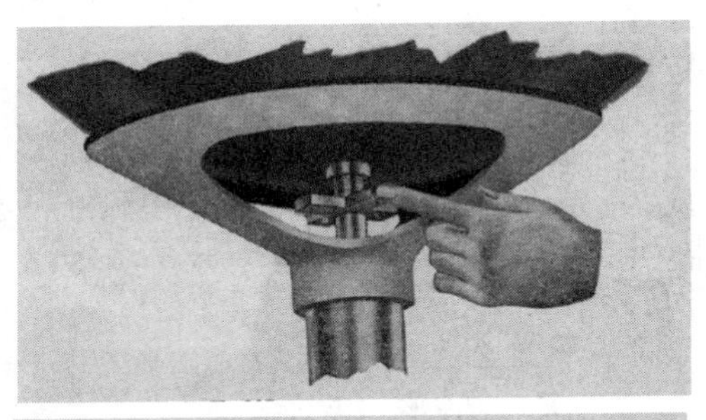

ONE SCREW SET UP

As simple as all that. One screw at base of kettle assembles the bowl and base mechanism. Set up or detached in a few moments—it's the quickest and easiest set-up in the tympani world.

POWER GRASP TUNING HANDLES

Symphonic experts have pronounced this feature highly important. Handles are large and full, form fit to hand for easy grasping, and provide quick, easy, hand tuning leverage. No skimping here—generous with all detail is a typical Slingerland tradition.

MICRO-CLUTCH PEDAL ACTION

Easy pedaling, positive lock and holding to pitch position are made possible by the Slingerland MICRO-CLUTCH pedal action. It provides FIVE TIMES the bearing surface of any other make for instant, positive, and the most delicate adjustment setting of the foot. Merely depress the toeboard forward and down for release, and reverse while pedaling for the sure-fire lock to hold to pitch desired. Easy, simple, and fool proof. Never any balancing or adjustment required on the foot-board for weather changes.

DEEPER PARABOLIC BOWLS

The true parabolic design produces focused reflection of sound waves for tonal response. This feature of added depth and parabola is found only on the Slingerland Philharmonic models. Bowls are of genuine copper, one piece, seamless type.

PLAYING CLEARANCE HANDLE

This is another Philharmonic feature exclusively on Slingerland typmani. The handle nearest beating spot is hinged to flip clear when playing. Thus it IS OUT OF THE WAY, and eliminates the accidental knock of beaters against the handle in rapid passages or where passing rolls are being played. This clearance handle tunes and adjusts like the fixed handles yet clears in an instant.

PEDAL SET LOW FOR EASY TUNING

The special Slingerland design coupled with the MICRO-CLUTCH principle permits the pedal to be set low to the floor for comfort, better foot control, and quicker pedal tunning.

1962–1979 *The "PHILHARMONIC GRAND" Pedal Timpani*

Most of the improvements to this model in the late 50's to early 60's were due to the designs acquired when Slingerland bought the Leedy drum division from Conn in 1955. The leg design, the ball-bearing clutch, the "bump on the kettle" were all here exactly as they had been as Leedy timpani just a few years earlier. The 1962 catalog drawings below, in fact, were hand drawn by George Way while he was a Conn employee. Way had participated in the development of the ball-bearing clutch.

THE BALL-BEARING CLUTCH

THAT DEFINITELY HOLDS IN ANY POSITION AND WILL NOT SLIP

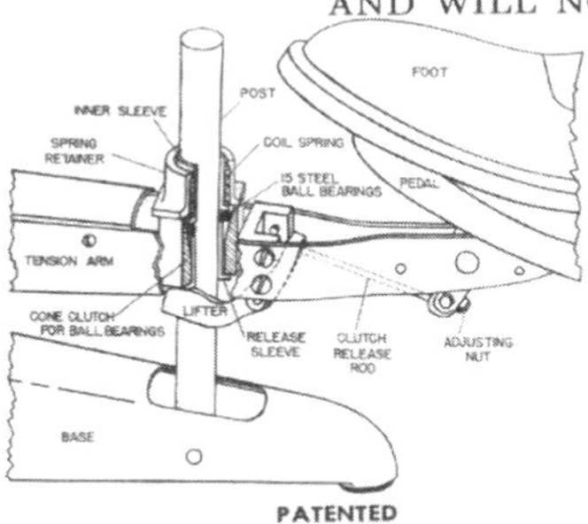

The outstanding feature that places this tympani far in advance of all others is the Silent Ball-Bearing Clutch. Fifteen ball bearings lie in a cone-shaped solid steel housing. These bearings surround the "range post" and create a vice-like grip. This precision (patented) mechanism holds positive in any position. The holding positions are as flexible as a finger on a fiddle string—a hair's breadth movement does it.

THE IMPORTANT "BUMP" ON THE KETTLE BRACKET

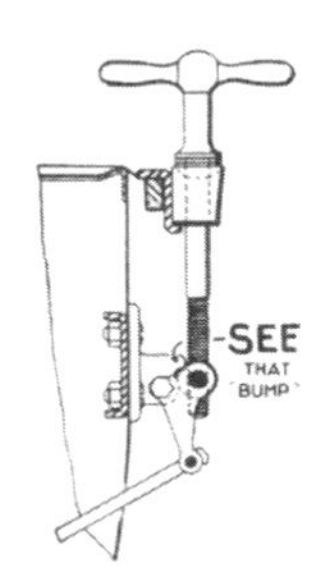

When the pedal is up as far as it will go (only 8"), the bell-cranks come to a stop at the "bump" built into the kettle bracket. This stop allows no strain on the inside rods when they are in this position. Therefore, when the player turns the handles to "iron out" the head tone to the lowest note, the strain is applied to the brackets and does not disturb the rods. All six inside tension rods are under EQUAL strain when the pedal starts to travel downward to create the various tones on up the scale and enables the player to KEEP even tension over the entire head surface at all times. This is a big factor in preventing that "pulled-down-on-one-side" condition seen on so many tympani which seriously interferes with true tone and tuning ease. The "bump" on the kettle brackets is a patented feature.

features added in 1970

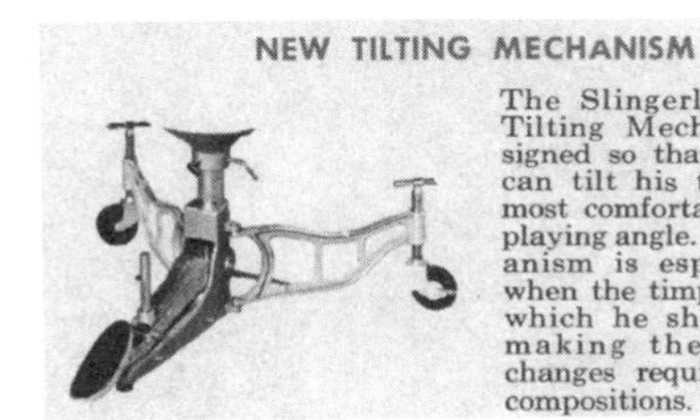

The Slingerland Timpani-Tilting Mechanism* is designed so that the timpanist can tilt his timpani to the most comfortable and easiest playing angle. This new mechanism is especially useful when the timpanist is seated, which he should be, while making the rapid pedal changes required in modern compositions.

1958–1979 Olympic/Supreme

Introduced in 1958 as the Olympic, the name was changed to the Supreme in 1961. (This may have been in response to a looming legal problem with Premier, who marketed in the U.S. a line of drums with the "Olympic" name. Beginning in 1977 this model was offered in fiberglass as well as copper.

COPPER		FIBRE GLASS	
402	26" and 29"	402F	26" and 29"
40223	23"	40223F	23"
40226	26"	40226F	26"
40229	29"	40229F	29"
40232	32"	40232F	32"

RHAPSODY FIBERGLASS 1962–1976

Introduced at the University of Michigan's School Bandmaster Clinic in Ann Arbor in January 1962, these inexpensive utilitarian models were an immediate hit.

Rhapsody
PEDAL TIMPANI
WITH THE PATENTED BALL BEARING CLUTCH THAT HOLDS IN ANY POSITION AND DEFINITELY WILL NOT SLIP

•

SUPPLIED WITH PLASTIC HEADS UNLESS OTHERWISE SPECIFIED

• Rhapsody Timpani are another Slingerland First. They sound great, look great, weigh less and cost less. The new Fibre-glass Bowls, with non-scratching, simulated copper finish, are strong, sturdy and resist denting. The only Fibre-glass Timpani with a hard Gel-coat Finish!

SQUARE HEAD TENSION RODS SUPPLIED AT NO ADDITIONAL COST, IF DESIRED

No. 350 25″ & 28″. Pedal Timpani, per Pair with Chrome Plated Hardware, Fibre-glass Bowls, Brake Wheels, Head Protectors, Beaters and No. 1204 Instruction Book **$510.00B**

No. 351 26″ & 29″. Pedal Timpani, per Pair with Chrome Plated Hardware, Fibre-glass Bowls, Brake Wheels, Head Protectors, Beaters and No. 1204 Instruction Book **$520.00B**

ADDITIONAL SIZES OF RHAPSODY MODEL

No. 35023 . . . 23″ Fibre-Glass Timpani with Brake Wheels and Fibre Head Protector **$260.00B**

No. 35030 . . . 30″ Fibre-Glass Timpani with Brake Wheels and Fibre Head Protector **$290.00B**

INDEX

note; there is a separate index of endorsers, pages 81–85

INDEX

INDEX

Appendix 1 Colors (see pp. 136–139)

An alphabetical listing of Slingerland colors with the approximate dates of production.

Abalone Pearl	1936
Antique (Two colors of lacquer)	1934–1938
This technique continued through the 1960s, though the term "Antique Finish" was used only until 1938. Most common combinations were silver & blue, gold & blue, silver & black, and gold & black.	
Aqua Sparkle Pearl	1959
Black Diamond Pearl	1928–1995
Black Beauty (Solid black pearl)	1953–1994
(called Black Gloss 1981–1994)	
Black Enamel	1928–1941
Black Sparkle	1958–1979
Blackrome	1977–1979
Blue Agate Pearl	1965–1977
Blue Gloss	1976–1986
Blue Ripple	1961–1967
Blue Satin Flame	1964–1977
Brilliant Gold	1928–1979
(called Sparkling Gold after 1929)	
Brown Aztec	1976
Capri Pearl	1958–1963
Cherrywood Lacquer	1979
Cherrywood Oil	1979
Combination Pearl Finishes	1961–1973
Chrome	1979–1994
Copper	1973
Coral Pearl	1934–1938
Fiesta	1961–1967
Gold Satin Flame	1964–1977
Gold Veiled Ebony	1958–1963
Green Aztec	1976
Green Satin Flame	1964–1973
Grey Agate Pearl	1956–1967
Knotty Pine Lacquer	1955–1957
Lavendar	1929
Lavender Satin Flame Pearl	1973
Light Blue Pearl	1958–1979
Mahogany	1928–1986
Maple	1976–1986
Mardi Gras Pearl	1961–1963
Marble Lacquer	1955–1957
Marine Pearl	1928–1994
Oakwood Lacquer	1979
Oakwood Oil	1979
Opal Pearl	1929–1938
Also called Peacock Pearl, 1936.	
Oyster Pink	1961–1967
Peacock Pearl	see Opal Pearl
Pewter Silk	1981–1986
Red Aztec	1976
Red Gloss	1976–1986
Red Ripple	1965
Red Satin Flame	1964–1977
Red Tiger Pearl	1973
Rose Pearl	1929
Rosewood Lacquer	1979
Rosewood Oil	1979
Sea Green	1928–1938
Silver Silk	1979–1986
Silver Veil Pearl	1958–1960
Smokey (Sparkling) Pearl	1958–1960
Sparkling Black	See Black Sparkle
Sparkling Blue	1948–1986
Sparkling Green	1934–1986
Sparkling Maroon Pearl	1973
Sparkling Orange Pearl	1973
Sparkling Peacock Pearl	1961–1963
Sparkling Pink	1959–1967
Sparkling Pink Champagne	1961–1973
Sparkling Purple Pearl	1973
Sparkling Red	1934–1986
Sparkling Silver	1934–1986
Sparkling White	1976–1979
Tangerine Satin Flame Pearl	1973
Teakwood Laquer	1979
Teakwood Oil	1979
Turquoise Veil Pearl	1958–1960
Tutone This term is sometime used by collectors to describe the Antique (two colors of lacquer) finish. Early catalogs use the term to identify a series of snare and bass drums offered in walnut, mahogany, white enamel, and black ebonized finishes, all with artgold hardhare.	
Violin Red Finish	1976–1986
Walnut	1928–1939, 1976–1986
White Aztec	1976
White Enamel	1928–1941
White Gloss	1976–1986
White Marine Pearl	see Marine Pearl
White Satin Flame	1967
White Tiger Pearl	1973–1977
Yellow Gloss	1979–1986
Yellow Tiger	1968

Appendix 2 Catalogs (pages 133–135)

The importance of old catalogs to drum historians can hardly be overstated. However useful, catalogs can also throw you off the track. Slingerland used old artwork and copy whenever they could, even repeating "new" designations in successive catalogs. Badges illustrated in catalogs are sometimes not the badges actually being installed on drums at the time the catalog was distributed.

Identifying and dating catalogs can be challenging and frustrating. One catalog, B, was identified by a letter designation, while most were given number designations which approximated the year of publication. Others can be identified by copyright year, while still others require research to date. Page counts here do not include the inside or outside cover pages. Like drums, the vintage catalogs will be appreciating in value. The values listed are what the author has seen these catalogs selling for at the retail level in 1995.

1928 5½"x8½", 80 pages Slingerland's first drum catalog. $250.00

Catalog B 1930 5½"x8½", 64 pages It's difficult to state with certainty that this undated catalog was published in 1930. That year, however, fits a two-year publication schedule Slingerland seems to have started with. This catalog was distributed in 1932 with an insert introducing new products and listing new prices. $250.00

1934 5½"x8½", 96 pages This is the only catalog to feature the Duall snare drum. $200.00

1936 5½"x8½", 96 pages First catalog with Gene Krupa on the cover, first Radio King snare drums and first tunable tom toms. Among the rarest of Slingerland catalogs. $300.00

1937 5½"x8½", 20 pages First catalog to feature streamlined lugs on tom-toms. $150.00

1938 5½"x8½", 96 pages One of the few catalogs with an early Buddy Rich endorsee photo; he was with Slingerland from 1937–1940. $200.00

1939 5½"x8½", 42 pages This one was tough to date! Collector Rich Kalinsky pointed out that Krupa instructional book pictured is copyrighted 1938. $175.00

1940 5½"x8½", 80 pages The first catalog with beavertail lugs. $125.00

1941 5½"x8½", 32 pages Clamshell strainer introduced. $125.00

WARTIME! No full catalogs were published between 1941 and 1948, just brochures on the wartime drums.

1947 8"x11", 22 pages HH pedal introduced, first floor tom legs (floor toms were held in basket-cradles previously), no more toms with tacked-on heads. $100.00

1948 8½"x11", 24 pages Pedal timpani were introduced in this catalog, which lists 49 endorsees. $100.00

#51, 1949 8½"x11", 30 pages Cocktail drums introduced,54 endorsees on roster. $100.00

1951 8½"x11", 32 pages Virtually identical to 1949 except for cover, higher prices, and back-cover roster of 57 endorsees. $100.00

#54 1953 8½"x11", 32 pages Knotty-pine lacquer finish introduced. Otherwise nearly identical to 1951.$100.00

#55 1955 8½"x11", 36 pages The first catalog to feature the "1955 lug". Introduces the short-lived (through 1957) finish Marble Lacquer. $100.00 A shortened version,

#555, 22 pages Was published as a supplement for bandmasters and drum corps. $50.00

#57 1957 (April 1, 1957) 8½"x11", 36 pages Nearly identical to #55; slightly higher prices and different layout of the parade drum section. $100.00
#57 1957 (not shown with other covers p. 161) Nearly identical to earlier (April 1) 1957 catalog: Rose and red cover instead of tan and green, and updated snare drum kits.

LEEDY 1956 8½"x11", 24 pages First "Slinger-Leedy" catalog. $100.00
LEEDY 1958 8½"x11", 28 pages First catalog with new Leedy design double-end lugs. Shelley Manne outfit introduced. $125.00
LEEDY #60, 1959 8½"x11", 32 pages Cocktail drum added, Leedy braced hardware replaced with Slingerland flat-base hardware.Numerous new snare drum models. $125.00
LEEDY #62, 1962 8½"x11", 32 pages Nearly identical to #60. $125.00

#59 1958, #60 1959, #61 1960, #61A 1961 8½"x11", 40 pages The only Slingerland catalogs to use exactly the same covers except for the catalog number. Very few changes were made in the Slingerland line during this era. A few colors were introduced and discontinued, plastic heads were introduced, and a few snare drum models changed. #59 & #60 (More rare than the others) $125.00, #61 $125.00, #61A $100.00

#63 1962 8½"x11", 56 pages Much more color than previous catalogs. Zoomatic strainer and Sound King snare drums. $90.00
#63A 1963 8½"x11". 56 pages Same as #63 except for a couple of staff and personnel changes. $80.00

LEEDY #70 1965 8½"x11", 36 pages The last Leedy catalog. Lots of full-color. Same color-swatch page (back cover) as Slingerland #67. $75.00

#65 1964 8½"x11", 64 pages Satin flame finishes introduced, Gene Krupa brass snare and parade drum outfits added. $75.00
#67 1965 8½"x11", 64 pages Same as #65 except for a few price increases. $75.00

#68 1967 8½"x11", Jenco mallet instruments introduced. $60.00

#69 1968 8½"x11", 72 pages Set-O-Matic tom holder introduced. New colors: White Tiger, Red Tiger, Yellow Tiger, Lavendar Satin Flame Discontinued: Red ripple, Fiesta, Oyster Pink, Sparkling pink $75.00

#71 1970 8½"x11", 80 pages Some new outfits, but otherwise very similar to #69. $75.00A separate outfit catalog was also published, called Drum Outfit Supplement Catalog #71. (14 pages, same cover, $35.00)

1973 8½"x11", 80 pages First catalog to include Deagan. New prices lists to go with this catalog were printed in 1974 and 1975. $50.00

1976 8½"x11", 84 pages First Slingerland catalog since 1928 to not list Zildjian cymbals; Kashian cymbals in this one. TDR strainer appears. Lots of new finishes and a few large rock outfit configurations.Expanded parts section. $50.00

1977-1978 8½"x11", 72 pages The first catalog to include no prices, which were printed in separate price list. Zildjian back in the catalog. $50.00

1979 8½"x11", 90 pages All new outfits, a number of new finishes, Two-to-one snare drum. $50.00

1983 8½"x11", 34 pages Magnum hardware and outfits introduced Artist outfits and Spirit outfits introduced. Built-in May-EA mike system. Sabian cymbals catalogued. $20.00
1985 8½"x11", 22 pages An abbreviated version of 1983, and the last Chicagoland catalog. Fred Gretsch Enterprises used this catalog, putting a Gretsch sticker over the Chicago address. $15.00

Appendix 3 Sam Rowland Notes

(see page 31)

Slingerland may well have given up on the drum business had Sam Rowland not joined the firm in 1930. The following is a transcription of Sam Rowland's handwritten notes in the 1936 Slingerland catalog; the last catalog to be published before he left Slingerland to join the Ludwig family in starting the WFL company. Many, but not all, of these comments refer to products which are shown on the pages of this book. Many are identified with this balloon:

Sam says... pages 239-242

Catalog page #, *Slingerland Book page #*

2,*184* Metal Radio King *Never matched heads! Rods poorly threaded casings full of pits and poorly plated.* (With line to snare cord:) *Cord stretches. This extended attachment is not a good thing. Drummers are having trouble and many complaints are coming in.*

2,*184* Wood Radio King *Counter hoops are made of too light a guage brass and dent and bend under rim shots and use. The strainer itself is poorly engineered and binds. Many replacements are required.*

2,*184* Radio King Badge *Should be plated to match drum finish.*

3,*184* Metal Radio King *Lugs will not fit metal shell.*

3,*184* Wood Radio King *This sells best in Antique Silver & Blue, some mahogany.*

3,*184* Wrapped Radio King *Best of all models.*

3,*184* All Radio Kings *All plating is notoriously bad.*

4,*183* Artist's Model, Metal *Average about 2 per month. (With lines to strainer arm and top shell screw:) Strainer N/G. This drum illustrated with tubular lugs because S forgot to make his streamlined lugs fit metal shells.*

4,*183* Artist's Model, Wood *Sales negligible.*

5 Bass Drum T's *The tympani handles on B.D. rods are aluminum so he won't have to chrome plate them. Thus they are always off color or nickel and chrome-plated rods. They are fragil (sic) also.*

6,*185* Gene Krupa Radio King Snare
Heads are never matched because these heads are poor and cut from B.D. head sizes, scraped and sanded and never really white. This is the #1 drum of the S. line. Sells 15 to 1 over the Pollack model below. (With line to Gene Krupa name:) A subsidized name in exchange for free equipment. (With line to Ben Pollack name:) Has never paid his bill.40% off given.

6,*185* Ben Pollack Model Radio King
Fair item, worth keeping but needs revision. Ben P. wants shell made of metal. Lugs do not fit properly, thus rods shoot intoward center.

7,*186* Bernie Mattison Model Radio King *Fair model, but other illustration could cover. He was given 40% off to list.*

7,*186* Band Master Model Radio King *Sells around six pieces/month in December and January. Seasonal model. Too bad they couldn't ask advice when these lugs were made. They are all too low.*

8,*182* Professional, Metal *This is sort of inbetween misfit and sells poorly in 4x14. The 5 and 6.5 sell fair and probably should be listed.*

8,*182* Professional, Wood *The wood model does not sell. Illustration taking up valuable space.*

9,*182* Universal, Metal *Finest of all cheap models. Sells 50 to 2 over the wood models. No illustration needed for wood.*

10 Junior, Metal *A good seasonal Xmas number.*

10 Junior, Wood *12 sold for Xmas 1936, not so good.*

10 (Junior) Orchestra *A pet model of theirs that does not sell. Kill it! A Montgomery Ward model.*

11 Juvenile Snare Drum *Excellent. They use any kind of head for their drums. Goat skins (back hides), lacquered* (underlined) *white were shipped out to the 1936 Xmas trade.*

11 Juvenile Parade Drum *Excellent.*

11 Juvenile Bass Drums *Only fair but deserves listing.*

12,*174* Bass drum 3 and 5-ply shell diagrams *The 5-ply does not sell.*

12 Bass Drum shell ruggedness explanation
If this were only true! All the S. bass drums aren't bad. The heads are their worst feature and the aluminum handles the next worse.

13 Artists' Model Bass Drums, 5-ply *Don't list it! Started out giving wood inlay. Now uses paper inlay. This drum costs too much and is too heavy and isn't that much better than 3-ply.*

14 Artists' Model Bass Drums, 3-ply *Good seller. Drummers want lugs to match streamlined lugs or R-K snare drums. S. won't go to the cost of new dies* *for die casting them.*

15 Artists' Model Bass Drums, 3-ply Single Tension *Good Seller*

16 Universal Model Bass Drums *Fine selling model in 14x28 size*

17,*196* "Premier" Outfit *Kill this.*

18,*196* "Radio" Outfit *Not so good.*

19,*196* "Broadway" Outfit *Best of the plain outfits and an all year round seller.*

20,*196* "School" Outfit *7 of these were sold last Christmas*

21,*196* Special Jobbing Outfit *A new item. Starting out at rate average of 6 sets per month.*

22,*196* "Junior" Outfit *A good Christmas outfit.*

22,*196* "American Boy" Outfit *Excellent Christmas outfit*

23,*156* Snare stands:

816 *This 816 does not sell.*

801 *W. & A. Should be made in plant.*

896-897 *All are good sellers*

23 #938 Bass Drum Stand *Scratches drum.*

24 #940 Pedal *Stolen from Heyn Pedal but binds and does not have Heyn action. Leedy XL is better. Pedals not properly tested.*

24 #731 Spurs *There is a need for a disappearing spur that can conveniently be left in drum.*

24 #1343 Cymbal Holder *Clamp stolen from Strupe model.*

26,*154* #1550 New Era Pedal *This is a flop but high-pressure road men stick dealers with them. The road men know less than nothing about drums and less about drummers.*

26,*154* #939 Frisco Pedal *No good at all. Sells in West Coast and W-C dealers order them from Mortenson "Frisco D Shop."*

27,*154* #724 Pedal *This sells and why it does is a major mystery. I believe since it's the first pedal of S. that road men must push it. Terrible action!*

27 #729 Spur (next to upper section rod) *To see is to know!*

27,*154* #726 Pedal *No, and it won't and doesn't sell well.*

28 #1203 Trap Rail *KILL!*

28 #1226 Temple Blocks *Being pushed. Old Leedy idea cleaned up a bit.*

28 #1269 Trap Table *None sold so far. No reason for existence.*

29 #1220,1223 Clamps *These have all been stolen from Leedy*

29 #1230 Tom Holder *Should be revised.*

29 #1235 Wood Block Holder *Not so good, but should be revised.*

29 #1240 Triangle Holder *Not so good.*

29 #1245 Cymbal Arm *ok*

29 #1235 Wood Block Holder *ok*

29 #1260 Tambourine Holder *ng*

29 #1265 Cow Bell Clamp *ok need a new idea*

30 Cymbals *All cymbals here are good.*

31 Cymbals *All good here*

31 #1206 Cymbal Holder *ok*

31 #1207 Choke Cymbal Holder *ok*

31 #1206 Assembly *ok*

32 #945 Bock-a-da-Bock Cymbals *No good now.*

32 #947 Bock-a-da-Bock Cymbals *Disc.*

32 #1108 Egyptian Cymbals and Holders *ok*

32 #913 Chinese Gong *Not selling now.*

32 #1113 Band Bass Drum Cymbal Holder *This is a good item.*

32 #934 Band Wire Cymbal Beater *Worthless. Might change by using heavier wire.*

33 #1836 Overhanging Cymbal Holder Obsolete

33 #765 Spring Cymbal Holder *Fairly good.*

33 #1052 New Universal Cymbal Holder *28 sold the first month.*

33 #918 Cymbal Strap Suspender *NG*

33 #1335 Drum Stand Cymbal Holder *good*

34 #1007 Gong Stand *None so far in January 1.5 months after it's introduction*

34 #1325 "Epic" Cymbal Holder ok

34 #761 Simplex Cymbal Holder *ok, but need to modernize*

35,*152* #1468 Duncan Sock Cymbal Pedal *dying out and being replaced by (arrow pointing to 1114)*

35,*152* #1114 Duncan pressed steel pedal *W&A Model sells well*

35,*152* #804 "High-Hat" sock pedal *good*

35 #805 Low Sock Cymbal Pedal *good, but not like 804*

36 #954 Trap Table *This table will probably outsell any on the market*

36 #1200 Trap Table *Still good.*

36 #1228 Trap Table *This is new and will go over.*

37,*152* #839 Holmes Afterbeat *Will average about 12 per month.*

37,*152* #835 Featherweight High Hat *12 sets sold first month. This is new and will go.*

37,*152* #837 Wowsock Cymbal Pedal *Results indeterminate so far. Questionable.*

37 #857 Drummer's Folding Chair *This will be a good item.*

38,*172* Pax-All Console *Stolen directly from Leedy. Probably will sell.*

39,*172* #1755 Goose Neck Cymbal Holder Ac*tual photo of a Leedy Co. holder*

39,*172* #1757 Gong Ring *Actual photo of a Leedy ring.*
39 #1759 Snare Drum Holder *This is an improvement over Leedy's*
41 Bass Drum Sticks *All are selling well but need for revision here*
42 Mallets *Selling good*
42 #1095 Trap Rail *16 sold first month's listing*
43 #1117 Maracas *This is of poor proposition and an injustice to sell*
43 #1129 Cuban Maracas *Good*
43 #1168, 1130 Cuban Gourds, Claves *Could be listed for convenience only*
43 #929 Dog Bark *Dead item.*
43 #911 Orchestra Bell Stand *Dead item*
44 Brushes *All are good sellers but 728x is impractical. Losing money on 728A and 728-O.*
45,*150* "Patrician" outfit *Very bad selling item. Not worth the space allotted.*
46 Sparkling Gold Models *Fairly good, but illustration should not be here at sacrifice of Marine Pearl the fastest selling of all models*
47,*136* Abalone Pearl Models *This is too effeminate and drummers admire but won't buy. Only one or two sold so far in 1.5 months.*
50,*196* "Hollywood Boulevard" outfit *Sells #1 of high priced pearl sets, sells #3 of colored outfits. A "natural" and should be listed*
51,*150,195* Improved "Monarch" outfit *Sells #4 of colored outfits. A good one to list.*
52,*150,196* Improved "Metropolitan" outfit *#2 of colored outfits, another natural, sells #1 of expensive outfits in lacquer color.*
53 #1370 Stick holder *n/g*
53,*167* #1465 "Shur-Grip" Snare Drum Muffler *n/g*
53,*168* #935 Deluxe "Shur-Grip" Bass Drum Muffler *will go well*
53,*168* #943 "Shur-Grip" Bass Drum Muffler *ok*
53,*168* #1115 "Epic" Bass Drum Muffler *ok*
54 Tambourines *All good except #1295*
55 Triangles *Fair, but needed*
55 #783 Piccolo Slap Sticks *NG*
55 Wood Blocks *good*
55 #1270 "Shur-Grip" Wood Block Holder *Badly in need of revision*
56,*26* Effects *Only fair. Debatable as to illustration. If listed they may as well be shown.*
57 Effects *Same for these. Neccessary evils*
58 #960 Cyclone Whistle *not selling*
58 #959 Cyclone Whistle *good item*
58 #769 Song Whistle *Very good selling since ring was put on. Objection being to wood plug. Hear they like Ludwig's better.*
58 Chinese Musettes *Rather good*
59 Sleigh Bells On Strap *Good.*
59 Sleigh Bells *Kill*
59 Four Tongued Wood Rattle with Crank *Kill*
59 Cowbell holders *Very good since advent of swing. Need better holders.*
60 Temple Blocks *These are good but too high priced. All holders stolen from Leedy.*
61 Chinese Tom Toms *Good*
61,*171* #1285 "Shur-Grip" Rotary Tom Tom holder *very good, expensive- could be revised to do same work.*
61,*171* #1280 Regular tom tom holder *ok, but in need of revision*
61,*171* #1290 "Shur-Grip" Combination Holder *N/G*
61 Giant Chinese Tom Toms *ok*
62,*169* Tunable tom toms *Could be revised by applying one lug in center so as to match construction of snare drums and bass drums.*
62 Top and Bottom tunable heads *This is a natural. I designed for Krupa, modernized them for catalog and they should be adopted immediately. Orders are coming in fast.*
63 Tunable tom toms
9x13 good for a cheap tunable
12x14, 16x16 not selling
63 "Shur Grip" Tom Tom Stands *There is a distinct need for a better and more modern stand.*
64,*169* Tenor Tymp Toms *Not selling because there is a lack of understnading among road men. Should be left to die unless tenor tymp is adopted where bottoms are adaptable for both. Dealers require education also. They will not read description.*
65 Professional Tympani *15 sets sold in 1936. Shows lack of school biz.*
66 Men standing on drum *Although true, this causes down doubt. No one will believe.*
66 Heads *Unfortunately due to disregard of drummers' needs and desires- and because no real heartfelt interest lies with the drummer himself these heads are the poorest I have ever seen. He averages four or five snare drum batter heads from one calf skin. This means flank skins, uneven, etc and as a result no quality; But, he thinks, profit.*
68 Books *Too many, but some are* neccessary.
69 #519 Drum Head Retainer *Seldom sold but proper education will determine future sales.*
70 Covers *Pax-All stolen from Leedy.*
71 #492,496,469 Cases *Stolen from Leedy*

71 #1017 Bass Drum Case *Not selling but needed*

73 #687 Double Claw Assembly *Screw head comes up too high. Hits drummer's hands.*

74 #953 Swivel Snap *Poorly plated. Stolen from Ludwig*

74 #970 Drum Key *Ludwig*

74 #949 Drum Key Holder *Won't hold up*

74 #447 Wood Hoop Snap Eye *Ludwig*

74 #673 Parade Drum Strainer *Stolen from Ludwig, as is #1 strainer.*

74,*159* #967 Speedy Strainer *poor strainer, wears out*

74,*157* #674 Shur-Grip Strainer *Stolen from Leedy. Not so good.*

75 Field Drum *Rods go inward. Lugs not high enough A lug is needed that fits street drums and bass drums and should be longer. Lugs stolen from Leedy.*

85 Lyras *Going very well but poorly tuned and poorly cast and poorly finished.*

86 #1046 Knobel Brass Bugle *France made*

86 #1074 Tenor Bugle *Kill*

86 #1037 Fan Fare Junior Baritone Bugle *Kill*

86 #1084 D-Crook Jr. Baritone Bugle *Kill*

87 #1600-V Knobel Piston Soprano Bugle *Kill*

87 #1090-V Alto Voice Piston Bugle *Kill- Takes expert to blow. Even LaMonaca threw them out. Most sales returned for credit.*

89 #1600-T Rowland Piston G-D Bugle *Good item. Not selling so well but a convenience.*

90 #1027 Drum Major Baton *poor*

#1028 Drum Major Baton *poor*

#1029 Drum Major Baton *very good*

#1030 Drum Major Baton *poor but needed*

#1031 Drum Major Baton *very bad*

#598 Drum Major Baton *very bad*

#570 Drum Major Baton *Not at all saleable due to wood ball and poor appearance*

#572 Drum Major Baton *questionable*

91 #1178 Drum Major Baton *(Cloos) good, due to Ludwig's efforts*

#1177 Drum Major Baton (Cloos) *will be good, due to Ludwig's efforts*

#1174 Drum Major Baton *Hammond will be good if pushed.*

#1170 Drum Major Baton *Questionable but probably needed for plain models*

#1180 Drum Major Baton *no sale, not needed*

92 top 4 cymbals *good*

#1157 Cymbal Handle *n/g*

#782 Practice Pad *good*

#952 Ideal Practice Pad *ok*

#1058 Practice Pad *bad*

#1158 Practice Pad on stand *Stand not selling.*

93 #1113 Bass Drum Cymbal Holder *Good*

#934 Wire Cymbal Beater *Kill or change*

#1066 Rain Cover *needed*

#1011 Bass Drum Lyre *Very good, revise*

#1143,1145 Bugle Cord *ok*

94 #589 Cadet Sling *None of these sell well enough to justify their space*

95 #1153 *Good. Stolen from Ludwig and poorly assembled. Does not use clips.*

#1725 Leg Rest *Kill this one*

#1723 Leg Rest *Stolen from Ludwig and will eventually kill the 1725*

Outside back cover, Guitar Page *Which ruins an otherwise good drum catalog and shows exceedingly bad taste, but also shows that they are still cheap guitar manufacturers at heart. Not personal opinion but that expressed by a few thinking drummers.*

Back Cover, 1936 Slingerland catalog

RESOURCES

John Aldridge (whose favorite gigging kit is is Radio King outfit) was the first to publish a vintage drum newsletter. It developed into a fullblown magazine, *NotSoModernDrummer*. At about the same time that he was starting his newsletter, Aldridge began to teach himself how to hand-engrave decorative patterns on metal. That talent eventually earned him a place in Slingerland history, see page 75. He has also engraved drums for Ludwig, Tama, Yamaha, DW, Craviotto, and other companies and personalized drums for numerous top players such as Bun E. Carlos and Kenny Aronoff.

Harry Cangany is a drum historian with a great deal of Slingerland expertise. Harry is the resource historian for Modern Drummer magazine as well as the proprietor of the Drum Center Of Indianapolis, which specializes in vintage drums. Harry has refurbished and supplied drums and drum outfits for a number of Hollywood movies. The Drum Center's online forum is a great place to pose your Slingerland questions.

SHOPS, DEALERS

A Drummer's Tradition
Robert Bowler 1619 Fourth St, San Rafael, CA 94901
415-458-1688

Donn Bennett's Drum Studios
4742 42nd Ave SW #207, Seattle, WA. 98116 425-747-6145

Drum Center of Indianapolis
5874 East 71st St., Indianapolis, IN 46220 317-594-8989
drumcenter.com

The Drum Detective
Todd Remmy 6977 Rosemary Ln, Cincinnati, OH 45236
513-791-1993

Drum Headquarters
Marty Monson, 7241 Manchester, St Louis, MO. 63143
314-644-0235

Memphis Drum Shop
Jim Pettit, 878 S. Cooper, Memphis, TN 38104, 888-276-2331

Steve Maxwell's Vintage & Custom Drums
410 S Michigan Ave, Ste 914, Chicago, IL 60505 630-865-6849

PUBLICATIONS

DRUM! www.drummagazine.com
Modern Drummer www.moderndrummer.com
NotSoModernDrummer www.notsomoderndrummer.com
Vintage Drummer www.vintagedrummer.com

AFTERMARKET PARTS

Jim Petty
817-268-2683
www.jp2creations.com

PROMINENT COLLECTORS

Gary Asher, Birmingham, AL. 800-841-8906
Dave Brown diddle@audiophile.com
Mike Curotto mike@curottodrums.com

SLINGERLAND GUITAR INFORMATION

Dave Kolars
dkolars@tbcnet.com
www.slingerlandguitar.com

Directions to Krupa's grave:
(from I-94, South side of Chicago)

Exit on Sibly Ave, East. Go East 1 mile to Torrence. Turn right (south) on Torrence, go about 3/4 mile to Michigan City Road. Turn left on Michigan City Road, continue about one mile, you'll see Holy Cross Cemetary on the right. Enter main gate, turn left at second opportunity after passing office.Watch the right side for Immaculata section. Krupa family has flush stone, hard to spot; they are behind the large Sadowski marker.

Story of the first edition Slingerland Book

About 1800 copies of this edition were distributed between 1996 and 2003. The drum featured on the cover belonged to Bun E. Carlos at the time the cover photo was shot by Gibson's Walter Carter.

About 400 copies of the first edition were produced with this cover, featuring a Nashville Radio King. (Cover photo and layout by Gibson's Walter Carter and Jim Landers.) 250 of those copies were distributed by Gibson, the rest by Rebeats.

The first edition of The Slingerland Book was printed by a high school drum buddy of mine, in a garage-based home printshop. He had previously done good work on several smaller projects for me and was delivering excellent product in both black & white and full color. This in spite of the fact that he was working with older equipment and technologies. (I had to provide original art for each photo, which he had to literally photograph to scale for the book, develop film, and burn plates from negatives. We had to send color photos out for separations, receiving four negatives for each color photo.) He gave me a quote to produce 3000 Slingerland books, and I took out a bank loan for the quoted amount. While he started work on the Slingerland project, he continued with smaller projects including ones that I brought to him. Among those projects were compilation printings of Not-So-Modern-Drummer back issues that I printed under an agreement with John Aldridge. One thing led to another, and soon the printer was printing every issue of NSMD magazine. It was way too much for him to handle. His equipment began to break down and the magazine was always behind schedule. The size of the magazine grew, as did circulation, which compounded the problem. A year went by and I still had no Slingerland books. I begged and pleaded for product, even offering to come and work in the print shop if it would expedite delivery. The printer said the only thing that would really help would be if I were to collate pages. He began bringing me boxes of pages as they were printed, and I spent literally thousands of hours over the next 6 years hand-collating every single book. I never had enough pages to put together more than several hundred copies at a time. When they were ready, I drove them to the bindery in Grand Rapids. At one point the printer suggested that if I were to invest in a used binding machine, he could do the binding and save me some time and expense. He found a used machine, for which I paid $2,000.00. The only books that ever got bound on that machine had pages falling out within weeks of being shipped.

Over the years, the frustration deepened as page delivery slowed and quality deteriorated. Although I only received 2200 of the 3000 copies plus lost money on the binder, it became time to shut the project down and start over. In less time than I could ever have collated the remaining 800 copies (if I had the neccessary pages, which I did not,) I have completely redone the project the right way.

The printer is not a bad or dishonest guy. He's been a pal of mine for nearly forty years, and I know he meant well. Litigation would not produce books. A judgement would not lead to compensation, it would only destroy the friendship. My apologies to customers who have purchased The Slingerland Book and found some of the pages too dark, or the color blurred, some pages falling out, or even some pages upside down. We meant well and did the best we could.

If you have a first edition, or have a chance to get one (at this writing several have recently sold on Ebay for over $100.00 per copy) you will find content changes in addition to the quality differences. The first edition included a reprint of a 1936 Gene Krupa fan magazine, while the 2004 edition has a totally revised Krupa section including several previously unpublished photos. The color swatch section has been updated, and the whole section of color collector pages is new. A few hundred of the first edition copies included pages provided by Gibson at the end; the pages featured the Nashville product and Gibson/Slingerland endorsers.

Rob Cook

also from Rob Cook....

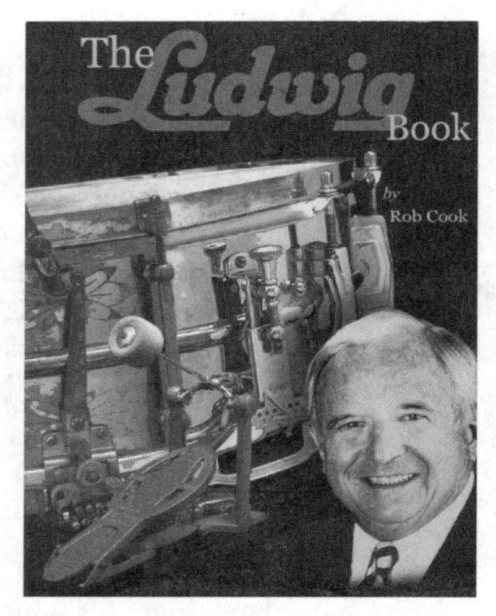

The Ludwig Book by Rob Cook (2003)
A complete business history and comprehensive dating guide. 302 pages, with 32 pages of color. Includes a CD-ROM produced by Selmer/Ludwig with the current Ludwig catalog, hi-rez scans of artist posters of the 70s and 80s, and audio of Wm. F. Ludwig and his father playing rudiments and solos.

The Making Of A Drum Company; the Autobiography of William F. Ludwig II edited by Rob Cook (2001)
The life story of one of the most important percussion figures of the 20th Century, told in his own words. A companion volume to *The Ludwig Book.*

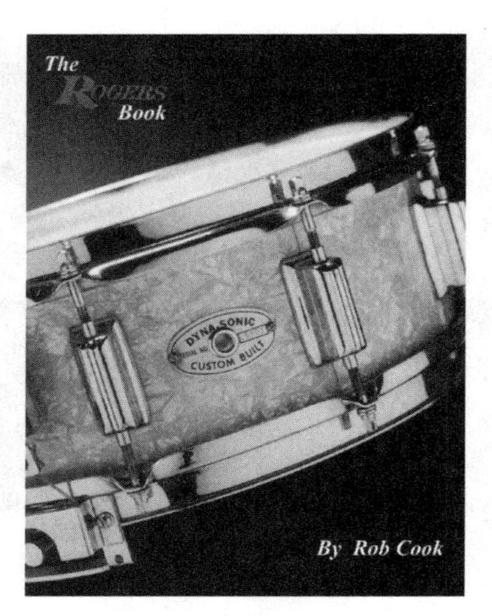

The Rogers Book by Rob Cook (1999)
Business history and dating guide in the same format as The Ludwig Book and The Slingerland Book. 221 pages with 16 pages of color.

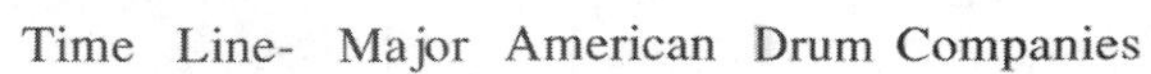

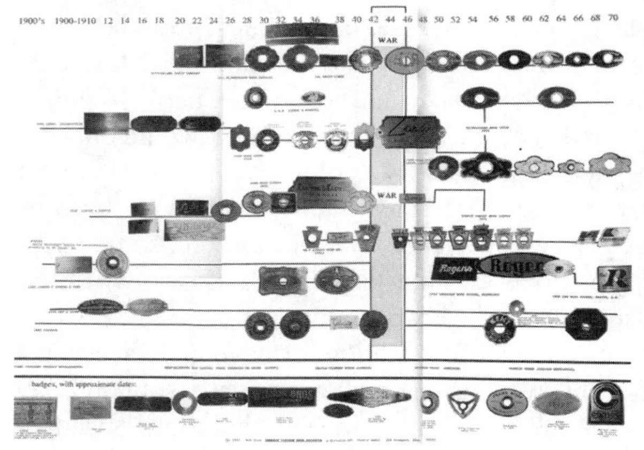

Drum Badge Timeline Poster
18"x24" full-color poster, suitable for framing. Features 85 badges arranged in chronological order, showing approximate production dates.

Complete History of The Leedy Drum Company by Rob Cook (Centerstream Pub., 1993)

George Way's Little Black Book (1992)
Capsule biography of Geo. Way and reproduction of Way's pocket notebook which contains his vendor directory, shell and stick production notes, etc.

Coming soon... *The Leedy Way* by Rob Cook; a full George Way biography with revised Leedy history (new dating guide, color section, etc.)

Rebeats Publications
219 Prospect, P.O. 6, Alma, Michigan, 48801
989-463-4757 (fax) 989-463-6545 www.rebeats.com email: Rob@rebeats.com